From "Bird Bones and Wood Ash"

At first, Jaime knows them only as women with the faces of animals: mare and deer, wild boar and bear, raven and toad. And others. So many others. Following her.

They smell like forest loam and open field, like wild apple blossoms and nuts crushed underfoot. Their arms are soft, but their hands are calloused and hard, the palms like leather. Where they have been, they leave behind a curious residue of dried blood and rose petals, tiny bird bones and wood ashes.

In those animal faces, their eyes are disconcertingly human, but not mortal. They are eyes that have seen decades pass as we see years, that have looked upon Eden and Hades. And their voices, at times a brew of dry African veldt whispers and sweet-toned crystal bells, looping through the clutter of city sound, echoing and ringing in her mind, heard only from a distance.

They hold Jaime in their soft arms, touch her hands with their calloused palms. Fairy godmothers in animal guises, bestowing their dangerous gifts.

By Charles de Lint from Tom Doherty Associates

THE
IVORY
AND THE
HORN

A NEWFORD COLLECTION

Charles de Lint

A TOM DOHERTY ASSOCIATES BOOK
NEW YORK

This is a work of fiction. All the characters and events portrayed in this book are fictitious, and any resemblance to real people or incidents is purely coincidental.

THE IVORY AND THE HORN

Cover art by Terri Windling
Edited by Terri Windling

Grateful acknowledgments are made to:

Happy Rhodes for the use of the lines from "Words Weren't Made for Cowards" from her album *Warpaint*. Copyright © 1991 by Happy Rhodes; lyrics reprinted by permission. For more information about Rhodes's music, contact Aural Gratification, P.O. Box 86458, Academy Station, Albany, NY 12208.

Kiya Heartwood for the use of a verse of "Wishing Well" from her album *True Frontiers*. Copyright © 1993 by Kiya Heartwood; lyrics reprinted by permission. For more information about Heartwood's music, contact Pame Kingfisher at Roaddog Booking & Management, (800) 382-5895.

A Tor Book
Published by Tom Doherty Associates, Inc.
175 Fifth Avenue
New York, NY 10010

Tor Books on the World Wide Web:
http://www.tor.com

Tor® is a registered trademark of Tom Doherty Associates, Inc.

ISBN: 0-812-53408-5
Library of Congress Card Catalog Number: 94-45340

First edition: April 1995
First mass market edition: March 1996

Printed in the United States of America

0 9 8 7 6 5 4 3 2 1

COPYRIGHT ACKNOWLEDGMENTS

for
Jane Yolen,
who showed me how to touch magic
and pass it on

ACKNOWLEDGMENTS

As anyone involved knows, contrary to the belief that artists create in the isolation of their workspaces, the act of creation is not a solitary endeavor. Without the inspiration and support I've received over the years, these stories wouldn't exist, so this time out I'd like to thank:

My wife, MaryAnn, for her help in the genesis of many of these stories and in their fine-tuning, always knowing when and where to say the right thing;

My editors at Tor, Terri Windling, Patrick Nielsen Hayden, Donald G. Keller and Greg Cox, for having enough faith in these stories to request a second volume sight unseen, and for making the publishing process so painless;

My agent, Richard Curtis, for finding me the spaces between novels when I could write these stories;

Altan, Tori Amos, Sarah Bauhan, Lisa Germano, Kiya Heartwood, Maria Kalaniemi, Peter Kater, Jon Mark, R. Carlos Nakai, Johnette Napolitano, Happy Rhodes and Ian Tamblyn, whose music keeps me sane;

All those editors who first asked for the stories collected herein: Kurt Busiak, Richard Chizmar, Pete Crowther, Bob

Garcia, Marty Greenberg, David Hartwell, Kit Kerr, Greg Ketter, Andre Norton, Jan and George O'Nale, Kris Rusch, Darrell Schweitzer, Erik Secker, Carol Serling and Dean Smith.

A few notes concerning individual stories:

In "The Bone Woman," the idea of *La Huesera* comes from the folklore of the American Southwest. My thanks to Clarissa Pinkola Estés for making me aware of the tale.

In "Where Desert Spirits Crowd the Night" the story of Coyote and the Buzzard is based upon traditional Kickapoo folklore.

"The Wishing Well" was written for MaryAnn, who wanted to know what was in the well, and for Jane Siberry, for her own "strange well" of songs. Special thanks to Dr. Sean Costello (a fine author in his own right) for technical advice.

—Charles de Lint
Ottawa, Canada

CONTENTS

FATHER, O FATHER, WHAT DO WE HERE
IN THIS LAND OF UNBELIEF AND FEAR?
THE LAND OF DREAMS IS BETTER FAR,
ABOVE THE LIGHT OF THE MORNING STAR.

—WILLIAM BLAKE

WE ARE ALL IN THE GUTTER, BUT SOME
OF US ARE LOOKING AT THE STARS.

—OSCAR WILDE

WAIFS AND STRAYS

Do I have to dig,
Do I have to prod;
Reach into your chest
And pull your feelings out?
    —Happy Rhodes, from "Words
        Weren't Made for Cowards"

1

There's a big moon glowing in the sky, a swollen circle of silvery-gold light that looks as though it's sitting right on top of the old Clark Building, balancing there on the northeast corner where the twisted remains of a smokestack rises up from the roof like a long, tottery flagpole, colors lowered for the night, or maybe like a tin giant's arm making some kind of semaphore that only other tin giants can understand. I sure don't.

But that doesn't stop me from admiring the silhouette of the smokestack against that fat moon as I walk through the rubble-strewn streets of the Tombs. I feel like a stranger and I think, That moon's a stranger, too. It doesn't seem real; it's more like the painted backdrop from some forties soundstage, except there's no way anybody ever gave paint and plywood this kind of depth. We're both strangers. That moon looks like it might be out of place anywhere, but I belonged here once.

Not anymore, though. I'm not even supposed to be here. I've got responsibilities now. I've got duties to fulfill. I should be Getting Things Done like the good little taxpaying citizen I'm trying to be, but instead I'm slumming, standing in front of my old squat, and I couldn't tell you why I've come. No, that's not quite right. I know, I guess; I just can't put it into words.

"You've got to see the full moon in a country sky sometime," Jackie told me the other day when she got back from her girlfriend's cottage. "It just takes over the sky."

I look up at it again and don't feel that this moon's at all diminished by being here. Maybe because in many respects this part of the city's just like a wilderness—about as close to the country as you can get in a place that's all concrete and steel. Some people might say you'd get that feeling more in a place like Fitzhenry Park, or on the lakefront where it follows the shoreline beyond the Pier, westward, out past the concession stands and hotels, but I don't think it's quite the same. Places like that are where you can only pretend it's wild; they look right, but they were tamed a long time ago. The Tombs, though, is like a piece of the city gone feral, the wild reclaiming its own—not asking, just taking.

In this kind of moonlight, you can feel the wilderness hiding in back of the shadows, lips pulled in an uncurbed, savage grin.

I think about that as I step a little closer to my old squat and it doesn't spook me at all. I find the idea kind of liberating. I look at the building and all I see is a big, dark, tired shape hulking in the moonlight. I like the idea that it's got a secret locked away behind its mundane façade, that's there's more to it than something that's been used up and then just tossed away.

Abandoned things make me feel sad. For as long as I can remember I've made up histories for them, cloaked them in stories, seen them as frog princes waiting for that magic kiss, princesses being tested with a pea, little engines that could if only they were given half a chance again.

But I'm pragmatic, too. Stories in my head are all well and fine, but they don't do much good for a dog that some guy's tossed out of a car when he's speeding through the Tombs and the poor little thing breaks a leg when it hits the pavement so it can't even fend for itself—just saying the feral dogs that run in these streets give it half a chance. When I can—if I get to it in time—I'm the kind of person who'll take it in.

People have tried to take me in, but it never quite works out right. Bad genes, I guess. Bad attitude. It's not the kind of thing I ever worried about much till the past few weeks.

I don't know how long I've been standing on the street, not even seeing the building anymore. I'm just here, a small shape in the moonlight, a stray dream from the safe part of the city that got lost and found itself wandering in this nightland that eats small dreams, feeds on hopes. A devouring landscape that fed on itself first and now preys on anything that wanders into its domain.

I never let it have me, but these days I wonder why I bothered. Living in the Tombs isn't much of a life, but what do you do when you don't fit in anywhere else?

I start to turn away, finally. The moon's up above the Clark Building now, hanging like a fat round flag on the smokestack, and the shadows it casts are longer. I don't want to go, but I can't stay. Everything that's important to me isn't part of the Tombs anymore.

The voice stops me. It's a woman's voice, calling softly from the shadows of my old squat.

"Hey, Maisie," she says.

I feel like I should know her, this woman sitting in the shadows, but the sense of familiarity I get from those two words keeps sliding away whenever I reach for it.

"Hey, yourself," I say.

She moves out into the moonlight, but she's still just a shape. There's no definition, nothing I can pin the sliding memories onto. I get an impression of layers of clothing that make a skinny frame seem bulky, a toque pulled down over hair that might be any color or length. She's dressed for winter though the night's warm and she's got a pair of shopping bags in each hand.

I've known a lot of street people like that. Hottest day of the summer and they still have to wear everything they own, all at once. Sometimes it's to protect themselves from space rays; sometimes it's just so that no one'll steal the little they've got to call their own.

"Been a long time," she says, and then I place her.

It's partly the way she moves, partly the voice, partly just the shape of her, though in this light she doesn't look any different from a hundred other bagladies.

The trouble is, she can't possibly wear the name I call up to fit her because the woman it used to belong to has been dead for four years. I know this, logically, intellectually, but I can't help trying it on for size all the same.

"Shirl?" I say. "Is that you?"

Shirley Jones, who everybody on the street knew as Granny Buttons because she carried hundreds of them around in the many pockets of her dresses and coats.

The woman on the street in front of me bobs her head, sticks her hands in the pockets of the raincoat she's wearing over all those layers of clothing, and I hear the familiar rattle of plastic against wood against bone, a soft *clickety-clickety-click* that I never thought I'd hear again.

"Jesus, Shirley—"

"I know, child," she says. "What am I doing here when I'm supposed to be dead?"

I'm still not spooked. It's like I'm in a dream and none of this is real, or at least it's only as real as the dream wants it to be. I'm just happy to see her. Granny Buttons was the person who first taught me that "family" didn't have to be an ugly word.

She's close enough now that I can even see some of her features. She doesn't look any different than she did when she died. She's got the same twinkle in her brown eyes—part charm and part crazy. Her coffee-colored skin's as wrinkled as a piece of brown wrapping paper that you've had in your back pocket for a few days. I see it isn't a toque she's wearing, but that same almost conical velour cap she always wore, her hair hanging out from below in dozens of unwashed, uncombed dreadlocks festooned with tiny buttons of every shape and description. She still smells the same as well—a combination of rosehip sachet and licorice.

I want to hug her, but I'm afraid if I touch her she'll just drift apart like smoke.

"I've missed you," I say.

"I know, child."

"But how . . . how can you *be* here . . . ?"

"It's like a riddle," she says. "Remember our treasure hunts?"

I nod my head. How can I forget? That's where I first learned about the freebies you can find in behind the bookstores, where I was initiated into what Shirley liked to call the rehab biz.

"If you cherish something enough," she told me, "it doesn't matter how old, or worn, or useless it's become; your caring for it immediately raises its value in somebody else's eyes. It's just like rehab—a body's got to believe in their own worth before anybody can start fixing them, but most people need someone to believe in them before they can start believing in themselves.

"You know, I've seen people pay five hundred dollars for something I took out of their trash just the week before—*only* because they saw it sitting on the shelf of some fancy antique shop. They don't even remember that it once was theirs.

" 'Course the dealer only paid me fifty bucks for it, but who's complaining? Two hours before I came knocking on his back door, it was sitting at the end of the curb in a garbage can."

Garbage days we went on our treasure hunts. Shirley probably knew more about collection days than the city crews did themselves: when each borough had its pickup, what the best areas were depending on the time of year, when you had to make your rounds in certain areas to beat the flea market dealers on their own night runs. We had dozens of routes, from Foxville down into Crowsea, across the river to Ferryside and the Beaches, from Chinatown over to the East End.

We'd head out with our shopping carts, sensei baglady

and her apprentice, on a kind of Grail quest. But what we found was never as important as the zen of our being out there in the first place. Each other's company. The conversation. The night's journey as we zigzagged from one block to another, checking out this alleyway, that bin, those Dumpsters.

We were like urban coyotes prowling the city's streets. At that time of night, nobody bothered us, not the cops, not muggers, not street toughs. We became invisible knights tilting against the remnants of other people's lives.

After Shirley died, it took me over a month to go out on my own and it was never quite the same again. Not bad, just not the same.

"I remember," I tell her.

"Well, it's something like that," she says, "only it's not entirely happenstance."

I shake my head, confused. "What are you trying to tell me, Shirley?"

"Nothing you don't already know."

Back of me, something knocks a bottle off a heap of trash—I don't know what it is. A cat, maybe. A dog. A rat. I can't help myself. I have to have a look. When I turn back to Shirley—you probably saw this coming—she's gone.

2

Pride goes before a fall, I read somewhere, and I guess whoever thought up that little homily had her finger on the pulse of how it all works.

There was a time when I wouldn't have had far to fall; by most people's standards, at seventeen, I was already on the bottom rung of the ladder, and all the rungs going up were broken as far as I'd ever be able to reach. I lived in a squat. I made my living picking garbage and selling the better stuff off to junk shops and the fancy antique places—only through the back door, if you would, yes it's a lovely piece but terribly worn, sorry that's my best offer, many thanks and do come again. I had a family that consisted of a bunch of old dogs so worn out that nobody wanted them, not to mention Tommy who's—what's the current euphemism? I lose track. Mentally handicapped, I guess you'd call him. I just call him Tommy and it doesn't matter how dim the bulb is burning in behind his eyes; like the dogs, he became family when I took him in and I love him.

I never thought much about pride back in those days, though I guess I had my share. Maybe I was just white trash to whoever passed me on the street, but I kept myself cleaner than a lot of those paying taxes and what I had then sure beat the hell hole I grew up in.

I hit the road when I was twelve and never looked back because up until then family was just another word for pain. Physical pain, and worse, the kind that just leaves your heart feeling like some dead thing is caught inside your chest. You know what pigeons look like once the traffic's been running over them for a couple of weeks and there's not much left except for a flat bundle of dried feathers that hasn't even got flies buzzing around it anymore?

That's like what I had in my chest until I ran away.

I was one of the lucky ones. I survived. I didn't get done in by drugs or selling my body. Shirley took me in under her wing before the lean men with the flashy suits and too much jewelry could get their hands on me. Don't know why she helped me—maybe when she saw me she was remembering the day she was just a kid stepping off a bus in some big city herself. Maybe, just looking at me, she could tell I'd make a good apprentice.

And then, after five years, I got luckier still—with a little help from the Grasso Street Angel and my own determination.

And that pride.

I was so proud of myself for doing the right thing: I got the family off the street. I was straightening out my life. I rejoined society—not that society seemed to care all that much, but I wasn't doing it for them anyway. I was doing it for Tommy and the dogs, for myself, and so that one day maybe I could be in a position to help somebody else, the way that Angel does out of her little storefront office on Grasso, the way that Shirley helped me.

I should've known better.

We've got a real place to live in—a tenement on Flood Street just before it heads on into the Tombs, instead of a squat. I had a job as a messenger for the QMS—the Quicksilver Messenger Service, run by a bunch of old hippies who got the job done, but lived in a tie-dyed past. Evenings, four times a week, I was going to night school to get my high school diploma.

But I just didn't see it as being better than what we'd had before. Paying for rent and utilities, food and for someone to come in to look after Tommy, sucked away every cent I made. Maybe I could've handled that, but all my time was gone too. I never really saw Tommy anymore, except on the weekends and even then I'd have to be studying half the time. I had it a little easier than a lot of the other people in my class because I always read a lot. It was my way of escaping—even before I came here to live on the streets.

Before I ran away I was a regular at the local library—it was both a source of books and refuge from what was happening at home. Once I got here, Shirley told me about how the bookstores'd strip the covers off paperbacks and just throw the rest of the book away, so I always made sure I stopped by the alleys in back of their stores on garbage days.

I hadn't read a book in months. The dogs were pining—little Rexy taking it the worst. He's just a cat-sized wiry-haired mutt with a major insecurity problem. I think someone used to beat on him, which made me feel close to him, because I knew what that was all about. Used to be Rexy was like my shadow; nervous, sure, but so long as I was around, he was okay. These days, he's just a wreck, because he can't come on my bike when I'm working and they won't let me bring him into the school.

The way things stand, Tommy's depressed, the other dogs are depressed, Rexy's almost suicidal, and I'm not in any great shape myself. Always tired, impatient, unhappy.

So I really needed to meet a ghost in the Tombs right

about now. It's doing wonders for my sense of sanity—or rather lack thereof, because I know I wasn't dreaming that night, or at least I wasn't asleep.

3

Everybody's worried about me when I finally get home—Rexy, the other dogs, Tommy, my landlady, Aunt Hilary, who looks after Tommy—and I appreciate it, but I don't talk about where I've been or what I've seen. What's the point? I'm kind of embarrassed about anybody knowing that I'm feeling nostalgic for the old squat and I'm not quite sure I believe who I saw there anyway, so what's to tell?

I make nice with Aunt Hilary, calm down the dogs, put Tommy to bed, then I've got homework to do for tomorrow night's class and work in the morning, so by the time I finally get to bed myself, Shirley's maybe-ghost is pretty well out of my mind. I'm so tired that I'm out like a light as soon as my head hits the pillow.

Where do they get these expressions we all use, anyway? Why out like a light and not on like one? Why do we hit the pillow when we go to sleep? Logs don't have a waking/sleeping cycle, so how can we sleep like one?

Sometimes I think about what this stuff must sound like when it gets literally translated into some other language. Yeah, I know. It's not exactly Advanced Philosophy 101 or anything, but it sure beats thinking about ghosts, which is what I'm trying not to think about as I walk home from the subway that night after my classes. I'm doing a pretty good job, too, until I get to my landlady's front steps.

Aunt Hilary is like the classic tenement landlady. She's a widow, a small but robust grey-haired woman with more energy than half the messengers at QMS. She's got lace hanging in her windows, potted geraniums on the steps going down to the pavement, an old black-and-white tabby named Frank that she walks on a leash. Rexy and Tommy are the only ones in my family that Frank'll tolerate.

Anyway, I come walking down the street, literally dragging my feet I'm so tired, and there's Frank sitting by one of the geranium pots giving me the evil eye—which is not so unusual—while sitting one step up is Shirley—which up until last night I would have thought was damned well impossible. Tonight I don't even question her presence.

"How's it going, Shirl?" I say as I collapse beside her on the steps.

Frank arches his back when I go by him, but deigns to give my shoulder bag a sniff before he realizes it's only got my school books in it. The look he gives me as he settles down again is less than respectful.

Shirley's leaning back against a higher step. She's got her hands in her pockets, *clickety-clickety-click,* her hat pushed back from her forehead. Her rosehip-and-licorice scent has to work a little harder against the cloying odor of the geraniums, but it's still there.

"Ever wonder why there's a moon?" she asks me, her voice all dreamy and distant.

I follow her gaze to where the fat round globe is ballooning in the sky above the buildings on the opposite side of the street. It looks different here than it did in the Tombs—safer, maybe—but then everything does. It's the second night that it's full, and I find myself wondering if ghosts are like werewolves, called up by the moon's light, only nobody's quite clued to it yet. Or at least Hollywood and the authors of cheap horror novels haven't.

I decide not to share this with Shirley. I knew her pretty well, but who knows what's going to offend a ghost? She doesn't wait for me to answer anyway.

"It's to remind us of Mystery," she says, "and that makes it both a Gift and a Curse."

She's talking like Pooh in the Milne books, her inflection setting capital letters at the beginning of certain words. I've never been able to figure out how she does that. I've never been able to figure out how she knows so much about books, because I never even saw her read a newspaper all the time we were together.

"How so?" I ask.

"Grab an eyeful," she says. "Did you ever see anything so mysteriously beautiful? Just looking at it, really Considering it, has got to fill the most jaded spirit with awe."

I think about how ghosts have that trick down pretty good, too, but all I say is, "And what about the curse?"

"We all know it's just an over-sized rock hanging there in the sky. We've sent men to walk around on it, left trash on its surface, photographed it and mapped it. We know what it weighs, its size, its gravitational influence. We've sucked all the Mystery out of it, but it still maintains its hold on our imaginations.

"No matter how much we try to deny it, that's where poetry and madness were born."

I still don't get the curse part of it, but Shirley's already turned away from this line of thought. I can almost see her ghostly mind unfolding a chart inside her head and plotting a new course for our conversation. She looks at me.

"What's more important?" she asks. "To be happy or to bring happiness to others?"

"I kind of like to think they go hand in hand," I tell her. "That you can't really have one without the other."

"Then what have you forgotten?"

This is another side of Shirley I remember well. She gets into this one-hand-clapping mode, asking you simple stuff that gets more and more complicated the longer you think about it, but if you keep worrying at it, the way Rexy'll take on an old slipper, it gets back to being simple again. To get there, though, you have to work through a forest of words and images that can be far too zen-deep and confusing—especially when you're tired and your brain's in neutral the way mine is tonight.

"Is this part of the riddle you were talking about last night?" I ask.

She sort of smiles—lines crinkle around her eyes, fingers work the pocketed buttons, *clickety-clickety-click*. There's a feeling in the air like there was last night just before she vanished, but this time I'm not looking away. I hear a car turn onto this block, its headbeams washing briefly over us, bright lights flicker, then it's dark again, with one solid flash of real deep dark just before my eyes adjust to the change in illumination.

Of course she's gone once I can see properly again and there's only me and Frank sitting on the steps. I forget for a moment about where our relationship stands and reach out to give him a pat. I'm just trying to touch base with reality, I realize as I'm doing it, but that doesn't matter to him. He doesn't quite hiss as he gets up and jumps down to the side-walk.

I watch him swagger off down the street, watch the empty pavement for a while longer, then finally I get up myself and go inside.

4

There's a wariness in Angel's features when I step into her Grasso Street office. It's a familiar look. I asked her about it once, and she was both precise and polite with her explana-tion: "Well, Maisie. Things just seem to get complicated whenever you're around."

It's nothing I plan.

Her office is a one-room walk-in storefront off Grasso Street, shabby in a genteel sort of way. She has a rack of filing cabinets along one wall, an old beat-up sofa with a matching chair by the bay window, a government surplus desk—one of those massive oak affairs with about ten mil-lion scratches and dents—a swivel chair behind the desk and a couple of matching oak straightbacks sitting to one side. I remember thinking they looked like a pair I'd sold a few years ago to old man Kemps down the street, and it turns out that's where she picked them up.

A little table beside the filing cabinets holds a hot plate, a kettle, a bunch of mismatched mugs, a teapot and the vari-ous makings for coffee, hot chocolate and tea. The walls have cheerful posters—one from a travel agency that shows this wild New Orleans street scene where there's a carnival going on, one from a Jilly Coppercorn show—cutesy little flower fairies fluttering around in a junkyard.

I like the one of Bart Simpson best. I've never seen the show, but I don't think you have to to know what he's all about.

The nicest thing about the office is the front porch and steps that go down from it to the pavement. It's a great place from which to watch the traffic go by, vehicular and pedestrian, or just to hang out. No, that's not true. The nicest thing is Angel herself.

Her real name's Angelina Marceau, but everyone calls her Angel, partly on account of her name, I guess, but mostly because of the salvage work she does with street kids. The thing is, she looks like an angel. She tries to hide it with baggy pants and plain T-shirts and about as little makeup as you can get away with wearing and still not be considered a Baptist, but she's gorgeous. Heart-shaped face, hair to kill for—a long, dark waterfall that just seems to go forever down her back—and soft warm eyes that let you know straight-away that here's someone who genuinely cares about you. Not as a statistic to add to her list of rescued souls, but as an individual. A real person.

Unless she's giving you the suspicious once-over she's giving me as I come in. It's a look you have to earn, because normally she'll bend over backwards to give you the benefit of the doubt.

I have to admit, there was a time when I'd push her, just to test the limits of her patience. It's not something I was particularly prone to, but we used to have a history of her trying to help me and me insisting I didn't need any help. We worked through all of that, eventually, but I keep finding myself in circumstances that make her feel as though I'm still testing the limits.

Like the time I punched out the booking agent at the Harbour Ritz my first day on the job that Angel had gotten for me at QMS.

I'm not the heartstopper that Angel is, but I do okay in the looks department. My best feature, I figure, is my hair. It's not as long as Angel's, but it's as thick. Jackie, the dispatch girl at QMS, says it reminds her of the way they all wore their hair in the sixties—did I mention that these folks are living in a time warp? I've never bothered to tell them that the sixties have been and gone, it's only the styles that are making yet another comeback.

Anyway, my hair's a nice shade of light golden brown and hangs halfway down my back. I do okay in the figure department, too, though I lean more towards Winona Ryder, say, than Kim Basinger. Still, I've had guys hit on me occasionally, especially these days, since I don't put out the impression that I'm some assistant baglady-in-training anymore.

The Harbour Ritz booking agent doesn't know any of this. He just sees a messenger girl delivering some documents and figures he'll give me a thrill. I guess he's either hard up, or figures anyone without his equipment between their legs is just dying to have him paw them, because that's what he does to me when I try to get him to sign for his envelope. He ushers me into his office and then closes the door, leans back against it and pulls me toward him.

What was I supposed to do? I just cocked back a fist and broke his nose.

Needless to say, he raised a stink, it's his word against mine, etcetera, etcetera. Except the folks at QMS turn out to be real supportive and Angel comes down on this guy like he's some used condom she's found stuck to the bottom of her shoe when she's walking through the Combat Zone. I keep my job, and don't get arrested for assault like the guy's threatening, but it's a messy situation, right?

The look Angel's wearing says, "I hope this isn't more of the same, but just seeing you kicks in this bad feeling. . . ."

It's not more of the same, I want to tell her, but that's about as far as my reasoning can take it. What's bothering me isn't exactly something I can just put my finger on. Do I tell her about Shirley, do I tell her about the malaise I've got eating away at me, or what?

I'd been tempted to bring the whole family with me—I spend so little time with them as it is—but settled on Rexy, mostly because he's easier to control. It's hard to think when you're trying to keep your eye on six of them and Tommy, too.

Today I could be alone in a padded cell and I'd still find it hard to think.

I take a seat on the sofa and after a moment Angel comes around from behind her desk and settles on the other end. Rexy's being real good. He licks her hand when she reaches out to pet him, then curls up on my lap and pretends to go to sleep. I know he's faking it because his ears twitch in a way they don't when he's really conked out.

Angel and I do some prelims—small talk which is always relaxed and easy around her, but eventually we get to the nitty-gritty of why I'm here.

"I've got this problem," I say, thinking of Shirley, but I know it's not her. I kind of like having her around again, dead or not.

"At work?" Angel tries when I'm not more forthcoming.

"Not exactly."

Angel's looking a little puzzled, but curious, too.

"Your grades are good," she says.

"It's not got anything to do with grades," I tell her. Well, it does, but only because the high school diploma's part and parcel of the whole problem.

"Then what *does* it have to do with?" Angel wants to know.

It's a reasonable request—more so because I'm the one who's come to her, taking up her time. I know what I want to say, but I don't know how to phrase it.

My new life's like a dress I might have wished after in a store window, saved for, finally bought, only to find out that while it's the right size, it still doesn't quite fit properly. It's the wrong color. The sleeves are too long, or maybe too short. The skirt's too tight.

It's not something Angel would understand. Intellectually, maybe, but not how I feel about it. Angel's one of those people that sees everyone having a purpose in life, you've just got to figure out what it is. I don't even know where to begin figuring out that kind of stuff.

"Nothing really," I say after a few moments.

I get up suddenly, startling Rexy who jumps to the floor and then gives me this put-upon expression of his—he should take out a patent on it.

"I've got to go," I tell Angel.

"Maisie," she starts, rising herself, but I'm already heading for the door.

I pretend I don't hear her. I pretend she's not following me to the street and calling after me as I head down the block at a quick walk that you might as well call running.

I'm not in good shape, I realize. Angel's the only person I know that I could have talked with about something like this, but I couldn't do it. I couldn't even start.

All I felt like doing was crying, and that really would have freaked her, because I never cry.

Not where people can see.

5

"So what are you really doing here?" I ask.

We're sitting on a bench in the subway station at Williamson and Stanton, Shirley and I, with little Rexy sleeping on the toes of my running shoes. We're at the far end of the platform. It's maybe ten o'clock and there's hardly anybody else down here with us. I see a couple of yuppies, probably coming back from an early show. A black guy in a three-piece checking out papers in his briefcase. Two kids slouched against a wall, watching a companion do tricks with her skateboard that bring her perilously close to the edge of the platform. My heart's in my throat watching her, but her friends just look bored.

I wonder what they see when they look down this way. A baglady and me, with my dog dozing on my feet, or just me and Rexy on our own?

Shirley's gaze is on the subway system grid that's on the opposite side of the tracks, but I doubt she's really seeing it.

She always needed glasses but never got herself a pair, even when she could afford them.

"When I first got to the city," she says, "I always thought that one day I'd go back home and show everybody what an important person I had become. I wanted to prove that just because everyone from my parents to my teachers treated me like I was no good, didn't mean I really was no good.

"But I never went back."

Ghosts always want to set something right, I remember from countless books and stories. Revenge, mistakes, that kind of thing. Sometimes just to say goodbye. They're here because of unfinished business.

This is the first time I ever realized that Shirley'd had any.

I mean, I wasn't stupid, even when I was twelve and she first took me in under her wing. Even then I knew that normal people didn't live on the streets wearing their entire wardrobe on their backs. But I never really thought about why she was there. She always seemed like a part of the street, so full of smarts and a special kind of wisdom, that it simply never occurred to me that she'd been running away from something, too. That she'd had dreams and aspirations once, but all they came to was a homeless wandering to which the only end was a mishap like falling down the stairs in some run-down squat and breaking your neck.

That's what your life'll be like, I tell myself, if you don't follow through on what Angel's trying to do for you.

Maybe. But I'd respected Shirley, for all her quirks, for all that I knew she wasn't what anybody else would call a winner. I'd just always thought that whatever she lacked, she had inner peace to make up for it.

I slouch lower on the bench, legs crossed at the ankles, the back of my head leaning against the top of the bench. I'm wearing my fedora and the movement pushes it forward so that the brim hangs low over my eyes.

"Is that why you're back?" I ask Shirley. "Because you still had things left to do here?"

She shrugs, an eloquent Shirley-like gesture, for all the layers of clothes she's wearing.

"I don't really feel I ever went anywhere or came back," she says.

"But you died," I say.

"I guess so."

I try a different tack. "So what's it like?"

She smiles. "I don't really know. When I'm here, I don't feel any different from before I died. When I'm not here, I'm . . . I don't know where I am. A kind of limbo, I suppose. A place where nothing moves, nothing changes, months are minutes."

I don't say anything.

"I guess it's like the bus I never took back home," she adds after a moment. "I missed out on wherever it was I was supposed to go, and I don't know how to go on, where to catch the next bus, or if they're even running anymore. For me at least. They don't leave a schedule lying around for people like me who arrive too late.

"Story of my life, I guess."

I start to feel so bad for her that I almost wish she'd go back to throwing cryptic little riddles at me the way she'd done the first couple of times we'd met.

"Is there anything I can do?" I say, but the subway roars into the station at the same time as I speak, swallowing my words with its thunder.

I'm about to repeat what I said but when I turn to look at Shirley, she's not there anymore. I only just make it through the doors of the car, Rexy under my arm, before they hiss closed behind me and the train goes roaring off again into the darkness.

The story of her life, I think. I wonder, what's the story of mine?

6

I should tell you about Tommy.

He's a big guy, maybe six feet tall and running close to a hundred and eighty pounds. And he's strong. He's got brown hair, a dirtier shade than mine, though I try to keep it looking clean, and guileless eyes. He couldn't keep a secret if he knew one.

The thing is, he's simple. A ten-year-old in an adult's body. I'm not sure how old he is, but the last time I took him in for a checkup at the clinic, the doctor told me he was in his early thirties, which makes him older than me.

When I say simple, I don't mean stupid, though I'll admit Tommy's not all that bright by the way society reckons intelligence. I like to think of him as more basic than the rest of us. He's open with his feelings, likes to smile, likes to laugh. He's the happiest person I know, which is half the reason I love him the way I do. He may be mentally impaired, but sometimes I figure the world would be a better place if we all maintained some of that sweet innocence that makes him so endearing.

I inherited Tommy the same way I did the rest of my family: I found him on the streets, abandoned. I worried some at first about keeping him with me, but when I started asking around about institutions, I realized he'd have something with me and the dogs that he couldn't get anywhere else: a family. All a guy like Tommy needs is someone willing to put the time into loving him. You don't get that in places like the Zeb, which is where he lived until they discharged him so that someone with more pressing problems, read money, could have his bed.

One of the things I hate about the way my life's going now is that I hardly ever see him anymore. Our landlady knows him better than I do these days and that's depressing.

The day after I talk to Shirley in the subway, I get off early from work. There's a million things I should be doing—like the week's grocery shopping and research for a history essay at the library—but I decide the hell with it. It's a beautiful day, so I'm going to pack up a picnic lunch and take the family to the park.

I find Tommy and Aunt Hilary in the backyard. She's working on her garden, which for a postage-sized tenement lot is a work of art, a miniature farm and English garden all rolled into about a twenty by twenty foot yard of sunflow-

ers, rosebushes, corn, peas, every kind of squash, tomatoes
and flowerbeds aflame with color and scent. Tom's playing
with the paper people that I cut out of magazines and then
stick onto cardboard backings for him. The dogs are
sprawled all over the place, except for Rexy, who's dogging
Aunt Hilary's heels. You don't understand how apt an expression like that is until you see Rexy do his I-always-have-
to-be-two-inches-away-from-you thing.

Tommy looks up when he hears the dogs starting to yap,
and suddenly I'm inundated with my family, everybody trying to get a piece of hello from me at the same time. But the
best thing is seeing that kind of sad expression that Tommy's wearing too much these days broaden into the sweet-
est, happiest smile you can imagine. I don't figure I've ever
done anything to deserve all this unadulterated love, but
I accept it—on credit, I guess. It makes me try harder to be
good to them, to be worthy of that love.

I've got the trick down pat by now, ruffling the fur of six
dogs and giving Tommy a hug without ever letting anybody
feel left out. Aunt Hilary's straightening up from her garden, hands at the small of her back as she stretches the kinks
from her muscles. She's smiling, too.

"We had a visitor," she tells me when the pandemonium
settles down into simple chaos.

Tommy's leading me over to the big wooden tray on a
patch of grass to show me what his paper people have been
up to while I was gone this morning, and the dogs sort of
mooch along beside us in an undulating wave.

"Anybody I know?" I ask Aunt Hilary.

"I suppose you must," my landlady says, "but she didn't
leave a name. She just said she wanted to drop by to see how
your family was making out—especially your son."

I blink with surprise at that. "You mean Tommy?"

"Who else?"

Well, I guess he is like my kid, I think.

"What did she look like?" I ask, half-anticipating the answer.

"A bit like a homeless person, if you want to know the

truth," Aunt Hilary says. "She must have been wearing three or four dresses under her overcoat."

"Was she black?"

"Yes, how did you—"

"Hair in dreadlocks with lots of buttons attached to them?"

Aunt Hilary nods. "And she kept fiddling with something in her pockets that made a rattle-y sort of sound."

"That's Shirley," I say.

"So you do know her."

"She's an old friend."

Aunt Hilary starts to say something else, but I lose the thread of her conversation because all I'm thinking is, I'm not crazy. Other people *can* see her. I was being pretty cool whenever Shirley showed up, but I have to admit to worrying that her presence was just the first stage of a nervous breakdown.

Suddenly I realize that I'm missing everything my landlady's telling me about Shirley's visit.

"I'm sorry," I tell her. "What did you say?"

Aunt Hilary smiles. She's used to my spacing out from time to time.

"Your friend didn't stay long," she says. "She just told Tommy what a handsome young man he was and patted each of the dogs with utter concentration, as though she wanted to remember them, and then she left. I asked her to stay for some lunch, or at least a cup of tea, because she looked so—well, hungry, I suppose. But she just shook her head and said, 'That's very kind of you, but I don't indulge anymore.'"

Aunt Hilary frowns. "At least I think that's what she said. It doesn't really make a lot of sense, when you consider it."

"That's just Shirley," I tell her.

I can tell Aunt Hilary wants to talk some more about it, but I turn the conversation to my plan for an outing to the park, inviting her along. She hasn't got the time, she says— is probably looking forward to a few hours by herself, is what I hear, and I don't blame her—but she gets right into helping me get a knapsack of goodies organized.

We have a great day. Nothing's changed. I've still got to deal with my malaise, I've still got the ghost of a dead friend hanging around, but for a few hours I manage to put it all aside and it's like old times again.

I haven't seen Tommy this happy since I can't remember when, and that makes me feel both glad and depressed.

There's got to be a better way to live.

7

I decide it's time to get some expert advice, so the next day I call in sick at work and head off down to Fitzhenry Park instead.

Everybody who spends most of their time on the streets isn't necessarily a bum. Newford's got more than its share of genuinely homeless people—the ones who don't have any choice: winos, losers, the hopeless and the helpless, runaways, and far too many ordinary people who've lost their jobs, their homes, their future through no fault of their own. But it's also got a whole subculture, if you will, of street musicians, performance artists, sidewalk vendors and the like.

Some are like me: They started out as runaways and then evolved into something like when I was making cash from trash. Others have a room in a boarding house or some old hotel and work the streets because that's where their inclination lies. There's not a whole lot of ways to make a living playing fiddle tunes or telling fortunes in other outlets, and the overhead is very affordable.

Fitzhenry Park is where a lot of that kind of action lies. It's close to the Combat Zone, so you get a fair amount of hookers and even less-reputable types drifting down when they're, let's say, off-shift. But it's also close to the Barrio, so the seedy element is balanced out with mothers walking in pairs and pushing strollers, old women gossiping in tight clusters, old men playing dominoes and checkers on the benches. Plus you get the lunch crowds from the downtown core which faces the west side of the park.

The other hot spot is down by the Pier, on the lakefront, but that's geared more to the tourists, and the cops are tight-assed about permits and the like. If you're going to get arrested for busking or hawking goods from a sidewalk cart or just plain panhandling, that's the place it'll happen.

The kind of person I was looking for now would work the park crowds and I found him without hardly even trying. He was just setting up for the day.

Bones is a Native American—a full-blooded Kickaha with dark coppery skin, broad features and a braid hanging down his back that's almost as long as Angel's hair. He got his name from the way he tells fortunes. He'll toss a handful of tiny bones onto a piece of deerskin and read auguries from the pattern they make. He doesn't really dress for the part, eschewing buckskins and beads for scuffed old work-boots, faded blue jeans and a white T-shirt with the arms torn off, but it doesn't seem to hurt business.

I don't really hold much with any of this mumbo-jumbo stuff—not Bones's gig, nor what his girlfriend Cassie does with Tarot cards, nor Paperjack's Chinese fortune-telling devices. But while I don't believe that any of them can fore-tell the future, I still have to admit there's something differ-ent about some of the people who work this schtick.

Take Bones.

The man has crazy eyes. Not crazy, you-better-lock-him-up kind of eyes, but crazy because maybe he sees something we can't. Like there really is some other world lying draped across ours, and he can see right into it. Maybe he's even been there. Lots of times, I figure he's just clowning around, but sometimes that dark gaze of his locks onto you and then you see this seriousness lying behind the laughter and it's like the Tombs all over again—a piece of the wilderness bid-ing on a city street, a dislocating sensation like not only is anything possible, but it probably already exists.

Besides, who am I to make judgments these days? I'm being haunted by a ghost.

"How do, Maisie?" he says when I wheel my mountain bike up to the edge of the fountain where he's sitting.

I prop the bike up on its kickstand, hang my helmet from one of the handlebars and sit down beside him. He's fiddling with his bones, letting them tumble from one hand to the other. They make a sound like Shirley's buttons, only more muted. I find myself wondering what kind of an animal they came from. Mice? Birds? I look up from his hands and see the clown is sitting in his eyes, laughing. Maybe with me, maybe at me—I can never tell.

"Haven't seen you around much these days," he adds.

"I'm going to school," I tell him.

"Yeah?"

"And I've got a job."

He looks at me for this long heartbeat and I get that glimpse of otherness that puts a weird shifting sensation in the pit of my stomach.

"So are you happy?" he asks.

That's something no one ever asks when I tell them what I'm doing now. I pick at a piece of lint that's stuck to the cuff of my shorts.

"Not really," I tell him.

"Want to see what Nanabozo's got in store for you?" he asks, holding up his bones.

I don't know who Nanabozo is, but I get the idea.

"No," I say. "I want to ask you about ghosts."

He doesn't even blink an eye. Just grins.

"What about them?"

"Well, what are they?" I ask.

"Souls that got lost," he tells me, still smiling, but serious now, too.

I feel weird talking about this. It's a sunny day, the park's full of people, joggers, skateboarders, women with baby carriages, a girl on the bench just a few steps away who probably looks sexy at night under a streetlight, the way she's all tarted up, but now she just looks used. Nothing out of the ordinary, and here we are, talking about ghosts.

"What do you mean?" I ask. "How do they get lost?"

"There's a Path of Souls, all laid out for us to follow when we die," he tells me. "But some spirits can't see it, so they wander the earth instead. Others can't accept the fact that they're dead yet, and they hang around too."

"A path."

He nods.

"Like something you walk along."

"Inasmuch as a spirit walks," Bones says.

"My ghost says she missed a bus," I tell him.

"Maybe it's different for white people."

"She's black."

He sits there, not looking at me, bones trailing from one hand to the other, making their tiny rattling sound.

"What do you really want to know?" he asks me.

"How do I help her?"

"Why don't you try asking her?"

"I did, but all she gives me back are riddles."

"Maybe you're just not listening properly," he says.

I think back on the conversations I've had with Shirley since I first saw her in the Tombs a few nights ago, but I can't seem to focus on them. I remember being with her, I remember the feeling of what we talked about, but the actual content is muddy now. It seems to shift away as soon as I try to think about it.

"I've really seen her," I tell Bones. "I was there when she died—almost four years ago—but she's back. And other people have seen her, too."

"I know you have," he says.

I don't even know why I was trying to convince him—it's not like he'd be a person that needed convincing—but what he says, stops me.

"What do you mean?" I ask. It's my question for the day.

"It's in your eyes," he says. "The Otherworld has touched you. Think of it as a blessing."

"I don't know if I like the idea," I tell him. "I mean, I miss Shirley, and I actually feel kind of good about her being back, even if she is just a ghost, but it doesn't seem right somehow."

"Often," he says, "what we take from the spirit world is only a reflection of what lies inside ourselves."

There's that look in his eyes, a feral seriousness, like it's important, not so much that I understand, or even believe what he's saying, but *that* he's saying it.

"What . . . ?" I start, but then I figure it out. Part of it anyway.

When I first came to the city, I was pretty messed up, but then Shirley was there to help me. I'm messed up again, so. . . .

"So I'm just projecting her ghost?" I ask. "I need her help, so I've made myself a ghost of her?"

"I didn't say that."

"No, but—"

"Ghosts have their own agendas," he tells me. "Maybe you both have something to give to each other."

We sit for awhile, neither of us speaking. I play with the whistle that hangs from a cord around my neck—all the messengers have them to blow at cars that're trying to cut us off. Finally, I get up and take my bike off its kickstand. I look at Bones and that feral quality is still lying there in his grin. His eyes seem to be all pupil, dark, dark. I'm about to say thanks, but the words lock up in my throat. Instead I just nod, put on my helmet and go away to think about what he's told me.

8

Tommy's got this new story that he tells me after we've cleaned up the dinner dishes. We sit together at the kitchen table and he has his little paper people act it out for me. It's about this Chinese man who falls down the crack in the pavement outside Aunt Hilary's house and finds himself in this magic land where everybody's a beautiful model or movie star and they all want to marry the Chinese guy except he misses his family too much, so he just tells them he can't marry any of them—not even the woman who won the Oscar for her part in *Misery,* who for some reason, Tommy's really crazy about.

I've got the old black lab Chuckie lying on my feet, Rexy

snuggled up in my lap. Mutt and Jeff are tangled up in a heap on the sofa so that it's hard to tell which part of them's which. They're a cross between a German Shepherd and who knows what; I found Jeff first and gave the other old guy his name because the two were immediately inseparable. Jimmie's part dachshund, part collie—I know, go figure—and his long, furry body is stretched out in front of the door like he's a dust puppy. Patty's mostly poodle, but there's some kind of placid mix in there as well because she's not at all high-strung. Right now she's sitting in the bay window, checking the traffic and pretending to be a cat.

The sad thing, Tommy tells me, is that the Chinese man knows that he'll never be able to get back home, but he's going to stay faithful to his family anyway.

"Where'd you get that story?" I ask Tommy.

He just shrugs, then he says, "I really miss you, Maisie."

How can I keep leaving him?

I feel like a real shit. I know it's not my fault, I know I'm trying to do my best for all of us, for our future, but Tommy's mind doesn't work very well considering the long term and my explanations don't really register. It's just me going out all the time, and not taking him or the dogs with me.

There's a knock on the door. Jimmie gets laboriously to his feet and moves aside as Aunt Hilary comes in. She gives her wristwatch an obvious look.

"You're going to be late for school," she says, not really nagging, she just knows me too well.

I feel like saying, Fuck school, but I put Rexy down, shift Chuckie from my feet and stand up. Six dogs and Tommy all give me a hopeful look, like we're going out for a walk, faces all dropping when I pick up my knapsack, heavy with school books.

I give Tommy a hug and kiss then make the goodbye rounds of the dogs. They're like Tommy; long term means nothing to them. All they know is I'm going out and they can't come. Rexy takes a few hopeful steps in the direction of the door, but Aunt Hilary scoops him up.

"Now, now, Rexy," she tells him. "You know Margaret's got to go to school and she can't take you."

Margaret. She's the one who goes to school and works at QMS and deserts her family five days and four nights a week. She's the traitor.

I'm Maisie, but I'm Margaret, too.

I say goodbye, trying not to look anyone in the eye, and head for the subway. My eyes are pretty well dry by the time I get there. I pause on the platform. When the southbound train comes, I don't get off at the stop for my school, but ride it all the way downtown. I walk the six blocks to the bus depot.

I get a piece of gum stuck to the bottom of my sneaker while I'm waiting in line at the ticket counter. I'm still trying to get it off with an old piece of tissue I find in my pocket—not the most useful tool for the job—when the guy behind the counter says, "Next," in this really tired voice.

Who's he got waiting at home for him? I wonder as I move toward the counter, sort of shuffling the foot with the gum stuck on it so it doesn't trap me to another spot.

"How much for a ticket?" I ask him.

"Depends where you're going."

He's got thinning hair lying flat against his head, parted way over on the left side. Just a skinny little guy in a faded shirt and pants that are too baggy for him, trying to do his job. He's got a tic in one eye and I keep thinking that he's giving me a wink.

"Right," I say.

My mind's out of sync. Of course he needs the destination. I let my thoughts head back into the past, looking for the name of the place I want, trying to avoid the bad times that are hiding there in my memories, just waiting to jump me, but it's impossible to do.

That's another thing about street people, whether they put the street behind them or not: The past holds pain. The present may not be all that great, but it's usually better than what went before. That goes for me, for Shirley, for pretty well everybody I know. You try to live here and now, like the people who go through twelve-step, taking it day by day.

Mostly, you try not to think at all.

"Rockcastle," I tell the guy behind the counter.

He does something mysterious with his computer before he looks up.

"Return or one-way?"

"One-way."

More fiddling with the computer before he tells me the price. I pay him and a couple of minutes later I'm hop-stepping my way out of the depot with a one-way ticket to Rockcastle in my pocket. I sit on a bench outside and scrape off the gum with a popsicle stick I find on the sidewalk, and then I'm ready.

I don't go to my class; I don't go home, either. Instead I take the subway up to Gracie Street. When I come up the steps from the station I stand on the pavement for a long time before I finally cross over and walk into the Tombs.

9

The moon seems smaller tonight. It's not just that it's had a few slivers shaved off one side because its waning; it's like it got tamed somehow.

I can't say the same for the Tombs. I see kids sniffing glue, shooting up, some just sprawled with their backs against a pile of rubble, legs splayed out in front of them, eyes staring into nothing. I pass a few 'bos cooking God-knows-what over a fire they've got rigged up in an old jerry can. A bag-lady comes lurching out between the sagging doors of an old office building and starts to yell at me. Her voice follows me as I pick a way through the litter and abandoned cars.

The bikers down the street are having a party. The buckling pavement in front of their building has got about thirty-five chopped-down street hogs parked in front of it. The place is lit up with Coleman lights and I can hear the music and laughter from where I'm sitting in the bay window of my old squat in the Clark Building.

They don't bother me; I never exactly hung out with them

or anything, but they used to consider me a kind of mascot after Shirley died and let the word get out that I was under their protection. It's not the kind of thing that means a lot everywhere, but it helped me more than once.

No one's taken over the old squat yet, but after five months it's already got the same dead feel to it that hits you anywhere in the Tombs. It's not exactly dirty, but it's dusty and the wind's been blowing crap in off the street. There's a smell in the air; though it's not quite musty, it's getting there.

But I'm not really thinking about any of that. I'm just passing time. Sitting here, waiting for a piece of the past to catch up to me.

I used to sit here all the time once I'd put Tommy to bed, looking out the window when I wasn't reading, Rexy snuggled close, the other dogs sprawled around the room, a comforting presence of soft snores and twitching bodies as they chased dream-rabbits in their sleep.

There's no comfort here now.

I look back out the window and see a figure coming up the street, but it's not who I was expecting. It's Angel, with Chuckie on a leash, his black shadow shape stepping out front, leading the way. As I watch them approach, some guy moves from out of the shadows that've collected around the building across the street and Chuckie, worn out and old though he is, lunges at him. The guy makes a fast fade.

I listen to them come into the building, Chuckie's claws clicking on the scratched marble, the leather soles of Angel's shoes making a scuffley sound as she comes up the stairs. I turn around when they come into the squat.

"I thought I'd find you here," Angel says.

"I didn't know you were looking."

I don't mean to sound put off, but I can't keep the punkiness out of my voice.

"I'm not checking up on you, Maisie. I was just worried."

"Well, here I am."

She undoes the lead from Chuckie's collar and he comes across the room and sticks his face up against my knees. The feel of his fur under my hand is comforting.

"You really shouldn't be out here," I tell Angel. "It's not safe."

"But it's okay for you?"

I shrug. "This was my home."

She crosses the room as well. The window sill's big enough to hold us both. She scoots up and then sits across from me, arms wrapped around her legs.

"After you came by the office, I went by your work to see you, then to your apartment, then to the school."

I shrug again.

"Do you want to talk about it?" she asks.

"What's to say?"

"Whatever's in your heart. I'm here to listen. Or I can just go away, if that's what you prefer, but I don't really want to do that."

"I . . ."

The words start locking up inside me again. I take a deep breath and start over.

"I'm not really happy, I guess," I tell her.

She doesn't say anything, just nods encouragingly.

"It's . . . I never really told you why I came to see you about school and the job and everything. You probably just thought that you'd finally won me over, right?"

Angel shakes her head. "It was never a matter of winning or losing. I'm just there for the people who need me."

"Yeah, well, what happened was—do you remember when Margaret Grierson died?"

Angel nods.

"We shared the same postal station," I tell her, "and the day before she was killed, I got a message in my box warning me to be careful, that someone was out to do a serious number on me. I spent the night in a panic and I was so relieved when the morning finally came and nothing had happened, because what'd happen to Tommy and the dogs if anything ever happened to me, you know?"

"What does that have to do with Margaret Grierson?" Angel asks.

"The note I got was addressed to 'Margaret'—just that,

nothing else. I thought it was for me, but I guess whoever sent it got his boxes mixed up and it ended up in mine instead of hers."

"But I still don't see what—"

I can't believe she doesn't get it.

"Margaret Grierson was an important person," I say. "She was heading up that AIDS clinic, she was doing things for people. She was making a difference."

"Yes, but—"

"I'm nobody," I say. "It should've been me that died. But it wasn't, so I thought well, I better do something with myself, with my life, you know? I better make my having survived meaningful. But I can't cut it.

"I've got the straight job, the straight residence, I'm going back to school and it's like it's all happening to someone else. The things that are important to me—Tommy and the dogs—it's like they're not even a part of my life anymore."

I remember something Shirley's ghost asked me, and add, "Maybe it's selfish, but I figure charity should start at home, you know? I can't do much for other people if I'm feeling miserable myself."

"You should've come to me," Angel says.

I shake my head. "And tell you what? It sounds so whiny. I mean there's people starving not two blocks from where we're sitting, and I should be worried about being happy or not? The important stuff's covered—I'm providing for my family, putting a roof over their heads and making sure they have enough to eat—that should be enough, right? But it doesn't feel that way. It feels like the most important things are missing.

"I used to have time to spend with Tommy and the dogs; now I have to steal a minute here, another there. . . ."

My voice trails off. I think of how sad they all looked when I left the apartment tonight, like I was deserting them, not just for the evening, but forever. I can't bear that feeling, but how do you explain yourself to those who can't possibly understand?

"We could've worked something out," Angel says. "We still can."

"Like what?"

Angel smiles. "I don't know. We'll just have to think it through better than we have so far. You'll have to try to open up a bit more, tell me what you're *really* feeling, not just what you think I want to hear."

"It's that obvious, huh?"

"Let's just say I have a built-in bullshit detector."

We don't say anything for awhile then. I think about what she's said, wondering if something could be worked out. I don't want special dispensation because I'm some kind of charity case—I've *always* earned my own way—but I know there've got to be some changes or the little I've got is going to fall apart.

I can't get the image out of my mind—Tommy with his sad eyes as I'm going out the door—and I know I've got to make the effort. Find a way to keep what was good about the past and still make a decent future for us.

I put my hand in my pocket and feel the bus ticket I bought earlier.

I have to open up a bit more? I think, looking at Angel, What would her bullshit detector do if I told her about Shirley?

Angel stretches out her legs, then lowers them to the floor.

"Come on," she says, offering me her hand. "Let's go talk about this some more."

I look around the squat and compare it to Aunt Hilary's apartment. There's no comparison. What made this place special, we took with us.

"Okay," I tell Angel.

I take her hand and we leave the building. I know it's not going to be easy, but then nothing ever is. I'm not afraid to work my butt off; I just don't want to lose sight of what's really important.

When we're outside, I look back up to the window where

we were sitting. I wonder about Shirley, how's she's going to work out whatever it is that she's got to do to regain her own sense of peace. I hope she finds it. I don't even mind if she comes to see me again, but I don't think that'll be part of the package.

I left the bus ticket for her, on the window sill.

10

I don't know if we've worked everything out, but I think we're making a good start. Angel's fixed it so that I've dropped a few courses which just means that it'll take me longer to get my diploma. I'm only working a couple of days a week at QMS—the Saturday shift that nobody likes and a rotating day during the week.

The best thing is I'm back following my trade again, trash for cash. Aunt Hilary lets me store stuff in her garage because she doesn't have a car anyway. A couple of nights a week, Tommy and I head out with our carts, the dogs on our heels, and we work the bins. We're spending a lot more time together and everybody's happier.

I haven't seen Shirley again. If it hadn't been for Aunt Hilary telling me about her coming by the house, I'd just think I made the whole thing up.

I remember what Bones told me about ghosts having their own agendas and how maybe we both had something to give each other. Seeing Shirley was the catalyst for me. I hope I helped her some, too. I remember her telling me once that she came from Rockcastle. I think wherever she was finally heading, Rockcastle was still on the way.

There isn't a solution to every problem, but at the very least, you've got to try.

I went back to the squat the day after I was there with Angel, and the bus ticket was gone. Logic tells me that someone found it and cashed it in for a quick fix or a bottle of cheap wine. I'm pretty sure I just imagined the lingered scent of rosehip and licorice, and the button I found on the floor was probably from one of Tommy's shirts, left behind when we moved.

But I'd like to think that it was Shirley who picked the ticket up, that this time she got to the depot on time.

MR. TRUEPENNY'S BOOK
EMPORIUM AND GALLERY

*The constellations were consulted
for advice, but no one understood them.*
—attributed to Elias Canetti

My name's Sophie and my friend Jilly says I have faerie
blood. Maybe she's right.

Faeries are supposed to have problems dealing with mod-
ern technology and I certainly have trouble with anything
technological. The simplest appliances develop horrendous
problems when I'm around. I can't wear a watch because
they start to run backwards, unless they're digital; then they
just flash random numbers as though the watch's inner
workings have taken to measuring fractals instead of time.
If I take a subway or bus, it's sure to be late. Or it'll have a
new driver who takes a wrong turn and we all get lost.

This actually happened to me once. I got on the number 3
at the Kelly Street Bridge and somehow, instead of going
downtown on Lee, we ended up heading north into Foxville.

I also have strange dreams.

I used to think they were the place that my art came from,
that my subconscious was playing around with images, tossing them up in my sleep before I put them down on canvas
or paper. But then a few months ago I had this serial dream

that ran on for a half dozen nights in a row, a kind of fairy tale that was either me stepping into faerie, and therefore real within its own parameters—which is what Jilly would like me to believe—or it was just my subconscious making another attempt to deal with the way my mother abandoned my father and me when I was a kid. I don't really know which I believe anymore, because I still find myself going back to that dream world from time to time and meeting the people I first met there.

I even have a boyfriend in that place, which probably tells you more about my usual ongoing social status than it does my state of mind.

Rationally, I know it's just a continuation of that serial dream. And I'd let it go at that, except it feels so damn real. Every morning when I wake up from the latest installment, my head's filled with memories of what I've done that seem as real as anything I do during the day—sometimes more so.

But I'm getting off on a tangent. I started off meaning just to introduce myself, and here I am, giving you my life story. What I really wanted to tell you about was Mr. Truepenny.

The thing you have to understand is that I made him up. He was like one of those invisible childhood friends, except I deliberately created him.

We weren't exactly well-off when I was growing up. When my mother left us, I ended up being one of those latchkey kids. We didn't live in the best part of town; Upper Foxville is a rough part of the city and it could be a scary place for a little girl who loved art and books and got teased for that love by the other neighborhood kids, who couldn't even be bothered to learn how to read. When I got home from school, I went straight in and locked the door.

I'd get supper ready for my dad, but there were always a couple of hours to kill in between my arriving home and when he finished work—longer if he had to work late. We didn't have a TV, so I read a lot, but we couldn't afford to buy books. On Saturday mornings, we'd go to the library and I'd take out my limit—five books—which I'd finish by Tuesday, even if I tried to stretch them out.

To fill the rest of the time, I'd draw on shopping bags or the pads of paper that dad brought me home from work, but that never seemed to occupy enough hours. So one day I made up Mr. Truepenny.

I'd daydream about going to his shop. It was the most perfect place that I could imagine: all dark wood and leaded glass, thick carpets and club chairs with carved wooden-based reading lamps strategically placed throughout. The shelves were filled with leather-bound books and folios, and there was a small art gallery in the back.

The special thing about Mr. Truepenny's shop was that all of its contents existed only within its walls. Shakespeare's *The Storm of Winter. The Chapman's Tale* by Chaucer. *The Blissful Stream* by William Morris. Steinbeck's companion collection to *The Long Valley, Salinas. North Country Stoic* by Emily Brontë.

None of these books existed, of course, but being the dreamy sort of kid that I was, not only could I daydream of visiting Mr. Truepenny's shop, but I could actually read these unwritten stories. The gallery in the back of the shop was much the same. There hung works by the masters that saw the light of day only in my imagination. Van Goghs and Monets and da Vincis. Rossettis and Homers and Cézannes.

Mr. Truepenny himself was a wonderfully eccentric individual who never once chased me out for being unable to make a purchase. He had a Don Quixote air about him, a sense that he was forever tilting at windmills. He was tall and thin with a thatch of mouse-brown hair and round spectacles, a rumpled tweed suit and a huge briar pipe that he continually fussed with but never actually lit. He always greeted me with genuine affection and seemed disappointed when it was time for me to go.

My imagination was so vivid that my daydream visits to his shop were as real to me as when my dad took me to the library or to the Newford Gallery of Fine Art. But it didn't last. I grew up, went to Butler University on student loans and the money from far too many menial jobs—"got a life," as the old saying goes. I made friends, I was so busy, there was no time, no *need* to visit the shop anymore. Eventually I simply forgot all about it.

Until I met Janice Petrie.

Wendy and I were in the Market after a late night at her place the previous evening. I was on my way home, but we'd decided to shop for groceries together before I left. Trying to make up my mind between green beans and a head of broccoli, my gaze lifted above the vegetable stand and met that of a little girl standing nearby with her parents. Her eyes widened with recognition though I'd never seen her before.

"You're the woman!" she cried. "You're the woman who's evicting Mr. Truepenny. I think it's a horrible thing to do. You're a horrible woman!"

And then she started to cry. Her mother shushed her and apologized to me for the outburst before bustling the little girl away.

"What was all *that* about, Sophie?" Wendy asked me.

"I have no idea," I said.

But of course I did. I was just so astonished by the encounter that I didn't know what to say. I changed the subject and that was the end of it until I got home. I dug out an old cardboard box from the back of my hall closet and rooted about in it until I came up with a folder of drawings I'd done when I still lived with my dad. Near the back I found the ones I was looking for.

They were studies of Mr. Truepenny and his amazing shop.

God, I thought, looking at these awkward drawings, pencil on brown grocery-bag paper, ballpoint on foolscap. The things we forget.

I took the drawings out onto my balcony and lay down on the old sofa I kept out there, studying them, one by one. There was Mr. Truepenny, writing something in his big leather-bound ledger. Here was another of him, holding his cat, Dodger, the two of them looking out the leaded glass windows of the shop. There was a view of the main aisle of the shop, leading down to the gallery, the perspective slightly askew, but not half bad considering I was no older when I did them than was the little girl in the Market today.

How could she have *known?* I found myself thinking. Mr. Truepenny and his shop were something I'd made up. I couldn't remember ever telling anyone else about them— not even Jilly. And what did she mean about my evicting him from the shop?

I could think of no rational response. After a while, I just set the drawings aside and tried to forget about it. Exhaustion from the late night before soon had me nodding off, and I fell asleep only to find myself, not in my boyfriend's faerie dream world, but on the streets of Mabon, the made-up city in which I'd put Mr. Truepenny's Book Emporium and Gallery.

⟶

I'm half a block from the shop. The area's changed. The once-neat cobblestones are thick with grime. Refuse lies everywhere. Most of the storefronts are boarded up, their walls festooned with graffiti. When I reach Mr. Truepenny's shop, I see a sign in the window that reads, CLOSING SOON DUE TO LEASE EXPIRATION.

Half-dreading what I'll find, I open the door and hear the familiar little bell tinkle as I step inside. The shop's dusty and dim, and much smaller than I remember it. The shelves are almost bare. The door leading to the gallery is shut and has a CLOSED sign tacked onto it.

"Ah, Miss Etoile. It's been so very long."

I turn to find Mr. Truepenny at his usual station behind the front counter. He's smaller than I remember as well, and looks a little shabby now. Hair thinning, tweed suit threadbare and more shapeless than ever.

"What . . . what's happened to the shop?" I ask.

I've forgotten that I'm asleep on the sofa out on my balcony. All I know is this awful feeling I have inside as I look at what's become of my old childhood haunt.

"Well, times change," he says. "The world moves on."

"This—is this my doing?"

His eyebrows rise quizzically.

"I met this little girl and she said I was evicting you."

"I don't blame you," Mr. Truepenny says, and I can see in his sad eyes that it's true. "You've no more need for me or my wares, so it's only fair that you let us fade."

"But you . . . that is . . . well, you're not real."

I feel weird saying this, because while I remember now that I'm dreaming, this place is like one of my faerie dreams that feel as real as the waking world.

"That's not strictly true," he tells me. "You did conceive of the city and this shop, but we were drawn to fit the blueprint of your plan from . . . elsewhere."

"What elsewhere?"

He frowns, brow furrowing as he thinks.

"I'm not really sure myself," he tells me.

"You're saying I didn't make you up, I just drew you here from somewhere else?"

He nods.

"And now you have to go back?"

"So it would seem."

"And this little girl—how can she know about you?"

"Once a reputable establishment is open for business, it really can't deny any customer access, regardless of their age or station in life."

"She's visiting my daydream?" I ask. This is too much to accept, even for a dream.

Mr. Truepenny shakes his head. "You brought this world into being through your single-minded desire, but now it has a life of its own."

"Until I forgot about it."

"You had a very strong will," he says. "You made us so real that we've been able to hang on for decades. But now we really have to go."

There's a very twisty sort of logic involved here, I can see. It doesn't make sense by way of the waking world's logic, but I think there are different rules in a dreamscape. After all, my faerie boyfriend can turn into a crow.

"Do you have more customers, other than that little girl?" I ask.

"Oh yes. Or at least, we did." He waves a hand to encompass the shop. "Not much stock left, I'm afraid. That was the first to go."

"Why doesn't *their* desire keep things running?"

"Well, they don't have faerie blood, now do they? They can visit, but they haven't the magic to bring us across or keep us here."

It figures. I think. We're back to that faerie-blood thing again. Jilly would love this.

I'm about to ask him to explain it all a little more clearly when I get this odd jangling sound in my ears and wake up back on the sofa. My doorbell's ringing. I go inside the apartment to accept what turns out to be a FedEx package.

"Can dreams be real?" I ask the courier. "Can we invent something in a dream and have it turn out to be a real place?"

"Beats me, lady," he replies, never blinking an eye. "Just sign here."

I guess he gets all kinds.

⸺

So now I visit Mr. Truepenny's shop on a regular basis again. The area's vastly improved. There's a café nearby where Jeck—that's my boyfriend that I've been telling you about—and I go for tea after we've browsed through Mr. Truepenny's latest wares. Jeck likes this part of Mabon so much that he's now got an apartment on the same street as the shop. I think I might set up a studio nearby.

I've even run into Janice—the little girl who brought me back here in the first place. She's forgiven me, of course, now that she knows it was all a misunderstanding, and lets me buy her an ice cream from the soda fountain sometimes before she goes home.

I'm very accepting of it all—you get that way after a while. The thing that worries me now is, what happens to Mabon when I die? Will the city get run down again and eventually disappear? And what about its residents? There's all these people here; they've got family, friends, lives. I get the feeling it wouldn't be the same for them if they have to go back to that elsewhere place Mr. Truepenny was so vague about.

So that's the reason I've written all this down and had it printed up into a little folio by one of Mr. Truepenny's friends in the waking world. I'm hoping somebody out there's like me. Someone's got enough faerie blood not only to visit, but to keep the place going. Naturally, not just anyone will do. It has to be the right sort of person, a book lover, a lover of old places and tradition, as well as the new.

If you think you're the person for the position, please send a résumé to me care of Mr. Truepenny's Book Emporium and Gallery, Mabon. I'll get back to you as soon as I can.

THE FOREST IS CRYING

———

There are seven million homeless children
on the streets of Brazil. Are vanishing
trees being reborn as unwanted children?
—Gary Snyder, from *The Practice of the Wild*

The real problem is, people think life
is a ladder, and it's really a wheel.
—Pat Cadigan, from "Johnny Come Home"

Two pairs of footsteps, leather soles on marble floors. Listening to the sound they made, Dennison felt himself wondering, What was the last thing that Ronnie Egan heard before he died? The squeal of tires on wet pavement? Some hooker or an old wino shouting, "Look out!" Or was there no warning, no warning at all? Just the sudden impact of the car as it hit him and flung his body ten feet in the air before it was smeared up against the plate glass window of the pawn shop?

"You don't have to do this," Stone said as they paused at the door. "One of the neighbors already IDed the body."

"I know."

Looking through the small window, glass reinforced with metal mesh, Dennison watched the morgue attendant approach to let them in. Like the detective at Dennison's side, the attendant was wearing a sidearm. Was the security to keep people out or keep them in? he wondered morbidly.

"So why—" Stone began, then he shook his head. "Never mind."

It wasn't long before they were standing on either side of

a metal tray that the attendant had pulled out from the wall at Stone's request. It could easily hold a grown man, twice the 170 pounds Dennison carried on his own six-one frame. The small body laid out upon the metal surface was dwarfed by the expanse of stainless steel that surrounded it.

"His mother's a heavy user," Dennison said. "She peddles her ass to feed the habit. Sometimes she brings the man home—she's got a room at the Claymore. If the guy didn't like having a kid around, she'd get one of the neighbors to look after him. We've had her in twice for putting him outside to play in the middle of the night when she couldn't find anybody to take him in. Trouble is, she always put on such a good show for the judge that we couldn't make the neglect charges stick."

He delivered the brief summary in a monotone. It didn't seem real. Just like Ronnie Egan's dead body didn't seem real. The skin so ashen, the bruises so dark against its pallor.

"I read the file," Stone said.

Dennison looked up from the corpse of the four-year-old boy.

"Did you bring her in?" he asked.

Stone shook his head. "Can't track her down. We've got an APB out on her, but . . ." He sighed. "Who're we kidding, Chris? Even when we do bring her in, we're not going to be able to find a charge that'll stick. She'll just tell the judge what she's told them before."

Dennison nodded heavily. I'm sorry, Your Honor, but I was asleep and I never even heard him go out. He's a good boy, but he doesn't always listen to his momma. He likes to wander. If Social Services could give her enough to raise him in a decent neighborhood, this kind of thing would never happen. . . .

"I should've tried harder," he said.

"Yeah, like your caseload's any lighter than mine," Stone said. "Where the fuck would you find the time?"

"I still should've . . ."

Done something, Dennison thought. Made a difference.

Stone nodded to the attendant, who zipped up the heavy

plastic bag, then slid the drawer back into the wall. Dennison watched until the drawer closed with a metal click, then finally turned away.

"You're taking this too personally," Stone said.

"It's always personal."

Stone put his arm around Dennison's shoulders and steered him toward the door.

"It gets worse every time something like this happens," Dennison went on. "For every one I help, I lose a dozen. It's like pissing in the wind."

"I know," Stone said heavily.

⟶

The bright daylight stung Dennison's eyes when he stepped outside. He hadn't had breakfast yet, but he had no appetite. His pager beeped, but he didn't bother to check the number he was supposed to call. He just shut off the annoying sound. He couldn't deal with whatever the call was about. Not today. He couldn't face going into the office either, couldn't face all those hopeless faces of people he wanted to help; there just wasn't enough time in a day, enough money in the budget, enough of anything to make a real difference.

Ronnie Egan's lifeless features floated up in his mind.

He shook his head and started to walk. Aimlessly, but at a fast pace. Shoe leather on pavement now, but he couldn't hear it for the sound of the traffic, vehicular and pedestrian. Half an hour after leaving the morgue he found himself on the waterfront, staring out over the lake.

He didn't think he could take it anymore. He'd put in seven years as a caseworker for Social Services, but it seemed as though he'd finally burned out. Ronnie Egan's stupid, senseless death was just too much to bear. If he went into the office right now, it would only be to type up a letter of resignation. He decided to get drunk instead.

Turning, he almost bumped into the attractive woman who was approaching him. She might be younger, but he put her at his own twenty-nine; she just wore the years better. A soft fall of light-brown hair spilled down to her shoulders in untidy tangles. Her eyes were a little too large for the rest of her features, but they were such an astonishing greygreen that it didn't matter. She was wearing jeans and a "Save the Rainforests" T-shirt, a black cotton jacket overtop.

"Hi there," she said.

She offered him a pamphlet that he reached for automatically, before he realized what he was doing. He dropped his hand and stuck it in his pocket, leaving her with the pamphlet still proffered.

"I don't think so," he said.

"It's a serious issue," she began.

"I've got my own problems."

She tapped the pamphlet. "This is everybody's problem."

Dennison sighed. "Look, lady," he said. "I'm more interested in helping people than trees. Sorry."

"But without the rainforests—"

"Trees don't have feelings," he said, cutting her off. "Trees don't cry. Kids do."

"Maybe you just can't hear them."

Her gaze held his. He turned away, unable to face her disappointed look. But what was he supposed to do? If he couldn't even be there for Ronnie Egan when the kid had needed help the most, what the hell did she expect him to do about a bunch of trees? There were other people, far better equipped, to deal with that kind of problem.

"You caught me on a bad day," he said. "Sorry."

He walked away before she could reply.

—

Dennison wasn't much of a drinker. A beer after work a couple of times a week. Wine with a meal even more occasionally. A few brews with the guys after one of their weekend softball games—that was just saying his pager left him alone long enough to get through all the innings. His clients' needs didn't fit into a tidy nine-to-five schedule, with weekends off. Crises could arise at any time of the day or night—

usually when it was most inconvenient. But Dennison had never really minded. He'd bitch and complain about it like everybody else he worked with, but he'd always be there for whoever needed the help.

Why hadn't Sandy Egan call him last night? He'd told her to phone him, instead of just putting Ronnie outside again. He'd promised her, no questions. He wouldn't use the incident as pressure to take the boy away from her. Ronnie was the first priority, plain and simple.

But she hadn't called. She hadn't trusted him, hadn't wanted to chance losing the extra money Social Services gave her to raise the boy. And now he was dead.

Halfway through his fourth beer, Dennison started ordering shots of whiskey on the side. By the time the dinner hour rolled around, he was too drunk to know where he was anymore. He'd started out in a run-down bar somewhere on Palm Street; he could be anywhere now.

The smoky interior of the bar looked like every other place he'd been in this afternoon. Dirty wooden floors, their polish scratched and worn beyond all redemption. Tables in little better condition, chairs with loose legs that wobbled when you sat on them, leaving you unsure if it was all the booze you'd been putting away that made your seat feel so precarious, or the rickety furniture that the owner was too cheap to replace until it actually fell apart under someone. A TV set up in a corner of the bar where game shows and soap operas took turns until they finally gave way to the six o'clock news.

And then there was the clientele.

The thin afternoon crowd was invariably composed of far too many lost and hopeless faces. He recognized them from his job. Today, as he staggered away from the urinal to blink at the reflection looking back at him from the mirror, he realized that he looked about the same. He couldn't tell himself apart from them if he tried, except that maybe they could hold their drink better.

Because he felt sick. Unable to face the squalor of one of the cubicles, he stumbled out of the bar, hoping to clear his head. The street didn't look familiar, and the air didn't help. It was filled with exhaust fumes and the tail end of rush-hour noise. His stomach roiled and he made his slow way along the pavement in front of the bar, one hand on the wall to keep his balance.

When he reached the alleyway, it was all he could do to take a few floundering steps inside before he fell to his hands and knees and threw up. Vomiting brought no relief. He still felt the world doing a slow spin and the stink just made his nausea worse.

Pushing himself away from the noxious puddle, the most he could manage was to fall back against the brick wall on this side of the alley. He brought his knees slowly up, wrapped his arms around them and leaned his head on top. He must have inadvertently turned his pager back on at some point in the afternoon, because it suddenly went off, its insistent beep piercing his aching head.

He unclipped it from his belt and threw it against the far wall. The sound of it smashing was only slightly more satisfying than the blessed relief from its shrill beeping.

"You don't look so good."

He lifted his head at the familiar voice, half-expecting that one of his clients had found him in this condition, or worse, one of his coworkers. Instead he met the grey-green gaze of the woman he'd briefly run into by the lakefront earlier in the day.

"Jesus," he said. "You . . . you're like a bad penny."

He lowered his head back onto his knees again and just hoped she'd go away. He could feel her standing there, looking down at him for a long time before she finally went down on one knee beside him and gave his arm a tug.

"C'mon," she said. "You can't stay here."

"Lemme alone."

"I don't just care about trees, either," she said.

"Who gives a fuck."

But it was easier to let her drag him to his feet than to fight her offer of help. She slung his arm over her shoulder and walked him back to the street where she flagged down a cab. He heard her give his address to the cabbie and wondered how she knew it, but soon gave up that train of thought as he concentrated on not getting sick in the back of the cab.

He retained the rest of the night in brief flashes. At some point they were in the stairwell of his building, what felt like a month later he was propped up beside the door to his apartment while she worked the key in the lock. Then he was lying on his bed while she removed his shoes.

"Who . . . who are you?" he remembered asking her.

"Debra Eisenstadt."

The name meant nothing to him. The bed seemed to move under him. I don't have a water bed, he remembered thinking, and then he threw up again. Debra caught it in his wastepaper basket.

A little later still, he came to again to find her sitting in one of his kitchen chairs that she'd brought into the bedroom and placed by the head of the bed. He remembered thinking that this was an awful lot to go through just for a donation to some rainforest fund.

He started to sit up, but the room spun dangerously, so he just let his head fall back against the pillow. She wiped his brow with a cool, damp washcloth.

"What do you want from me?" he managed to ask.

"I just wanted to see what you were like when you were my age," she said.

That made so little sense that he passed out again trying to work it out.

━

She was still there when he woke up the next morning. If anything, he thought he actually felt worse than he had the night before. Debra came into the room when he stirred and gave him a glass of Eno that helped settle his stomach. A couple of Tylenol started to work on the pounding behind his eyes.

"Someone from your office called and I told her you were sick," she said. "I hope that was okay."

"You stayed all night?"

She nodded, but Dennison didn't think she had the look of someone who'd been up all night. She had a fresh-scrubbed glow to her complexion and her head seemed to catch the sun, spinning it off into strands of light that mingled with the natural highlights already present in her light-brown hair. Her hair looked damp.

"I used your shower," she said. "I hope you don't mind."

"No, no. Help yourself."

He started to get up, but she put a palm against his chest to keep him lying down.

"Give the pills a chance to work," she said. "Meanwhile, I'll get you some coffee. Do you feel up to some breakfast?"

The very thought of eating made his stomach churn.

"Never mind," she said, taking in the look on his face. "I'll just bring the coffee."

Dennison watched her leave, then straightened his head and stared at the ceiling. After meeting her, he thought maybe he believed in angels for the first time since Sunday school.

It was past ten before he finally dragged himself out of bed and into the shower. The sting of hot water helped to clear his head; being clean and putting on fresh clothes helped some more. He regarded himself in the bathroom mirror. His features were still puffy from alcohol poisoning and his cheeks looked dirty with twenty-four hours worth of dark stubble. His hands were unsteady, but he shaved all the same. Neither mouthwash nor brushing his teeth could quite get rid of the sour taste in his mouth.

Debra had toast and more coffee waiting for him in the kitchen.

"I don't get it," he said as he slid into a chair across the table from her. "I could be anyone—some maniac for all you know. Why're you being so nice to me?"

She just shrugged.

"C'mon. It's not like I could have been a pretty sight

when you found me in the alley, so it can't be that you were attracted to me."

"Were you serious about what you said last night?" she asked by way of response. "About quitting your job?"

Dennison paused before answering to consider what she'd asked. He couldn't remember telling her that, but then there was a lot about yesterday he couldn't remember. The day was mostly a blur except for one thing. Ronnie Egan's features swam up in his mind until he squeezed his eyes shut and forced the image away.

Serious about quitting his job?

"Yeah," he said with a slow nod. "I guess I was. I mean, I am. I don't think I can even face going into the office. I'll just send them my letter of resignation and have somebody pick up my stuff from my desk."

"You do make a difference," she said. "It might not seem so at a time like this, but you've got to concentrate on all the people you have helped. That's got to count for something, doesn't it?"

"How would you know?" Dennison asked her. No sooner did the question leave his mouth, than it was followed by a flood of others. "Where did you come from? What are you doing here? It's got to be more than trying to convince me to keep my job so that I can afford to donate some money to your cause."

"You don't believe in good Samaritans?"

Dennison shook his head. "Nor Santa Claus."

But maybe angels, he added to himself. She was so fresh and pretty—light years different from the people who came into his office, their worn and desperate features eventually all bleeding one into the other.

"I appreciate your looking after me the way you did," he said. "Really I do. And I don't mean to sound ungrateful. But it just doesn't make a lot of sense."

"You help people all the time."

"That's my job—*was* my job." He looked away from her steady gaze. "Christ, I don't know anymore."

"And that's all it was?" she asked.

"No. It's just . . . I'm tired, I guess. Tired of seeing it all turn to shit on me. This little kid who died yesterday . . . I could've tried harder. If I'd tried harder, maybe he'd still be alive."

"That's the way I feel about the environment, sometimes," she said. "There are times when it just feels so hopeless, I can't go on."

"So why do you?"

"Because the bottom line is I believe I can make a difference. Not a big one. What I do is just a small ripple, but I know it helps. And if enough little people like me make our little differences, one day we're going to wake up to find that we really did manage to change the world."

"There's a big distinction between some trees getting cut down and a kid dying," Dennison said.

"From our perspective, sure," she agreed. "But maybe not from a global view. We have to remember that everything's connected. The real world's not something that can be divided into convenient little compartments, like we'll label this, 'the child abuse problem,' this'll go under 'depletion of the ozone layer.' If you help some homeless child on these city streets, it has repercussions that touch every part of the world."

"I don't get it."

"It's like a vibe," she said. "If enough people think positively, take positive action, then it snowballs all of its own accord and the world can't help but get a little better."

Dennison couldn't stop from voicing the cynical retort that immediately came into his mind.

"How retro," he said.

"What do you mean?"

"It sounds so sixties. All this talk about vibes and positive mumbo-jumbo."

"Positive thinking brought down the Berlin Wall," she said.

"Yeah, and I'm sure some fortune teller predicted it in the pages of a supermarket tabloid, although she probably got the decade wrong. Look, I'm sorry, but I don't buy it. If the world really worked on 'vibes,' I think it'd be in even worse shape than it already is."

"Maybe that's what *is* wrong with it: too much negative energy. So we've got to counteract it with positive energy."

"Oh, please."

She got a sad look on her face. "I believe it," she said. "I learned that from a man that I came to love very much. I didn't believe him when he told me, either, but now I know it's true."

"*How* can you know it's true?"

Debra sighed. She put her hand in the back pocket of her jeans and pulled out a piece of paper.

"Talk to these people," she said. "They can explain it a whole lot better than I can."

Dennison looked at the scrap of paper she'd handed him. "Elders' Council" was written in ballpoint. The address given was City Hall's.

"Who are they?"

"Elders from the Kickaha Reservation."

"They've got an office at City Hall?"

Debra nodded. "It's part of a program to integrate alternative methods of dealing with problems with the ones we would traditionally use."

"What? People go to these old guys and ask them for advice?"

"They're not just men," she said. "In fact, among the Kickaha—as with many native peoples—there are more women than men sitting on an elders' council. They're the grandmothers of the tribe who hold and remember all the wisdoms. The Kickaha call them 'the Aunts.' "

Dennison started to shake his head. "I know you mean well, Debra, but—"

"Just go talk to them—please? Before you make your decision."

"But nothing they say is going to—"

"Promise me you will. You asked me why I helped you last night, well, let's say this is what I want in return: for you just to talk to them."

"I . . ."

The last thing Dennison wanted was to involve himself with some nut-case situation like this, but he liked the woman, despite her flaky beliefs, and he did owe her something. He remembered throwing up last night and her catching the vomit in his garbage can. How many people would do that for a stranger?

"Okay," he said. "I promise."

The smile that she gave him seemed to make her whole face glow.

"Good," she said. "Make sure you bring a present. A package of tobacco would be good."

"Tobacco."

She nodded. "I've got to go now," she added. She stood up and shook his hand. "I'm really glad I got the chance to meet you."

"Wait a minute," Dennison said as she left the kitchen.

He followed her into the living room where she was putting on her jacket.

"Am I going to see you again?" he asked.

"I hope so."

"What's your number?"

"Do you have a pen?"

He went back into the kitchen and returned with a pencil and the scrap of paper she'd given him. She took it from him and quickly scribbled a phone number and address on it. She handed it back to him, gave him a quick kiss on the cheek, and then she was out the door and gone.

Dennison stood staring at the door after it had closed behind her. The apartment had never seemed so empty before.

Definitely flaky, he thought as he returned to the kitchen. But he thought maybe he'd fallen in love with her, if that was something you were allowed to do with angels.

He finished his coffee and cleaned up the dishes, dawdling over the job. He didn't know anything about the Kickaha except for those that he saw in his office, applying for welfare, and what he'd seen on the news a couple of years ago when the more militant braves from the reservation had

blockaded Highway 14 to protest logging on their land. So
he had only two images of them: down and out, or dressed
in khaki, carrying an assault rifle. Wait, make that three.
There were also the pictures in the history books of them
standing around in ceremonial garb.

He didn't want to go to this Elders' Council. Nothing
they could tell him was going to make him look at the world
any differently, so why bother? But finally he put on a light-
weight sportsjacket and went out to flag a cab to take him to
City Hall, because whatever else he believed or didn't believe, the one thing he'd never done yet was break a promise.

He wasn't about to start now—especially with a promise
made to an angel.

━

Dennison left the elevator and walked down a carpeted hallway on the third floor of City Hall. He stopped at the door
with the neatly lettered sign that read ELDERS' COUNCIL. He
felt surreal, as though he'd taken a misstep somewhere
along the way yesterday and had ended up in a Fellini film.
Being here was odd enough, in and of itself. But if he was
going to meet a native elder, he felt it should be under pine
trees with the smell of wood smoke in the air, not cloistered
away in City Hall, surrounded by miles of concrete and
steel.

Really, he shouldn't be here at all. What he should be
doing was getting his affairs in order. Resigning from his
job, getting in touch with his cousin Pete, who asked Dennison at least every three or four months if he wanted to go
into business with him. Pete worked for a small shipping
firm, but he wanted to start his own company. "I've got the
know-how and the money," he'd tell Dennison, "but
frankly, when it comes to dealing with people, I stink.
That's where you'd come in."

Dennison hesitated for a long moment, staring at the
door and the sign affixed to its plain wooden surface. He
knew what he should be doing, but he'd made that promise,
so he knocked on the door. An old native woman answered

as he was about to lift his hand to rap a second time.

Her face was wrinkled, her complexion dark; her braided hair almost grey. She wore a long brown skirt, flat-soled shoes and a plain white blouse that was decorated with a tracing of brightly coloured beadwork on its collar points and buttoned placket. The gaze that looked up to meet his was friendly, the eyes such a dark brown that it was hard to differentiate between pupil and iris.

"Hello," she said and ushered him in.

It was strange inside. He found himself standing in a conference room overlooking the parking garage behind City Hall. The walls were unadorned and there was no table, just thick wall-to-wall on the floor and a ring of chairs set in a wide circle, close to the walls. At the far side of the room, he spied a closed door that might lead into another room or a storage closet.

"Uh . . ."

Suddenly at a loss for words, he put his hand in his pocket, pulled out the package of cigarette tobacco that he'd bought on the way over and handed it to her.

"Thank you," the woman said. She steered him to a chair, then sat down beside him. "My name is Dorothy. How can I help you?"

"Dorothy?" Dennison replied, unable to hide his surprise.

The woman nodded. "Dorothy Born. You were expecting something more exotic such as Woman-Who-Speaks-With-One-Hand-Rising?"

"I didn't know what to expect."

"That was my mother's name actually—in the old language. She was called that because she'd raise her hand as she spoke, ready to slap the head of those braves who wouldn't listen to her advice."

"Oh."

She smiled. "That's a joke. My mother's name was Ruth."

"Uh . . ."

What a great conversationalist he was proving to be

today. Good thing Pete couldn't hear him at this moment.
But he just didn't know where to begin.

"Why don't you just tell me why you've come," Dorothy
said.

"Actually, I feel a little foolish."

Her smile broadened. "Good. That is the first step on the
road to wisdom." She put a hand on his knee, dark gaze
locking with his. "What is your name?"

"Chris—Chris Dennison."

"Speak to me, Chris. I am here to listen."

So Dennison told her about his job, about Ronnie Egan's
death, about getting drunk, about Debra Eisenstadt and
how she'd come to send him here. Once he started, his awkwardness fled.

"Nothing seems worth it anymore," he said in conclu-
sion.

Dorothy nodded. "I understand. When the spirit de-
spairs, it becomes difficult to see clearly. Your friend's
words require too much faith for you to accept them."

"I guess. I'm not sure I even understand them."

"Perhaps I can help you there."

She fell silent for a moment, her gaze still on him, but she
no longer seemed to see him. It was as though she saw
beyond him, or had turned to look inward.

"The Kickaha way to see the world," she finally said, "is
to understand that everything is on a wheel: Day turns to
night. The moon waxes and wanes. Summer turns to autumn. A man is born, he lives, he dies. But no wheel turns by
itself. Each affects the other, so that when the wheel of the
seasons turns to winter, the wheel of the day grows shorter.
When the day grows shorter, the sweetgrass is covered with
snow and the deer must forage for bark and twigs rather
than feast on its delicate blades. The hunter must travel far-
ther afield to find the deer, but perhaps the wolf finds her
first."

She paused, sitting back in her chair. "Do you see?"

Dennison nodded slowly. "I see the connection in what
you're saying, but not with what Debra was trying to tell

me. It was so vague—all this talk about positive energy."

"But the energy we produce is very powerful medicine," Dorothy said. "It can work great good or ill."

"You make it sound like voodoo."

She frowned for a moment as though she needed to think that through.

"Perhaps it is," she said. "From the little I know of it, *voudoun* is a very basic application of the use of one's will. The results one gains from its medicine become positive or negative only depending upon one's intention."

"You're saying we make bad things happen to ourselves?"

Dorothy nodded. "And to our sacred trust, the earth."

"I still don't see how a person can be so sure he's really making a difference."

"What if the child you save grows up to be the scientist who will cure AIDS?"

"What if the child I don't get to in time was supposed to be that scientist, and so she never gets the chance to find the cure?"

Dorothy lifted her hand and tapped it against his chest. "You carry so much pain in here. It wasn't always so, was it?"

Dennison thought about how he'd been when he first got into social work. He'd been like Debra then, so sure he knew exactly what to do. He'd believed utterly in his ability to save the world. That had changed. Not because of Ronnie Egan, but slowly, over the years. He'd had to make compromises, his trust had been abused not once, or twice, but almost every day. What had happened to Ronnie had forced him to see that he fought a losing battle.

Perhaps it was worse than that. What he felt now was that the battle had been lost long ago and he was only just now realizing the futility of continuing to man the frontlines.

"If you were to see what I have to work with every day," he said, "you'd get depressed, too."

Dorothy shook her head. "That is not our way."

"So what is your way?"

"You must learn to let it go. The wheel must always turn. If you take upon yourself the sadness and despair from those you would help, you must also learn how to let it go. Otherwise it will settle inside you like a cancer."

"I don't know if I can anymore."

She nodded slowly. "That is something that only you can decide. But remember this: You have given a great deal of yourself. You have no reason to feel ashamed if you must now turn away."

She had just put her finger on what was making the decision so hard for him. Futile though he'd come to realize his efforts were, he still felt guilty at the idea of turning his back on those who needed his help. It wasn't like what Debra had been saying: The difference he made didn't have far-reaching effects. It didn't change what was happening in the Amazon, or make the hole in the ozone layer any smaller. All it did was make one or two persons' misery a little easier to bear, but only in the short term. It seemed cruel to give them hope when it would just be taken away from them again.

If only there really were something to Debra's domino theory. While the people he helped wouldn't go on to save the environment, or find that cure for AIDS, they might help somebody else a little worse off than themselves. That seemed worthwhile, except what do you do when you've reached inside yourself and you can't find anything left to give?

Dorothy was watching him with her dark gaze. Oddly enough, her steady regard didn't make him feel self-conscious. She had such a strong personality that he could feel its warmth as though he was holding his hands out to a fire. It made him yearn to find something to fill the cold that had lodged inside him since he'd looked down at Ronnie Egan's corpse.

"Maybe I should get into environmental work instead," he said. "You know, how they say that a change is as good as a rest?"

"Who says you aren't already doing environmental work?" Dorothy asked.

"What do you mean?"

"What if the dying trees of the rainforest are being reborn as unwanted children?" she asked.

"C'mon. You can't expect me to believe—"

"Why not? If a spirit is taken from its wheel before its time, it must go somewhere."

Dennison had a sudden vision of a tenement building filled with green-skinned children, each of them struggling to reach the roof of the building to get their nourishment from the sun, except when they finally got up there, the smog cover was so thick that there was nothing for them. They got a paler and paler green until finally they just withered away. Died like so many weeds.

"Imagine living in a world with no more trees," Dorothy said.

Dennison had been in a clear-cut forest once. It was while he was visiting a friend in Oregon. He'd stood there on a hilltop and for as far as the eye could see, there were only tree stumps. It was a heartbreaking sight.

His friend had become an environmentalist after a trip to China. "There are almost no trees left there at all now," he'd told Dennison. "They've just used them all up. Trees clean the environment by absorbing the toxins from carbon dioxide and acid rain. Without them, the water and air become too toxic and people start to die off from liver cancer. China has an incredibly high mortality rate due to liver cancer.

"That's going to happen here, Chris. That's what's going to happen in the Amazon. It's going to happen all over the world."

Dennison had felt bad, enough so that he contributed some money to a couple of relevant causes, but his concern hadn't lasted. His work with Social Services took too much out of him to leave much energy for other concerns, no matter how worthy.

As though reading his mind, Dorothy said, "And now

imagine a world with no more children."

Dennison thought they might be halfway there. So many of the children he dealt with were more like miniature adults than the kids he remembered growing up with. But then he and his peers hadn't had to try to survive on the streets, foraging out of trash cans, maybe taking care of a junkie parent.

"I have a great concern for Mother Earth," Dorothy said. "We have gravely mistreated her. But when we speak of the environment and the depletion of resources, we sometimes forget that our greatest resource is our children.

"My people have a word to describe the moment when all is in harmony—we call it Beauty. But Beauty can find no foothold in despair. If we mean to reclaim our Mother Earth from the ills that plague her, we must not forget our own children. We must work on many levels, walk many wheels, that lives may be spared—the lives of people, and the lives of all those other species with whom we share the world. Our contributions, no matter how small they might appear, carry an equal importance, for they will all contribute to the harmony that allows the world to walk the wheel of Beauty."

She closed her eyes and fell silent. Dennison sat quietly beside her for a time.

"What . . . what advice would you give me?" he asked finally.

Dorothy shrugged. Her eyes remained closed.

"You must do what you believe is right," she said. "We have inside of each of us a spirit, and that spirit alone knows what it is that we should or should not do."

"I've got to think about all of this," Dennison said.

"That would be a good thing," Dorothy told him. She opened her eyes suddenly, piercing him with her gaze. "But hold onto your feelings of foolishness," she added. "Wisdom never comes to those who believe they have nothing left to learn."

Dennison found an empty bench when he left City Hall. He sat down and cradled his face in his hands. His headache had returned, but that wasn't what was disturbing him. He'd found himself agreeing with the Kickaha elder. He also thought he understood what Debra had been telling him. The concepts weren't suspect—only the part he had to play in them.

He felt like one of those biblical prophets, requiring the proof of a burning bush or some other miracle before they'd go on with the task required of them. If he could just have the proof that he'd made a real and lasting difference for only one person, that would be enough. But it wasn't going to come.

The people he helped continued to live hand to mouth because there was no other way for them to live. Caught up in a recession that showed no sign of letting up, they considered themselves lucky just to be surviving.

And that was why his decision was going to have to stand. He'd given of himself, above and beyond what the job required, for years. The empty cold feeling inside told him that he had nothing left to give. It was time to call Pete and see about that shipping business. He wasn't sure he could bring Pete's enthusiasm to it, but he'd do his best.

But first he owed Debra a call: Yeah, I went and saw the elder, she was a wonderful woman, I understand what you were saying, but I haven't changed my mind. He knew he'd be closing the door on the possibility of a relationship with her, but then he didn't feel he had even that much of himself to give someone anyway.

He dug a quarter out of his pocket and went to the pay phone on the corner. But when he dialed the number she'd given him, he got a recorded message: "I'm sorry, but the number you have dialed is no longer in service."

"Shit," he said, stepping back from the phone.

An older woman, laden down with shopping bags, gave him a disapproving glare.

"Sorry," he muttered.

Flagging down a cab, he gave the driver the address that

Debra had written down to accompany her bogus phone number, then settled back in his seat.

⟶

The building was a worn, brownstone tenement, indistinguishable from every other one on the block. They all had the same tired face to turn to the world. Refuse collected against their steps, graffiti on the walls, cheap curtains in the windows when there were any at all. Walking up the steps, the smell of urine and body odor was strong in the air. A drunk lay sleeping just inside the small foyer.

Dennison stepped over him and went up to the second floor. He knocked on the door that had a number matching the one Debra had written down for him. After a moment or two, the door opened to the length of its chain and a woman as worn down as the building itself was looking at him.

"What do you want?"

Dennison had been expecting an utter stranger, but the woman had enough of a family resemblance to Debra that he thought maybe his rescuing angel really did live here. Looking past the lines that worry and despair had left on the woman's face, he realized that she was about his own age. Too young to be Debra's mother. Maybe her sister?

"Are you . . . uh, Mrs. Eisenstadt?" he asked, trying the only name he had.

"Who wants to know?"

"My name's Chris Dennison. I'm here to see Debra."

The woman's eyes narrowed with suspicion. "What'd she do now?"

"Nothing. That is, she gave me some help yesterday and I just wanted to thank her."

The suspicion didn't leave the woman's features. "Debra!" she shouted over her shoulder. Turning back to Dennison, she added, "I've got lots of neighbors. You try anything funny, I'll give a scream that'll have them down here so fast you won't know if you're coming or going."

Dennison doubted that. In a place like this, people would

just mind their own business. It wouldn't matter if somebody was getting murdered next door.

"I'm not here to cause trouble," he said.

"Deb-*ra!*" the woman hollered again.

She shut the door and Dennison could hear her unfastening the chain. When she opened the door once more, it swung open to its full width. Dennison looked down the hall behind the woman and saw a little girl of perhaps nine coming slowly down the hallway, head lowered, gaze on the floor.

"I thought you told me you were in school yesterday," the woman said to her.

The girl's gaze never lifted. "I was."

She spoke barely above a whisper.

"Man here says you were helping him—doing what, I'd like to know." She turned from her daughter back to Dennison. "Maybe you want to tell me, mister?"

The girl looked at him then. He saw the grey-green eyes first, the features that might one day grow into ones similar to those of the woman he'd met yesterday, though this couldn't be her. The discrepancy of years was too vast. Then he saw the bruises. One eye blackened. The right side of her jaw swollen. She seemed to favor one leg as well.

His training kept him silent. If he said something too soon, he wouldn't learn a thing. First he had to give the woman enough room to hang herself.

"This is Debra Eisenstadt?" he asked.

"What, you need to see her birth certificate?"

Dennison turned to the woman and saw then what he hadn't noticed before. The day was warm, but she was wearing slacks, long sleeves, her blouse buttoned all the way up to the top. But he could see a discoloration in the hollow of her throat that the collar couldn't quite hide. Abrasive or not, she was a victim, too, he realized.

"Where is your husband, Mrs. Eisenstadt?" he asked gently.

"So now you're a cop?"

Dennison pulled out his ID. "No. I'm with Social Services. I can help you, Mrs. Eisenstadt. Has your husband been beating you?"

She crossed her arms protectively. "Look, it's not like what you're thinking. We had an argument, that's all."

"And your daughter—was he having an argument with her as well?"

"No. She . . . she just fell. Isn't that right, honey?"

Dennison glanced at the girl. She was staring at the floor again. Slowly she nodded in agreement. Dennison went down on one knee until his head was level with the girl's.

"You can tell me the truth," he said. "I can help you, but you've got to help me. Tell me how you got hurt and I promise you I won't let it happen to you again."

What the hell are you doing? he asked himself. You're supposed to be quitting this job.

But he hadn't turned in his resignation yet.

And then he remembered an odd thing that the other Debra had said to him last night.

I just wanted to see what you were like when you were my age.

He remembered puzzling over that before he finally passed out. And then there was the way she'd looked at him the next morning, admiring, then sad, then disappointed. As though she already knew him. As though he wasn't matching up to her expectations.

Though of course she couldn't have any expectations because they'd never met before. But what if this girl grew up to be the woman who'd helped him last night? What if her being here, in need of help, was his prophetic sign, his burning bush?

Yeah, right. And it was space aliens who brought her back from the future to see him.

"Look," the girl's mother said. "You've got no right, barging in here—"

"No right?" Dennison said, standing up to face her. "Look at your daughter, for Christ's sake, and then tell me that I've got no right to intervene."

"It's not like what you think. It's just that times are hard, you know, and what with Sam's losing his job, well he gets a little crazy sometimes. He doesn't mean any real harm. . . ."

Dennison tuned her out. He looked back at the little girl. It didn't matter if she was a sign or not, if she'd grow up to be the woman who'd somehow come back in time to help him when his faith was flagging the most. What was important right now that he get the girl some help.

"Which of your neighbors has a working phone?" he asked.

"Why? What're you going to do? Sam's going to—"

"Not do a damned thing," Dennison said. "It's my professional opinion that this child will be in danger so long as she remains in this environment. You can either come with us, or I'll see that she's made a ward of the court, but I'm not leaving her here."

"You can't—"

"I think we'll leave that for a judge to decide."

He ignored her then. Crouching down beside the little girl, he said, "I'm here to help you—do you understand? No one's going to hurt you anymore."

"If I . . . he said if I tell—"

"Debra!"

Dennison shot the mother an angry look. "I'm losing my patience with you, lady. Look at your daughter. Look at those bruises. Is that the kind of childhood you meant for your child?"

Her defiance crumbled under his glare and she slowly shook her head.

"Go pack a bag," he told the woman. "For both of you."

As she slowly walked down the hall, Dennison returned his attention to the little girl. This could all go to hell in a hand basket if he wasn't careful. There were certain standard procedures to deal with this kind of a situation and badgering the girl's mother the way he had been wasn't one of them. But he was damned if he wasn't going to give it his best shot.

"Do you understand what's happening?" he asked the

girl. "I'm going to take you and your mother someplace where you'll be safe."

She looked up at him, those so-familiar grey-green eyes wide and teary. "I'm scared."

Dennison nodded. "It's a scary situation. But tell you what. On the way to the shelter, maybe we get you a treat. What would you like?"

For one long moment the girl's gaze settled on his. She seemed to be considering whether she could trust him or not. He must have come up positive, because after that moment's hesitation, she opened right up.

"For there still to be trees when I grow up," she said. "I want to be a forest ranger. Sometimes when I'm sleeping, I wake up and I hear the trees crying because their daddies are being mean to them, I guess, and are hurting them and I just want to help stop it."

Dennison remembered himself saying to the older Debra, *Trees don't cry. Kids do.* And then Debra's response.

Maybe you just can't hear them.

Jesus, it wasn't possible, was it? But then how could they look so similar, the differences caused by the passage of years, not genetics. And the eyes—the eyes were exactly the same. And how could the old Debra have known the address, the phone number—

He got up and went over to the phone he could see sitting on a TV tray beside the battered sofa. The number was the same as on the scrap of paper in his pocket. He lifted the receiver, but there was no dial tone.

"I . . . I've packed a . . . bag."

Debra's mother stood in the hallway beside her daughter, looking as lost as the little girl did. But there was something they both had—there was a glimmer of hope in their eyes. He'd put that there. Now all he had to do was figure out a way to keep it there.

"Whose phone can we use to call a cab?" he asked.

"Laurie—she's down the hall in number six. She'd let us use her phone."

"Well, let's get going."

As he ushered them into the hall, he was no longer thinking about tendering his resignation. He had no doubt the feeling that he had to quit would rise again, but when that happened he was going to remember a girl with grey-green eyes and the woman she might grow up to be. He was going to remember the wheels that connect everything, cogs interlocked and turning to create a harmonious whole. He was going to remember the power of good vibes.

He was going to learn to believe.

I believe it. I learned that from a man that I came to love very much. I didn't believe him when he told me, either, but now I know it's true.

But most of all he was going to make sure that he earned the respect of the angel that had visited him from the days still to come.

Dennison knew there was probably a more rational explanation for it all, but right then, he wanted to believe in angels.

THE WISHING WELL

*Do you think it's better to do the right
thing for the wrong reason or the wrong
thing for the right reason?*
—Amy Luna, Sumner, WA,
from *Sassy,* May 1991

Beyond the mountains, more mountains.
—Haitian proverb

1

There are always ghosts in the well. I can't call them echoes,
because the sounds I hear all were made too long ago.

The splash of coins in the water.

Voices whispering their wishes.

Secrets.

Nobody was supposed to hear them.

But I do.

2

"It's been almost two weeks," Brenda said, "and he still
hasn't called."

She butted out a cigarette in the ashtray on the table between them and immediately lit another. Wendy sighed, but
didn't say anything about her friend's chain-smoking. If
you listened to Brenda, there was always something going
wrong in her life, so Wendy had long ago decided that there
was no point in getting on her case about yet one more negative aspect of it. Besides, she already knew the argument
Brenda would counter with: "Right, quit smoking and gain

twenty pounds. As if I don't already look like a pig."

Self-esteem wasn't Brenda's strong point. She was an attractive woman, overweight only in the sense that everyone was when compared to all those models who seemed to exist only in the pages of a fashion magazine. But that didn't stop Brenda from constantly worrying over her weight. Wendy never had to read the supermarket tabloids to find out about the latest diet fad—Brenda was sure to tell her about it, often before it appeared in newsprint along with stories of recent Elvis sightings, Bigfoot's genealogy and the like.

Sometimes it all drove Wendy a little crazy. In her unending quest for the perfect dress size, what Brenda seemed to forget was her gorgeous green eyes, the mane of naturally curly red-gold hair and the perfect complexion that people would kill for. She had a good job, she dressed well—perhaps too well, since her credit cards were invariably approaching, if not over, their limit—and when she wasn't beating on herself, she was fun to be around. Except Brenda just didn't see it that way, and so she invariably tried too hard. To be liked. To look better. To get a man.

"Was this the guy you met at the bus stop?" Wendy asked.

Brenda nodded. "He was so nice. He called me a couple of days later and we went out for dinner and a movie. *I* thought we had a great time."

"And I suppose you sent him flowers?"

Sending small gifts to men she'd just met was Brenda's thing. Usually it was flowers.

"I just wanted to let Jim know that I had a good time when we went out," Brenda said, "so I sent him a half-dozen roses. What's so wrong about that?"

Wendy set down her wine glass. "Nothing. It's just that you—I think maybe you come on too strong and scare guys off, that's all."

"I can't help it. I get compulsive."

"Obsessively so."

Brenda looked at the end of her cigarette, took a final drag, then ground it out. She dropped the butt on top of the half-dozen others already in the ashtray.

"I just want to be in love," she said. "I just want a guy to be in love with *me.*"

"I know," Wendy replied, her voice gentle. "But it's never going to happen if you're always trying too hard."

"I'm starting to get *old,*" Brenda said. "I'm almost thirty-five."

"Definitely middle-aged," Wendy teased.

"That's not funny."

"No. I guess it's not. It's just—"

"I know. I have to stop coming on so strong. Except with the nice guys, it seems like the woman always has to make the first move."

"This is too true."

3

Sunday afternoons, I often drive out of town, up Highway 14. Just before I get into the mountains proper, I pull off into the parking lot of a derelict motel called The Wishing Well. The pavement's all frost-buckled and there are weeds growing up through the cracks, refuse everywhere, but I still like the place. Maybe because it's so forsaken. So abandoned. Just the way I feel half the time.

The motel's all boarded up now, though I'm sure the local kids use it for parties. There are empty cans and broken beer bottles all over the place, fighting for space with discarded junk food packaging and used condoms. The rooms are set out in a horseshoe, the ends pointing back into the woods, embracing what's left of the motel's pool. Half the boards have been torn off the windows and all of the units have been broken into, their doors hanging ajar, some torn right off their hinges.

The pool has a little miniature marsh at the bottom of it— mud and stagnant water, cattails and reeds and a scum of algae covering about two feet of water. I've seen minnows in the spring—god knows how they got there—frogs, every kind of water bug you can imagine. And let's not forget the trash. There's even a box spring in the deep end with all the beer cans and broken glass.

The lawn between the pool and the forest has long since been reclaimed by the wilderness. The grass and weeds grow thigh-high and the flowerbeds have mostly been overtaken by dandelions and clover. The forest has sent a carpet of young trees out into the field, from six inches tall to twenty feet. Seen from the air, they would blur the once-distinct boundary between forest and lawn.

The reason I come here is for the motel's namesake. There really is a wishing well, out on the lawn, closer to the forest than the motel itself. The well must have been pretty once, with its fieldstone lip, the shingled roof on wooden supports, the bucket hanging down from its cast iron crank, three wrought-iron benches set facing the well and a flower garden all around.

The shingles have all pretty much blown off now; the bucket's completely disappeared—either bagged by some souvenir-hunter, or it's at the bottom of the well. The garden's rosebushes have taken over everything, twining around the wooden roof supports and covering the benches like Sleeping Beauty's thorn thicket. The first time I wandered out in back of the motel, I didn't even know the well was here, the roses had so completely overgrown it. But I found a way to worm through and by now I've worn a little path. I hardly ever get nicked by a thorn.

The fieldstone sides of the well are crumbling and I suppose they're not very safe, but every time I come, I sit on that short stone wall anyway and look down into the dark shaft below. It's so quiet here. The bulk of the motel blocks the sound of traffic from the highway and there's not another building for at least two miles in either direction.

Usually I sit there a while and just let the quiet settle inside me. Then I take out a penny—a lucky penny that I've found on the street during the week, of course, head side facing up—and I drop it into the darkness.

It takes a long time to hear the tiny splash. I figure dropping a penny in every week or so as I do, I'll be an old lady and I still won't have made a noticeable difference in the water level. But that's not why I'm here. I'm not here to make a wish either. I just need a place to go, I need—

A confessor, I guess. I'm a lapsed Catholic, but I still carry my burdens of worry and guilt. What I've got to talk about, I don't think a priest wants to hear. What does a priest know or care about secular concerns? All they want to talk about is God. All they want to hear is a tidy list of sins so that they can prescribe their penances and get on to the next customer.

Here I don't have to worry about God or Hail Marys or what the invisible face behind the screen is really thinking. Here I get to say it all out loud and not have to feel guilty about bringing down my friends. Here I can have a cathartic wallow in my misery, and then . . . then . . .

I'm not sure when I first started to hear the voices. But after I've run out of words, I start to hear them, coming up out of the well. Nothing profound. Just the ghosts of old wishes. The echoes of other people's dreams, paid for by the simple dropping of a coin, down into the water.

Splash.

I guess what I want is for Jane to love me, and for us to be happy together.

Splash.

Just a pony and I swear I'll take care of her.

Splash.

Don't let them find out that I'm pregnant.

Splash.

Make John stop running around on me and I promise I'll make him the best wife he could ever want.

Splash.

I don't know why it makes me feel better. All these ghost voices are asking for things, are dreaming, are wishing, are needing. Just like me. But I do come away with a sense of, not exactly peace, but . . . less urgency, I suppose.

Maybe it's because when I hear those voices, when I know that, just like me, they paid their pennies in hopes to make things a little better for themselves, I don't feel so alone anymore.

Does that make any sense?

4

"So what're you doing this weekend, Jim?" Scotty asked.

Jim Bradstreet cradled the phone against his ear and leaned back on his sofa.

"Nothing much," he said as he continued to open his mail. Water bill. Junk flyer. Another junk flyer. Visa bill. "I thought maybe I'd give Brenda a call."

"She the one who sent you those flowers?"

"Yeah."

"You can do better than that," Scotty said.

Jim tossed the opened mail onto his coffee table and shifted the receiver from one ear to the other.

"What's that supposed to mean?" he asked.

"I'd think it was obvious—you said she seemed so desperate."

Jim regretted having told Scotty anything about his one date with Brenda Perry. She *had* seemed clingy, especially for a first date, but he'd also realized from their conversation throughout the evening that she didn't exactly have the greatest amount of self-esteem. He'd hesitated calling her again—especially after the flowers—because he wasn't sure he wanted to get into a relationship with someone so dependent. But that wasn't exactly fair. He didn't really know her and asking her for another date wasn't exactly committing to a relationship.

"I still liked her," he said into the receiver.

Scotty laughed. "Just can't get her out of your mind, right?"

"No," Jim replied in all honesty. "I can't."

"Hey, I was just kidding, you know?" Before Jim could reply, Scotty added, "What do you say we get together for a few brews, check out the action at that new club on Lakeside."

"Some other time," Jim told him.

"I'm telling you, man, this woman's trouble. She sounds way too neurotic for you."

"You don't know her," Jim said. "For that matter, *I* don't really know her."

"Yeah, but we know her kind. You're not going to change your mind?"

"Not tonight."

"Well, it's your loss," Scotty said. "I'll give the ladies your regrets."

"You do that," Jim said before he hung up.

It took him a few moments to track down where he'd put Brenda's number. When he did find it and made the call, all he got was her answering machine. He hesitated for a brief moment, then left a message.

"Hi, this is Jim. Uh, Jim Bradstreet. I know it's late notice and all, but I thought maybe we could get together tonight, or maybe tomorrow? Call me."

He left his number and waited for a couple of hours, but she never phoned back. As it got close to eight-thirty, he considered going down to that new club that Scotty had been so keen on checking out, but settled instead on taking in a movie. The lead actress had red hair, with the same gold highlights as Brenda's. The guy playing the other lead character treated her like shit.

That just added to the depression of being alone in a theater where it seemed as though everyone else had come in couples.

5

Sometimes I feel as though there's this hidden country inside me, a landscape that's going to remain forever unexplored because I can't make a normal connection with another human being, with someone who might map it out for me. It's my land, it belongs to me, but I'm denied access to it. The only way I could ever see it is through the eyes of someone outside this body of mine, through the eyes of someone who loves me.

I think we all have these secret landscapes inside us, but I don't think that anybody else ever thinks about them. All I know is that no one visits mine. And when I'm with other people, I don't know how to visit theirs.

6

Wendy wasn't on shift yet when Brenda arrived at Kathryn's Cafe, but Jilly was there. Brenda had first met the two of them when she was a reporter for *In the City*, covering the Women in the Arts conference with which they'd been involved. Jilly Coppercorn was a successful artist, Wendy St. James a struggling poet. Brenda had enjoyed the panels that both women were on and made a point of talking to them afterwards.

Their lives seemed to be so perfectly in order compared to hers that Brenda invariably had a sense of guilt for intruding the cluttered mess of her existence into theirs. And they were both such small, enviably thin women that, when she was with them, she felt more uncomfortable than usual in her own big fat body.

This constant focusing on being overweight was a misperception on her part, she'd been told by the therapist her mother had made her go see while she was still in high school.

"If anything, you could stand to gain a few pounds," Dr. Coleman had said. "Especially considering your history."

Brenda's eating disorders, the woman had gone on to tell her, stemmed from her feelings of abandonment as a child, but no amount of lost weight was going to bring back her father.

"I *know* that," Brenda argued. "I know my father's dead and that it's not my fault he died. I'm not stupid."

"Of course you're not," Dr. Coleman had patiently replied with a sad look in her eyes.

Brenda could never figure out why they wouldn't just

leave her alone. Yes, she'd had some trouble with her weight, but she'd gotten over it. Just as she knew it was a failing business that had put the gun in her father's mouth, the bitter knowledge that he couldn't provide for his family that had pulled the trigger. She'd dealt with *all* of that.

It was in the past, over and done with long ago. What wouldn't go away, though, was the extra weight she could never quite seem to take off and keep off. Nobody she knew seemed to understand how it felt, looking in a mirror and always seeing yourself on the wrong side of plump.

She'd asked Jilly once how she stayed so thin.

"Just my metabolism, I guess," Jilly had replied. "Personally, I'd like to gain a couple of pounds. I always feel kind of . . . skin-and-bonesy."

"You look perfect to me," Brenda had told her.

Perfect size, perfect life—which wasn't really true, of course. Neither Jilly nor Wendy was perfect. For one thing, Jilly was one of the messiest people Brenda had ever met. But at least she wasn't in debt. Brenda was tidy to a fault, but she couldn't handle her personal finances to save her life. She'd gone from reporter to the position of *In the City*'s advertising manager since she'd first become friends with Wendy and Jilly. At work, she kept her books and budgeting perfectly in order. So why couldn't she do the same thing in her private life?

There was only one other customer in the restaurant, so after Jilly had served him his dinner, she brought a pot of herbal tea and a pair of mugs over to Brenda's table. She sat down with a contented sigh before pouring them each a steaming mugful. Brenda smiled her thanks and lit a cigarette.

"So whatever happened with that guy you met at the bus stop?" Jilly asked as she settled back in her chair.

"Didn't Wendy tell you?"

Jilly laughed. "You know Wendy. Telling her something personal is like putting it into a Swiss bank vault and you're the only person who's got the account number."

So Brenda filled her in.

"Then when I got home on Friday," she said as she finished up, "there was a message from him on my machine. But I decided to take Wendy's advice and play it cool. Instead of calling him back, I waited for him to call me again."

"Well, good for you."

"I suppose."

"And did he?"

Brenda nodded. "We made a date for Saturday night and he showed up at my door with a huge box of chocolates."

"That was nice of him."

"Right. Real nice. Give the blimp even more of what she doesn't need. You'd think he'd be more considerate than that. I mean, all you have to do is look at me and know that the last thing I need is chocolate."

"Jesus, Brenda. The last thing you are is fat."

"Oh, right."

Jilly just shook her head. "So what did you do?"

"I ate them."

"No, I meant where did you go?"

"Another movie. I can't even remember what we saw now. I spent the whole time trying to figure out how he felt about me."

"You should try to just relax," Jilly told her. "Let what happens, happen."

"I guess." Brenda butted out her cigarette and lit another. Blowing a wreath of blue-grey smoke away from the table, she gave Jilly a considering look, then asked, "Do you believe in wishing wells?"

Wendy took that moment to arrive in a flurry of blonde hair and grocery bags. She dumped the bags on the floor by the table and pulled up a chair.

"Better to ask, what *doesn't* she believe in," she said. "This woman's mind is a walking supermarket tabloid."

"Ah," Jilly said. "The poet arrives—only fifteen minutes late for her shift."

Wendy grinned and pointed at Jilly's tangle of brown ringlets.

"You've got paint in your hair," she said.

"You've got ink on your fingers," Jilly retorted, then they stuck out their tongues at each other and laughed.

Their easy rapport made Brenda feel left out. Where did a person learn to be so comfortable with other people? she wondered, not for the first time. She supposed it started with feeling good about yourself—like losing a little weight, getting out of debt, putting your love life in order. She sighed. Maybe it started with not always talking about your own problems all the time, but that was a hard thing to do. There were times when Brenda thought her problems were the only things she did have to talk about.

"Earth to Brenda," Jilly said. Under the table, the point of her shoe poked Brenda's calf to get her attention.

"Sorry."

"Why were you asking about wishing wells?" Jilly asked.

"Oh, I don't know. I was just wondering if anybody still believes that wishes can come true."

"I think there are magical things in the world," Wendy said, "but hocus-pocus, wishes coming true—" she shook her head "—I doubt it."

"I do," Jilly said. "It just depends on how badly you want them to."

7

Most wishing wells started out simply as springs or wells that were considered sacred. I found this out a while ago when I was supposed to be researching something else for the paper. I had just meant to look into the origin of wishing wells, but I ended up getting caught up in all the folklore surrounding water and spent most of that afternoon in the library, following one reference which led me to another. . . .

All the way back to primitive times, a lake or well was the place that the sick were taken to be healed. Water images show up in the medicinal rites of peoples at an animistic level, where those being healed are shown washing their hands, breast and head. At the water's edge, reeds grow and shells are found, both symbols of water as salvation—something that Christian symbolism took to itself with a vengeance.

But even before the spread of Christianity, the well of refreshing and purifying water had already gained all sorts of fascinating associations. It was symbolic of sublime aspirations, thought of as a "silver cord" which attached a human to the center of all things. The corn goddess Demeter or other deities would often be shown standing beside a well. The act of drawing water from a well was like fishing, drawing out and upward the numinous contents of the deeps. Looking into its still waters, like looking into a placid lake, was seen as equivalent to meditation or mystic contemplation. The well symbolized the human soul and was considered an attribute of all things feminine.

It's no wonder the Christians came to include it in their baptismal rituals; Christianity has had a long history of taking popular older beliefs and assimilating into its own— even I knew that. But there was so much here that I had never heard of before; fascinating stuff, even though it ended up taking me way off my initial topic. And anyway, the idea of making a wish at a well is tied up in all those tangled stories.

Throughout Europe sacred wells were given new names after various saints. But as the centuries passed and religious beliefs changed, many of these saints' wells became less esteemed and pilgrims no longer approached them with the same feelings of devotion they once had. People stopped offering prayers to the saints and made a wish instead.

And the associated rituals often survived. In some places the wish-maker had to dip her bare hands into the water up to her wrists, make a silent wish, then withdraw her hands and swallow the water held in them. Other places, one left a pin, often bent, or the ever-popular coin. In some ways, wishing wells are a reversion to paganism, the serious wishes made at them being reminiscent of when people approached the sacred water to make an offering or benediction to some god or other, or to the spirit of the water.

Of course water wasn't seen just as the home of benevolent spirits. Folklore throughout the world relates the dangers of water witches and sirens, kelpies and other malevolent creatures whose sole existence seems to rely on drowning those they manage to snare with their various wiles. Everybody knows the story of how Ulysses confronted the sirens and most have probably heard of the Rhine maiden Lorelei—although, oddly enough, she entered folkloric tradition through Clemens Brentano's ballad "Lore Lay." He was so convincing that people just assumed it was based on true folklore.

Among the creepiest of the water witches are the Russian *rusalki*. They're lake spirits in female form—very beautiful and very deadly. They were supposed to bring a weird kind of ecstatic death when they drowned their victims, although some stories said it wasn't actually death they brought, but rather passage to another world. Another book I read said that before their current place in folklore tradition, they were considered to be fertility spirits. I found one reference where some Russian peasants were quoted as saying that "where the *rusalki* trod when dancing, there the grass grew thicker and the wheat more abundant."

That's the weird thing about folklore. Everything gets stirred up so you don't know which story's the original one anymore. Whatever comes along, be it a church or a new government, usually assimilates into their own the traditions and beliefs that existed before they came, and that's what creates the tangle.

This bit with the *rusalki* being psychopomps—leading human souls into the afterworld—makes them reminiscent of angels or Valkyries. Certain birds and animals could also act as "good shepherd" spirits. All of which might make the *rusalki* seem less scary, except I saw a representation of one in a book, and it gave me a serious case of the willies. The picture showed a tall, scowling woman dressed in a tattered green dress, with claw-like hands and burning eyes. In another book I ran across a painting of a Scottish waterwraith that could have been the *rusalka*'s twin sister.

It's funny how the same inspirational source can make for opposite beliefs. Fertility goddess from one point of view, harbinger of death from another. Benevolent spirit or collector of souls. Weird.

Anyway, through all my reading, I never did discover anything interesting about the wishing well at the motel. It wasn't erected on some sacred site; it wasn't the central crossroad of a bunch of ley lines or the home of some Kickaha corn goddess. It was just a gimmick to get people to stop at the motel. But that makes for another funny thing— funny strange, still, not ha-ha. Jilly once told me that if you get enough people to agree that something is a certain way, then it becomes that way.

It almost makes sense. For one thing, it would explain how Elvis or JFK can be as much a spiritual avatar for some people as Jesus is for others. Or how a gimmicky wishing well could really grant wishes—just saying it did. Doesn't do much to explain the voices, though.

Or the ghosts.

Here's something I've never told anybody before: One day, about a month or so ago when I'm at the well, I get this weird compulsion to close my eyes and try to imagine the faces that once went with those long-lost voices I now hear.

All I want is for Timmy to look at me the way he looks at Jennifer.

That girl—was she pretty, or fat like me?

Please make Daddy stop shouting at Mommy the way he does.

That child—I can't tell, is it a boy or a girl?

We'll love each other forever.

Did they? They sound so young, that couple. Don't they know that nothing ever lasts? Nothing is forever. Except maybe loneliness. Or does being lonely just feel as though it lasts forever?

The air is thick with the scent of rose blossoms, the hum of bees. I look down at my legs and see them crisscrossed with the shadows of rose thorns and tiny jagged leaves. The faces rise easily in my imagination, but later I realize that maybe it wasn't such a good idea, calling them up the way I did.

Lying in bed that night, it's as though I've actually summoned their ghosts to me by imagining them. I dream about them, about their lives, about wishes that were granted and ones that weren't. About how the wishes some received weren't what they really wanted, how others are happy they never got theirs. . . .

It all seems so real.

I learn to put them aside in the morning, but lately it's gotten harder. These last few days I can feel my life tangling with theirs. They're not dead people, I think, but then I realize some of them might be. The Wishing Well closed its doors twenty years ago. A lot can happen to a person in twenty years. I really could be living with their ghosts—if there really were such things.

Jilly believes in ghosts. As Wendy says, Jilly believes in all kinds of things that nobody else would. Not exactly tabloid fodder, but close. Everything's got a ghost, she says. A spirit. And if you look closely enough, if you pay attention and really learn to *see,* you'll be able to recognize it.

While Jilly can be persuasive, I don't think I can quite believe in ghosts. But I do believe in memories.

Jilly's friend Christy Riddell—the writer—made the connection between ghosts and memories for me. He told me it's not just people that have memories; places have them, too.

"If you think of ghosts as a kind of recording," he says, "a memory that's attached itself to a certain place or an object, then they don't become quite so farfetched after all."

"So why don't we see them everywhere?" I ask. "Why doesn't everyone see them?"

"People's minds are like radio receivers," he explains. "They're not all capable of tuning into every station."

I still don't believe in ghosts and I tell him so.

"Look at the stars," he says.

This is happening in the middle of a party at Wendy's house. Christy and I are having a smoke in the backyard, thrown together because we're the only ones with the habit in Wendy's circle of friends.

"What about them?" I ask, my gaze roving from star to star in the darkness overhead.

"Did you ever think about how many of them are ghosts?"

"I don't get it."

"We're not seeing the stars as they are right now," he says. "We're seeing them as they were thousands of years ago, maybe millions of years ago—however long it took their light to reach us. Some of them don't exist anymore. What we see when we look at them right now aren't the stars themselves, but the light that they gave off—images of themselves, of what they once were."

"So . . . ?"

"So maybe that's what ghosts are."

I hate to admit it, but I can almost buy this.

"Then how come ghosts are so scary?" I ask.

"They're not always," he says. "But memories can be like wounds. They're not easily forgotten because they leave a scar as a constant reminder. It's the moments of strongest emotions that we remember the most: a love lost or won; anger, betrayal, vengeance. I think it's the same for ghosts, the strength of their emotions at the time of their death is what allows them to linger, or go on."

If strong emotions can linger on, I think, then so might desperate wishes.

8

"So I met this woman at the Carlisle," Scotty said as he and Jim were having lunch on Monday, "and she's stunning. She's so hot I can't believe she's interested in me."

"Really?" Jim asked, looking up from his soup with curiosity.

"Oh, yeah. Tight red leather miniskirt, legs like you wouldn't believe, and she snuggles right up next to me at the bar, rubbing her calf against my leg. And let me tell you, the place is *not* crowded. I'm thinking, if we don't get out of this place soon, she's going to jump me right here on the bar stool."

"So what happened?"

A sheepish look came over Scotty's features. "Turns out she's a hooker."

Jim laughed.

"Hey, it's not funny. I could've caught a *disease* or something, you know?"

"So you didn't take her up on her . . . offer."

"Get real. What about you?"

"No hookers for me, thanks all the same."

"No, I mean with what's-her-name, Brenda. Did you see her?"

Jim nodded. "She was different this time," he said. "A little cooler, I guess."

"What? Now she's playing hard to get?"

"I don't think that's it. She just wasn't all that up. I asked her if something was bothering her, but she just changed the subject. After the movie she perked up, though. We stopped for a drink at the Rusty Lion and she had me in stitches, talking about some of the weird people she met back when she was a reporter, but then when I took her home she was all withdrawn again." Jim toyed with his spoon for a moment, slowly stirring his soup. "I'm not really sure what makes her tick. But I want to find out."

"Well, good luck," Scotty said. "But just before you get in too deep, I want you to think of two words: manic depressive."

"Thanks a lot, pal."

"Don't tell me the thought hasn't crossed your mind."

Jim shrugged. "The only down side I see is that she smokes," he said, and then returned to his soup.

9

Jim calls me on Tuesday night and he's really sweet. Tells me he's been thinking about me a lot and he wants to see me again. We talk for a while and I feel good—mostly because he can't see me, I guess. After I get off the phone, I take a bath and then I look at myself in the mirror and wonder how he could possibly be interested in me.

I know what I see: a cow.

What's he going to think when he sees me naked? What's going to happen when he realizes what a fuck-up I am? He hasn't said anything yet, but I don't think he much cares for me smoking, and while he's not stingy or anything, I get the feeling he's careful with his money. What's he going to think about *my* finances?

I'm such a mess. I can't quit smoking, I can't stick to a diet, I can't stop spending money I don't have. Where does it stop? I keep thinking, if I just lose some weight, everything'll be okay. Except I never do, so I keep buying new clothes that I hope will make me look thinner, and makeup and whatever else I can spend money I haven't got on to trick myself into thinking things'll be different. I decide if I get out of debt, everything'll be okay, but first I have to lose some weight. I think if I get a man in my life . . . it goes on and on in an endless downward spiral.

I'd give anything to be like Wendy or Jilly. Maybe if I had a wish . . .

But while I might be starting to believe in ghosts, I side with Wendy on the wish question. Hocus-pocus just doesn't work. If I want to solve my problems, I'm going to have to do it by myself. And I can't keep putting it off. I have to make some real changes—*now*, not when I feel like it, because if I wait until then, I'll never do it.

First thing tomorrow I'm going to make an appointment with my bank manager. And I'll start a serious diet.

10

"Frankly, Ms. Perry," the manager of the Unity Trust said, "your finances are a mess."

Brenda nodded. The nameplate on his desk read "Brent Cameron." He'd given her That Look when she came into his office, the one that roved carelessly up her body before his gaze finally reached her face. Now he didn't seem to be interested in her looks at all.

She'd been upset when he gave her the once-over; now she was upset because he'd obviously dismissed her. She knew just what he was thinking. Too fat.

"But I think we can help you," he went on. "The first thing I want you to do is to destroy your credit cards—all of them."

He gave her an expectant look.

"Um, did you want me to do that now?" Brenda asked.

"That might be best."

He handed her a pair of scissors and one by one she clipped her credit cards in two—Visa, Mastercard, gas and department store cards. The only one she didn't touch was her second Visa card.

"You can't keep any of them, Ms. Perry."

"This isn't mine," she explained. "It's from work. I'll hand it in to them when I get back."

He nodded. "Fine. Now I know this isn't going to be easy, but if we start with making a list of all your monthly requirements, then I think we can come up with a plan that will . . ."

The rest of the meeting went by in a blur. She got the loan. She also came out with a sheaf of paper which held her financial plan for the next three years. Every bit of her income was accounted for, down to the last penny. God, it was depressing. She was going to have to do all her shopping in thrift shops—if she could even afford to do that. To make things worse, she hadn't even mentioned the six-hundred-dollar repair bill she owed her garage for work they'd done on her car last month.

What she could really use right now was a cigarette, she thought, but she hadn't had one since last night and this time she was determined to quit, once and for all. She was starving, too. She'd skipped breakfast and all she'd had for lunch was a bag of popcorn that she'd eaten on the way to her interview with Mr. Cameron.

It hadn't done much to quell the constant gnaw of hunger

inside. All she could do was think of food—food and cigarettes and not necessarily in that order. She'd been feeling
grumpy all morning. The interview hadn't done much to im-
prove her mood. Her nerves were all jangled, her stomach
was rumbling, her body craved a nicotine fix, she was broke
for at least the next three years. . . .

How come doing the right thing felt so bad?

Her route back to the office took her by her favorite clothing store, Morning Glory, and naturally they were having a
huge sale—UP TO 40% OFF EVERYTHING! the banner read. She
hesitated for a long moment before finally going in, just to
have a look at what she could no longer afford. Then of
course there were three dresses that she just had to have and
the next thing she knew she was standing at the counter with
them.

"Will that be cash or charge?" the sales clerk asked her.

It'd be her last splurge before the austerity program went
into affect, she vowed.

But she didn't have enough money with her to pay for
them. Nor could she write a check that wouldn't bounce—
wouldn't *that* impress Mr. Cameron with how well she was
following the guidelines of his budget? Finally she used her
In the City Visa card.

She'd make it up from her next pay. Her first loan pay-
ment wasn't due for three weeks, and she had another paycheck due before that. Conveniently, she'd managed to forget the unpaid bill due her garage.

11

Thursday after work I drive up Highway 14 and pull into
the parking lot of The Wishing Well. By the time I've
walked around back and made my way through the rose
bushes, the evening's starting to fall. I've never been here so
late in the day before. I sit on the crumbly stone wall and
lean against one of the roof supports. It's even more peaceful than on a Sunday afternoon, and I just drink in the tran-
quillity for a long time.

I need something good in my life right now. I've already lost a couple of pounds, and I still haven't had a cigarette since Tuesday night, but I feel terrible. My jaw aches from being clenched so much and all I can think of is cigarettes and food, food and cigarettes. Whenever I turned around at work, someone was stuffing a Danish into their mouth, chewing a sandwich, eating cookies or donuts or a bag of chips. The smoke from Keith's cigarettes—one desk over from mine—is a constant reminder of what I can't do anymore.

Sitting here, just letting the quiet soak into me, is the first real down time I feel I've had in the last two days. It's dark when I finally reach into the pocket of my dress and take out the penny I found in front of the trust company the other day.

Splash.

"So there's this guy," I say finally. My voice sounds loud, so I speak more softly. "I think I like him a lot, but I'm afraid I'm just going to get hurt again. . . ."

It's the same old litany, and even I'm getting tired of it. If the well had a wish for itself, it'd probably be for me just to go away and leave it alone.

Wishes. I don't believe in them, but I'd like to. I think of what Jilly said about them.

It just depends on how badly you want them.

To come true.

For all the times I've visited the well, I've never actually made a wish myself. I don't know why. It's not just because I don't believe in them. Because there's *something* here, isn't there? Why else would I be able to hear all those old wishes? Why else would the ghosts come walking through my sleep every night? Truth is, I've been thinking about wishes more and more lately, it's just that . . .

I don't know. Two days into my new healthy Brenda regime, yes, I'm still hanging in with the diet and not smoking, but it's like I'm conspiring against myself at the same time, trying to undermine what I am accomplishing with other messes. Can't eat, can't smoke? Then, why not blow some money you don't have?

I made the mistake of stopping at one of the sidewalk jewelry vendors on Lee Street and I used my *In the City* Visa card to buy fifty dollars' worth of earrings. I didn't even *know* those vendors took credit cards. Then, when I got back to work, there was a guy from a collection agency waiting for me. The garage got tired of waiting for the money I owed them. The collection agency guy had a talk with Rob—my boss, the paper's editor—and I had to agree to letting them garnishee my wages until the collection agency's paid off.

Which is going to leave me desperately short. *Where* am I going to get the money to pay off the bank loan I took out earlier this week, not to mention the money I borrowed on the paper's Visa card? This diet and no-smoking business is saving me money, but not *that* much money.

Whatever good I'm supposed to get out of doing the right thing still seems impossibly out of reach. Even though I haven't smoked in two days, my lungs seem more filled with phlegm than ever and my mouth still tastes terrible. All I had was popcorn again today, and a quarter of a head of lettuce. I'm losing weight, according to my bathroom scale, but I can feel the fat cells biding their time in my body, ready to multiply as soon as I stick a muffin or a piece of chocolate in my mouth. I'm worse than broke.

I guess the reason I haven't ever made a wish is that this is the only place I know where I don't feel so bad. If I make a wish it'll be like losing the genie in the bottle. You know, you've always got him in reserve—for company, if nothing else—until you make your final wish.

What would I wish for? To be happy? I'd have to become a completely different person for that to work. Maybe to be rich? But how long before I'd blow it all?

The only thing I'd really want to wish for is to see my dad again, but I know that's something that'll never happen.

12

Monday morning found Jilly sitting on the wooden bench in front of Amos & Cook's Arts Supplies, impatiently waiting for the store to open. She amused herself as she usually did in this sort of a situation by making up stories about the passersby, but it wasn't as much fun without somebody to share the stories with. She liked telling them to Geordie best, because she could invariably get the biggest rise out of him.

She'd been up all night working on the preliminary sketches for an album cover that the Broken Hearts had commissioned from her, only to discover when she finally started on the canvas that she'd used up all her blues the last time she'd worked with her oils. So here she sat, watching the minute hand on the clock outside the delicatessen across the street slowly climb to twelve, dragging the slower hour hand up to the nine as it went.

Eventually Amos & Cook's opened and she darted inside to buy her paints. It was while she was heading back up Yoors Street to her studio that she ran into Brenda coming the other way.

"You're looking good," she said when they came abreast of each other.

"Well, thanks a lot," Brenda said sarcastically.

Jilly blinked in confusion. "What's that supposed to mean?"

"You and Wendy are always telling me how I shouldn't worry about being fat—"

"We never said you were—"

"—but now as soon as I find a diet that's actually letting me lose some weight, I'm 'looking great.' "

"Whoa," Jilly said. "Time out. I have never said that you needed to lose weight."

"No, but now that I have I look so much better, right?"

"I was just being—"

Friendly, Jilly had been about to say, but Brenda interrupted her.

"Honest for a change," Brenda said. "Well, thanks for nothing."

She stalked off before Jilly could reply.

"You have a nice day, too," Jilly said as she watched Brenda go.

Wow, talk about getting up on the wrong side of the bed this morning, she thought. She'd never seen Brenda running on such a short fuse.

She was a little hurt from the confrontation until she realized that besides Brenda's bad mood, there'd been something else different about her this morning: no cigarette in her hand, no smell of stale smoke on her clothes. Knowing that Brenda must have recently quit smoking made Jilly feel less hurt about the way Brenda had snapped at her. She'd quit herself years ago and knew just how hard it was—and how cranky it made you feel. Add that to yet another new diet. . . .

Quitting cigarettes was a good thing, but Jilly wasn't so sure about the diet. Brenda didn't need to lose weight. She had a full figure, but everything was in its proper proportion and place. Truth was, she often felt envious of Brenda's fuller shape. It was so Italian Renaissance, all rounded and curved—and lovely to paint, though she had yet to get Brenda to sit for her. Perhaps if this latest diet helped raised Brenda's self-esteem enough, Brenda would finally agree to pose for some quick studies at the very least.

She knew Brenda needed a boost in the self-esteem department, so she supposed a diet that worked couldn't hurt. Just so long as she doesn't get *too* carried away with it, Jilly thought as she continued on home.

13

Even I'm getting tired of my bitchiness. I can't believe the way I jumped on Jilly this morning. Okay, I know why. I was not having a good morning. The ghosts kept me up all night, going through my head even when I wasn't asleep. By the time I ran into Jilly, I was feeling irritable and running late, and I didn't want to hear what she had to say.

Thinking it over, none of that seems like much of an excuse. It's just that, even though I knew she was just trying to be nice, I couldn't help feeling this rage toward her for being so two-faced. You'd think a friend would at least be honest right from the start.

Yes, Brenda, you are starting to seriously blimp on us. Do everybody a favor and lose some weight, would you?

Except nobody was going to say something like that to a friend. I wouldn't even say it to an enemy. It's bad enough when you've got to haul that fat body around with you, never mind having somebody rub your face in the fact of its existence.

I think the best thing I could do right now is just to avoid everybody I know so that I'll have some friends to come back to if I ever make it through this period of my life.

I wonder how long I can put Jim off. He called me three times this past weekend. I played sick on Friday and Saturday. When he called on Sunday, I told him I was going out of town. Maybe I really should go out of town, except I can't afford to travel. I don't even have transit fare this week. Too bad the paper won't pay my parking the way it does Rob's. Of course, I'm not the editor.

When it comes right down to it, I don't even know why I'm working at a newspaper—even a weekly entertainment rag like *In the City*. How did I get here?

I was going to be a serious writer like Christy, but somehow I got sidetracked into journalism—because it offered the safety of a regular paycheck, I suppose. I'm still not sure how I ended up as an advertising manager. I don't even write anymore—except for memos.

The girl I was in college wouldn't even recognize me now.

14

Jim looked up to find Scotty approaching his desk. Scotty sat down on a corner and started to play with Jim's crystal ball paperweight, tossing it from hand to hand.

"So," Scotty said. "How goes the romance?"

Jim grabbed the paperweight and replaced it on his desk. "One of these days you're going to break that," he said.

"Yeah, right. It wasn't me that missed the pop fly at the last game."

"Wasn't me who struck out."

"Ouch. I guess I deserved that." Scotty started to reach for the paperweight again, then settled for a ballpoint pen instead. He flipped it into the air, caught it again. "But seriously," he went on. "Was Brenda feeling better on Sunday?"

Jim nodded. "Except she said she's going to be out of town for a few weeks. She had to pack, so we couldn't get together."

"Too bad. Hey, did Roger tell you about the party he's throwing on Friday? He told me he's invited some seriously good-looking, *single* women."

"I think I'll pass."

Scotty raised his eyebrows. "How serious *is* this thing?" he asked. "She's out of town, so that means you have to stay in?"

"It's not like that."

"When do I get to meet her, anyway?"

Jim shrugged. "When she gets back, I guess."

Scotty gave him a long considering look, the pen still in his hands for a moment.

"I think you've got it bad, pal," he said finally.

"I guess I do."

"How does she feel about you?"

"I think she likes me," Jim said.

Scotty set the pen back down on Jim's desk.

"You're a lucky stiff," he said.

15

I've decided that the ghosts are simply hallucinations, brought on by my hunger. Never mind what Jilly or Christy would say. That's all that makes sense. If anything makes sense anymore.

I've been on this diet for almost four weeks now. Popcorn and lettuce, lettuce and popcorn. A muffin on Wednesday, but I won't let that happen again because I'm *really* losing weight and I don't want to screw anything up. From a hundred and twenty-six to a hundred and four this morning.

Once I would have been delirious with joy to weigh only a hundred and four again, but when I look in the mirror I know it's not enough. All I still see is fat. I can get rid of more. I don't have to be a cow all my life.

I still haven't had a cigarette either and it hasn't added anything to my weight. It's as bad as I thought it'd be—you never realize what a physical addiction it really is until you try to quit—but at least I'm not putting on the pounds, stuffing my face with food because I miss sticking a cigarette in my mouth.

I'm so cranky, though. I guess that's to be expected. My whole body feels weird, like it doesn't belong to me anymore. But I kind of like it. There's a down side, like my clothes don't fit right anymore, but I can deal with it. Since I can't afford to buy new ones, I've been taking them in—skirts and jeans. My T-shirts and blouses are all getting really loose, but I don't mind. I feel so good about the way I'm starting to look now I know that I can never let myself get fat again. I'm just going to lose a few more pounds and then I'm going to go on a bit of a more normal diet. I'm sick of popcorn and lettuce.

The diet's probably making me cranky as well, but I know I'll get past it, just like I'll get past the constant need to have a cigarette. Already it's easier. Now all I've got to do is deal with the financial mess I'm in. I don't know *how* to handle it. I'm not spending any money at all—mine *or* the paper's—but I'm in deep. My phone got cut off yesterday. I just didn't have the money to pay the bill after covering my other expenses. I guess I should've told the bank manager about it when I went in for that loan, but I'd forgotten I was overdue and I don't want to go back to his office.

What I really want to do is just go away for awhile—the way I'm pretending to Jim that I have. Before my phone got cut off, I was calling him from these "hotels" I'm supposed to be staying in and we'd have nice long talks. It's the weirdest romance I've ever had. I can't wait to see his face when he finally sees the new and improved me.

But I'm not ready yet. I want to trim the last of the fat away and put the no-smoking jitters aside first. I know I can do it. I'm feeling a lot more confident about everything now. I guess it really is possible to take charge of your life and make the necessary changes so that you're happy with who you are. What I want now is some time to myself. Go away and come back as an entirely new person. Start my life over again.

Last night one of the ghosts gave me a really good idea.

16

Wendy slouched in the window seat of Jilly's studio while Jilly stood at her easel, painting. She had her notebook open on her lap, but she hadn't written a word in it. She alternated between watching Jilly work, which was fairly boring, and taking in the clutter of the studio. Paintings were piled up against one another along the walls. Everywhere she looked there were stacks of paper and reference books, jars and tins full of brushes, tubes of paint and messy palettes for all the different media Jilly worked in. The walls were hung with her own work and that of her friends.

One of the weirdest things in the room was a fabric mâché self-portrait that Jilly had done. The life-size sculpture stood in a corner, dressed in Jilly's clothes, paint brush in hand and wearing a Walkman. No matter how often Wendy came over, it still made her start.

"You're being awfully quiet," Jilly said, stepping back from her canvass.

"I was thinking about Brenda."

Jilly leaned forward to add a daub of paint, then stepped back again.

"I haven't seen much of her myself," she said. "Of course I've been spending twenty-six hours a day trying to get this art done for this album cover."

"Do they still make albums?"

Jilly shrugged. "CD, then. Or whatever. Why are you thinking about Brenda?"

"Oh, I don't know. I just haven't seen her for ages. We used to go down to the Dutchman's Bakery for strudels every Saturday morning, but she's begged off for the last three weeks."

"That's because she's on a diet," Jilly said.

"How do you know?"

Jilly stuck her brush behind her ear and used the edge of her smock to rub at something on the canvass.

"I ran into her on the way to the art store the other day," she said as she fussed with the painting. "She looked so thin that she's got to be on another diet—one that's working, for a change."

"I don't know why she's so fixated on her weight," Wendy said. "She thinks she's humongous, and she's really not."

Jilly shrugged. "I've given up trying to tell her. She's like your friend Andy in some ways."

"Andy's a hypochondriac," Wendy said.

"I know. He's always talking about what's wrong with him, right?"

"So?"

"So Brenda's a little like that. Did you ever know her to not have a problem?"

"That's not really being fair," Wendy said.

Jilly looked up from her painting and shook her head. "It might not be a nice thing to say," she said, "but it is fair."

"Things just don't work out for her," Wendy protested.

"And half of the reason is because she won't let them," Jilly said. "I think she lives for extremes."

Putting her palette and brush down on the wooden orange crate that stood beside her easel for that purpose, she dragged another orange crate over to the window and sat down.

"Take the way she is with men," Jilly said. "Either nobody's interested in her, or she's utterly convinced some guy's crazy about her. She never gives a relationship a chance to grow. It's got to be all or nothing, right off the bat."

"Yeah, but—"

"And it's not just guys. It's everything. She either has to be able to buy the best quality new blouse or dress, or she won't buy it at all. She either has to eat five desserts, or not have dinner at all."

Wendy found herself reluctantly nodding in agreement. There were times when Brenda could just drive her crazy, too.

"So does it bug you?" she asked.

"Of course it bugs me," Jilly said. "But you have to put up with your friends' shortcomings—just like you hope they'll put up with yours. Under all her anxieties and compulsive behavior has got to be one of the nicest, warmest people I know. What's saddest, I suppose, is that *she* doesn't know it."

"So what should we do?"

"Just like we always do—be there for her when she needs us."

"I suppose," Wendy said. "You know, I hate to say this, but I think what she really needs is a man in her life—a good, solid, dependable man who cares about her. I think that'd straighten up half the problems in her life."

"I think she's got one," Jilly said. "That is, unless she screws this one up by going to the other extreme and suddenly playing too hard to get."

"What do you mean?"

Jilly leaned forward. "You know the guy she met at the bus stop?"

"Jim?"

"Uh-huh. Well, it turns out he works at the Newford School of Art."

"He's an artist?"

Jilly shook her head. "No, he works in admin. I dropped by to see how the registration was coming along for that drawing class I'm going to be teaching next semester, and he started talking to me about Brenda."

"How'd he know you knew her?"

"She'd talked to him about us, I suppose. Anyway, he was wondering if I knew when she'd get back and I almost blew it by saying I'd just run into her on Yoors Street that week, but I caught myself in time. Turns out, he thinks she's out of town on business. She calls him every few days—supposedly from this hotel where she's staying—but she's been very evasive about when she's due back."

"That is so not like Brenda," Wendy said.

"Ignoring a nice guy who's showing some interest in her?"

"That, too. But I meant lying."

"I thought so, too, but who knows what's going on with her sometimes. Did you know she quit smoking?"

"Go on."

"Really. And that last time at the restaurant—before you showed up—she was telling me how she was finally taking your advice to heart and wasn't going to throw herself all over some guy anymore."

"Yeah, but she always says that," Wendy said. She swung her legs down to the floor and hopped down from the window seat. "I'm going to give her a call," she added.

Jilly watched her dial, wait a moment with the receiver to her ear, then frown and hang up.

"She didn't leave her answering machine on?" she asked as Wendy slowly walked back to the window seat.

"The number's not in service anymore," Wendy said slowly. "Her phone must be disconnected."

"Really?"

Wendy nodded. "I guess she didn't pay her phone bill. You know how she's always juggling her finances."

"I don't get it," Jilly said. "If she was that short of cash, why didn't she just come to one of us? We're not rich, but we could've helped out."

"Has she *ever* asked you for a loan?"

Jilly shook her head.

"Me, neither. I think she'd die before she did that."

Wendy packed her notebook away in her knapsack. Turning from the window, she added, "I think I'm going to go by her apartment to see how she's doing."

"Let me clean my brushes," Jilly said, "and I'll come with you."

17

Well, I didn't have to ask Rob if I could get a leave of absence from the paper for a couple of weeks. After I left work last night, it came out how I'd been using *In the City*'s Visa card. Rob confronted me with it this morning, and since I couldn't tell him when, or even if, I'd be able to pay it back, he gave me my pink slip.

"You've been impossible to work with," he told me. "I realize you've just quit smoking—"

I hadn't told anybody, wanting to do it on my own without the pressure of feeling as though I were living in a fishbowl, but I suppose it was obvious.

"—and I can certainly empathize with you. I went through the same thing last year. But I've had complaints from everyone and this business with the Visa is just the final straw."

"No one said anything to me."

"Nobody felt like getting their head bitten off."

"I'm sorry—about everything. I'll make it up to you. I promise."

"It's not just about money," Rob said. "It's about trust."

"I know."

"If you needed a loan, why didn't you come talk to me about it?" he asked. "We could've worked something out."

"It . . . it just happened," I said. "Things have been getting out of control in my life lately."

He gave me a long, considering look. "Do you have a problem with drugs?" he asked.

"No!" That was one of the few areas of my life where I hadn't screwed up. "God, how could you even think that?"

"Because frankly, Brenda, you're starting to look like a junkie."

"I'm on a diet, that's all."

The concern in his eyes seemed to say that he genuinely cared. The next thing he said killed that idea dead in the water.

"Brenda, you need help."

Yeah, like he cared. If firing me was his idea of compassion, I'd hate to see what happened if he really started to be helpful. But I was smart this time and just kept my mouth shut.

"I'm sorry," was all I said. "I'll pay you back. It's just going to take some time."

I got up and left then. He called after me, but I pretended I didn't hear him. I was afraid of what I might say if he kept pushing at me.

I was lucky, I guess. He could have pressed charges—misappropriation of the paper's funds—but he didn't. I should have felt grateful. But I didn't walk out of there thinking how lucky I'd been. I felt like dirt. I'd never been so embarrassed in all my life.

That was Friday. I'm trying to put it behind me and not think about it. That's easier said than done. I've been only partially successful, but by this morning I don't feel as bad as I did yesterday. I'm still a little light-headed, but I'm down another couple of pounds and I still haven't had a cigarette. Day twenty-nine into my new life and counting.

I've moved into The Wishing Well, in unit number twelve—that's the last one on the north wing. I didn't bring much with me—just a few necessities. A few changes of clothing. Some toiletries. A sleeping bag and pillow. A kazillion packages of popcorn, a couple of heads of lettuce and some bottled water. A box of miscellaneous herb teas and a Coleman stove to boil water on. A handful of books.

I also brought along my trusty old manual typewriter that I used all through college, because I think I might try to do some writing again—creative writing like I used to do before I got my first job on the paper. I would've brought my computer, but there's no electricity here, which is also why I've got a flashlight and an oil lamp, though I wasn't sure I could use either until I checked if they could be seen from the highway at night. It turns out all I had to do was replace a couple of boards on the window facing the parking lot.

And of course I brought along my bathroom scale, so I can monitor my weight. This diet's proving to be one of the few successes of my life.

I've hidden my car by driving it across the overgrown lawn and parking it between the pool and my unit. After I got it there, I went back and did what I could with the grass and weeds the wheels had crushed to try and make it look as though no one had driven over them. A frontier woman I'm not, but I didn't do that bad a job. I doubted anybody would notice unless they really stopped to study the area.

Once I had the car stashed, I worked on cleaning up the unit. I had to keep resting because I didn't seem to have much stamina—I still don't—but by nine o'clock last night, I had my little hideaway all fixed up. It still has a musty smell, but either it's airing out, or I'm getting used to it by now. The trash is swept out and bagged in the unit next to mine, along with the mattress and a bundle of towels I found rotting in the bathroom. The plumbing doesn't work, so I'm going to have to figure out where I can get water to mop the floors—not to mention keep myself clean. I found an old ping-pong table in what must have been the motel's communal game room, and I laid that on top of the bed with my sleeping bag unrolled on top of it. It'll be hard, but at least it's off the floor.

I finally made myself a cup of tea, boiling the water on my Coleman stove, and settled down to do a little reading before I went to bed. That's when things got a little weird.

Now usually I'm asleep when the well's ghosts come visiting, but last night . . . last night . . .

I'm not really sure what she is, if you want to know the truth.

I was rereading my old journal—the one I kept when I was still a reporter—kind of enjoying all the little asides and notes I'd made to myself in between the cataloguing of a day's events, when the door to my unit opened. One of the reasons I'd chosen number twelve was because it had a working door; I just never expected anybody else to use it.

I almost died at the sound of the door. The fit's a little stiff, and the wood seemed to screech as it opened. The journal fell from my hands and I jumped to my feet, ready to do I don't know what. Run out the front door into the parking lot. Pick up something to defend myself with. Freeze on the spot and not be able to move.

I picked the latter—through no choice of my own, it just happened—and in walked this woman. The first thought that came to mind was that she was some old hillbilly, drawn down from the hills after seeing the light that spilled out of the window on the pool side of the room. When I was cleaning up the unit, I took the boards off that window and, miracle of miracles, the glass panes were still intact. I never did bother to tack the boards back up when night fell.

She had to be in her seventies at least. She looked wiry and tough, face as wrinkled as an unironed handkerchief, hair more white than grey and standing up from around her head in a wild tangle. Her eyes were her strongest feature—a pale blue, slightly protruding and bird-bright. She was wearing a faded red flannel shirt and baggy blue jeans, scuffed work boots on her feet, with a ratty-looking grey cardigan sweater draped over her shoulders, the sleeves hanging down across the front of her shirt.

She looked vaguely familiar—the way someone you might have gone to school with looks familiar: The features have changed, but not enough so as to render them unrecognizable. I couldn't place her, though. When I was a reporter I met more new people in a month than I could ever hope to remember, so my head's a jumble of people I can only vaguely recognize. Most of them were involved in the arts, mind you, and she didn't look the type. I could more easily picture her sitting on a rocking chair outside some hillbilly cabin, smoking a corncob pipe.

I wasn't thinking about ghosts, then.

She seemed to recognize me, too, because she stood there in the doorway, studying me for what seemed like the longest time, before she finally came in and shut the door behind her.

"You're the one who comes to the well on Sundays," she said as she sat down on the end of my bed. She moved like a man and sat with her legs spread wide, hands on her knees.

I nodded numbly and managed to sit back down on my chair again. I left my journal where it lay on the floor.

"Got a smoke?" she asked.

How I wished.

"No," I told her, finally finding my voice. "I don't smoke."

"Don't eat much either, seems."

"I'm on a diet."

She made a hrumphing sound. I wasn't sure if it was a comment on dieting or if she was just clearing her throat.

"Who . . . who are you?" I asked.

The sense of familiarity was still nagging at me. Having pretty well exhausted everyone I could think of that I knew, I'd actually found myself flipping through the faces of the ghosts I'd called up from the well.

"No reason to call myself much of anything anymore," she said, "but once I went by the name of Carter. Ellie Carter."

As soon as she said her name, I knew her. Or at least I knew where I'd seen her before. After I first found the motel and then started coming by more or less regularly, I'd tried looking up its history. There was nothing in the morgue at *In the City,* but that didn't surprise me once I tracked down a twenty-five-year-old feature in the back issues of *The Newford Star.*

I'd had a copy made of the article, and it was pinned up above my desk back home. There was a picture of Ellie accompanying the article, with the motel behind her. She looked about the same, except shrunk in on herself a little.

She'd been the owner until—as an article dated five years later told me—business had dropped to such an extent that she couldn't make her mortgage payments and the bank had foreclosed on her.

"So've you made yourself a wish yet?" she asked.

I shook my head.

"Well, don't. The well's cursed."

"What do you mean?"

"Don't you clean your ears, girl? Or is that a part of your diet as well?"

"My name's Brenda."

"How long are you planning to stay, Brenda?"

"I . . . I don't know."

"Well, the rate's a dollar a day. You can give me a week in advance and I'll refund what you've got coming back to you if you don't stay that long."

This was insane, I thought, but under her steady gaze I found myself digging the seven dollars out of my meager resources and handing it over to her.

"You need a receipt?"

I shook my head slowly.

"Well, have yourself a nice time," she said, standing up. "Plumbing's out, so you'll have to use the outhouse at the back of the field."

I hadn't got around to thinking much about that aspect of the lack of bathroom facilities yet. When I'd had to pee earlier, I'd just done it around the corner near some lilac bushes that had overgrown the south side of the motel.

"Wait," I said. "What about the well?"

She paused at the door. "I'd tell you to stay away from it, but you wouldn't listen to me anyway, would you? So just don't make a wish."

"Why not?"

She gave me a tired look, then opened the door and stepped out into the night.

"Listen to your elders, girl," she said.

"My name's Brenda."

"Whatever."

She closed the door before I could say anything else. By the time I had reached it and flung it open again, there was no one to be seen. I started out across the parking lot's pavement until I saw headlights approaching on the highway and quickly ducked back into my room and shut the door. Once the car had passed, I slipped out again, this time shutting the door behind me.

I walked all around the motel, but I could find no sign of the woman. I wasn't really expecting to. I hadn't found any recent sign of anyone when I'd explored the motel earlier in the day, either.

That's when I started thinking about ghosts.

So tonight I'm waiting to see if Ellie's going to show up again. I want to ask her more about the well. Funny thing is, I'm not scared at all. Ellie may be a ghost, but she's not frightening. Just a little cranky.

I wonder how and when she died. I don't have to guess where. I've read enough ghost stories to be able to figure out that much.

I also wonder if the only reason I saw her last night is because I'm so light-headed from my diet. I'd hate to find out that I've suddenly turned into one of those people that Jilly calls "sensitives." I've got enough problems in my life as it is without having to see ghosts every which way I turn when I'm awake as well as when I'm asleep.

Besides, if I'm going to meet a ghost, I wouldn't pick one from the wishing well. I'd call up my dad—just to talk to him. I know I can't bring him back to life or anything, but that doesn't stop me from wanting to know why he quit loving my mom and me.

18

Brenda's apartment was the second story of a three-floor brick house with an attached garage in Crowsea. It stood on a quiet avenue just off Waterhouse, a functional old building, unlike its renovated neighbors. The porch was cluttered with the belongings of Brenda's downstairs neighbor, who appeared to use it as a sitting room-cum-closet. At the moment it held a pair of mismatched chairs—one wooden, one wicker and well past its prime—several plastic milk crates that appeared to serve as tables or makeshift stools, three pairs of shoes and one Wellington boot, empty coffee mugs, books, magazines and any number of less recognizable items.

Jilly and Wendy picked their way to the front door and into the foyer which was, if anything, even more messy than the porch. The clutter, Jilly knew, would drive Brenda crazy, she who was so tidy herself. At the second landing, Wendy pressed Brenda's doorbell. When there was no answer after Wendy had rung the bell for the fifth time, she fished her key ring out of her pocket and unlocked the door. Jilly put her hand on Wendy's arm, holding her back.

"I don't think we should be doing this," she said.

"It's not like we're breaking in," Wendy said. "Brenda gave me a spare key herself."

"But it doesn't seem right."

"Well, I'm worried," Wendy told her. "For all we know she fell in the shower and she's been lying there unconscious for days."

"For all we know she's in bed with Jim and doesn't want to be disturbed."

"We wish," Wendy said as she went in ahead.

Jilly followed, reluctantly.

It was, of course, as tidy inside Brenda's apartment as it was messy on the porch. Everything was in its place. Magazines were neatly stacked in a squared-off pile on a table beside Brenda's reading chair. The coasters were all in their holder. There wasn't one shoe or sock off adventuring by itself on the carpet.

Her desk was polished until the wood gleamed, and the computer sitting dead center looked as though it had just come out of the showroom. If it weren't for the corkboard above the desk, bristling with the snarl of papers, pictures and the like pinned to it, Jilly might have thought that Brenda never used her desk at all.

"Brenda?" Wendy called.

Jilly's sympathies lay with the downstairs neighbor. Tidiness wasn't exactly her own strong point.

As Wendy went down the hall toward the kitchen, still calling Brenda's name, Jilly wandered over to the desk and looked at what the corkboard held. It was the only area that made her feel comfortable. Everything thing else in the room was just too perfect. It was as though no one lived here at all.

Old newspaper clippings vied for space with photographs of Brenda's friends, shopping lists, an invitation for an opening to one of Jilly's shows that Brenda hadn't been able to make, a letter that Jilly dutifully didn't read, although she wanted to. She liked the handwriting.

"This place gives me the creeps," she said as Wendy returned to the living room. "I feel like a burglar."

Wendy nodded. "But it's not just that."

Jilly thought about it for a moment. Being in somebody else's apartment when they weren't always gave one a certain empty feeling, but Wendy was right. This was different. The place felt abandoned.

"Maybe she really has gone out of town," Jilly said.

"Well, her toothbrush is gone, but her makeup bag is still here, so she can't have gone far."

"We should go," Jilly said.

"Just let me leave a note."

Jilly wandered over to the window to look out at the street below while Wendy foraged for paper and a pen in the desk. Jilly paused when she looked at Brenda's plants. They were all drooping. The leaves of one in particular, which grew up along the side of the window, had wilted. Jilly couldn't remember what it was called, but Geordie had once given her a plant just like it, so she knew it needed to be watered religiously, at least every day. This one looked exactly like hers had if she went away for the weekend and forgot to water it.

"This isn't like Brenda," Jilly said, pointing to the plants. "The Brenda I know would have gotten someone to look after her plants before she left."

Wendy nodded. "But she never called me."

"Her phone's been disconnected, remember?"

Jilly and Wendy exchanged worried glances.

"I'm getting a really bad feeling about this," Wendy said.

Jilly hugged herself, suddenly chilled. "Me, too. I think we should go by her office."

⟶

"She didn't tell you?" Greg said.

Both Jilly and Wendy shook their heads. Jilly leaned closer to his desk, expectantly.

"I don't know if I should be the one," he said.

"Oh, come on," Jilly said. "You owe me. Who got you backstage at the Mellencamp show last year when you couldn't get a pass?"

"We could've been arrested for the way you got us in!"

Jilly gave him a sweet smile. "I didn't break the window— it just sort of popped open. Besides, you got your story, didn't you?"

Greg Sommer was *In the City*'s resident music critic and one of its feature writers. He was so straight-looking with his short hair, horn-rimmed glasses and slender build that Jilly often wondered how he ever got punk or metal musicians to talk to him.

"Yeah, I did," he admitted. "And I got double use of the material when I covered Lisa Germano's solo album."

"Isn't it wonderful?" Jilly said. "It's nothing like what I expected. I never knew that she sang, which is weird, considering what a really great voice she—"

"Jilly!" Wendy said.

"Oh. Sorry." It was so easy for Jilly to get distracted. She shot Wendy a slightly embarrassed look before she turned back to Greg. "You were saying about Brenda?" she prompted him.

"I wasn't, actually, but I might as well tell you. She got canned first thing yesterday morning."

"What?"

"Weird, isn't it? She's the last person I would've thought to get fired—she's usually so damn conscientious it makes the rest of us look bad. But she's been acting really strange for the past few weeks. I heard a rumor that she's got a really bad drug problem and I believe it. She looks completely strung out."

Wendy shook her head. "No way does Brenda do drugs."

"Well, she's doing something to herself, because there's not much left but skin and bones. And it's happened so fast—just over the last few weeks." He got a funny look. "Jesus, you don't think she has AIDS, do you?"

Just the mention of the disease made all of Jilly's skin go tight and her heartbeat jump. She'd had three friends die of the disease over the past year. Another two had recently tested HIV-positive. It seemed to be sweeping through the arts community, cutting down the brightest and the best.

"Oh, God, I hope not," she said.

Wendy stood up. "Brenda doesn't do drugs and she hasn't got AIDS," she said. "Come on, Jilly. We've got to go."

"But you heard what Greg said about the way she looks," Jilly said as she rose to join her.

Wendy nodded. "It sounds like she's finally found a diet that works," she said grimly. "Except it works too well."

She left Greg's office and walked briskly down the hall towards the stairwell. Jilly only had enough time to quickly thank Greg before she hurried off to catch up to her.

"I don't even know where to begin looking for her," she said as she followed Wendy down the stairs.

"Maybe we should start with this Jim guy she's been seeing."

Jilly nodded, then looked at her watch. It was past five.

"He'll be off work by now," she said. "The admin staff usually leaves at five."

"We can still call the school," Wendy said. "Somebody there will give you his number."

━━

"I haven't seen her in over two weeks," Jim told Jilly when she got him on the line. "And she hasn't called for a couple of days now."

"That's just great."

"What's wrong? Is Brenda in some kind of trouble?"

Jilly put her hand over the mouthpiece and turned to Wendy who was standing outside the phone booth. "He wants to know what's going on. What do I tell him?"

"The truth," Wendy said. "We don't know where she is and we're worried because of what we've been hearing."

"Right. And if there's nothing the matter she's really going to appreciate our blabbing all her problems to a potential boyfriend."

"Hello?" Jim's voice was tiny in the receiver. "Jilly? Are you still there?"

"What do I tell him?" Jilly asked, hand still over the mouthpiece.

"Give it to me," Wendy said.

Jilly exchanged places with her but leaned in close so that she could listen as Wendy made up some story about needing to pick up a dress at Brenda's apartment and they were sorry to have bothered him.

"Right. Tell him the truth," Jilly said when Wendy had hung up. "I could've told him that kind of truth."

"What was I supposed to say? Once you reminded me of how Brenda would react if we did lay it all on him, I didn't have any other choice."

"You did fine," Jilly assured her.

They crossed the sidewalk and sat down on a bench. The

tail end of rush hour crept by on McKennitt, making both of them happy that they didn't own a car.

"Could you imagine putting yourself through that every day?" Jilly said, indicating the crawling traffic with a lazy wave of her hand. "I'd go mad."

"But a car is still nice to have when you want to get out of the city," Wendy said. "Remember when Brenda drove us out to Isabelle's farm this spring?"

"Mmm. I could've stayed there for a month. . . ." Jilly's voice trailed off and she sat up on the bench. "We never checked if Brenda's car was in the garage."

➤

The car was gone.

"Of course that doesn't prove anything," Jilly said.

She and Wendy walked slowly back up the driveway. When they reached the front of Brenda's building, they sat down on the bottom steps of the porch, trying to think of what to do next.

"Just because she's gone for a drive somewhere on a Saturday afternoon," Jilly tried, "doesn't mean anything sinister's going on."

"I suppose. But remember what Greg told us about how she looked?"

"She looked fine when I saw her," Jilly said. "Thinner, and a little jittery from having quit smoking, but not sickly."

"But that was a few weeks ago," Wendy said. "Now people are talking about her looking emaciated, like she's a junkie or something."

Jilly nodded. "I'm not as close to her as you are. I know she's always going on about her weight and diets, but does she actually have an eating disorder?"

The Brenda Jilly knew had never weighed under a hundred and twenty-five.

"She was in therapy in high school," Wendy said. "Which is when she first started suffering from anorexia. The one time she talked to me about it, she told me that the therapist

thought her problems stemmed from her trying to get her
father back: If she looked like a little girl instead of a
woman, then he'll love her again.''

"But her father didn't abandon his family, did he?" Jilly
asked. "I thought he died when she was eight or nine."

"He did, which is a kind of abandonment, don't you
think? Anyway, she doesn't buy into the idea at all, doesn't
think she has a problem anymore."

"A classic symptom of denial."

Wendy nodded. "All of which makes me even more worried. The way Greg was talking, she's down to skin and
bones.''

"I wouldn't have thought it was possible to lose so much
weight so fast," Jilly said.

"What if you just stopped eating?" Wendy said. "Your
basic starvation diet."

Jilly considered that for a moment. "I suppose. You'd
have to drink a lot of liquids, though, or the dehydration'd
get to you.''

"It's still going to leave you weak."

Jilly nodded. "And spacey."

"I wonder if we should report her as missing?" Wendy
wondered aloud.

"I've been that route before," Jilly said. "There's not
much the police can do until she's been gone for at least
forty-eight hours.''

"We don't know *how* long she's been gone."

"Let's give it until tomorrow," Jilly said. "If she's just
gone somewhere for the weekend, she'll be back in the afternoon or early evening.''

"And if she's not?"

"Then we'll see my pal Lou. He'll cut through the red
tape for us.''

"That's right, he's a cop, isn't he?"

Jilly nodded.

"I might still try calling the hospitals," Wendy said. She
gave Jilly a pained look. "God, I sound like a parent, don't
I?''

"You're just really worried."

Wendy sighed. "What gets me is that Brenda's always so . . . so organized. If she was going somewhere, she'd be talking about it for weeks in advance. She'd ask me to drop by to look after her plants. She'd—oh, I don't know. I thought we were close, but she's been avoiding me these past few weeks—nothing I can really point to, it's only when I look back on it I can see there was something more going on. Whenever I called, she was just on her way out, or working overtime, or doing something. I thought it was bad timing on my part, but now I'm not so sure."

She gave Jilly a worried look. "The idea that she's gone on some weird diet really scares me."

Jilly put her arm around Wendy's shoulders and gave her a hug.

"Things'll work out," she said, wishing she felt as confident as she sounded.

Wendy's anxiety had become contagious.

19

I wait until it's past ten and then realize Ellie's going to pull a no-show. Waiting for her, I find myself wondering about my reaction to all of this. From the voices rising up out of the well and their lost faces manifesting in my dreams to the ghost of the motel's old proprietor . . . I seem to accept it all so easily. Why doesn't it freak me as much as it should?

I don't have an answer—at least I don't have one that makes me feel comfortable. Because either the ghosts are all real and I'm far more resilient than I'd ever have imagined myself to be, or I'm losing it.

I'm tired, but I'm not quite ready to go to bed. Maybe weak would be a better way to put it. I've had a busy day. Since there's no maid service—along with everything else this place hasn't got—the first thing I did after I got up was go exploring for water. There was the well, of course, but it was deep and I'd no way to bring water up its shaft. I wasn't so sure I'd even want to if I could. Bad enough I called up ghosts, just by thinking of them. I didn't want to know what would show up if I took some water from that well.

Turns out I didn't have to worry. Not a half dozen yards into the forest, on this side of an old set of railway tracks, I found a stream. The water's clear and cold, even at this time of year. Using a battered tin pail that I discovered inside what must have been a tool shed, I carried water back to my unit and scrubbed the floors and walls. It sounds pretty straightforward, but it took a long time, because I had to rest a lot.

I'll be glad when I've regained my strength. I think I've caught some bug—a summer flu or something—because I keep getting these waves of dizziness that makes the room do a slow spin. It only goes away when I rest my head.

I forgot to mention: I checked my weight this morning, and I'm right at a hundred pounds even. When I look in the mirror, I still see some flab I could lose, but I really think I'm getting there. Once I hit a comfortable ninety-six or seven, I'll switch to a hold-and-maintain diet. Well, maybe ninety-five. No point in going halfway.

I just wish I didn't still want a cigarette. You'd think the urge would be gone by now.

Jim's been on my mind a lot. I'd really been enjoying our telephone conversations. I find I can relate to him so much better knowing that he can't see what I look like when we're talking. It seems to free me up and I found myself talking about all sorts of things—the kinds of conversations I had when I was in college, when we were all going to change the world.

A couple of miles back towards Newford, there's a diner and garage sitting on the corner where a county road crosses the highway. I noticed a pay phone in its parking lot when I drove by. I'm thinking of driving down tomorrow evening and giving Jim a call. This time I'll really be out of town. The only thing I worry about is moving the car too often. If I keep driving over the lawn, anyone with half a brain will be able to see that someone's staying at the motel.

Then I laugh. What am I worrying about? I'm not trespassing. I paid for my room.

I wonder what a ghost does with money.

I give Ellie a little longer to show up, but when the minute hand's crept to quarter past ten, I finally put on a jacket and go outside. I want to clear my head. It takes my eyes a few moments to adjust to the dark. The night gets absolutely black out here. The stars seem so close it's like they're hanging from a ceiling the height of the one in my unit, rather than in the sky.

But you get used to the dark. Your eyes have to work harder to take in light, but after a while you can differentiate between shapes and start to make out details.

I look around, listening to the crickets and June bugs, the frogs down at the bottom of the pool. My gaze crosses the lawn to where the rose bushes have overgrown the wishing well. After a while I cross the lawn. The tall grass and weeds make swishing noises against my jeans. My legs are damp from the dew, right up to the knee, and my sneakers are soon soaked.

I use my flashlight to light my way as I squeeze through the rose bushes, but it's a more awkward process than it is by day and I'm nursing a few thorn pricks before I make it all the way inside to the well. I shut off the light then and put a match to the candle I brought. There's not much of a wind at all, just a slight movement in the air so that the candle casts shadows that make the rose thicket seem even denser than it really is. I pretend I'm—well, not Sleeping Beauty, but one of her handmaidens, say, hidden away behind the wall of thorns. Did they all sleep straight through the hundred years? I find myself wondering. Or did they wake from time to time and glance at their watches, thinking, "When *is* that prince coming?"

It's weird what'll go through your mind when you're in a situation such as this. There are people who pay good money to go away on spiritual retreats. I always thought it was kind of weird, but now it's starting to make a little sense. When all you've got is yourself, it changes the way you think. You have the freedom to consider anything you want, for as long as you want, because there aren't any distractions. You don't have to go to work. The phone won't ring. Nobody drops by your apartment. It's just—

"So what are you hiding from, girl?" a voice asks.

I'm so startled I jump about a foot off the fieldstone wall. This is getting to be a bad habit of hers, but I've got to admit, Ellie sure knows how to make an entrance.

I see her sitting on the edge of one of the benches, the candle's light playing a thorny pattern on her white hair. She never made a sound, coming through the bushes, but then I guess a ghost would just float through.

"Who says I'm hiding?" I ask.

"Everything about you says it."

I shake my head. "I just need some time to be by myself, that's all."

"You're not a very good liar," Ellie says. "I think the only person who believes you is yourself."

"I'm not lying," I tell her, but the words ring as false to me as they obviously do to her.

If I stop to think about it, I know she's right. I have been lying—most of all to myself.

I look at her, half-hidden in the dark, and find myself telling her what's brought me here: all the messy baggage that I seem to drag around with me wherever I go. I have to laugh at myself as I'm doing it. In the stories, it's always the ghosts that unburden themselves.

"What makes you think hiding'll make it all go away?" Ellie asks when I'm done.

"It won't, I guess. There's a lot I'll have to face up to when I get back. I know that. But at least I'll be able to do it with a little self-esteem."

"Seems to me you're just going to the other extreme," she says.

Like she knows me so well.

"You don't know what I'm like," I say. "You don't know how hard it is, just trying to be normal. To fit in."

She seems to consider that. "It's easier when you're my

age," she says finally. "Nobody expects you to be pretty or fashionable. You can be as pushy or as cantankerous as you want, and they don't blink an eye."

"I suppose."

"It was easier when I was younger, too," she goes on. "Oh, we had movie stars and singers to look up to, the pretty girls in the Coca-Cola adverts and all, but there didn't seem to be as desperate a need for a girl to make herself over into one of them. We all wanted to, but we didn't *have* to, if you get my meaning."

I shake my head.

"You didn't have to be pretty to land yourself a husband and raise a family. You just had to be a good person."

"Like the best looking girls didn't get the best men," I say.

"If you think the girls you see as pretty are any happier than you are, you don't know much about anything."

"Yeah, well—"

Ellie doesn't give me a chance to speak; she just barrels along over the top of what I was about to say.

"What you don't understand," she tells me, "is that all these problems you've got—none of them are your own fault."

"Oh, right. The old cop-out: Society's to blame."

"It is, girl."

"Brenda. My name's Brenda."

I hate the way she keeps calling me "girl."

"Society makes you get all these expectations for yourself and then, when you can't meet up to them, it screws up your life. You spend money you don't have because you're trying to comfort yourself. You smoke because you imagine it relieves your stress. You lose weight, not because you need to, but because you think if you can look like some woman in a magazine your life's suddenly going to be perfect. But it's not going to work that way.

"First you have to accept yourself—just as you are. Until that happens, nothing's going to get better for you."

At least she's not going on about my father, the way the

therapists always do, but it still all sounds so pat. And how much did she make of her life? Working her ass off trying to keep her business afloat, having to declare bankruptcy, probably dying broke in some alleyway, one more burned-out baglady.

"What would you know about why I'm doing anything?" I say.

"Because I've been there—" she hesitates for a moment "—Brenda. I spent too much of my own life trying to be somebody that everybody else thought I should be, instead of who I am. If there's anything I regret, if there's anything that really gets me riled up still, it's all those years I wasted."

Is this my future I see sitting in front of me? I wonder. Because I know all about that feeling of having wasted my life. But then I shake my head. There's a difference. I'm *doing* something about my problems.

Still, I think maybe I know what's keeping Ellie here now. Not vengeance, not any need. Just regret.

"You really are dead, aren't you?" I say.

"Land sakes, girl. Whatever gave you that idea?"

I'm not going to let her put me off this time.

"I know you're a ghost," I tell her. "No different from the voices in the well."

"You've heard voices in the well?" she asks.

"First the voices," I say, "and then the ghosts. I dream about them. I started wondering what they looked like—the people those voices once belonged to—and now I can't get them out of my head. They've been getting stronger and stronger until now—well, here you are."

It makes sense, I think as I'm talking. The closer I am to the well, the stronger an influence the ghosts would have on me—so strong now that I'm seeing them when I'm awake. I look over at Ellie, but she's staring off into nowhere, as though she never even heard what I was saying.

"I never considered ghosts," she says suddenly. "I used to dream about spacemen coming to take me away."

This is so weird, it surprises a "You're kidding" out of me.

Ellie shakes her head. "No. I'd be vacuuming a room, or cleaning the bathroom, and suddenly I'd just get this urge to lay down. I'd stare up at the ceiling and then I'd dream about these silver saucers floating down from the hills, flying really low, almost touching the tops of the trees. They'd land out on the lawn by the wishing well here and these shapes would step out. I never quite knew what exactly they looked like; I just knew I'd be safe with them. I'd never have to worry about making ends meet again."

I wait a few moments, but she doesn't go on.

"Are there ghosts in the well?" I ask.

She looks at me and smiles. "Are there spacemen in the hills?"

I refuse to let her throw me off track again.

"Are *you* a ghost?" I ask.

Now she laughs. "Are we back to that again?"

"If you're not a ghost, then what are you doing here?"

"I live here," she says. "Just because the bank took it away from me, it didn't mean I had to go. I've got a place fixed up above the office—nothing fancy, but then I'm not a fancy person. I sleep during the day and do my walking around at night when it's quiet—except for when the kids come by for one of their hoolies. I get my water from the stream and I walk along the railway tracks out back in the woods, following them down to the general store when I run short of supplies."

I hadn't gone further into the office than the foyer, with its sagging floorboards and the front desk all falling in on itself. That part of the motel looks so decrepit I thought the building might fall in on me if I went inside. So I suppose it's possible. . . .

"What do you do in the winter?" I ask.

"Same as I always did—I go south."

She's so matter-of-fact about it all that I start to feel crazy, even though I know she's the one who's not all there. If she's not a ghost, then she's *got* to be crazy to be living here the way she does.

"And you've been doing this for twenty years?" I ask.

"Has it been that long?"

"What do you live on?"

"That's not a very polite question," she says.

I suppose it isn't. She must feel as though I'm interrogating her.

"I'm sorry," I say. "I'm just . . . curious."

She nods. "Well, I make do."

I guess it's true. She seems pretty robust for someone her age. I decide to forget about her being a ghost for the moment and get back to the other thing that's been bothering me.

"I know there's something strange about this well," I say. "You told me last night that it's cursed. . . ."

"It is."

"How?"

"It grants you your wish—can you think of anything more harmful?"

I shake my head. "I don't get it. That sounds perfect."

"Does it? How sure can you be that what you want is really the right thing for you? How do you know you haven't got your ideas all ass-backwards and the one thing you think you can't live without turns out to be the one thing that you can't live with?"

"But if it's a good wish . . ."

"Nothing's worth a damn thing unless you earn it."

"What if you wished for world peace?" I ask. "For an end to poverty? For no one ever to go hungry again? For the environment to be safe once more?"

"It only grants personal wishes," she says.

"Anybody's?"

"No. Only those of people who want—who need—a wish badly enough."

"I still don't see how that's a bad thing."

Ellie stands up. "You will if you make a wish."

She walks by me then and pushes her way through the roses. I hear the rasp of cloth against twig as she moves through the bushes, the thorns pulling at her jeans and her shirt.

"Ellie!" I call after her, but she doesn't stop.

I grab my candle, but the wind blows it out. By the time I get my flashlight out and make it out onto the lawn, there's no one there. Just me and the crickets.

Maybe she isn't a ghost, I find myself thinking. Maybe she was just sitting here all along and I never noticed her until she spoke to me. That makes a lot more sense, except it doesn't feel quite right. Do ghosts even know that they're ghosts? I wonder.

I think about the way she comes and goes. Did she have enough time to get out of sight before I got through the bushes? Who else but a ghost would hang around an abandoned motel, year after year for twenty years?

I get dizzy worrying at it. I don't know what to think anymore. All it does is make my head hurt.

I decide to follow the railway tracks through the woods to the general store where Ellie says she buys her groceries. I'll use the pay phone in the parking lot to call Jim. And maybe, if they're still open, I'll ask them what they know about Ellie Carter and her motel.

20

Jim picked up the phone when it rang, hoping it was Brenda calling. He hadn't heard from her for a few days now, and Jilly's odd call this afternoon had left him puzzled and just a little worried. But it was Scotty on the other end of the line.

"I thought you had a date tonight," Jim said.

He carried the phone over to the sofa. Sitting down, he put his feet up on the coffee table and rested the phone on his chest.

"I did," Scotty told him, "but she stood me up."

"That's low."

He could almost see Scotty's shrug.

"I can't say's I really blame her," Scotty said, "if you really want to know the truth. I'm coming on so strong these days, I think I'd stand myself up if I was given the chance."

"What are you talking about?"

"Ah, you know. All I do is think with my cock. I should be like you—take it slow, take it easy. Be friends with a woman first instead of trying to jump her bones the minute we're alone. But I can't seem to help myself. First chance I get and I'm all over her."

"Yeah, well don't hold me up as some paradigm of virtue," Jim said. "And besides, I get the feeling I'm getting a version of the old runaround myself."

He told Jim about the call he'd gotten from Jilly this afternoon and how it had sounded as though she hadn't known Brenda was away on business.

"When you put that together with how Brenda won't even leave me the number of where she's staying, it's . . . I don't know. I just get a weird feeling about it."

"Sounds like a scam to me," Scotty said.

Jim switched the receiver from one ear to another. "What's that supposed to mean?"

"Think about it. It's obvious that she's put her friends up to call you—just to get a rise out of you. To make you more interested."

"How much more interested can I seem? Whenever she calls, we're on the phone for at least an hour. I'd take her out in a minute, but I can't seem to get the chance. She was too sick before she left and now she's out of town."

"Supposedly."

Jim sighed. "Supposedly," he repeated, somewhat reluctantly.

"Maybe she's just getting back at you for not calling her after she sent you those flowers."

"You really think so?"

"Hey, what do I know? Dear Abby I'm not. I'm just a guy who can't get a date and when I do, the girl dumps me before we even go out." He paused, then added, "Next time she calls, just ask her what's going on."

"What if there's nothing? I'd hate to screw things up. I figure not calling her back right away was already one strike against me. I don't want to add to it now because—"

A sudden beep on the line interrupted him.

"Just a sec," Jim said. "That's my call waiting. It might be Brenda calling."

"I've got to go anyway," Scotty said. "Call me tomorrow and let me know how things worked out."

"Will do," Jim told him.

Cutting the connection with Scotty, he took the other call.

21

I was really looking forward to talking to Jim tonight. I just wanted to hear his voice and connect with a world that didn't involve ghosts or diets or strange voices that come out of a haunted wishing well.

Following the railway tracks really cuts the distance to the general store. The highway takes a curve, but the tracks go straight through the woods. They're overgrown, but not so much that they're not easy to follow. I didn't even need to use my flashlight. I just stepped from wooden rail to wooden rail, one foot, then the other, but slowly, every step an effort. I was so tired.

This flu bug I've caught made it seem as though I was walking all the way back to Newford. I kept having to stop and rest. I would've given up and just gone back, but by the time I started thinking along those lines, I'd already come so far that going back no longer made much sense. And besides, I had this real *need* to step outside myself and my problems—if only for a few minutes.

But now I wish I'd never called Jim, because it seems as though all my lies are coming home tonight: the ones Ellie pointed out that I'd used on myself, and the ones I'd told Jim. He didn't come right out and say he didn't believe I was out of town, but he kept asking all these questions about what my day had been like, had I got to see the sights, that kind of thing. Innocent enough questions, but I couldn't help but feel there was an agenda behind them, as though he was trying to catch me up in my lies.

And then there was this business with Jilly calling him

and Wendy wanting to pick up a dress from my apartment.

I don't have any of Wendy's dresses—God knows they'd never fit me anyway. At least they wouldn't have before the diet. I could get into one of them now, I suppose; it'd just be a little short in the skirt and sleeves. But even if I did have something of Wendy's, she's got a key to my place anyway.

As soon as Jim started talking about their having called him I knew what was really going on. They were worried about me. They'd probably found out about my phone being cut off. Or that I'd lost my job. Or both. Wendy was probably upset anyway because of the way I've been avoiding her these past few weeks. . . .

What a mess I've made of things.

I get off the phone as quickly as I can. Once I hang up, though, I don't have the energy to go back to the motel. The general store is closed, gas pumps and all, so I just sit down on the steps running up to its porch and lean my head against the railing. I want to rest for a couple of minutes.

Once I'm sitting down I feel as though I'll never be able to move again, but I know I can't stay here. It's not that I'm scared of running into the people who own the place or anything—there's no law against using a public phone and then having a rest before heading back home.

No. It's that I can't shake the feeling that I'm being watched. At first I think it's Ellie, but the watching has a hungry feeling about it, as though I'm being stalked, and I can't see Ellie wanting to hurt me. If she ever did, she's already had plenty of opportunities before now.

Logically, I know I'm safe. I'm just a little sick, weak from this flu bug I've caught. Maybe it's the flu that's making me feel paranoid. But logic doesn't help me feel any better because, logically, there shouldn't be ghost voices in the well and ghosts running through my dreams. Logically, I shouldn't keep having conversations with the deceased proprietor of an abandoned motel.

Finally, I drag myself to my feet and start back. I have to rest every fifty feet or so because I just don't have any strength left in me at all. The feeling of being watched gets stronger, but I'm feeling so sick it's as though I don't even care about it anymore. I have cramps that come and go in painful waves. I want to throw up, but I've got nothing in my stomach to bring up. I can't even remember if I had any dinner or not. When all you eat is the same thing, popcorn and lettuce, lettuce and popcorn, day in and day out, it's hard to differentiate between meals.

I don't know how I make it back to my room, but finally I do. Dawn's pinking the eastern horizon, casting long shadows as I stumble to my bed. The birds are making an incredible racket, but I almost can't hear them.

My bed seems to sway, back and forth, back and forth, as I lie on it. I keep hearing ominous sounds under the morning bird calls. A floorboard creaking. A shutter banging. I'm too sick even to turn my head to see if there's someone there. There's a wet, musty smell in the air—part stagnant water, part the smell you get when you turn over a rotting log.

I really want to turn to look now, but the cramps have come back and I double up from the pain. When they finally ease off, I fall asleep and the ghosts are waiting for me.

They're not familiar any longer—or rather, I recognize them, but they look different. It's so awful. All I can see is drowned people, bloated corpses shambling toward me. Their faces are a dead white and grotesquely swollen. Their clothes are rotting and hang in tatters, they have wet weeds hanging from them, dripping on the floor. Their hair is plastered tight against their distended faces. They have only sunken sockets, surrounded by puffs of dead white flesh where they should have eyes.

You're only dreaming, I try to tell myself. You're sick and you have a fever and this is only a dream.

I manage to come out of it. The light's bright in my eyes— must be mid-morning already. It's impossible to focus on anything. I have some dry heaves which only makes me weaker. I try to fight it, but eventually I fall back into the dreams again.

That's when I finally see her, rising up from behind the

ranks of the drowned dead. She looks just like the picture of the *rusalka* in that book. A water-wraith. The deadly spirit of the well.

22

Wendy stayed over at Jilly's studio Saturday night. She slept on the Murphy bed while Jilly camped out on the sofa— over Wendy's protests. "I'll be up early working," Jilly insisted, and refused to discuss it any further. And sure enough, when Wendy woke the next morning, Jilly was already behind her easel, frowning at her current work in progress.

"I can't decide," she said when she saw that Wendy was awake. "Have I made it too dark on this side, or too light on the other?"

"Please," Wendy said. She put on the kimono that Jilly used as a bathrobe and shuffled across the studio toward the kitchen area, looking for the coffee. "At least give me a chance to wake up."

The door buzzer sounded as she was halfway to the coffee carafe sitting on the kitchen counter.

"Would you mind getting that?" Jilly asked. "It's probably Geordie coming by to mooch some breakfast."

"Wonderful," Wendy said.

She was barely awake and now she had to put up with Geordie's ebullient morning cheer on top of Jilly's. She considered writing a sign saying, "Quiet, please, some people are still half asleep," and holding it up when she opened the door, but she didn't have the energy to do more than unlock the door. When she swung it open it was to find a stranger standing there in the hallway.

"Um, is Jilly here?"

Wendy gathered the kimono more closely about her neck and looked over her shoulder. "It's for you," she told Jilly. Turning back to the stranger, she added, "Come on in."

"Thanks."

Jilly looked around the side of her easel, her welcoming smile turning puzzled.

"Jim?" she said.

"I hope I'm not interrupting anything," he said.

So this was Jim Bradstreet, Wendy thought as she continued on her quest for a caffeine hit. He wasn't as handsome as she'd imagined he'd be, but there was a warmth about him that was directly evident. Mostly, it had to do with his eyes, she decided, the laugh lines around them and the way his gaze had immediately sought her own.

Behind her, Jilly laid down the paintbrush she'd been using. Wiping her hands on her jeans, which left new streaks of a dark red on top of the other paint already on the material, she sat Jim down on the sofa and introduced him to Wendy. Wendy offered him coffee which he luckily refused, since there was barely one cup left in the carafe.

"Well, this is a pleasant surprise," Jilly said. "I didn't think you even knew where I lived."

Wendy brought her coffee over to where they were sitting and curled up on the end of the sofa opposite Jim. That was Jilly, she thought. Always happy to see anybody. Sometimes Wendy thought Jilly must know every third person living in the city—with plans already formed to meet the rest.

"I looked the address up in the phone book," Jim said. He cleared his throat. "Uh, maybe I should get right to the point. I've been kind of worried about Brenda ever since you called yesterday. You see, I got the impression that you didn't even know she was out of town."

Jilly's eyebrows rose quizzically, but she didn't say anything. Wendy stared down at her coffee. She hated getting caught in a lie—even one so well-intentioned.

"Anyway," Jim went on, "when she called me last night, I tried to find out where she was staying, how long she'd be gone—that kind of thing. I was trying to be surreptitious, but I could tell she felt I was grilling her and she acted very evasive. We hardly talked for more than five minutes before she was off the phone."

Nice-looking and kindhearted, too, Wendy thought. Obviously concerned. She wondered if he had a brother.

Jilly sighed. "Well, it's true," she said. "We didn't know anything was wrong until yesterday when we found out her phone was cut off and she'd lost her job."

"But it's the paper that's sent her out of town," Jim began before his voice trailed off. He nodded. "I get it," he added, almost to himself. "She just didn't want to see me."

"I don't think it's quite like that," Jilly said.

"She's been avoiding everybody," Wendy said. "I haven't seen her in three weeks."

"And you say she's lost her job?"

Jilly nodded. "Brenda will probably hate us for telling you about any of this, but you seem to care for her and right now I get the feeling she needs all the people she can get to care about her."

"What—what's the matter with her?" Jim asked.

"We don't know exactly," Jilly said.

With Jilly having opened the Pandora's box, Wendy realized she couldn't hold back herself now. She just hoped that it wouldn't put Jim off and that Brenda would forgive them.

"Brenda's got a serious case of low self-esteem," she said. "Way serious. She's always had money problems, but now we think she's quit smoking *and* gone on some weird crash diet. If you've done either, you probably know how it can make you a little crazy. With everything coming down at once on top of that—losing her job, obviously way broke— God knows what she's thinking right now."

"She never said anything. . . ."

"Well, she wouldn't, would she?" Wendy said. "Do you lay all your problems on a woman you've just met— especially someone you might like a lot?"

"She said that?" Jim asked. "That she likes me a lot?"

Wendy and Jilly exchanged amused glances. It was almost like talking to Brenda, Wendy thought. That'd be the first thing she'd center on as well.

"When you were talking to Brenda," Jilly asked. "Did she say where she was staying?"

Jim shook his head.

"Well, I might be able to fix that," Jilly said. "Or at least, Lou might."

She got up and dug her phone out from under a pile of newspapers and art magazines and dialed a number.

"Who's Lou?" Jim asked Wendy.

"A cop she knows."

"Yes, hello?" Jilly said into the phone. "Could I speak to Detective Fucceri, please? It's Jilly Coppercorn calling." She listened for a moment, then put her hand over the mouthpiece. "Great," she told them. "He's in." She removed her hand before either Wendy or Jim could say anything and spoke into the phone again.

"Lou? Hi. It's Jilly. I was wondering if you could do me a favor.

"That's not true—I called you just last week to ask you out for lunch but you were too busy, remember?

"How soon we forget.

"What? Oh, right. I want to get an address to go with a phone number.

"Well, no. I don't have the number yet. I need that as well."

Wendy sat fascinated as she listened to Jilly deal with number traces and the like as though she were some TV private eye who did this all the time. Jilly passed on Jim's number and the approximate time of Brenda's call to Lou, then finally hung up and gave Jim and Wendy a look of satisfaction.

"Lou'll have the address for us in about half an hour," she said.

"Can anybody do that?" Jim asked.

Wendy just looked at him. "What do you think?" she asked.

"What's the big deal?" Jilly asked. "All I did was ask a friend to do us a favor."

"But only *you* would think of tracing Brenda's call," Wendy said.

"But everybody knows that the phone company keeps records on that kind of thing—don't they?"

"And only you would know who to ask and have them actually do it for you," Wendy finished.

Jilly waved her hand dismissively. "Anybody want some breakfast?" she asked.

Jim glanced at his watch. "But it's almost noon."

"It's also Sunday," Wendy told him. "Normal people are only just waking up about now."

"So call it brunch," Jilly said.

━

It took Lou closer to an hour to get back to Jilly, by which time they'd all eaten the somewhat complicated Mexican omelet that Jilly had whipped up for them with her usual careless aplomb. Wendy and Jim were cleaning the dishes and Jilly was back behind the easel when the phone finally rang.

"You're sure?" Jilly said when she had finished writing down the information he had given her. "No, no. I'd never think that. I really appreciate your doing this, Lou. It's just such a weird place. Yes, I'll tell you all about it next week. Thanks again."

She hung up the phone and then stared at what she'd written.

"*Well?*" Wendy said. "Aren't you going to tell us where she is?"

Jilly shrugged. "I don't know. The call was made from a public phone booth in the parking lot of a general store up Highway 14."

"A general store?" Wendy said.

" 'Ada & Bill's General Store.' It's almost in the mountains."

Wendy's hopes fell. "That doesn't tell us anything."

Jilly nodded her head in glum agreement.

"I've got a car," Jim said. "Anybody want to take a drive up there to see if we can find out more?"

All Jilly had to do was change her jeans for a clean pair and comb her tangled hair with her fingers. Wendy was dressed and ready to go in a record five minutes.

23

Everything stands still when the *rusalka* appears. She's tall and gaunt, a nightmare of pale flesh clad in the remains of a tattered green dress, hair matted and tangled, the color of dried blood, the eyes burning so that looking at them is like looking into the belly of a furnace.

She's what's been haunting me, I realize. She's the curse of the well. It's not her granting wishes that makes her so terrible, but that she steals your vitality as a vampire would. She sucks all the spirit out of you and then drags your body down into the bottom of the well where you lie with all the other bodies of her victims.

I can see the mound of them in the water, a mass of drowned flesh spotted with the coins that have been dropped on top of them. I know that's where I'm going, too.

She steps up to me, clawed hands reaching out. I try to scream but it's as though my mouth's full of water. And then she touches me. Her flesh is so cold it's like a frost burn. Her claws dig into my shoulders, cutting easily through the skin like sharp knives. She starts to haul me up toward her in an awful embrace and finally I can scream.

But it's too late, I know.

That's all I can think as she drags my face up toward her own. It's too late.

She's got jaws like a snake's. Her mouth opens wider than is humanly possible—but she's not human, is she? She's going to swallow me whole . . . but suddenly I'm confused. I feel like I'm standing on the edge of the wishing well and it's the mouth of the well that's going to swallow me, not the *rusalka,* except they're one and the same and all I can do is scream, and even that comes out like a jagged whisper of sound because I've got no strength in me, no strength left at all.

24

"That was it!" Jilly cried as Jim drove by a small gas bar and store on the right side of the highway. "You went right by it."

Jim pulled over to the side of the road. He waited until there was a break in the traffic, then made a U-turn and took them back into the parking lot. The name of the store was written out in tiny letters compared to the enormous GAS sign above it. The building itself was functional rather than quaint—cinderblock walls with a flat shingled roof. All that added a picturesque element was the long wooden porch running along the front length of the building. It was simply furnished, with a pair of plastic lawn chairs, newspaper racks for both *The Newford Star* and *The Daily Journal*, and an ancient Coca-Cola machine belonging to an older time when the soft drink was sold only in its classic short bottles.

Jim parked in front of the store, away from the pumps, and killed the engine. Peering through the windshield, they could see an old woman at the store's counter.

"I'll go talk to her," Jilly said. "Old people always seem to like me."

"*Everybody* likes you," Wendy said with a laugh.

Jilly gave a "can I help it" shrug before she opened her door and stepped out onto the asphalt.

"I'm coming," Wendy added, sliding over across the seat.

In the end they all trooped inside. The store lived up to its name, selling everything from dried and canned goods and fresh produce to fishing gear, flannel shirts, hardware and the like. The goods were displayed on shelves that stood taller than either Jilly or Wendy, separated by narrow aisles. It was dim inside as well—the light seeming almost nonexistent compared to the bright sunlight outside.

The old woman behind the counter—she must be Ada, Jilly decided—looked up and smiled as they came in. She was grey-haired and on the thin side, dressed in rather tasteless orange polyester pants and a blouse that was either an off white or a very pale yellow—Jilly couldn't quite decide which. Her hair was done up in a handkerchief from which stray strands protruded like so many dangling vines.

"I wish I could be of more help," Ada said when Jilly showed her the photograph of Brenda that she'd brought along, "but I've never seen her before. She's very pretty, isn't she?"

Jilly nodded. "Are there any motels or bed-and-breakfasts nearby?" she asked.

"The closest would be Pine Mountain Cabins up by Sumac Lake," Ada told her. "But that's another fifteen or so miles up the highway."

"Nothing closer?"

"Afraid not. Pine Mountain is certainly the closest—other than The Wishing Well, of course, but that's been boarded up ever since the early seventies when the bank foreclosed on Ellie Carter."

"That's the place where Brenda goes on her Sunday drives," Wendy put in.

Jilly nodded. She could remember Brenda having spoken of the place before. "And she's got a newspaper clipping of it up above her desk in her apartment," she added.

"I doubt your friend would be staying there," Ada said. "The place is a shambles."

"Let's try it anyway," Jilly said. "We've got nothing to lose. Thank you," she added to Ada as she headed for the door with Jim in tow.

Wendy stopped long enough to buy a chocolate bar, before following them to the car. Jilly had already slid in beside Jim so this time Wendy got the window seat.

"What would Brenda be doing at an abandoned motel?" Wendy asked as Jim started up the car.

"Who knows?" he said.

"Besides," Jilly said, "with the way this idea panned out, our only other option is to go back home."

←

The motel was easy to find. They followed the long curve of the highway as it led away from the store and came upon it almost immediately as the road straightened once more.

"I don't see a car," Jim said.

He parked close to the highway and they all piled out of his car again. The soles of their shoes scuffed on the buckling pavement as they approached the motel proper. The tumbled-down structure looked worse the closer they came to it.

"Maybe she parked it around back," Jilly said. "Out of sight of the highway."

She was trying to sound hopeful, but the place didn't look encouraging—at least not in terms of finding Brenda. It was so frustrating. She kicked at a discarded soda can and watched it skid across the parking lot until it was brought up short by a clump of weeds growing through the asphalt.

"God, it's so creepy-looking," Wendy said. "Way abandoned."

It did have a forlorn air about it, but Jilly rather liked it—maybe because of that. She'd always had a soft spot in her heart for the abandoned and unwanted.

"I think it's great," she said.

"Oh, please."

"No, really. I've got to come back here and do some paintings. Look at the way that shed's almost leaning right into the field. The angle's perfect. It's like it's pointing back at the motel sign. And the lattice work on that roofline—over there. It's just—"

"What's that weird *sound?*" Jim broke in.

Jilly fell silent and then both she and Wendy both heard it as well—an eerie mix of a high-pitched moan and a broken whisper. It was so quiet that it disappeared completely when a car passed on the highway behind them. Once the car was gone, though, they could hear it again.

"It . . . it must be some kind of animal," Wendy said. "Caught in a trap or something."

Jilly nodded and set off around the side of the motel at a run, quickly followed by the other two.

"Oh, shit," Wendy said. "That's Brenda's car."

Jilly had recognized it as well, but she didn't bother replying. She had a bad feeling about all of this—the motel, Brenda's car, that *sound.* Worry formed a knot in the pit of her stomach, but she ignored the discomfort as best she could. Head cocked, she tried to place where the sound originated. It made her shiver, crawling up her spine like a hundred little clawed feet.

"It's coming from over there," Jim said, pointing toward a thick tangle of rose bushes.

"That's where Brenda said the well is," Wendy said.

But Jilly wasn't listening. She'd already taken the lead again and so it was she who, after pushing her way through a worn path in the rose bush tangle, first found Brenda.

Jilly almost didn't recognize her. Brenda was wasted to the point of emaciation—a gaunt scarecrow version of the woman Jilly had known. Her clothes hung on her as though they were a few sizes too large, her hair seemed to have lost its vibrancy and was matted against her scalp and neck. She was leaning over a crumbling stone wall, head and shoulders in the well, thin arms pushing on the stones as though something was dragging her down. But there was nothing there. Only Brenda and the terrible soft keening sound she was making.

Afraid of startling her, Jilly waited until Jim and Wendy had pushed through the roses as well so that they could lend her a hand in case Brenda fell forward when she was touched. Speaking softly—just uttering meaningless comforting sounds, really—Jilly pulled Brenda back from the well with Jim's help. When they laid her on the ground, Brenda's eyes gazed sightless up at them, vision turned inward. But the sound she'd been making slowly faded away.

"Oh my God," Wendy said as she took in the change that had been wrought on Brenda in just a few weeks. "There's nothing left of her."

Jilly nodded grimly. "We have to get her to a hospital."

She and Wendy took Brenda's legs, Jim her shoulders, then they carried her back through the rose bushes, all of them suffering scratches and cuts from the sharp thorns since the path was too narrow for this sort of maneuver. Brenda seemed to weigh nothing at all. Once they had her out on the lawn, Jim hoisted her up in his arms and they hurried back to his car.

"What about Brenda's car?" Wendy said as they passed it on the way back to the motel's parking lot.

"We'll come back for it," Jilly said.

25

I don't remember much about the hospital. I feel like I was underwater the whole time—from when I hung up the phone on Jim Saturday night until a few days later, when I found myself in a hospital bed in Newford General. I don't know where the lost time went—down some dark well, I guess.

The doctor told me I'd been starving myself to death.

I was in the hospital forever and I've been in therapy ever since I got out. I'm really just starting to come to grips with the fact that I have an eating disorder. Have one, had one, and always have to guard against its recurrence.

Thank god I had my health insurance premiums paid up.

The thing that's hardest to accept is that it's not my fault. This is something Ellie told me and my therapist keeps returning to. Yes, I'm responsible for the messes I've made in my life, but I have to understand where the self-destructive impulses come from. The reason I feel so inadequate, so fat, so ugly, so mixed up, is because all my life I've had certain images pounded into my head—the same way that everybody does. Perfect ideals that no one can match. Roles to play that—for whatever reason—we can't seem to adjust to. When you don't toe the line, it's not just the outside world that looks askance at you; you feel in your own head that you've let yourself down.

Logically, it all makes sense, but it's still a hard leap of faith to accept that the person I am is a good person and deserves recognition for that, rather than trying to be somebody I'm not, that I can never be, that it would even be wrong to be.

But though that's part of my problem, it's not the real root of it. Every woman has to deal with those same social strikes against her. For me, it all comes back to my dad, to this belief that if I'd been better, prettier, he wouldn't have killed himself; that if I could somehow regain the sexless body of a child—look like a child, be the perfect child—I could win him back again.

Understanding that is even harder.

I weigh a hundred and twenty-seven pounds now, but I still haven't taken up smoking again. As for my finances— I'm working on them. I had to declare personal bankruptcy, but I'm going to pay everybody back. I have to, because I don't think anybody else should have to pay for my mistakes—no matter what the extenuating circumstances leading up to those mistakes. A friend of Jilly's got me a job at *The Daily Journal* doing proofing, copyediting, that sort of thing. The pay's not great, but there's room to move up.

Things never really worked out between Jim and me—my fault again, but I'm trying not to feel guilty about it. I just couldn't accept that he cared for me after he'd seen how screwed up I can get. I know it wasn't pity he felt—I mean, he obviously liked me before things got really weird—but I could never look at him without wondering what he was seeing: me, or that creature I became by the well. Jilly says he still asks about me. Maybe one day I'll feel confident enough to look him up again.

There was no *rusalka*—that's pretty much the general consensus, myself included. Sort of. Wendy says I must have seen a reflection of myself in the window of the motel room and just freaked out. My therapist simply says there's no such thing, but won't offer explanations for what I thought I saw except to tell me that I was in a disturbed state of mind and that people are liable to experience anything in such a situation.

I don't quite buy it. I don't know if there really was a water-wraith or not, but there's something in water that's still haunting me. Not a bad something, not a nightmare creature like the *rusalka,* but still something not of this world. When I talked about it with Jilly once, she said, "You know the way Christy talks about ghosts being a kind of audiovisual memory that a place holds? Well, water's supposedly the best conductor for that sort of a thing. And that's why there are so many holy wells and sacred lakes and the like."

I suppose. The ghosts in my head are gone, but I hear water all the time and my dreams always seem to take me underwater. I'm never scared, it's never spooky. Just . . . strange. Dark and cool. Peaceful in a way that I can't explain.

Wendy says I shouldn't let Jilly fill my head with her weird ideas, but I don't know. The interesting thing about Jilly is that she's totally impartial. She accepts everything with the same amount of interest and tolerance, just as she seems to love everybody the same—which is why I think she's never really had a steady boyfriend. She never quite has that extra amount of love it would take to make a relationship with just one person work.

Wendy disagrees with that. She says that Jilly just can't get close to a man that way. I get the feeling it's got to do with something that happened to Jilly when she was growing up, but Wendy's as closemouthed about that as she is with any bit of privileged information, and I've never quite got up the nerve to ask Jilly herself. I'd hate to remind her of some really awful thing in her past—if that's truly the case.

Whatever it was, she's moved beyond it now. Her life is so contained, so steady, for all her fey impulses. I think I envy that about her more than her thinness now.

I wonder if there's anything she envies in other people.

━

It's autumn now—months later. Like I said, the ghosts don't come to me anymore, but sometimes I still hear voices drifting up from out of the well when I go for my Sunday drives up to the motel. Or maybe it's only the wind. All I know is that I still like to come sit on the old stone wall here by the well and when I leave, I feel . . . different. It's as though the calmness that's hidden away in that well enclosed by its rose bushes imparts something to me: maybe no more than simply another way of seeing things.

I don't worry about it; I just appreciate it. And if I come back a little spacey, saying odd things which seem very insightful to me, but are confusing to other people, nobody seems to mind. Or at least they don't say anything about it to me.

As for Ellie, I went up into the rooms above the office where she said she lived and there was nothing there. No Ellie, no sign of anyone living there, except it was very clean, as though someone took the trouble to sweep it out regularly and maybe put some wildflowers in a vase on the window sill when they're in season. There was a glass jar with dried flowers in it when I was there, and it didn't smell musty the way the other rooms do.

I tried to find an obit for her, but as someone pointed out to me, she could have died anywhere. If she didn't die in or around the city, there wouldn't be an obit in the morgues of any of our local papers. Still, I looked.

Jilly's got another answer, of course. She says she knows what Ellie meant about the well being cursed: Ellie must have wished that she'd always be at The Wishing Well, so after she died, her ghost was forever doomed to haunt the motel. Which, as Wendy put it, is par for the course, considering the way Jilly sees the world.

I like to think Ellie's just gone south for the winter.

—

The first time I go back to the wishing well, I find four dollar bills held down by a stone on the wall of the well. I look at them and wonder, a refund for the days I'd paid for, but didn't stay at the motel?

I drop them down into the shaft, one after the other, but I don't make a wish. My life's not perfect, but then whose is? All I can do is forget about miracles and try to take things one day at a time. I'm the only one who can empower myself—I don't need my therapist to tell me that.

━

I don't think the well ever was cursed. The only curse comes from the ghosts a person brings to it.

━

I still think about my dad a lot. I guess we had more in common than I thought, since we both screwed up our lives pretty badly. I think he'd be proud of me for finding a solution different from the one he did.

━

WKPN's on the radio when I drive home. "Rock and gold, without the hard rock and rap." They're playing Buddy Holly.

Wella, wella.

I turn the dial, chasing static and stations until I hear a black woman's voice, clipped rhymes, ghetto poetry riding the back of a sliding beat that's so contagious my pulse can't help but keep time with it. She's talking about standing up for herself, being herself, facing the world with what she calls a buffalo stance.

You can keep your "rock and gold," I think. I'm tired of living in the past. I'm like the wishing well, in a lot of ways, full of old ghosts that I just can't seem to exorcise. They're what keeps dragging me down. It's when I listen to them, when I start to believe that all the unhappy things they're saying about me is true, that I'm at my worst.

What I want is what this woman's singing about, something that's here and now. What I need is my own buffalo stance.

I think I'm finally on the right road to finding it.

DEAD MAN'S SHOES

*There are people who take the heart
out of you, and there are people who
put it back.*

—Elizabeth David

In her office, her head rests upon her arms, her arms upon the desk. She is alone. The only sounds are those of the clock on the wall, monotonously repeating its two-syllable vocabulary, and the faint noise of the street coming in through her closed windows. Her next appointment isn't until nine P.M.

She meant merely to rest her eyes for a few moments; instead, she has fallen asleep.

In her dream, the rain falls in a mist. It crouches thicker at knee level, twining across the street. The dead man approaches her through the rain with a pantherlike grace he never displayed when alive. He is nothing like Hollywood's shambling portrayals of animated corpses; confronted by the dead man, she is the one whose movements are stuttered and slow.

Because she is trapped in flesh, she thinks.

Because in this dreamscape, he is pure spirit, unfettered by gravity or body weight, while she still carries the burden of life. The world beyond this night's dreams retains a firm grip, shackling her own spirit's grace with the knowledge of its existence and her place in it.

Not so the dead man.

The rain has pressed the unruly thicket of his hair flat against his scalp. His features are expressionless, except for the need in his eyes. He carries a somewhat bulky object in his arms, bundled up in wet newspapers. She can't quite identify it. She knows what he carries is roundish, about the size of a soccer ball, but that is all. All other details have been swallowed in the play of shadow that the rain has drawn from the neon signs overhead and the streetlight on the corner.

She is not afraid of the dead man, only puzzled. Because she knows him in life. Because she has seen him glowering from the mouths of alleyways, sleeping in doorways. He has never been truly dangerous, despite his appearance to the contrary.

What are you doing here? she wants to ask him. What do you want from me? But her voice betrays her as much as her body, and what issues forth are only sounds, unrecognizable as words.

She wakes just as he begins to hand her what he is carrying.

—

The dream was very much upon Angel's mind as she later looked down at the pathetic bundle of rag-covered bones Everett Hoyle's corpse made at the back of the alley. But since she had always believed that the supernatural belonged only to the realm of fiction, film and the tabloids, she refused to allow the dream to take root in her imagination.

Jilly would call what she had experienced prescience; she thought of it only as an unhappy coincidence, and let it go no further. Instead she focused her attention on the latest addition to the city's murder-victim statistics.

No one was going to miss Everett, she thought, least of all her. Still, she couldn't help but feel sorry for him. It was an alien reaction insofar as Everett was concerned.

The streets were filled with angry individuals, but the reasons behind their anger usually made sense: lost homes, lost jobs, lost families. Drink, or drugs. Institutions turning out their chronic psychiatric patients because the government couldn't afford their care. Victims of neglect or abuse who discovered too late that escaping to a life on the street wasn't the answer.

But Everett was simply mean-spirited.

He had a face that would make children cry. He wasn't deformed, he simply wore a look of rage that had frozen his features into a roadmap of constant fury. He stood a cadaverous six-four, which was more than merely intimidating to those from whom he was trying to cadge spare change; it could be downright frightening. With that manner, with his matted shock of dirty grey hair and tattered clothing, he didn't seem so much a man down on his luck as some fearsome scarecrow that had ripped itself free from its support pole and gone out to make the world around him as unpleasant as he felt himself. Which put him about one step up from those men who had to kill their families before they put the gun in their own mouth and pulled the trigger.

No, Angel corrected herself. Think in the past tense now, because Everett had terrorized his last passerby.

Surprisingly, death had brought a certain calm to his features, smoothing away the worst of the anger that normally masked them. This must be what he looked like when he was sleeping, Angel thought. Except he wasn't asleep. The blood pooled around his body bore stark testimony to that. She'd already checked for a pulse and found none. Having called the police before she left the office, now it was simply a matter of waiting for them to arrive.

The scene laid out before her held an anomaly that wouldn't stop nagging her. She took a step closer and studied the body. It was like a puzzle with one piece missing, and it took her a few minutes before she could finally pinpoint what was bothering her. She turned to the young white boy who'd come to her office twenty minutes ago and brought her back to where he'd found the body.

"What happened to his boots, Robbie?" she asked.

Everett's footwear had been distinctive: threadbare Oxfords transformed into boots by stitching the upper half of a pair of Wellingtons onto the leather of each of the shoes. Olive green with yellow trim on the left; black with red trim on the right. The Oxfords were so old and worn that they were devoid of any recognizable color themselves.

"I guess Macaulay took 'em," the boy replied.

"You never said Macaulay was here with you."

Robbie shrugged.

She waited for him to elaborate, but Robbie simply stood beside her, face washed pale by the streetlight coming in from the mouth of the alley, thin shoulders stooped, one Dr. Marten kicking at the trash underfoot. His dirty-blonde hair was so short it was no more than stubble. He wouldn't meet her gaze.

Angel sighed. "All right," she said. "I'll bite. Why did Macaulay take the boots?"

"Well, you know what the homes are saying, Miz Angel. Man gets nined, you got to take away his shoes or he's gonna go walkin' after he's dead. He'll be lookin' for who took him down, usually, but Everett now—he's so mean I suppose anybody'd do."

With all her years of working with street people, dealing with the myriad superstitions that ran rampant through the tenements and squats, Angel thought she'd heard it all. But this was a new one, even on her.

"You don't believe that, do you?" she asked.

"No, ma'am. But I'd say Macaulay surely do."

Robbie spoke casually enough, but Angel could tell there was more to what had happened here tonight than he was letting on. He was upset—a natural enough reaction, considering the circumstances. Keeping Everett's corpse company until the police arrived had upset her as well. But the tension underlying Robbie's seeming composure spoke of more.

Before she could find just the right way to persuade him to open up to her, one of the sirens that could be heard at all hours of the day or night in this part of the city disengaged itself from the general hubbub of night sounds and became more distinct. Moments later, a cruiser pulled up, blocking the mouth of the alley. The cherry-red lights of its beacons strobed inside the alley, turning the scene into a macabre funhouse. Backlit, the two officers who stepped out of the cruiser took on menacing shapes: shadows, devoid of features.

At Angel's side, Robbie began to tremble, and she knew she wouldn't get anything from him now. Hands kept carefully in view, she went to meet the approaching officers.

Angelina Marceau ran a youth distress center on Grasso Street, from which she got her nickname, the Grasso Street Angel. She looked like an angel as well: heart-shaped face surrounded by a cascade of dark curly hair, deep warm eyes, next to no makeup because she didn't need it with her clear complexion. Her trim figure didn't sport wings, and she leaned more toward baggy pants, T-shirts and hightops than she did harps and white gowns, but that didn't matter to those living on the streets of Newford. So far as they were concerned, all she lacked was a visible halo.

Angel wasn't feeling particularly angelic by the time three A.M. rolled around that night. She sat wearily in her office, gratefully nursing a mug of coffee liberally spiked with a shot of whiskey, which Jilly had handed to her when she walked in the door.

"I appreciate your looking after the place while I was at the precinct," she said.

"It wasn't a problem," Jilly told her. "No one showed up."

Angel nodded. Word on the street moved fast. If the Grasso Street Angel was at the precinct, *no one* was going to keep his appointment and take the chance of running into one of the precinct bulls. The only one of her missed appointments that worried her was Patch. She'd spent weeks trying to convince him at least to look into the sponsorship program she administered, only to have this happen when she'd finally gotten him to agree. Patch was so frail now that

she didn't think the boy would survive another beating at
the hands of his pimp.

"So how'd it go?" Jilly asked.

It took Angel a moment to focus on what she'd been
asked. She took a sip of her coffee, relaxing as the warmth
from the whiskey reached her stomach.

"We were lucky," she said. "It was Lou's shift. He made
sure they went easy on Robbie when they took our state-
ments. They've got an APB out on Macaulay."

"Robbie. He's the skinny little peacenik that looks like a
skinhead?"

Angel smiled. "That's one way of putting it. There's no
way he could have killed Everett."

"How *did* Everett die?"

"He was stabbed to death—a half-dozen times at least."

Jilly shivered. "They didn't find the knife?"

"They didn't find the weapon and—I find this really
odd—they didn't find Everett's boots either. Robbie says
Macaulay took them so that Everett's ghost wouldn't be
able to come after anyone." She shook her head. "I guess
they just make them up when they haven't got anything better to do."

"Actually, it's a fairly old belief," Jilly said.

Angel took another sip of her whiskey-laced coffee to for-
tify herself against what was to come. For all her fine traits,
and her unquestionable gifts as an artist, Jilly had a head
filled with what could only charitably be called whimsy.
Probably it was *because* she was an artist and had such a
fertile imagination, Angel had eventually decided. Still,
whatever the source, Jilly was ready to espouse the oddest
theories at the drop of a hat, everything from Victorian-
styled fairies living in refuse dumps to Bigfoot wandering
through the Tombs.

Angel had learned long ago that arguing against them
was a fruitless endeavor, but sometimes she couldn't help
herself.

"Old," she said, "and true as well, I suppose."

"It's possible," Jilly said, plainly oblivious to Angel's lack of belief. "I mean, there's a whole literature of superstition surrounding footwear. The one you're talking about dates back hundreds of years and is based on the idea that shoes were thought to be connected with the life essence, the soul, of the person to whom they belonged. The shoes of murdered people were often buried separately to prevent hauntings. And sorcerers were known to try to persuade women to give them their left shoes. If the woman did, the sorcerer would have power over her."

"Sorcerers?" Angel repeated with a cocked eyebrow.

"Think what you want," Jilly told her, "but it's been documented in old witch trials."

"Really?"

"Well, it's been documented that they were accused of it," Jilly admitted.

Which wasn't quite the same thing as being true, Angel thought, but she kept the comment to herself.

Jilly put her feet up on a corner of Angel's desk and started to pick at the paint that freckled her fingernails. There always were smudges of paint on her clothes, or in her tangled hair. Jilly looked up to find Angel watching her work at the paint and shrugged unselfconsciously, a smile waking sparks of humor in her pale blue eyes that made them seem as electric as sapphires.

"So what're you going to do?" Jilly asked.

"Do? I'm not going to do anything. I'm a counselor, not a cop."

"But you could find Macaulay way quicker than the police could."

Angel nodded in agreement. "But what I do is based on trust—you know that. If I found Macaulay and turned him over to the police, even though it's just for questioning, who's going to trust me?"

"I guess."

"What I am going to do is have another talk with Robbie," Angel said. "He's taken all of this very badly."

"He actually liked Everett?"

Angel shook her head. "I don't think anyone liked Everett. I think it's got to do with finding the body. He's probably never seen a dead man before. I have, and I'm still feeling a little queasy."

She didn't mention that Robbie had seemed to be hiding something. That was Robbie's business, and even if he did share it with her, it would still be up to him who could know about it and who could not. She just prayed that he hadn't been any more involved in Everett's death than having stumbled upon the body.

"Actually," she said after a moment's hesitation, "there was another weird thing that happened tonight."

Although she knew she'd regret it, because it was putting a foot into the strange world Jilly inhabited, where fact mixed equally with fantasy, she told Jilly about her dream. As Angel had expected, Jilly accepted what she was told as though it were an everyday occurrence.

"Has this ever happened to you before?" she asked.

Angel shook her head. "And I hope it never happens again. It's a really creepy feeling."

Jilly seemed to be only half-listening to her. Her eyes had narrowed thoughtfully. Chewing at her lower lip, she cocked her head and studied the ceiling. Angel didn't know what Jilly saw up there, but she doubted it was the cracked plaster that anybody else would see.

"I wonder what he wanted from you," Jilly finally said. Her gaze dropped and focused on Angel's. "There has to be a reason he sent his spirit to you."

Angel shook her head. "Haven't you ever dreamed that someone you know died?"

"Well, sure. But what's that—"

"And did they turn out to be dead when you woke?"

"No, but—"

"Coincidence," Angel said. "That's all it was. Plain and simple coincidence."

Jilly looked as though she was ready to argue the point, but then she simply shrugged.

"Okay," she said, swinging her feet down from the desk. "But don't say you weren't warned when Everett's spirit comes back to haunt you again. He wants something from you and the thing with ghosts is they can be patient forever. He'll keep coming back until you figure out what he wants you to do for him and you do it."

"Of course. Why didn't I think of that?"

"I'm serious, Angel."

Angel smiled. "I'll remember."

"I just bet you will," Jilly said, returning her smile. She stood up. "Well, I've got to run. I was in the middle of a new canvas when you called."

Angel rose to her feet as well. "Thanks for filling in."

"Like I said, it was no problem. The place was dead." Jilly grimaced as the word came out of her mouth. "Sorry about that. But at least a building doesn't have shoes to lose, right?"

After Jilly left, Angel returned to her desk with another spiked coffee. She stared out the window at Grasso Street where the first touch of dawn was turning the shadows to grey, unable to get Everett's stockinged feet out of her mind. Superimposed over it was an image of Everett in the rain, holding out a shadowed bundle towards her.

One real, one from a dream. Neither made sense, but at least the dream wasn't supposed to. When it came to Everett's boots, though . . .

She disliked the idea of someone believing superstitions almost as much as she did the superstitions themselves. Taking a dead man's shoes so he wouldn't come back seeking revenge. It was so patently ludicrous.

But Macaulay had believed enough to take them.

Angel considered Jim Macaulay. At nineteen, he was positively ancient compared to the street kids such as Robbie whose company he kept, though he certainly didn't look it. His cherubic features made him seem much younger. He'd been in and out of foster homes and juvie hall since he was seven, but the experiences had done little to curb his minor criminal ways, or his good humor. Macaulay always had a smile, even when he was being arrested.

Was he good for Everett's murder? Nothing in Macaulay's record pointed to it. His crimes were always nonviolent: B&Es, minor drug dealing, trafficking in stolen goods. Nothing to indicate that he'd suddenly upscaled to murder. And where was the motive? Everett had carried nothing of value on his person—probably never had—and everyone knew it. And while it was true he'd been a royal pain in the ass, the street people just ignored him when he got on a rant.

But then why take the boots?

If Macaulay believed the superstition, why would he be afraid of Everett coming after him unless he *had* killed him?

Too tired to go home, Angel put her head down on the desk and stared out the window. She dozed off, still worrying over the problem.

━

Nothing has changed in her dream.

The rain continues to mist. Everett approaches her again, no less graceful, while she remains trapped in the weight of her flesh. The need is still there in Everett's eyes, the mysterious bundle still cradled against his chest as he comes up to her. But this time she finds enough of her voice to question him.

Why is he here in her dream?

"For the children," he says.

It seems such an odd thing for him to say: Everett, who's never had a kind word for anyone, so far as Angel knows.

"What do you mean?" she asks him.

But then he tries to hand the bundle to her and she wakes up again.

━

Angel sat up with a start. She was disoriented for a long moment—as much by her surroundings as from the dream—before she recognized the familiar confines of her office and remembered falling asleep at her desk.

She shook her head and rubbed at her tired eyes. Twice in the same night. She had to do something about these hours, but knew she never would.

The repetition of the dream was harder to set aside. She could almost hear Jilly's voice, I-told-you-so plain in its tone.

Don't say you weren't warned when Everett's spirit comes back to haunt you again.

But it had been just a dream.

He wants something from you, and the thing with ghosts is they can be patient forever.

A disturbing dream. That shadowed bundle Everett kept trying to hand to her and his enigmatic reply, "For the children."

He'll keep coming back until you figure out what it is he wants you to do for him and you do it.

She didn't need this, Angel thought. She didn't want to become part of Jilly's world, where the rules of logic were thrown out the door and nothing made sense anymore. But this dream . . . and Macaulay taking those damn boots. . . .

She remembered Jilly asking her what she was going to do and what her own reply had been. She still didn't want to get involved. Her job was helping the kids, not playing cop. But the image of the dream-Everett flashed in her mind, the need in his eyes and what he'd said when she'd asked him why he was there in her dream.

For the children.

Whether she wanted it or not, she realized that she was involved now. Not in any way that made sense, but indiscriminately, by pure blind chance, which seemed even less fair. It certainly wasn't because she and Everett had been friends. For God's sake, she'd never even *liked* Everett.

For the children.

Angel sighed. She picked up her mug and looked down at the cold mixture of whiskey and coffee. She started to call Jilly, but hung up before she'd finished dialing the number. She knew what Jilly would say.

Grimacing, she drank what was left in her mug, then left her office in search of an answer.

Macaulay had a squat in the same abandoned tenement where Robbie lived, just a few blocks north of Angel's office on the edge of the Tombs. Angel squinted at the building, then made her way across the rubble-strewn lot that sided the tenement. The front door was boarded shut, so she went around the side and climbed in through a window the way the building's illegal inhabitants did. Taking a moment to let her eyes adjust to the dimmer light inside, she listened to the silence that surrounded her. Whoever was here today, was obviously asleep.

She knew Macaulay's squat was on the top floor, so she found the stairwell by the boarded-up entrance and climbed the two flights to the third floor. She looked in through the doorways as she passed by the rooms, heart aching with what she saw. Squatters, mostly kids, were curled up in sleeping bags, under blankets or in nests of newspaper. What were they going to do when winter came and the coolness of late summer nights dropped below the freezing mark?

Macaulay's room was at the end of the hall, but he wasn't in. His squat had a door, unlike most of the other rooms, but it stood ajar. Inside it was tidier than Angel had expected. Clean, too. There was a mattress in one corner with a neatly-folded sleeping bag and pillow on top. Beside it was an oil lamp, sitting on the wooden floor, and a tidy pile of spare clothes. Two crates by the door held a number of water-swelled paperbacks with their covers removed. On another crate stood a Coleman stove, a frying pan and some utensils. Inside the crate was a row of canned goods while a cardboard box beside it served to hold garbage.

And then there were the shoes.

Although Angel didn't know Macaulay's shoe size, she doubted that any of them would fit him. She counted fifteen pairs, in all shapes and sizes, from a toddler's tiny sneakers to a woman's spike-heeled pumps. They were lined up against the wall in a neat row, a miniature mountain range, rising and falling in height, with Everett's bizarre boots standing like paired peaks at the end closest to the door.

It was a perfectly innocent sight, but Angel felt sick to her stomach as she stood there looking at them. They were all the shoes of children and women—except for Everett's. Had Macaulay killed all of their—

"Angel."

She turned to find him standing in the doorway. With the sun coming through the window, making his blonde hair look like a halo, he might have been describing himself as much as calling her name. Her gaze shifted to the line of shoes along the wall, then back to his face. His blue eyes were guileless.

Angel forwent the amenities.

"These . . . these shoes . . . ?" she began.

"Shoes carry the imprint of our souls upon their own," he replied. He paused, then added, "Get it?"

All she was getting was a severe case of the creeps. What had she been thinking to come here on her own? She hadn't told anyone where she was going. Her own hightops could be joining that line of shoes, set in place beside Everett's.

Get out while you can, she told herself, but all she could do was ask, "Did you kill him?"

"Who? Everett?"

Angel nodded.

"Do I look like a killer to you?"

No, he looked as though he was on his way to mass—not to confess, but to sing in the choir. But the shoes, something about the way the shoes stood in their tidy, innocuous line, said differently.

"Why did you take them?"

"You're thinking they're souvenirs?"

"I . . . I don't know what to think."

"So don't," he said with a shrug, then disconcertingly changed the subject. "Well, it's a good thing you're here. I was just going out to look for you."

"Why?"

"Something terrible's happened to Robbie."

The flatness of his voice was completely at odds with his choir-boy appearance. Angel's gaze dropped to his hands, but they were empty. She'd been expecting to see him holding Robbie's shoes.

"What . . . ?"

"You'd better come see."

He led the way down to the second floor, on the other side of the building, then stood aside at the open door to Robbie's room. It was as cluttered as Macaulay's was tidy, but Angel didn't notice that as she stepped inside. Her gaze was drawn and riveted to the small body hanging by a rope from the overhead light fixture. It turned slowly, as though Robbie's death throes were just moments past. On the floor under him, a chair lay on its side.

Angel turned to confront Macaulay, but he was gone. She stepped out into the hallway to find it empty. Part of her wanted to run him down, to shake the angelic smugness from his features, but she made herself go back into Robbie's room. She righted the chair and stood on it. Taking her pen knife from the back pocket of her jeans, she held Robbie against her as she sawed away at the rope. When the rope finally gave, Robbie's dead weight proved to be too much for her and he slipped from her arms, landing with a thud on the floor.

She jumped down and straightened his limbs. Forcing a finger between the rope and his neck, she slowly managed to loosen the pressure and remove the rope. Then, though she knew it was too late, though his skin was already cooling, she attempted CPR. While silently counting between breaths, she called for help, but no one stirred in the building around her. Either they were sleeping too soundly, or they just didn't want to get involved. Or maybe, a macabre part of her mind suggested, Macaulay's already killed them all. Maybe she hadn't walked by sleeping runaways and street kids on her way to Macaulay's room, but by their corpses. . . .

She forced the thought out of her mind, refusing to let it take hold.

She worked until she had no more strength left. Slumping

against a nearby wall, she stared at the body, but couldn't see it for the tears in her eyes.

It was a long time before she could get to her feet. When she left Robbie's room, she didn't go downstairs and leave the building to call the police. She went upstairs, to Macaulay's room. Every room she passed was empty, the sleeping figures all woken and fled. Macaulay's room was empty as well. It looked the same as it had earlier, with one difference. The sleeping bag and the clothes were gone. The line of shoes remained.

Angel stared at them for a long time before she picked up Everett's boots. She carried them with her when she left the building and stopped at the nearest pay phone to call the police.

⟶

There was no note, but the coroner ruled it a suicide. But there was still an APB out on Macaulay, and no longer only in connection with Everett's death. Two of the pairs of shoes found in his squat were identified as belonging to recent murder victims; they could only assume that the rest did as well. The police had never connected the various killings, Lou told Angel later, because the investigations were handled by so many different precincts and, other than the missing footwear, the M.O. in each case was completely different.

Behind his cherubic features, Macaulay proved to have been a monster.

What Angel didn't understand was Robbie's suicide. She wouldn't let it go and finally, after a week of tracking down and talking to various street kids, she began to put together another picture of Macaulay. He wasn't just a killer; he'd also made a habit of molesting the street kids with whom he kept company. Their sex made no difference—just the younger the better. Coming from his background, Macaulay was a classic case of "today's victim becoming tomorrow's predator"—a theorem put forth by Andrew Vachss, a New York lawyer specializing in juvenile justice and child abuse with whom Angel had been in correspondence.

Even more startling was the realization that Macaulay probably hadn't killed Everett for whatever his usual reasons were, but because Everett had tried to help Robbie stand up to Macaulay. In a number of recent conversations Angel had with runaways, she discovered that Everett had often given them money he'd panhandled, or shown them safe places to flop for a night.

Why Everett had needed to hide this philanthropic side of himself, no one was ever going to find out, but Angel thought she now knew why Robbie had killed himself: It wasn't just the shame of being abused—a shame that kept too many victims silent—but because Everett had died trying to protect him. For the sweet soul that Robbie had been, Angel could see how he would be unable to live with himself after what had happened that night.

But the worst was that Macaulay was still free. Two weeks after Everett's death, he still hadn't been apprehended. Lou didn't hold out much hope of finding him.

"A kid like that," he told Angel over lunch the following Saturday, "he can just disappear into the underbelly of any big city. Unless he gets picked up someplace and they run his sheet, we might never hear from him again."

Angel couldn't face the idea of Macaulay in some other city, killing, sexually abusing the runaways on its streets, protected by his cherubic features, his easy smile, his guileless eyes.

"All we can hope," Lou added, "is that he picks himself the wrong victim next time—someone meaner than he is, someone quicker with a knife—so that when we do hear about him again, he'll be a number on an ID tag in some morgue."

"But this business of his taking his victims' shoes," Angel said.

"We've put it on the wire. By this time, every cop in the country has had their duty sergeant read it to them at roll call."

And that was it. People were dead. Kids already feeling

hopeless carried new scars. She had a dead man visiting her in her dreams, demanding she do she didn't know what. And Macaulay went free.

Angel couldn't let it go at that, but there didn't seem to be anything more that she could do.

All week long, as soon as she goes to sleep, Everett haunts her dreams.

"I know what you were really like," she tells him. "I know you were trying to help the kids in your own way."

For the children.

"And I know why Macaulay killed you."

He stands in the misting rain, the need still plain in his eyes, the curious bundle held against his chest. He doesn't try to approach her anymore. He just stands there, half swallowed in mist and shadow, watching her.

"What I don't know is what you want from me."

The rain runs down his cheeks like tears.

"For God's sake, *talk* to me."

But all he says is, "Do it for the children. Not for me. For the children."

"Do *what?*"

But then she wakes up.

Angel dropped by Jilly's studio on that Sunday night. Telling Jilly she just wanted some company, for a long time she simply sat on the Murphy bed and watched Jilly paint.

"It's driving me insane," she finally said. "And the worst thing is, I don't even believe in this crap."

Jilly looked up from her work and pushed her hair back from her eyes, leaving a steak of Prussian blue on the errant locks.

"Even when you dream about him every night?" she asked.

Angel sighed. "Who knows what I'm dreaming, or why."

"Everett does," Jilly said.

"Everett's dead."

"True."

"And he's not telling."

Jilly laid down her brush and came over to the bed. Sitting down beside Angel, she put an arm around Angel's shoulders and gave her a comforting hug.

"This doesn't have to be scary," she said.

"Easy for you to say. This is all old hat for you. You like the fact that it's real."

"But—"

Angel turned to her. "I don't want to be part of this other world. I don't *want* to be standing at the checkout counter and have to seriously consider which of the headlines are real and which aren't. I can't deal with that. I can barely deal with this . . . this haunting."

"You don't have to deal with anything except for Everett," Jilly told her. "Most people have a very effective defensive system against paranormal experiences. Their minds just automatically find some rational explanation for the unexplainable that allows them to put it aside and carry on with their lives. You'll be able to do the same thing. Trust me on this."

"But then I'll just be denying something that's real."

Jilly shrugged. "So?"

"I don't get it. You've been trying to convince me for years that stuff like this is real and now you say just forget it?"

"Not everybody's equipped to deal with it," Jilly said. "I just always thought you would be. But I was wrong to keep pushing at you about it."

"That makes me feel inadequate."

Jilly shook her head. "Just normal."

"There's something to be said for normal," Angel said.

"It's comforting," Jilly agreed. "But you do have to deal with Everett, because it doesn't look like he's going to leave you alone until you do."

Angel nodded slowly. "But do what? He won't tell me what he wants."

"It happens like that," Jilly said. "Most times spirits can't communicate in a straightforward manner, so they have to talk in riddles, or mime, or whatever. I think that's where all the obliqueness in fairy tales comes from: They're memories of dealing with real paranormal encounters."

"That doesn't help."

"I know it doesn't," Jilly said. She smiled. "Sometimes I think I just talk to hear my own voice." She looked across her studio to where finished paintings lay stacked against the wall beside her easel, then added thoughtfully, "I think I've got an idea."

Angel gave her a hopeful look.

"When's the funeral?" Jilly asked.

"Tomorrow. I took up a collection and raised enough so that Everett won't have to be buried in a pauper's grave."

"Well, just make sure Everett's buried with his boots on," Jilly told her.

"That's *it?*"

Jilly shrugged. "It scared Macaulay enough to take them, didn't it?"

"I suppose. . . ."

For all she's learned about his hidden philanthropic nature, she still feels no warmth towards the dead man. Sympathy, yes. Even pity. But no warmth.

The need in his eyes merely replaces the anger they wore in life; it does nothing to negate it.

"You were buried today," she says. "With your boots on."

The slow smile on the dead man's face doesn't fit well. It seems more a borrowed expression than one his features ever knew. For the first time in over a week, he approaches her again.

"A gift," he says, offering up the newspaper-wrapped bundle. "For the children."

For the children.

He's turned into a broken record, she thinks, stuck on one phrase.

She watches him as he moves into the light. He peels away the soggy newspaper, then holds up Macaulay's severed head. He grips it by the haloing blonde hair, a monstrous, bloody artifact that he thrusts into her face.

➤

Angel woke screaming. She sat bolt upright, clutching the covers to her chest. She had no idea where she was. Nothing looked right. Furniture loomed up in unfamiliar shapes, the play of shadows was all wrong. When a hand touched her shoulder, she flinched and screamed again, but it was only Jilly.

She remembered then, sleeping over, going to bed, late, late on that Sunday night, each of them taking a side of the Murphy bed.

"It's okay," Jilly was telling her. "Everything's okay."

Slowly, Angel felt the tension ease, the fear subside. She turned to Jilly and then had to smile. Jilly had been a street kid once—she was one of Angel's success stories. Now it seemed it was payback time, their roles reversed.

"What happened?" Jilly asked.

Angel trembled, remembering the awful image that had sent her screaming from her dream. Jilly couldn't suppress her own shivers as Angel told her about it.

"But at least it's over," Jilly said.

"What do you mean?"

"Everett's paid Macaulay back."

Angel sighed. "How can you *know* that?"

"I don't know it for sure. It just feels right."

"I wish everything was that simple," Angel said.

➤

The phone rang in Angel's office at mid-morning. It was Lou on the other end of the line.

"Got some good news for you," he said.

Angel's pulse went into double-time.

"It's Macaulay," she said. "He's been found, hasn't he? He's dead."

There was a long pause before Lou asked, "Now how the hell did you know that?"

"I didn't," Angel replied. "I just hoped that was why you were calling me."

It didn't really make anything better. It didn't bring Robbie back, or take away the pain that Macaulay had inflicted on God knew how many kids. But it helped.

—

Sometimes her dreams still take her to that street where the neon signs and streetlights turn a misting rain into a carnival of light and shadow.

But the dead man has never returned.

BIRD BONES AND WOOD ASH

—

> *It's a wonder we don't dissolve*
> *in our own bath water.*
> —attributed to Pablo Picasso

1

At first, Jaime knows them only as women with the faces of animals: mare and deer, wild boar and bear, raven and toad. And others. So many others. Following her.

They smell like forest loam and open field, like wild apple blossoms and nuts crushed underfoot. Their arms are soft, but their hands are callused and hard, the palms like leather. Where they have been, they leave behind a curious residue of dried blood and rose petals, tiny bird bones and wood ashes.

In those animal faces, their eyes are disconcertingly human, but not mortal. They are eyes that have seen decades pass as we see years, that have looked upon Eden and Hades. And their voices, at times a brew of dry African veldt whispers and sweet-toned crystal bells, or half-mad, like coyotes and loons, one always rising above the others, looping through the clutter of city sound, echoing and ringing in her mind, heard only from a distance.

They never come near, they simply follow her, watching, figments of post-traumatic stress, she thinks, until they begin to leave their fetish residue in her apartment, in her car, on her pillow. They finally approach her in the grave-yard, when the mourners are all gone and she's alone by Annie's grave, the mound of raw earth a sharp blade that has already left a deep scar inside her.

They give her no choice, the women. When they touch her, when they make known their voiceless need, she tells them she's already made the choice, long before they came to her.

All she lacked was the means.

"We will give you the means," one of them says.

She thinks it's the one with the wolf's head who spoke. There are so many of them, it's hard to keep track, all shapes and sizes, first one in sharp focus, then another, but never all at the same time. One like a woodcock shifts nervously from foot to foot. The rabbit woman has a nose that won't stop twitching. The one like a salmon has gills in her neck that open and close rhythmically as though the air is water.

She must have stepped into a story, she thinks—one of Annie's stories, where myths mingle with the real world and the characters never quite know which is which. Annie's stories were always about the people, but the mythic figures weren't there just to add color. They created the internal resonance of the stories, brought to life on the inner landscapes of the characters.

"It's a way of putting emotions on stage," Annie explained to her once. "A way of talking about what's going on inside us without bogging the story down with all kinds of internal dialogue and long-winded explanations. The anima are so . . . immediate."

If she closes her eyes she can picture Annie sitting in the old Morris chair by the bay window, the sunlight coming in through the window, making a pre-Raphaelite halo around the tangle of her long hennaed hair as she leans her chin on a hand and speaks.

"Or maybe it's just that I like them," Annie would add, that pixie smile of hers sliding across her lips, her eyes luminous with secrets.

Of course she would, Jaime thinks. She'd like the animal women, too.

Jaime isn't so sure that she does, but she doesn't really question the women's presence—or rather the reality of their presence. Since Annie's death, nothing is as it was. The surreal seems normal. The women don't so much make her nervous as cause her to feel unbalanced, as though the world underfoot has changed, reality curling sideways into a skein of dreams.

But if the women are real, if they can help . . .

"I'll do it," she tells them. "I'll do it for Annie."

The rat-snake woman sways her head from side to side. Her human eyes have yellow pupils, unblinking in her scaled features.

"This is not about the storyteller," she says.

"It is for all those who have need of a strong mother," explains the wild boar, lisping around her tusks.

The ground seems more unbalanced than ever underfoot. Jaime puts out a hand and steadies herself on a nearby headstone. Annie's neighbor now. The scar inside is still so raw that it's all Jaime can do to blink back the tears.

"I don't understand," she tells them. "If it's not about Annie, then why have you come to me?"

"Because you are strong," the raven says.

"Because of your need," the salmon adds.

The mountain lion bares her fangs in a predatory grin.

"Because you will never forgive them," she says.

She lays her hand on Jaime's arm. The rough palm is warm and has the give of a cat's paw. Something invisible flickers between them—more than the warmth: a glow, a spark, a fire. Jaime's eyes widen and she takes a sharp breath. The lioness's gift burns in her chest, in her heart, in her belly, in her mind. It courses through her veins, drums in her temples, sets every nerve end quivering.

One by one, the others approach. They hold her in their soft arms, touch her hands with their callused palms. Fairy godmothers in animal guises, bestowing their gifts.

2

It's a night in late July and Karl thinks he's dreaming.

He's in that private place inside his head where everything is perfect. He doesn't have to be careful here. He can be as rough as he likes, he can leave a roadmap of bruises and cuts and welts, he can do any damn thing he wants and it doesn't make a difference because it's just in his head. He doesn't have to worry about his wife finding out, about what a neighbor or a teacher might say. Nobody's going to come around asking awkward questions because it's just in his head.

Here's he's hard forever and children do exactly what he tells them to do or he punishes them. How he punishes them.

Tonight's scenario has his youngest daughter tied to her bed. He's just come into the room and he's shaking his head.

"You've been a bad, bad girl, Judy," he tells her.

When she starts to cry, he brings his hand out from behind his back. He doesn't own a belt like this anywhere except for in his private place. The leather is thick, so thick the belt can barely bend, and covered with large metal studs.

Karl's problem is that it's not his daughter there on the bed tonight. He just doesn't know it yet.

I only caught the tail end of what really happened in Judy's bedroom earlier tonight. I heard her crying. I saw him zipping up his pants. I heard him remind her how if she ever told anybody about their special secret that bad people would take her and her sister away and put them in a horrible prison for bad girls. How they'd have to stay there forever and it would break their mother's heart and she would probably die.

I wanted to kill him right then and there, but I waited. I clung to the side of the tenement's wall and shivered with anger, but I've learned how to be patient. I've found a less messy way to deal with the monsters. I don't do it for them; I do it for those who are left behind. To save them the trauma of waking to find their loving husband/father/boyfriend/uncle disemboweled on the floor.

I wait until he's asleep, then I come in through his bedroom window. I pad over to the bed where he's lying beside his sleeping wife and step up, balancing my weight like a cat, so there's no give in the mattress, no indication at all that I'm crouched over the monster, hands free from their gloves, palms laid against his temples. The contact, skin to skin, makes me feel ill, but it lets me step into his private place.

It's only there, when he moves towards the bed with the belt, that I make myself known. I break the ropes tying my Judy-body to the bed as though they were tissue paper. When he looks at me he doesn't see a scared child's eyes anymore. He sees my eyes, the hot bear-rage, the unblinking snake-disdain, searing his soul.

And then I take him apart.

It's a tricky process, but I'm getting better at it with practice. The first few times I left a vegetable behind and that's no good either. Some of these families can barely keep a roof over their heads, food in their stomachs. No way they can afford the chronic hospital care for the empty monster shells I left behind.

So I've refined the process, emasculating them, making it impossible for them ever to hurt anybody again, but still functional. Barely. Scared of everything, including their own shadow. But no more likely to regress to their former selves than I am to forgive them.

Karl's wife never wakes as I leave their bedroom through the window. I make it to the roof and I have to rest. It would be easier just to kill them, but I know this way is better. It leaves me feeling weak, with a tear in my soul as though I've lost a piece of myself. I think I leave something behind each time—more than that anima residue of dried blood and rose petals, bird bones and wood ash. I leave some part of myself that I'll never be able to regain. But it's worth it. I just have to think of the sleeping child and know that, for her, at least, the monster won't be returning.

I want a shower so bad it hurts, but the night's young and it's still full of monsters. That's what breaks my heart. There are always more monsters.

3

It's cold for a September night, colder still on the rooftop where I crouch, and the wind can find me so easily, but I don't feel the chill.

I used to laugh at the comic books Annie would read, all those impossibly proportioned characters running around in their long underwear, but I don't laugh anymore. The costumes make perfect sense now. My bodysuit has a slick black weave with enough give to let me move freely, but nothing that'll catch on a cornice or in someone's grip. The Thinsulate lining keeps me warm, even below zero. Black gloves, lined hood and runners complete the outfit. Makes me look like one of those B-movie ninjas, but I don't care. It gets the job done.

I draw the line at a cape.

I never read superhero comics when I was a kid—not because they seemed such a guy thing, but because I just couldn't believe in them. I had the same questions for Superman as I did for God: If he was so powerful, why didn't he deal with some real problems? Why didn't he stop wars, feed the starving in Ethiopia, cure cancer? At least God had the Church to do His PR work for Him—if you can buy their reasoning, they have any number of explanations ranging from how the troubles of this life build character to that inarguable catchall, "God's will." And the crap in this life sure makes heaven look good.

When I was growing up, the writers and artists of Superman never even tried to deal with the problem. And since they didn't, I could only see Superman as a monster, not a hero. I couldn't believe his battles with criminals, superpowered geniuses and the like.

I never believed in God either.

If my business wasn't so serious, I'd have to laugh to see

myself wearing this getup now, climbing walls like a spider, all my senses heightened; faster, stronger, and more agile than a person has any right to be. It's like—remember the story of Gwion, when he's stirring Cerridwen's potion and it bubbles up and scorches him? He licks off those three drops, and suddenly he can understand the languages of animals and birds, he has all this understanding of the connections that make up the world, and he can change his shape into anything he wants—which proves useful when Cerridwen goes after him.

That's pretty well the way it is for me, except that I can't change my shape. What I've got are the abilities of the totem-heads the anima wore when they came to me. I just wish my fairy godmothers had made me a little smarter while they were at it. Then I wouldn't be in this mess.

I think I've figured out where they came from. I used to work for *The Newford Examiner*—I guess that makes me more like Superman than the Bat-guy, isn't that another laugh? And I guess I just blew any chance of maintaining a secret identity by revealing that much. Not that it matters. I was always pretty much a loner until I met Annie, and then most of our friends were hers. I liked them all well enough, but without our link with Annie, we've just kind of drifted apart. As for my family, well, they pretty much disowned me when I came out.

So I was working for *The Examiner,* and before you ask, it's true: We make up most of the stories. Our editor starts with a headline like "Please Adopt My Pig-Faced Son" and the writers take it from there. But sometimes we let other people make it up for us. You wouldn't believe the calls and letters that paper would get.

Anyway, a few months before Annie died, I find myself up in the mountains, interviewing this old hillbilly woman who claims to have a fairy ring on her property—you know, one of those places where the Little People are supposed to gather for dances at night? I'd brought Annie with me because she wouldn't stay home once I told her where I was going.

The interview goes a little strange—not the strange that's par for the course whenever I've been out in the field interviewing one of our loyal readers with her own take on the wild and the wacky, but strange in how it starts to make sense. Maybe it's because Annie's with me and fairy tales are her bread and butter. I don't know. But the fairy ring is amazing.

It's deep in the woods behind the old lady's trailer, this Disneylike glade surrounded by enormous old trees, with grass that's only growing about an inch high—naturally; I check to see if it's been cut and it hasn't—and the mushrooms. They form a perfect circle in the middle of the glade. These big, fat, umbrella-capped toadstools, creamy colored with blood-red spots on them standing anywhere from a foot to a foot-and-a-half high. The grass inside the mushroom ring is a dark, dark green.

I know, from having read up on them before coming out to do the interview, that fairy rings are due to the growth of certain fungi below the surface. The spawn of the fungi radiates out from the center at a similar rate every year, which is how the ring widens. The darker grass is due to the increased nitrogen produced by the fungus.

None of which explains the feeling I get from the place. Or the toadstools. The last time I saw one like that was when I was still in Brownies—you know the one the owl sits on?

"Do you have to believe in the fairies to see them?" Annie asks.

"Land's sakes, no," Betsy tells her.

She's this beautiful old woman, kind of gangly and pretty thin, but still robust and a real free spirit. I can't believe she's pushing eighty-two.

"They have to believe in you," she explains.

Annie nods like she understands, but the two of them have lost me.

"What do you mean?" I ask.

I'm not even remembering to take notes anymore.

"It's like this," Betsy says. "You don't think of them as

prissy little creatures with wings. That's plain wrong. They're earth spirits—and they don't really have shapes of their own; they just show up looking the way we expect them to look. Could be you'll see 'em as your Tinkerbells, or maybe they'll come to you looking like those Japanese robot toys that my grandson likes so much."

"But the fairy ring," I say. "That's just like in the stories. . . ."

"I didn't say the stories were all lies."

"So. . . ." I pause, trying to put it all together—for myself now, never mind the interview. "What is it that you're saying? What do these earth spirits do?"

"They don't *do* anything. They just are. Mostly they mind their own business, just like we mind ours. But sometimes we catch their attention and that's when you have to be careful."

Annie doesn't say anything.

"Of what?" I ask.

"Of what you're thinking when you're around them. They like to give gifts, but when they do hand 'em out, it's word for word. Sometimes, what you're asking for isn't what you really want."

At my puzzled look Betsy goes on.

"They give you what you really want," she says. "And that can hurt, let me tell you."

I stand there, the jaded reporter, and I can't help but believe. I find myself wondering what it was that she asked for and what it was that she got.

After a while, Betsy and Annie start back towards the trailer, but I stay behind for a few moments longer, just drinking in the feel of the place. It's so . . . so innocent. The way the world was when you were a kid, before it turned all crazy-cruel and confusing. Everybody loses their innocence sooner or later; for me and Annie it was sooner.

Standing there, I feel like I'm in the middle of a fairy tale. I forget about what Betsy has just been telling us. I think about lost innocence and just wish that it doesn't have to be that way for kids, you know? That they could *be* kids for as long as possible before the world sweeps them away.

I think that's why they came to me after Annie died. They mourn that lost innocence, too. They came to me, because with Annie gone, I have no real ties to the world anymore, nothing to hold me down. I guess they just figured that, with their gifts, I'd head out into the world and do what I could to make things right; that I'd make the perfect fairy crusader.

They weren't wrong.

The trouble is, when you can do the things I can do now, you get cocky. And in this business, cocky means stupid.

Crouching there on the rooftop, all I can find myself thinking about is another bit of fairy lore.

"The way it works," Annie told me once, explaining one of her stories that I didn't get, "is that there's always a price. Nothing operates in a vacuum: not relationships, not the ecology, and especially not magic. That's what keeps everything in balance."

If there's got to be a price paid tonight, I tell the city skyline, let it be me that pays it.

I don't get any answer, but then I'm not expecting one. All I know is that it's time to get this show on the road.

4

It starts to go wrong around the middle of August, when I meet this guy on the East Side.

His name's Christopher Dennison and he works for Social Services, but I don't find that out until later. First time I see him, he's walking through the dark back alleys of the Barrio, talking in this real loud voice, having a conversation, except there's no one with him. He's tall, maybe a hundred-and-seventy pounds, and not bad looking. Clean white shirt and jeans, red windbreaker. Nikes. Dressed pretty well for a loser, which is what I figure he must be, going on the way he is.

I dismiss him as one more inner-city soul who's lost it, until I hear what it is that he's saying. Then I follow along above him, a shadow ghosting from roof to roof while he makes his way through the refuse and crap that litters the ground below. When he pauses under some graffito that reads PRAISE GOD FOR AIDS, I make my way down a fire escape.

I want to tear out the heart of whoever spray-painted those words, but they're long gone, so I concentrate on the guy instead. I can see perfectly in the dark and my hearing's nothing to be ashamed of either. The wind changes and his scent comes to me. He's wearing some kind of cologne, but it's faint. Or maybe it's aftershave. I don't smell any fear.

"I just want to know how you do it," he's saying. "I've got a success rate of maybe one in thirty, but you . . . you're just shutting them down, right, left and center. And it sticks. I can tell when it's going bad. Can't always do something about it, but I can tell. The ones you help stay helped."

He's talking about me. He's talking *to* me. I don't get the impression he knows what I am—or even who I am and what exactly it is that I can do—but he knows there's something out in the city, taking back the night for those who aren't strong or old enough to do it for themselves. I've been so careful—I didn't think anybody had picked up on it yet.

"Let me in on the secret," he goes on. "I want to help. I can bring you names and addresses."

I let the silence hang for long moments. City silence. We can hear traffic from the street, the vague presences of TVs and stereos coming out of nearby windows, someone yelling at someone, a siren, but it's blocks away.

"So who died and made you my manager?" I finally say.

I hear his pulse quicken. His sudden nervousness is a sharp sting in my nostrils, but he's pretty quick at recovering. He looks above him, trying to spot me, but I'm just one more shadow in a dark alley, invisible.

"So you are real," he says.

A point for him, I think. He didn't *know* until I just confirmed it for him. How many nights has he been walking through these kinds of neighborhoods, talking to the night this way, wondering if he'll make contact or if he's just chasing a dream?

I make a deliberate noise coming down the fire escape and sit down near the bottom of it so that our heads are almost level. His heart rate quickens again, but settles fast.

"I wasn't sure," he says after I've sat there for a while not saying anything.

I've decided that I've already said enough. I'll let him do the talking. I'm in no hurry. I've got all night. I've got the rest of my life.

"Do you, ah, have a name?" he asks.

I give him nothing back.

"I mean, what do people call you?"

This is getting ridiculous.

"What?" I say. "Like the Masked Avenger?"

He takes a step closer and I tense up, but whether I'll fight back or flee if he comes at me, I'm not sure yet. The cat anima left me with a lot of curiosity.

"You're a woman," he says.

Shit. That's another bit of freebie information I've given him. I feel like just taking off, but it's too late now. I'm intrigued. I have to know what he wants from me.

"My name's Chris," he says. "Chris Dennison. I work with Social Services."

"So?"

"I want to help you."

"Why?"

He shakes his head. "Christ, you have to ask that? We're in the middle of a war and the freaks are winning—isn't that enough of a reason?"

I think of the child waiting in the dark for a boogieman that's all too real to come into her bedroom. I think of the woman whose last bruises have yet to heal, thrown across the kitchen, kicked and beaten. I think of the boy, victimized since he was an infant, turning on those weaker than himself because that's all he knows, because that's the only way he can regain any kind of self-empowerment.

It's not a war, it's a slaughter. Fought not just physically, but in the soul as well. It's about the loss of innocence. The loss of dignity and self-respect.

"What is it that you do to them?" he asks.

I don't know how to explain it. Using the abilities with which the anima have gifted me, I could literally tear the monsters apart, doesn't matter how big and strong they are—or think they are. But I don't. Instead, I pay them back, tit for tat.

But *how* do I do it? I'm not sure myself. I just know that it works. I look at this Boy Scout standing there, waiting for an answer, but I don't think he's ready to hear what I have to say, how everyone has a dreaming place inside them, a secret, private place that defines them. It's what I learned from Annie's stories. I just put that knowledge to a different use than I think Annie ever would have imagined someone could.

"I turn them off," I say finally. "I go into their heads and just turn them off."

He looks confused and I don't blame him.

"But how?" he asks.

I can tell it's not just curiosity that's driving him. What he wants is a weapon for his war—one that's more efficient than any he's had to work with so far.

"It's too weird," I tell him.

"I'm not a stranger to weird shit."

I'm not sure I want to get into wherever that came from.

"How did you figure out that I existed?" I asked to change the subject.

He takes the bait.

"I started to notice a drop of activity in some of our more habitual offenders," he says. "You know, cases where we're trying to prove that there's good reason to make the child a ward of the court, but we're still building up the evidence?"

I didn't, but I gave him an encouraging nod.

"It was weird," he goes on. "I mean we get more recants than we do testimony anyway, but when I investigated these particular cases I found that the offenders really *had* changed. Completely. I didn't make any kind of a connection, though, until I was interviewing a six-year-old boy named Peter. His mother's boyfriend had been molesting him on a regular basis, and we were working on getting a court order to deny the man access to the child and his mother as a forerunner to hopefully laying some charges.

"The mother was working with us—she was scared to death, if you want the truth, and was grasping at straws. She claimed she'd do anything to get out of this relationship. And then she suddenly retracted her offer to testify. The boyfriend had changed. He was good as gold now. Peter confirmed it when I interviewed him. He was the one who told me that he'd quote, 'seen a ninja angel who'd stolen away all of the boyfriend's badness.' "

I remembered Peter. He'd come into the room and caught me as I was getting up from his mother's bed, putting on my gloves. I almost bolted, but I didn't want to leave a different kind of night fear in the little tyke's head, so I told him what I'd done, couching the information in words I thought he'd understand. He'd been really brave and hadn't cried at all.

"He said he'd keep the secret," I say.

"Give the kid a break. He's only six."

I nod.

"Anyway," Chris says, "something clicked for me then. It seemed . . . well, impossible, but I couldn't stop thinking about it. What if there really *was* someone out there that could do what Peter had said his angel had done? I've been fighting the freaks for years with hardly anything to show for it. It's heartbreaking work."

I nod again. I've got a hundred percent success rate myself, but there's only so many places I can be at one time. I know all about heartbreak.

"I felt like a fool walking around out here, trying to get your attention, but I just had to know. And if it *was* real, I wanted a part of it."

I think of the anima that came to me all those long months ago.

"It's not something that can be shared," I tell him.

"But I can help, can't I?"

"I don't think that's such a good—"

"Look," he breaks in. "How do you figure out who to hit? I'll bet you just skulk around outside windows, hoping to get lucky. Am I right?"

Too right, but I don't answer.

"I can provide you with names and addresses," he says.

I remember him saying that earlier. It's part of what drew me down from the rooftops to hear him out.

"You won't have to waste your time guessing anymore," he goes on, voice so damn eager. "With what I give you, you can go right to the *known* offenders. Just think of how much more effective you can be."

It's tempting. Oh, who am I kidding? It's another gift, as unexpected, but as welcome, as those the anima gave me.

"Okay," I tell him. "We'll give it a try."

I barely get the words out of my mouth, then he's dragging a folded sheet of paper out of the pocket of his jacket.

"These are just some of the worst, ongoing situations that we've got on file," he begins.

My heart sinks. There must be fifty names and addresses on that one piece of paper.

So many monsters.

5

The relationship works better than I think it might. I was working blind before, hanging around on fire escapes and ledges outside windows, crawling down from rooftops, listening, watching, until I got a fix on one of the monsters. And even then I had to be careful. Not every domestic argument leads to spousal abuse. Not every child, crying in the lonely dark, has been molested.

I'm also careful with the tips I get from Chris. I may have taken on the roles of judge and jury, but I always make sure that I'm really dealing with a monster before I step into his head and turn him off. But Chris's information is usually good. We don't just use what he's collected on his own, either. He takes what we need from all the files in his office, his and the other caseworkers', as well as from Children's Aid and the like, to avoid suspicion falling on him the way it might if all the monsters I dealt with came from his caseload.

If Chris could make the connection, then so could someone else—someone perhaps not as sympathetic to my particular working methods. I've no idea how I'd deal with prison. I think the gifts of the anima would make it a thousand times worse for me. I think I'd rather die first.

A few weeks into our partnership, Chris asks me what got me started with all of this. I don't know what to say at first, but then I just tell him that I lost a good friend which leaves him with the impression that it's revenge motivating me. I let him believe that, even if it's not exactly true. What killed Annie isn't something anyone can fight against.

It's funny. I never think of Annie looking as she did when she died. It's like my mind's closed off the image of how frail she became toward the end. She was just skin and bones, a pale, pale ghost of herself lying there in the hospital ward. Chemotherapy had stolen that gorgeous head of hair, but she refused to wear a wig.

"This is who I am now," is all she'd say.

When I think of her, I see instead the woman I fell in love with. She could have been a model for one of those nineteenth-century painters whose work she so admired: Rosetti, Burne-Jones, Dixon—that crew. She was beautiful, but more importantly to me, she completed me. Until I was with Annie, I never felt whole. I was just an observer going through life, never a participant, which might be the reason I became a journalist.

I remember telling her that once and she just laughed.

"I don't think so, Jaime," she said. "If you really just wanted to report on life, you wouldn't have worked for *The Examiner*. I think, secretly, there's a novelist living inside you, just dying to get out. Why else would you be drawn to a job that has you making up such outlandish stories, day after day?"

Who knows what we secretly want—I mean, really, *seri-*

ously want? I knew that with Annie I had everything I could ask for, so I had no more need for secrets. When I came out, it didn't raise an eyebrow among my coworkers. The only people who changed toward me were my family. Ex-family. Can you get a divorce from your flesh and blood? To all intents and purposes, I certainly have.

But that's okay. I was never close to them anyway. See, that's the real revenge motive that let me take the anima's gift: lost innocence.

Both my parents were alcoholics. I'm surprised I even survived some of the beatings I got as a kid. It was different for Annie. Instead of being beaten, her father started molesting her when she was in the cradle. The nightmare lasted until she was in her teens.

"What's scariest," she told me once, "is that I didn't even *know* it was wrong. It didn't feel right, but I never knew any different. I thought that was how it was in every family."

What are the statistics? I think it's something like two out of every three women have been sexually assaulted by the time they're in their twenties. Everything from being abused as children to being raped when they're older.

Lost innocence.

Somehow, Annie regained hers, but most people aren't that lucky. I know I never have.

But that's why I think of what I'm doing as something I'm doing for her. So many monsters, and I've barely made a dent in their numbers. I wish there was a way to get rid of them all in one fell swoop. I wish I could deal with them before the damage is done. It kills me that it's all ending for me before I've really gotten started with my work.

See, by the beginning of July my savings finally run out and I begin to lose the amenities because I can't pay my bills anymore. The phone goes first, then the power. By the time I meet Chris, I've lost my apartment.

So I become a baglady superhero—do they ever deal with that in those comics? I know I'm obsessed, but I don't have anything else to do with my life. It was bad enough when I was on my own, tracking the monsters down by trial and error. I'd deal with one, maybe two in a week—three tops. But now, with Chris's help, I can hit that same number on a good night.

I'm proud of what I'm doing, but it's starting to take its toll. That little piece of myself I was losing every time I dealt with one of the monsters has escalated to where now it feels as though what I'm losing is falling off the way clumps of dirt can be shaken from a piece of sod. The empty patches inside me just keep getting bigger. It's as though my spirit is dissolving, bit by bit. I stare down at the anima residue I leave on their beds and want to pick it up and somehow stick it back onto me. I'm so wasted come morning now that I don't care where I sleep—on a park bench, in an alleyway, in some deserted building.

Chris offers to put me up, but I don't want to get that close to him. I let him buy me meals, though. Left on my own, I forget to eat half the time. When I do remember, I'm usually scrounging something from one of the monsters' kitchens—now there's something that really helps your appetite. God.

The cramps start in September, and I begin to get these sudden spells of weakness so often that even Chris notices the change. I mean, he can't see much of me, all clothed in black and hiding in the shadows most of the time, but what he can see tells him I'm not well.

"Maybe we should ease off a bit," he says.

"I'm fine."

"You look like shit."

I know. I caught a reflection of myself in a window on my way to meet him tonight. All the meat was gone, leaving just corded animal muscles over the bones. The real emptiness is inside.

"I tell you I'm fine," I repeat, trying to convince myself as much as him. "What've you got for me tonight?"

"Nothing."

I don't even realize that the growl's rumbling in my chest until I smell the sudden sting of his fear. I force myself to calm down, but he still backs away from me.

"I'm sorry," I say and I mean it.

He nods slowly, but he keeps his distance.

"Okay," I tell him. "We'll take a break tonight. Just give me one name."

I don't know why I'm pressing him like this. I could do it on my own. Skulk around until I found a monster. I might get lucky, you never know. But I think later that I want his complicity in this. I want someone to know what I'm doing—not to feed my ego. Just to remember me when I'm gone.

"One name," he says.

"That's all."

Chris sighs. He tries to talk me out of it for a little while longer, but finally gives in. One name and address.

"This one's a little weird," he says as he hands it over. "It came in from the guidance counselor at Redding High. Something about it being a sensitive case, but I couldn't find anything in the file to say why."

"That's okay. I can handle it."

Mistake—but I don't blame him.

6

Grant Newman is awake, only I don't realize it. I pull myself in through his window, third story, nice part of town, and creep soundlessly across the hardwood floor to where he's lying. He's alone in his bed. I scouted around earlier and discovered that he and his wife have separate bedrooms. Makes it easier for when he wants to pay little Susan a night visit, I guess.

I slip up onto the bed and he grabs me. It happens so suddenly that I just freeze up in surprise. Then when I try to fight him, I can't find the strength to break free. It's not that the anima's gifts have worn off; it's that I'm worn out. I've left too many pieces of myself behind in too many monsters' lairs. The shock of my sudden helplessness makes me feel dizzy.

"What the hell've we got here?" Newman says as I struggle to break his grip.

My heightened sense of smell makes his bad breath seem worse than it must really be. I know that smell. It's the way my old man used to stink before he took the belt to me.

I try to get my legs up between us so that I can kick him, but he rolls me over and pins me to the bed with his knees.

"Some kind of little ninja fuck," he says. "So what's the deal? Yukio getting tired of paying me off?"

He reaches for my mask until his gaze locks onto my chest.

"Jesus," he says. "Your boss must be really getting hard up if he's running woman assassins now."

I'm gaunt these days, just muscle and bone and the muscles aren't working tonight. But the bodysuit still shows I'm a woman. For some men, that's excuse enough for anything. Maybe Newman thinks he's in his private place and anything goes. For all I know we *are* in his private place, and I've just lost control of the situation.

Newman forgets about the mask, and reaches for the zipper of my suit instead.

"I've never fucked a ninja before," he says. "This'll be something to—"

I'm the wolf with its leg in a trap, the bear that's been shot, the puma that's been harassed until it has its back to the wall. Panic whips my head forward and I close my teeth on his hand, biting through fingers, straight to the bone. I'll give him this: He doesn't scream. But the pain makes him loosen his grip.

I whip up a leg from behind him and manage to hook it around his neck. I pull him back, off of me, heaving myself up to help the momentum. He falls backward out of the bed and I'm out of there. I almost lose it in the window frame, but my adrenalin lets me catch my balance before I go tumbling three stories down to the pavement below. By the time Newman gets to the window, I'm two floors above his apartment, spidering my way up the wall and onto the roof.

I make the jump from his building to its neighbor, and

then over one more before I collapse. The roof's covered with gravel, but I can barely feel it digging into my skin. Cramps pull me into a fetal position, and I've got the shakes so bad that my teeth start to rattle.

It's a long time before I calm down.

It's even longer before I'm scratching at Chris's window.

As I tell Chris about what happened, I start to remember things I saw in Newman's bedroom, things I hadn't noticed when I'd scouted the place out earlier.

"It's going to be okay," Chris tells me.

"But he's seen me."

By which I mean: Now the monsters know I exist.

"Don't worry," Chris says. "What's he going to do? All he saw was a masked woman. It's not like he can recognize you. It's not like there's any way he can find you. He's probably more scared of you than you are of him."

"I don't think so," I say.

On Newman's night table: The police-issue .38 in its well-worn holster. The billfold with the shape of a badge worn into the leather.

"Newman's a cop," I tell Chris.

I remember more: What he was saying about payoffs.

"A crooked cop," I add.

"Oh, shit."

We both know what can happen. Newman can have an APB put out on me. He can make up any old story he likes about why I'm wanted and they'll believe him. Christ, he can tell the truth and I'll still have every cop in the city out looking for me. The police don't take kindly to anyone assaulting one of their own.

I'm bone-tired, but I know what I have to do. Chris tries to stop me when I get up and head for the window, but I turn around and look at him.

"What else can I do?" I ask him.

"You're in no condition to—"

He's actually a really nice guy, even though he acts a bit too much like a mother. I can see why kids, even abused kids, like him and trust him.

"I know," I say. "But I don't have any choice."

I'm out the window before he can stop me. I make my way back across town to the roof of the building across from Newman's. The September wind's cold, but I can't feel it through my bodysuit. Don't need it to be chilled anyway. I've got a piece of ice inside me and that's what's making me shiver.

I know I should wait until I'm stronger, but I'm not so sure I'm ever going to get any stronger. I get the feeling that I'm wasting away, as inexorably as the cancer that took Annie.

I wait, crouching there on the rooftop, until I see the light in Newman's bedroom go off. I'm like a ghost coming down the side of the building and crossing the street. I don't feel strong, at least not physically. But I'm determined, and I hope that'll count for something.

7

When I get outside Newman's window, I realize he's not asleep. I can sense him sitting in a chair in the corner of the room, gun in hand, watching the window. He knew I'd be back.

So I go in through a window on the other side of the apartment. My entire being is focused on what I'm doing. Keeping silent. Staying strong—at least long enough to tidy up the mess I've made of things. His wife never stirs as I slip by her bed and out into the hall. I pass his daughter's bedroom and that helps. She makes a little moan in her sleep. The plaintive sound brings everything into sharper focus— why I'm here, what I'm doing—and makes it easier for me to concentrate on getting it over with.

Newman's attention is fixed on the window of his bedroom. He never hears me come in the door and sidle my way alongside the wall to where he's sitting. I'm sure of it. But something—sixth sense, cop smarts—has him turn just as I'm reaching for him.

"What the fuck *are* you?" he says as he brings up the gun.

The bandage on his hand is a white flash in the dark.

Stupid, I think. I'm so stupid. I still wanted to make a try at keeping this clean. Step into his private place and shut him down instead of cutting him open. And maybe I can.

I grab his hand, the one holding the gun, skin to skin. Contact.

Everything stops. He can't shoot me, I can't claw him. We're locked in a space between our heads. Not his private place, but somewhere else. There's a sudden shift of vertigo, a crazy quilt strobing in my eyes, and then we're somewhere else again. It takes me a few moments to realize what's happened.

We're in someone's head, all right, but it's mine. This is my own dreaming place.

I've never tried to step inside when the monster was awake before. It's so easy to make the transition when they're asleep, dreaming. But Newman was so focused, his will so strong, that even though he couldn't have a clue as to what he was doing, he's managed to push me out of his head and then follow me back into my own.

I can't seem to do anything right tonight.

I try to take us back out again, but it's no good. I give Newman a shove and he goes sprawling. As soon as he hits the ground, that crazy-quilt spinning starts up again. When it finally settles down, things have changed once more.

My dreaming place looks like the kitchen in the house where I grew up. I look for Newman, but he's gone. My father there in his place. He's standing there, weaving slightly from side to side, grinning at me, smelling like a brewery.

"Time to even the score," he says, slurring the words but not so much that I can't understand them.

He takes a step toward me, mad drunk gleam in his eyes, and I lose it. This is too much for me.

I never dealt with what happened to me as a child. I just left home as soon as I could. When I remade contact with my parents—before I told them I was gay—we all just pretended that all the drinking and screaming and beatings had never happened. That was just the way it worked, I thought.

Keep the family unit whole, no matter what the cost.

But I never forgot. And I never forgave. And seeing him like this now, it's like I've stepped right back into the past and all the years between were just a dream. Except I'm not powerless anymore. When he hits me, I don't have to take it. I don't have to cringe and try to hide from his fists. Not anymore. Not ever again.

With his first blow, all of my animal rage comes tearing through me and I lash back at him. My fingers are clawed, taloned, killing weapons. It's like I have rabies. I cut him down and I'm still slashing at him, long after he's fallen to the ground. Long after he's dead. There's blood everywhere. And there's this screaming that just goes on and on and on.

I think it's me screaming, I know it's me, until I fall out of my head and I'm back in Newman's bedroom. I'm crouched over his savaged corpse, snarling and growling, and then I realize how wrong I've been. It's not me screaming. It's not me at all.

I see her in the doorway, the monster's daughter. The screams stop when I turn to look at her, but then I see her go away. She folds away inside herself, going deeper and deeper, until there's just this blank-eyed child standing there, everything that ever animated her walled away against the night creature that snuck into her Daddy's bedroom and tore him apart.

Doesn't matter what he did to her. That's gone, swallowed by the more horrible image of what's been done to him.

I stagger to my feet, but I don't even think of trying to comfort her. I almost fall through the window, trying to get out. And then I just flee. Run blind. I'll do anything to get rid of those emptied eyes, their blank stare, but they follow me, out into the night.

I know I'll carry them with me for the rest of my life.

When I finally stop running, the cramps hit me. I lie on my side and throw up. I'm still dry-heaving long after my stomach's empty, but I can't get rid of what's inside me that easily. The guilt's just going to lie there and fester and never go away.

8

Nothing helps.

It comes out that Newman was on the payroll of Yukio Nakamura, the boss of Little Japan's biggest Yakuza gang.

It comes out that not only was Newman taking graft, he was using his badge to help Nakamura get rid of his competition. And when the badge didn't provide intimidation enough, Newman was happy to use his gun.

It comes out that he beat his wife, abused his daughter.

By the time the investigation's over, half the Yakuza in Little Japan are up on racketeering charges and there's not one person in the city who has an ounce of sympathy for the monster. If they knew I'd killed him, they'd probably give me a medal.

But all I can focus on is that fact that his daughter's lost to the world now, locked up inside her own head, and I put her there. I tried to help, but I all I did was make things worse.

"You can't beat yourself over this," Chris said the one time I let him find me. "It's unfortunate what happened to the girl—an awful, terrible thing—but there's still a war going on. The freaks are still out there.

"You can't walk away from the fight now."

He thinks I'm scared, but that's not it. I'm not anything. All I can think of is that little girl and what I put through, what I made her see.

Susan Newman didn't just lose her innocence. She had any hope of a normal life torn away.

"Do you need anything?" Chris asks. "Money? Food? A place to stay?"

I shake my head.

"Give this a little time," he says. "You're suffering from trauma too, you know."

I let him talk on, but I stop listening. I've regained my

strength. I can leap tall buildings with a single bound again—or at least spider my way up their walls—but I don't have the heart for it anymore. I don't have the heart to step into anybody's dreaming place and then shut him down. And I certainly can't see myself killing someone again—I don't care how much he deserves it.

After a while, Chris stops talking and I walk away. He starts to follow, but finally gives up when I keep increasing the distance between us.

I don't wear my bodysuit anymore; I don't look like some dimestore ninja. I just look like any other homeless person, wandering around the street in clothes that are more than a few weeks away from clean, looking for handouts at the shelters, cadging spare change from passersby.

A month goes by, maybe two. I don't know. I just know it's getting really cold at night. Then late one afternoon I'm standing over a grating by a used bookstore, trying to get warm, and I see, in amongst the motley selection of titles that crowd the display window, a familiar cover and byline.

When the Desert Dreams, by Anne Bourke.

I've got two dollars and eighty cents in my pocket. I'm planning to use it to get something to eat later, but I go into the bookstore. The guy behind the counter takes pity on me and sells me the book for what I've got, even though there's a price of fifteen bucks penciled in on the right-hand corner of the front endpaper.

I leave, holding the book to my chest, and I walk around like that all night, from one side of the city to the other. I don't need to read the stories. I was there when they were written—almost a lifetime ago.

Finally, I start walking up Williamson Street, just trudging on and on until the downtown stores give way to more residential blocks, which give way to drive-in fast-food joints and malls and the 'burbs, and then I'm finally out of the city. The sun's up for about an hour when I stick out my thumb.

It's a long time before someone stops, but when this guy does, he's going my way. He can take me right up into the

mountains. I find myself wanting to apologize for the way I
look, for the way I smell, but I don't say anything. I know if
I try to say anything more than where I'm going, I'm just
going to break down and cry. So I sit there and hold my
book. I nod and try to smile as the guy talks to me. Mostly, I
just look ahead through the windshield.

I don't know what I'm expecting or hoping to find when I
get there. I don't even know why I'm going. I just know that
I've run out of other options.

Without Annie, I don't know where to turn. Only she'd
be able to comfort me, only she'd be able to help me reclaim
my dreaming place. I've had to shut myself off from what's
inside me, because when I step into my private place, I get
no solace now; when I dream, I have only nightmares.

What was my only haven is home to monsters now.

9

"Are you sure this is where you want out?" my ride asks.

There's something in the tone of his voice that tells me he
doesn't think it's exactly the greatest idea. I don't blame
him. We're out in the middle of nowhere, and Betsy's trailer
looks deserted. The lawn's overgrown and thick with leaves.
Her vegetable and flower gardens are a jungle of weeds. The
trailer itself was never in the greatest shape, but now shutters are hanging loose and the door stands ajar. From the
road we can see that a thick carpet of forest debris has already worked its way inside.

I guess I'm not really surprised. Betsy was an old woman.
It's been over a year since I was here with Annie, and anything could have happened to her in that time. She could
have moved. Or died.

I don't like to think of her as dead. There are some people
who deserve to live forever, and although I only met her that
one afternoon, I knew that Betsy was one of them. Eternal
spirits, trapped in far too transient flesh.

Like Annie.

My ride clears his throat in case I didn't hear him. This

guy's so polite. I was lucky it was him that stopped for me and not some loser who thinks with his dick instead of his heart.

Or maybe, considering, it was lucky for those losers. I've still got the anima's gifts; I just don't use them anymore.

"Yeah, I'm sure," I tell him and get out. "Thanks for the ride."

I stand by the end of Betsy's overgrown driveway and watch the car until it's out of sight. There's something in the air that calms me, smoothing all my nervous edges. No longer summer, not quite winter, everything just hanging between the two. I take it all in until I hear another vehicle coming up the road, then I dart into the woods, Annie's book clutched to my chest.

The glade doesn't look anything like I remembered it, either, but I know it's just because I'm here in a different season. The surrounding trees have all lost their leaves and everything's faded and brown. Except for the fairy ring. The toadstools still stand in their circle, the grass is still a deep green, and there's not a leaf or twig lying within the circle.

I know there's probably a sound, scientific reason why this is so, but I don't have access to the paper's morgue anymore to look it up, and besides, I've seen the anima. I'm more likely to believe that fairies are keeping the ring raked and tidy.

I stand there, looking at it for a long time, before I finally step into the ring. I lay Annie's book in the middle and sit down on the grass.

I don't know what I'm doing here. Maybe I thought I could call up the anima. Or Annie's ghost. But now that I'm here, none of that matters. All the confusion and pain that's sent my life into its downward spiral after I killed Newman just fades away. My pulse takes on the slow heartbeat of the forest. I close my eyes and let myself go. I can feel myself drifting, edging up on that dreaming place inside me that I haven't been able to visit for months because I know the monsters are waiting for me there.

I'm just starting to get convinced that maybe there is a

way to regain one's innocence when I realize that I'm no longer alone.

It's neither the animal-headed fairy women nor Annie's ghost that I find watching me from the edge of the ring, but Betsy. I think for a minute that maybe she's a ghost, or a fairy woman, but then I see how frail she is, the cane she's used to get here, how her face is red from the effort she's made and her breathing is way too fast. She's as real as I am—maybe more so, because I don't know where I've been these last few months.

We don't say anything for a long time. I watch her lean on her cane and slowly catch her breath. The flush leaves her face.

"I read about your friend," she says finally. "That must have been hard for you."

Tears well in my eyes and I can't seem to find my voice. I manage a nod.

"It's always hardest for those of us who get left behind," she says, filling the silence that grows up between us. "I know."

"You . . . you've lost someone close to you?" I ask.

Betsy gives me this sad smile. "At my age, girl, I've just about lost them all." She pauses for a heartbeat, then asks, "You and your friend—you were . . . lovers?"

"Does that shock you?"

"Land's sake, no. I left my own husband for a woman—though that was years ago. Folks didn't look on it with much understanding back then."

They still don't, I think.

"I think it makes it that much harder when you love someone folks don't think you're supposed to and she dies. You don't get a period of mourning. Folks are just relieved that the situation's gone and fixed itself."

"But you still mourn," I say.

"Oh yes. But you have to do your crying on the inside."

My eyes fill again, not just for Annie and me now, but for Betsy and her long-gone lover. Betsy looks like she's about to lose it too; her eyes are all shiny, and the flush is returning to her cheeks, but then she wipes her eyes on her sleeve and straightens her back.

"So," she says, trying to sound cheery. "What brings you back? Another story for your newspaper?"

I shake my head even though I know she's only being kind. She can see the state I'm in—I look like the homeless person I've become, not the reporter I was.

"Remember when you were telling me about fairy gifts?" I say.

She nods slowly.

I want to tell her about the anima and what they gave me. I want to tell her about the ninja suit and climbing walls and leaping from rooftop to rooftop, looking for prey. I want to tell her about the dreaming places, and what I did to Newman when I pulled him into mine. I want to ask what the fairy women gave her. But none of it will come out.

Instead I just say, "I liked the idea of it."

"You did a lovely job writing it all up in your article," Betsy tells me. "It had a different . . . ring to it."

"As opposed to the stories *The Examiner* usually runs," I say dryly.

Betsy smiles. "I've still got it in my scrapbook."

That reminds me.

"I didn't think you—" were still alive. "—Still lived around here," I say. "When I saw the trailer . . ."

"After I had my stroke," she says, "I went to live across the road with my friend Alice."

I don't remember there being a place across the road from hers, but when she invites me back for tea, I see that it's because the evergreens hide it so well. As we walk up the little dirt track leading to it, Betsy tells me how it's a step up for her. I look from the run-down log cabin to her, the question plain in my eyes.

"It doesn't have wheels," she explains.

I never do any of the things that might have brought me up here. I don't talk about the anima to Betsy or what their coming into my life has done to me. I don't talk about how they might have affected her. I don't meet the anima again; I don't see Annie's ghost. But when Alice's daughter drives me back to the outskirts of the city where I can catch a bus, I realize the trip was still worthwhile, because I brought away with me something I hadn't had for so long I'd forgotten it had ever existed.

I brought away some human contact.

10

In Frank Estrich's private place there's a small dog, trembling in the weeds that grow up along the dirt road where Frank's walking. The dog is just a mutt, lost and scared. You see them far too often in the country—some poor animal that's outlived its welcome in a city home, so it gets taken for a ride, the car slows down, the animal's tossed out—"returned to nature"—and the problem's solved.

Frank found a stray the summer before, but his dad killed it when Frank brought it home and tried to hide it in the barn. And then his dad took the belt to Frank. His dad does that a lot, most of the time for no other reason than because he likes to do it.

Frank always feels so helpless. Everybody's bigger than him: his father, his uncles, his brothers, the other kids. Everybody can rag on him and there's not a thing he can do about it. But this dog's not bigger than him.

Frank knows it's wrong, he knows he should feel sorry for the little fella because the dog's as unwanted as Frank feels he is most of the time, but I can see in his head that he's thinking of getting his own back. And if he can't do it to those that are hurting him, then maybe he'll just do it to the dog.

Doesn't matter how it cringes down on its belly as he approaches it, eyes hopeful, body shaking. All Frank can think of is the beating he got earlier tonight. Dad took him out to the barn, made him take down his pants, made him bend over a bale of hay as he took off his belt. . . .

I've already dealt with the father, but I know now how that's not enough. The seed's still lying inside the victim.

Maybe it'll turn Frank into what his father calls a "sissy-boy," scared of his own shadow; more likely it'll make Frank grow up no different from his father, one more monster in a world that's got too many already.

So I have to teach Frank about right and wrong—not like his father did; not with arbitrary rules and punishments, but in a way that doesn't leave Frank feeling guilty for what was done to him, in a way that lets him understand that self-empowerment has got nothing to do with what you can do to someone else.

It's a long, slow process of healing that's as hard for me to put into words as it is for me to explain how I can step into other people's dreaming places. But it's worth it. Not just for the victims like Frank that I get to help, but for myself as well.

What happened to me before was that I was wearing myself out. I was putting so much out, but getting nothing back. I was living only in the shadows, living there so long that I almost forgot there was such a thing as sunlight.

That's what I do, I guess. I still step into the monsters' heads and turn them off, but then I visit the dreaming places of their victims and show them how to get back into the sunlight. The funny thing is, that when I'm with someone like Frank and he finally gets out of the shadows, I don't leave anything of myself behind. But they leave something in me.

Dried blood and rose petals.

Bird bones and wood ash.

It's all just metaphor for spirit—that's what Annie would say. I don't know. I don't need to put a name to it. I just use it all to reclaim my own dreaming place and keep it free of shadows.

A TEMPEST IN HER EYES

Remember all is but a poet's dream,
The first he had in Phoebus' holy bower,
But not the last, unless the first displease.
—John Lyly, from *The Woman in the Moone*

1

I've heard it said that there are always two sides to a story: There's the official history, the version that's set onto the page, then filed away in the archives where it waits for when the librarian comes to retrieve the facts to footnote some learned paper or discourse. Then there's the way an individual remembers the event; that version sits like an old woman on a lonely porch, creaking back and forth in her wicker rocker as she waits for a visitor.

I think there's a third version as well: that of the feral child, escaping from between the lines, from between how it's said the story went and how it truly took place.

I'm like that child. I'm invariably on the edge of how it goes for everyone else. I hear them tell the story of some event that I took part in and I can scarcely recognize it. I'd like to say that it's because I'm such a free spirit—the way Jilly is, always bouncing around from one moment to the next—but I know it's not true. The reason I'm not part of the official story is because I'm usually far from civilization, lost in wildernesses of my own making, unaware of either the library or the porch.

I'm just not paying attention—or at least not paying attention to the right thing. It all depends on your perspective, I suppose.

2

September was upon us and I couldn't have cared less, which is weird for me, because autumn's usually my favorite time of year. But I was living through one of those low points in my life that I guess everyone has to put up with at one time or another. I went through the summer feeling increasingly tired and discouraged. I walked hand in hand with a constant sense of foreboding, and you know what that's like: If you expect things to go wrong, they usually do.

I hadn't met a guy I liked in ages—at least not anyone who was actually available. Every time I sat down to write, my verses came out as doggerel. I was getting cranky with my friends, but I hated being home by myself. About the only thing I was still good at was waitressing. I've always liked my job, but as a lifelong career choice? I don't think so.

To cheer me up, Jilly and Sophie took me to the final performance of *A Midsummer Night's Dream* at the Standish. The play was a traditional production—Lysander and Demetrius hadn't been rewritten as bikers, say, and the actors had performed in costume, not in the nude. Being a poet myself, I lean toward less adventurous productions because they don't get in the way of the words.

I'd been especially taken with the casting of the fairy court tonight. The director had acquired the services of the Newford Ballet for their parts, which lent the characters a wonderfully fey grace. They were so light on their feet, I could almost imagine that they were flying at times, flitting about the stage, rather than constrained by gravity to walking its boards. The scene at the end where the fairies sport through the Duke's palace had been so beautifully choreographed that I was almost disappointed when the spotlight narrowed to capture Puck in his final speech, perched at the edge of the stage, fixing us in our seats with a half-mocking, half-feral gaze that seemed to belie his promise to "make amends."

The actor playing Robin Goodfellow had been my favorite among a talented cast, his mobile features perfectly capturing the fey charm and menace that the idea of fairy has always held for me. Oberon was the more handsome, but Puck had been simply magic. I found myself wishing that the play was just beginning its run, rather than ending it, so that I could go back another night, for his performance alone.

Jilly and Sophie didn't seem quite as taken with the production. They were walking a little ahead of me, arguing about the authorship of Shakespeare's works, rather than discussing the play we'd just seen.

"Oh, come on," Sophie was saying. "Just look at the names of some of these people: John Thomas Looney. S. E. Silliman. George Battey. How can anyone possibly take their theories seriously?"

"I didn't say they were necessarily right," Jilly replied. "It's just that when you consider the historical Shakespeare: a man whose father was illiterate, whose kids were illiterate, who didn't even bother to keep copies of his own work in his house . . . It's so obvious that whoever wrote the plays and sonnets, it wasn't William Shakespeare."

"I don't really see how it matters anyway," Sophie told her. "It's the work that's important, in the end. The fact that it's endured so long that we can still enjoy it today, hundreds of years after he died."

"But it's an interesting puzzle."

Sophie nodded in agreement. "I'll give you that. Personally, I like the idea that Anne Whately wrote them."

"But she was a *nun.* I can't *possibly* imagine a nun having written some of the bawdier lines."

"Maybe those are the ones old Will put in."

"I suppose. But then . . ."

Trailing along behind them, I was barely paying attention

and finally just shut them out. My own thoughts were circling mothlike around Titania's final promise:

> *Hand in hand with fairy grace*
> *Will we sing and bless this place.*

That was what I needed. I needed a fairy court to bless my apartment, to lift the cloud of gloom that had been thickening over me throughout the summer until it had gotten to the point where when I looked in the mirror, I expected to see a stranger's face looking back at me. I felt that different.

I think the weather had something to do with it. It rained every weekend and day off I had this summer. It never got hot—not that I like or missed the heat. But I think we need a certain amount of sunshine just to stay sane, never mind the UV risk. Who ever heard of getting cabin fever in the middle of the summer? But that's exactly the way I felt around the end of July—the way I usually feel in early March, when I don't think I can take one more day of cold and snow.

And it's just gotten worse for me as the summer's dragged on.

The newspapers blame the weird weather on that volcano in the Philippines—Mount Pinatubo—and say that not only did the eruption mess up the weather this year, but its effects are going to be felt for a few years to come. If that's true, I think I'll just go quietly mad.

I started wondering then about how the weather affects fairies, though if they did exist, I guess it might be the other way around. Instead of a volcano causing all of this trouble, it'd be another rift in the fairy court. As Titania put it to Oberon:

> *. . . the spring, the summer,*
> *The chiding autumn, angry winter change*
> *Their wonted liveries, and the mazéd world*
> *By their increase now knows not which is which.*
> *And this same progeny of evils comes*

> *From our debate, from our dissension,*
> *We are their parents and original.*

It certainly fits the way our weather's messed up. I heard it even snowed up in Alberta a couple of weeks ago—and not just a few flurries. The skies dumped some ten inches. In *August.*

"The seasons alter," indeed.

If there were fairy courts, if they *were* having an argument, I wished they'd just kiss and make up. Though not the way they did in *A Midsummer Night's Dream.*

Ahead of me, Sophie and Jilly came to a stop and I walked right into them.

"How's our dreamwalker?" Jilly asked.

She spoke the words lightly, but the streetlights showed the concern in her eyes. Jilly worries about people—seriously, not just for show. It's nice to know that someone cares, but sometimes that kind of concern can be as much of a burden as what you're going through, however well meant it might be.

"I'm fine," I lied. "Honestly."

"So who gets *your* vote as the author of Shakespeare's works?" Sophie asked.

I thought Francis Bacon looked good for it. After all, he was known as the most erudite man of his time. The author of the plays showed through his writing that he'd had a wide knowledge of medicine and law, botany and mythology, foreign life and court manners. Where would a glove maker's son from Stratford have gotten that kind of experience? But the argument bored me.

"I'd say it was his sister," I said.

"His *sister?*"

"Did he even have a sister?" Jilly asked.

A black Cadillac pulled up to the curb beside us before I could answer. There were three Hispanic boys in it, and for a moment I thought it was LaDonna's brother Pipo and a couple of his pals. But then the driver leaned out the window to give Jilly a leer and I realized I didn't recognize any of them.

"Hey, *puta*," he said. "Looking for a little of that kickin' action?"

Homeboys in a hot car, out for a joy ride. The oldest wasn't even fourteen. Jilly didn't hesitate. She cocked back her foot and kicked the Cadillac's door hard enough to make a dent.

"In your dreams," she told him.

If it had been anybody else, those homies would've been out of the car and all over us. We're all small women; Jilly's about my height, and I'm just topping five feet. We don't exactly look formidable. But this was Jilly, and the homie at the wheel saw something in her face that made him put the pedal to the floor and peel off.

The incident depressed all three of us. When we got to my apartment, I asked them in, but they just wanted to go home. I didn't blame them. I watched them go on off down the street, but sat down on the porch instead of going inside.

I knew I wasn't going to sleep because I started thinking about what a raw deal women always seem to get, and that always keeps me up. Even Titania in the play—sure, she and Oberon made up, but it was on *his* terms. Titania never even realized the crap he had put her through before their "reconciliation."

A Midsummer Night's Dream definitely hadn't been written by a woman.

3

A funny thing happened to me a few years ago. I caught a glimpse of the strange world that lies on the other side of the curtain we've all agreed is reality. Or at least I think I did.

The historical version of what happened is pretty straightforward: I met a street person—the old man on the bicycle that everybody calls the Conjure Man—and he got me to take an acorn from the big old tree that used to grow behind the library at Butler U. He had me nurture it over the winter, then plant it in Fitzhenry Park near the statue of the poet, Joshua Stanhold.

The version he tells is that he's this immortal who diminishes as the years go by, which is why he's only our height now. He was supposed to leave our world when its magic went away, but he got left behind. The tree that came down behind the library was a Tree of Tales, a repository of stories without which wonder is diminished in our world. The one I grew from an acorn and planted in the Silenus Gardens is supposed to be its replacement.

My version . . . I don't really know what my version is. There was something strange about the whole affair, I'll grant you that. And that little sapling I planted—it's already the size of a ten-year-old oak. Jilly told me she was talking to a botanist who was quite amazed at its appearance there. Seems that kind of oak isn't native to North America, and he was surprised to find it growing in the middle of the park that way.

"The only other one I've ever seen in the city," he told Jilly, "used to grow behind the Smithers Library, but they cut it down."

I haven't seen John—that's the Conjure Man's real name, John Windle. I haven't seen him for a while now. I like to think that he's finally made it home to wherever home is. Behind the curtain, I suppose. But I still go out to the tree and tell it stories—all kinds of stories. Happy ones, sad ones. Gossip. News. Just whatever comes to mind.

I'm not even sure why; I just do.

4

I'm not as brave—or maybe as foolish—as Jilly is. She doesn't seem to know the meaning of fear. She'll go anywhere, at any time of the day or night, and she never seems to get hurt. Like what happened earlier tonight. If I'd been on my own, or just with Sophie, when that car pulled up, who knows how it would have ended up? Not pleasant, that's for sure.

So I'm not nearly so bold—except when I'm on my bike. It's sort of like a talisman for me. It's nothing special, just an old ten-speed, but it gets me around. Sometimes I think I should become one of those messengers that wheel through the traffic on their mountain bikes, whistle between their lips, ready to let out a shrill blast if anybody gets in their way.

You think you're immortal, covering ground faster than anyone can walk, but you're not all locked up inside some motorized box that's spewing noxious fumes into the air. You feel as natural as a bird, or a deer, racing through your concrete forest. Maybe that's where John got that feeling from, riding through town on his bike, free as the wind, when all the other street people are just sort of shuffling along, gaze to the ground.

I started a poem about it once, but I couldn't get the words to fit the vision. That's been happening to me all too often this summer. Oh, who'm I kidding? Wordless pretty well sums me up these days. I look at the work I've had published, and I can't even imagine what it was like to write those verses, little say believe that it was me who did it.

Feeling sorry for myself is the one thing I have gotten good at lately. It's not a feeling I like. I hate the way it leaves me with this overpowering sense of being ineffectual. Worthless.

When I start getting into that kind of mood, I usually get on my bike and just ride. Which is how I found myself in Fitzhenry Park a few hours after Sophie and Jilly left me at my apartment.

I laid my bike down under the young Tree of Tales and sprawled on the grass beside it. I could see a handful of stars, looking up through the tree's boughs, but my mind was back in the Standish, listening to Puck warn Oberon of the coming dawn. I drifted off to the remembered sound of his voice.

5

Puck breaks off and looks at me. The play has faded, the hall is gone. It's just the two of us, alone in some copsy wood, as far from the city as the word orange is from a true rhyme.

"And who are you?" he says.

I make no reply. I'm too fascinated by his transformation. Falling asleep, the voice I heard, the face I imagined, was that of the actor from the Standish whom I'd seen earlier in the night. But he's gone along with the city and everything familiar. This Puck is more compelling still. I can't take my gaze from him. He has a beauty that no actor could replicate, but he's more inhuman, too. It's hard to say where the man ends and the animal begins. I think of Pan; I think of fauns.

"Your hair," he says, "is like moonlight, gracing your fair shoulders."

Maybe I should be thinking of satyrs. Legendary being or not, this is a come-on if ever I heard one.

"It's dyed," I tell him.

"But it looks so full of life."

"I mean, I color it. I'm not a natural blonde."

"And your eyes?" he asks. "Is that tempest of dream-starved color dyed as well?"

I have to admit, he's got a way about him. I don't know if I should assume "dream-starved" to be a compliment exactly, but the sound of his voice makes me wish he'd just take me in his arms. Maybe this is what they mean by fairy enchantment. I've only known him for the better part of a couple of minutes, and already he's got me feeling all warm and tingly inside. There's a musky odor in the air and my heartbeat has found a new, quicker rhythm.

It's a tough call, but I tell my libido to take five.

"What do you mean by 'dream-starved?' " I ask him.

He sits back on his furry haunches and the sexual charge that's built up between us eases somewhat.

"I see a storm in your soul," he says, "held at bay by a grey cloud of uncomfortable reason."

"What's that supposed to mean?" I ask.

But I know. I know exactly what he's talking about: how everything that ever made me happy seems to have been washed away. I smile, but there's no light behind the smile. I laugh, but the sound is hollow. I don't know how it happened, but it all went away. I do have a storm inside me, but it can't seem to get out and I don't know how to help it. All I do know is that I don't want to feel like a robot anymore, like I took a walk-on bit as a zombie for some B-movie only to find that I can't shake the part once my scene's in the can.

"When was the last time you felt truly alive?" he asks.

I look back through my memories, but everything seems dismal and grey. It's like walking into a room where all the furniture is covered with sheets, dust lies thick on the floor, all color has been sucked away.

"I . . . I can't remember. . . ."

"It was not always so."

A statement, not a question, but I still nod my head in slow agreement.

"What bedevils you," he says, "is that you have misplaced the ability to see—to truly see behind the shadow, into the heart of a thing—and so you no longer think to look. And the more you do not look, the less able you are to see. Wait long enough, and you'll wander the world as one blind."

"I already feel that way."

"Then open your eyes and see."

"See *what?*"

Puck shrugs. "It makes no difference. You can look upon the most common thing and see the whole of the cosmos reflected within."

"Intellectually, I know what you're talking about," I tell him. "I understand—really I do. But in here—" I lay the palm of one hand between my breasts and cover it with the palm of the other "—it's not so clear. My heart just feels too heavy to even think about sunshine and light, little say look for them in anything."

"Then free your heart from your mind," he says. "Embrace wonder for one moment without the need to consider how that wonder came to be, without the need to justify if it be real or not."

"I . . . I don't know how."

His lips shape that puckish smile then. "If you would forget thought for a time, let me love you."

He cups my chin with his hand and brings his lips close to mine. At the touch, being so close to those wild eyes of his, I can feel the warmth again, the fire in my loins that rises up into my belly.

"Let the storm loose," he whispers.

I want to, I'm going to, I can't seem to stop myself, yet I manage to pull back from him.

"I'll try," I say. "But first," and I don't know where this thought comes from, "first—tell me a story."

"A . . . story."

It's all happening too fast for me. I need to slow down.

"Tell me what happened when Titania found out that Oberon had taken her changeling into his court."

He smiles. He rests his back against a tree and pulls me close so that my head's on his shoulder. I need this breathing space. I need the quiet sound of his voice, the intimacy it builds between us. Without it, fairy enchantment or not, the act of making love with him would be no different than if I did it with one of those homeboys who pulled up beside the curb earlier in the evening.

He's a good storyteller. I hope the Tree's listening.

When the story's done, he sits quietly beside me, as taken away by the story he's let unfold between us as I am. I'm the one who has to unbutton my blouse, who reaches for his hand and puts it against my breast.

6

I woke with the morning sun in my eyes, stiff and chilled from having spent the night on the damp grass. I sat up and used my fingers as a comb to pull the grass and leaves from my hair. My dream was still vivid. Puck's advice rang like a clarion bell inside my mind.

You can look upon the most common thing and see the whole of the cosmos reflected within.

But I couldn't seem to do it. I could feel the storm inside me, yearning to be freed, but the veil was over my eyes again and everything seemed to be shrouded with the fine covering of its fabric.

Free your heart from your mind. Embrace wonder for one moment without the need to consider how that wonder came to be, without the need to justify . . . if . . . it . . .

Already the advice was fading. I found myself thinking, It was only a dream. There's no more wisdom in a dream than in anything you might make up. It's just shadows. Without substance.

I tried to tell myself that it wasn't true. I might make up my poems, but when they work, when the line of communication runs true between my heart and whoever's reading them, they touch a real truth.

But the argument didn't seem worth pursuing.

Above me, the sky was grey, overcast. The morning was cool and it probably wouldn't get much warmer. So much for summer. So much for my life. But it seemed so unfair.

I remembered the dream. I remembered Puck—my Puck, not Shakespeare's, not some actor, not somebody else's interpretation of him. I remembered the magic in his voice. The gentleness in his touch. The wild enchantment in his eyes. Somehow I managed, if only in a dream, to pull aside the curtain that separates strangeness from the world we've all agreed on, and find a piece of wonder that I could bring back with me. But now that I've woken, I find that all I've brought back is more of what it seems I've always had.

Greyness. Boredom. No meaning in anything.

And that seemed the most unfair thing of all.

I lay back down on the grass and stared up into the Tree of Tales, my gaze veiled with tears. I could see the gloom that had spread throughout me during the summer, just deepening and deepening until it swallowed me whole. I was so sick of feeling sorry for myself, but I just couldn't seem to stop myself.

And then a small bird landed on a branch above my head—I don't even know what kind. A sparrow? A wren? It lifted up its head and warbled a few notes and for no good reason at all, I felt happy.

I didn't see the singer as a small drab brown bird on an equally drab branch, but as a microcosm that reflected every living thing. I didn't hear its song as a few warbled notes, quickly swallowed by the sounds of traffic beyond the confines of the park, but as an echo of all the music that was ever sung.

I sat up and looked around and nothing seemed the same. It was as though someone had just told me some unbelievably good news and simply by hearing it, my perspective on everything was changed.

7

Someone once described the theory of right and left brain to me and I read up on it myself later. Basically, it boils down to this: The left brain is the logical one, the rationalist, the scientist, the one that sees us through the everyday. It's the one that lets us conduct normal business, walk safely across a busy street, that kind of thing. And it's the one we know best.

The right brain belongs to the artist and its mostly a stranger because we don't call on it very often. In the general course of our lives, we don't *need* to. But fey though it is, this stranger inside us is the one that keeps us sane. It's the one that imparts meaning to what we do, that allows us to see beyond the drone of the everyday.

It's always trying to remind us of its existence. It's the one that's responsible for synchronicities and other small wonders, strange dreams or really *seeing* a small drab brown bird. It'll do anything to shake us up. But mostly we don't pay attention to it. And when we sink low enough, we don't hear its voice at all.

And that's such a shame, because that stranger is the Puck in the midden, the part of us that makes gold out of trash, poetry out of nonsense. It calls art forth from common sights and music from ordinary sound and without it, the world would be a very grey place indeed. Trust me, I know—from my own all-too-unpleasant experience with that world. But I'm working on never going through a summer like that again.

The stranger, that Puck in my midden, showed me how.

When I think of that Puck now, I'm always reminded of how he came to me—not just from out of a dream, but from a dream that was based on someone else's dream, put to words, enacted on the stage, centuries after his death. And I believe now that Shakespeare did write the plays that bear his name.

I doubt we'll ever know for sure. In this case, the historical version's lost, while the stories everybody else has to tell contradict one another—as so often they do. But I'll pick from between the lines and say it was old Will.

Because the dream also reminds me of the Tree of Tales, and I think maybe that's what Shakespeare was: a kind of human Tree of Tales. He got told all these stories and then he reshaped them into his plays so that they wouldn't be forgotten.

It doesn't matter where he got those stories. What matters is that he was able to put them into the forms they have now so that they could and can live on: small sparks of wisdom and joy, drama and buffoonery, that touch the stranger inside us so that she'll remind us what we're all here for. Not just to plod through life, but to celebrate it.

But knowing all of that, believing in it as I do, the mystery of authorship still remains for most people, I suppose. The scholars and historians. But that's their problem; I've solved it to my own satisfaction. There's only one thing I'd ask old Will if I ever ran into him. I'd love to know who told him about Puck.

I'll bet she had a tempest in her eyes.

SAXOPHONE JOE AND THE
WOMAN IN BLACK

—

*A cat has nine lives. For three he
plays, for three he strays, and for
the last three he stays.*
                    —American folklore

I love this city.

Even now, with things getting worse the way they do: Too
many people hungry, or cold, or got nowhere to sleep, and
here's winter creeping up on us, earlier each year, and staying later. The warm grate doesn't do much when the sleet's
coming down, giving everything the picture-perfect pretti-
ness of a fairy tale—just saying you've got the wherewithal
to admire a thing like that, instead of always worrying how
the ends are going to meet.

But you've got to take the time, once in a while, or
what've you got? Don't be waiting for the lotto to come in
when you can't even afford the price of a ticket.

It's like all those stories that quilt the streets, untidy little
threads of yarn that get pulled together into gossiping
skeins, one from here, one from there, until what you've got
in your hand isn't a book, maybe, doesn't have a real beginning or end, but it tells you something. You can read the big
splashes that make their way onto the front page, headlines
standing out one inch tall, just screaming for your attention.
Sure, they're interesting, but what interests me more is the

little stories. Nothing so exciting, maybe, about losing a job, or looking for one. Falling in or out of love. New baby coming. Old grandad passed away. Unless the story belongs to you. Then it fills your world, and you don't have time even to glance at those headlines.

What gets me is how everybody's looking to make sense of things. Sometimes you don't want sense. Sometimes, the last thing in the world you need is sense. Work a thing through till it makes sense and you lose all the possibilities.

That's what runs this city. All those possibilities. It's like the heart of the city is this old coal furnace, just smoking away under the streets, stoked with all those might-yet-bes and who'd-a-thoughts. The rich man waking up broke and he never saw it coming. The girl who figures she's so ugly she won't look in a mirror, and she finds she's got two boys fighting over her. The father who surprises himself when he finds he likes his son better, now that he knows the boy's gay.

And the thing is, the account doesn't end there. One possibility just leads straight up to the next, with handfuls of story lying in between. Stoking the furnace. Keeping the city interesting.

You just got to know where to look. You just got to know *how* to look.

Got no time?

Maybe the measurement's different from me to you to that girl who gives you your ticket at the bus depot, but the one thing we've all got is time. You can use it or lose it, your choice. That's how come we've got that old saying about how it's not having a thing that's important, but how we went about getting it. Our time's the most precious thing we've got to offer folks, and the worst thing a body can do is to take it away from us.

So don't you go wasting it.

But I was talking about possibilities and little stories, things that maybe don't even make it into the paper. Like what happened to Saxophone Joe.

I guess everybody knows how a cat's got nine lives, and

I'm thinking a few more of you know how those lives are divided up: three to play, three to stray, and the last three to stay. Maybe that's a likeness for our own lives, a what-do-you-call-it, metaphor. I don't know.

But grannies used to tell their children's children how if a cat came to live with you of its own accord during one of its straying lives, why you couldn't ask for better luck in that household. And that cat'd stay, too, unless you called it by name. Not the name you gave it, or maybe the one it gave you—it comes wandering in off the fire escape with its little white paws, so you call it Boots, or maybe it's that deep orange like you'd spread on your toast, so you call it Marmalade.

I'm talking about its secret name, the one only it knows.

Anyway, Joe's playing six nights a week with a combo in the Rhatigan, a little jazz club over on Palm Street; him on sax, Tommy Morrison on skins, Rex Small bellied up to that big double bass, and Johnny Fingers tickling the ivories. The Rhatigan doesn't look like much, but it's the kind of place you never know who's going to be sitting in with the band, playing that long cool music.

Used to be people said jazz was the soul of the city, the rhythm that made it tick. A music made up of slick streets and neon lights, smoky clubs and lips that taste like whiskey. Now we've got hip hop and rap and thrash, and I hear people saying it's not music at all, but they're plain wrong. All these sounds are still true to the soul of the city; it's just changed to suit the times is all.

One night Joe's up there on the Rhatigan's stage, half-sitting on his stool, one long leg bent up, foot supported on a rung, the other pointing straight out across the stage to where Johnny's hunched over his piano, fingers dancing on the keyboard as they trade off riffs. There's something in the air that night, and they're seriously connected to it.

Joe takes a breath, head cocked as he listens to what Johnny's playing. Then, just as he tightens his lips around the reeds, he sees the woman sitting there off in a dark corner, alone at her table, black hair, black dress, skin the same midnight tone as Joe's own so that she's almost invisible, except for the whites of her eyes and her teeth, because she's looking right at him and she's smiling.

Dark eyes, she's got, like there's no pupils, watching him and not blinking, and Joe watches her back. He's got one eye that's blue and one eye that's brown, and the gaze of the two of them just about swallows her whole.

But Joe doesn't lose the music, doesn't hesitate a moment; his sax wails, coming in right when it should, only he's watching the woman now, Johnny's forgotten, and the music changes, turns slinky, like an old tomcat on the prowl. The woman smiles and lifts her glass to him.

She comes home with him that night, just moves in like she's always been there. She doesn't talk, she doesn't ever say a word, but things must be working out between them because she's there, isn't she, sharing that tiny room Joe's had in the Walker Hotel for sixteen years. Live together in a small space like that, and you soon find out if you can get along or not.

After a while, Joe starts calling her Mona because that's the name of the tune they were playing when he first saw her in the Rhatigan and, musicians being the way they are, nobody thinks it strange that she doesn't talk, that she's got no ID, that she answers to that name. It's like she's always been there, always been called Mona, always lived with Saxophone Joe and been his woman.

But if he doesn't talk to anyone else about it, Joe's still thinking about her, always thinking about her, if he's on stage or walking down a street or back in their room, who she is and where she came from, and he finds himself trying out names on her, to see which one she might've worn before he called her Mona, which one her momma and poppa called her by when she was just a little girl.

Then one day he gets it right, and the next morning she's gone, walked out of his life like the straying cat in the story the grannies tell, once someone's called her by her true, secret name. What was her name, this woman Joe started out calling Mona? I never learned. But Joe knows the story, too, cats and names, and he gets to thinking some more, he can't *stop* thinking about Mona and cats, and then he gets this crazy idea that maybe she really *was* a cat, that she could change, cat to woman, woman to cat, slipped into his life during her straying years, and now she's gone.

And then he gets an even crazier idea: The only way to get her back is if he gets himself his own cat skin.

So he goes to see the priest—not the man with the white collar, but the hoodoo man—except Papa Jo-el's dead, got himself mixed up with some kind of juju that even he couldn't handle, so when Joe goes knocking soft on Papa Jo-el's door, it's the gris-gris woman Ti Beau that answers and lets him in.

Friday night, Joe's back in the club, and he's playing a dark music now, the tone of his sax's got an undercurrent in it, like skinheaded drums played with the palm of your hand and a tap-tap of a drumstick on a bar of iron, like midnight at a crossroads and the mist's coming in from the swamp, like seven-day candles burning in the wind, but those candles don't flicker because the gateways are open and *les invisibles* are there, holding the flames still.

Saturday night, he's back again, and he's still playing music like no one's heard before—not displeasing, just unfamiliar. Tommy and Rex, they're having trouble keeping the rhythm, but Johnny's following, note for note. After the last set that Saturday night, he walks up to where Joe's putting his sax away in its case.

"You been to see the *mambo*?" Johnny asks, "playing music like that?"

Joe doesn't answer except to put his sax case in Johnny's hands.

"Hold on to this for me, would you?" he asks.

When he leaves the club that night, it's the last time anybody sees him. Sees the man. But Heber Brown, he's been working at the Walker Hotel for thirty years. When he's cleaning out Joe's room because the rent's two months due and nobody's seen him for most of that time, Heber sees an old tomcat on the fire escape, scratching at the window, trying to get in. Heber says this cat's so dark a brown it's almost black, like midnight settled in the corner of an alleyway, and it's got one blue eye, so you tell me.

You think Ti Beau's got the kind of gris-gris potion to turn a man into a cat, or maybe just an old cat skin lying about that'll work the same magic, someone says the right words over it? Or was it maybe that Joe just up and left town, nursing a broken heart?

Somebody taped that last set Joe played at the Rhatigan, and I'll tell you, when Johnny plays it for me, I hear hurting in it, but I hear something else, too, something that doesn't quite belong to this world, or maybe belonged here first but we kind of eased it out of the way once we got ourselves civilized enough. It's like one of the *loa* stepped into Joe that night, maybe freed him up, loosened his skin enough so that he could make the change, but first that spirit talked to us through Joe's sax, reminding us that we weren't here first, and maybe we won't be here the last either.

It's all part and parcel of the mystery that sits there, right under all the things we know for sure. And the thing I like about that mystery is that it doesn't show us more than a little piece at a time; but you touch it and you've just got to pass it on. So if Joe's not with Mona now, you can bet he's slipped into someone else's life and he's making them think. Sitting there on a windowsill, maybe looking lazy, but maybe looking like he knows something we don't, something important, and that person he's with, who took him in, well she stops the tumbling rush of her life for a moment to take the time to think about what lies under the stories that make up this city.

Things may be getting worse in some ways, but you can't deny that they're interesting, too, if you just stop to look at them a little closer.

Like that old man playing the clarinet in the subway station that you pass by every day. He's bent and old and his clothes are shabby and you can't figure out how he makes a living from the few coins that get tossed into the hat sitting on the pavement in front of him. So maybe he's just an old man, down on his luck, making do. Or maybe he's got a piece of magic he wants to pass on with that music he's playing.

Next time you go by, stop and give him a listen. But don't go looking for a tag to put on what you hear or, like that cat that runs off when you name her, it'll all just go away.

THE BONE WOMAN

—

No one really stops to think of Ellie Spink, and why should they?

She's no one.

She has nothing.

Homely as a child, all that the passing of years did was add to her unattractiveness. Face like a horse, jaw long and square, forehead broad; limpid eyes set bird-wide on either side of a gargantuan nose; hair a nondescript brown, greasy and matted, stuffed up under a woolen toque lined with a patchwork of metal foil scavenged from discarded cigarette packages. The angularity of her slight frame doesn't get its volume from her meager diet, but from the multiple layers of clothing she wears.

Raised in foster homes, she's been used, but she's never experienced a kiss. Institutionalized for most of her adult life, she's been medicated, but never treated. Pass her on the street and your gaze slides right on by, never pausing to register the difference between the old woman huddled in the doorway and a bag of garbage.

Old woman? Though she doesn't know it, Monday, two

weeks past, was her thirty-seventh birthday. She looks twice her age.

There's no point in trying to talk to her. Usually no one's home. When there is, the words spill out in a disjointed mumble, a rambling monologue itemizing a litany of misperceived conspiracies and other ills that soon leave you feeling as confused as she herself must be.

Normal conversation is impossible and not many bother to try it. The exceptions are few: The odd pitying passerby. A concerned social worker, fresh out of college and new to the streets. Maybe one of the other street people who happens to stumble into her particular haunts.

They talk and she listens, or she doesn't—she never makes any sort of a relevant response, so who can tell? Few push the matter. Fewer still, however well intentioned, have the stamina to make the attempt to do so more than once or twice. It's easier just to walk away; to bury your guilt, or laugh off her confused ranting as the excessive rhetoric it can only be.

I've done it myself.

I used to try to talk to her when I first started seeing her around, but I didn't get far. Angel told me a little about her, but even knowing her name and some of her history didn't help.

"Hey, Ellie. How're you doing?"

Pale eyes, almost translucent, turn toward me, set so far apart it's as though she can only see me with one eye at a time.

"They should test for aliens," she tells me. "You know, like in the Olympics."

"Aliens?"

"I mean, who cares who killed Kennedy? Dead's dead, right?"

"What's Kennedy got to do with aliens?"

"I don't even know why they took down the Berlin Wall. What about the one in China? Shouldn't they have worked on that one first?"

It's like trying to have a conversation with a game of Trivial Pursuit that specializes in information garnered from su-permarket tabloids. After a while, I'd just pack an extra sandwich whenever I was busking in her neighborhood. I'd sit beside her, share my lunch, and let her talk if she wanted to, but I wouldn't say all that much myself.

That all changed the day I saw her with the Bone Woman.

I didn't call her the Bone Woman at first; the adjective that came more immediately to mind was fat. She couldn't have been much more than five-one, but she had to weigh in at two-fifty, leaving me with the impression that she was wider than she was tall. But she was light on her feet—peculiarly graceful for all her squat bulk.

She had a round face like a full moon, framed by thick black hair that hung in two long braids to her waist. Her eyes were small, almost lost in that expanse of face, and so dark they seemed all pupil. She went barefoot in a shapeless black dress, her only accessory an equally shapeless shoul-der bag made of some kind of animal skin and festooned with dangling thongs from which hung various feathers, beads, bottlecaps and other found objects.

I paused at the far end of the street when I saw the two of them together. I had a sandwich for Ellie in my knapsack, but I hesitated in approaching them. They seemed deep in conversation, real conversation, give and take, and Ellie was—knitting? Talking *and* knitting? The pair of them looked like a couple of old gossips, sitting on the back porch of their building. The sight of Ellie acting so normal was something I didn't want to interrupt.

I sat down on a nearby stoop and watched until Ellie put away her knitting and stood up. She looked down at her companion with an expression in her features that I'd never seen before. It was awareness, I realized. She was completely *here* for a change.

As she came up the street, I stood up and called a greeting to her, but by the time she reached me she wore her usually vacuous expression.

"It's the newspapers," she told me. "They use radiation to print them and that's what makes the news seem so bad."

Before I could take the sandwich I'd brought her out of my knapsack, she'd shuffled off, around the corner, and was gone. I glanced back down the street to where the fat woman was still sitting, and decided to find Ellie later. Right now I wanted to know what the woman had done to get such a positive reaction out of Ellie.

When I approached, the fat woman was sifting through the refuse where the two of them had been sitting. As I watched, she picked up a good-sized bone. What kind, I don't know, but it was as long as my forearm and as big around as the neck of my fiddle. Brushing dirt and a sticky candy wrapper from it, she gave it a quick polish on the sleeve of her dress and stuffed it away in her shoulderbag. Then she looked up at me.

My question died stillborn in my throat under the sudden scrutiny of those small dark eyes. She looked right through me—not the drifting, unfocused gaze of so many of the street people, but a cold, far-off seeing that weighed my presence, dismissed it, and gazed further off at something far more important.

I stood back as she rose easily to her feet. That was when I realized how graceful she was. She moved down the side-walk as daintily as a doe, as though her bulk was filled with helium, rather than flesh, and weighed nothing. I watched her until she reached the far end of the street, turned her own corner and then, just like Ellie, was gone as well.

I ended up giving Ellie's sandwich to Johnny Rew, an old wino who's taught me a fiddle tune or two, the odd time I've run into him sober.

———

I started to see the Bone Woman everywhere after that day. I wasn't sure if she was just new to town, or if it was one of those cases where you suddenly see something or someone you've never noticed before and after that you see them all the time. Everybody I talked to about her seemed to know her, but no one was quite sure how long she'd been in the city, or where she lived, or even her name.

I still wasn't calling her the Bone Woman, though I knew by then that bones were all she collected. Old bones, found bones, rattling around together in her shoulderbag until she went off at the end of the day and showed up the next morning, ready to start filling her bag again.

When she wasn't hunting bones, she spent her time with the street's worst cases—people like Ellie that no one else could talk to. She'd get them making things—little pictures or carvings or beadwork, keeping their hands busy. And talking. Someone like Ellie still made no sense to anybody else, but you could tell when she was with the Bone Woman that they were sharing a real dialogue. Which was a good thing, I suppose, but I couldn't shake the feeling that there was something more going on, something if not exactly sinister, then still strange.

It was the bones, I suppose. There were so many. How could she keep finding them the way she did? And what did she do with them?

My brother Christy collects urban legends, the way the Bone Woman collects her bones, rooting them out where you'd never think they could be. But when I told him about her, he just shrugged.

"Who knows why any of them do anything?" he said.

Christy doesn't live on the streets, for all that he haunts them. He's just an observer—always has been, ever since we were kids. To him, the street people can be pretty well evenly divided between the sad cases and the crazies. Their stories are too human for him.

"Some of these are big," I told him. "The size of a human thighbone."

"So point her out to the cops."

"And tell them what?"

A smile touched his lips with just enough superiority in it to get under my skin. He's always been able to do that. Usually, it makes me do something I regret later, which I sometimes think is half his intention. It's not that he wants to see me hurt. It's just part and parcel of that air of authority that all older siblings seem to wear. You know, a raised eyebrow, a way of smiling that says "You have so much to learn, little brother."

"If you really want to know what she does with those bones," he said, "why don't you follow her home and find out?"

"Maybe I will."

———

It turned out that the Bone Woman had a squat on the roof of an abandoned factory building in the Tombs. She'd built herself some kind of a shed up there—just a leaning, ramshackle affair of castoff lumber and sheet metal, but it kept out the weather and could easily be heated with a woodstove in the spring and fall. Come winter, she'd need warmer quarters, but the snows were still a month or so away.

I followed her home one afternoon, then came back the next day when she was out to finally put to rest my fear about these bones she was collecting. The thought that had stuck in my mind was that she was taking something away from the street people like Ellie, people who were already at the bottom rung and deserved to be helped, or at least just left alone. I'd gotten this weird idea that the bones were tied up with the last remnants of vitality that someone like Ellie might have, and the Bone Woman was stealing it from them.

What I found was more innocuous, and at the same time creepier, than I'd expected.

The inside of her squat was littered with bones and wire and dog-shaped skeletons that appeared to be made from the two. Bones held in place by wire, half-connected ribs and skulls and limbs. A pack of bone dogs. Some of the figures were almost complete, others were merely suggestions, but everywhere I looked, the half-finished wire-and-bone skeletons sat or stood or hung suspended from the ceiling. There had to be more than a dozen in various states of creation.

I stood in the doorway, not willing to venture any further, and just stared at them all. I don't know how long I was there, but finally I turned away and made my way back down through the abandoned building and out onto the street.

So now I knew what she did with the bones. But it didn't tell me how she could find so many of them. Surely that many stray dogs didn't die, their bones scattered the length and breadth of the city like so much autumn residue?

⤙

Amy and I had a gig opening for the Kelledys that night. It didn't take me long to set up. I just adjusted my microphone, laid out my fiddle and whistles on a small table to one side, and then kicked my heels while Amy fussed with her pipes and the complicated tangle of electronics that she used to amplify them.

I've heard it said that all Uillean pipers are a little crazy—that they have to be to play an instrument that looks more like what you'd find in the back of a plumber's truck than an instrument—but I think of them as perfectionists. Every one I've ever met spends more time fiddling with their reeds and adjusting the tuning of their various chanters, drones and regulators than would seem humanly possible.

Amy's no exception. After a while I left her there on the stage, with her red hair falling in her face as she poked and prodded at a new reed she'd made for one of her drones, and wandered into the back where the Kelledys were making their own preparations for the show, which consisted of drinking tea and looking beatific. At least that's the way I always think of the two of them. I don't think I've ever met calmer people.

Jilly likes to think of them as mysterious, attributing all kinds of fairy-tale traits to them. Meran, she's convinced, with the green highlights in her nut-brown hair and her wise brown eyes, is definitely dryad material—the spirit of an oak tree come to life—while Cerin is some sort of wizard figure, a combination of adept and bard. I think the idea amuses them, and they play it up to Jilly. Nothing you can put your finger on, but they seem to get a kick out of spinning a mysterious air about themselves whenever she's around.

I'm far more practical than Jilly—actually, just about anybody's more practical than Jilly, God bless her, but that's another story. I think if you find yourself using the word magic to describe the Kelledys, what you're really talking about is their musical talent. They may seem preternaturally calm offstage, but as soon as they begin to play, that calmness is transformed into a bonfire of energy. There's enchantment then, burning on stage, but it comes from their instrumental skill.

"Geordie," Meran said after I'd paced back and forth for a few minutes. "You look a little edgy. Have some tea."

I had to smile. If the Kelledys had originated from some mysterious elsewhere, then I'd lean more toward them having come from a fiddle tune than Jilly's fairy tales.

"When sick is it tea you want?" I said, quoting the title of an old Irish jig that we all knew in common.

Meran returned my smile. "It can't hurt. Here," she added, rummaging around in a bag that was lying by her chair. "Let me see if I have something that'll ease your nervousness."

"I'm not nervous."

"No, of course not," Cerin put in. "Geordie just likes to pace, don't you?"

He was smiling as he spoke, but without a hint of Christy's sometimes annoying demeanor.

"No, really. It's just . . ."

"Just what?" Meran asked as my voice trailed off.

Well, here was the perfect opportunity to put Jilly's theories to the test, I decided. If the Kelledys were in fact as fey as she made them out to be, then they'd be able to explain this business with the bones, wouldn't they?

So I told them about the fat woman and her bones and what I'd found in her squat. They listened with far more reasonableness than I would have if someone had been telling the story to me—especially when I went on to explain the weird feeling I'd been getting from the whole business.

"It's giving me the creeps," I said, finishing up, "and I can't even say why."

"La Huesera," Cerin said when I was done.

Meran nodded. "The Bone Woman," she said, translating it for me. "It does sound like her."

"So you know her."

"No," Meran said. "It just reminds us of a story we heard when we were playing in Phoenix a few years ago. There was a young Apache man opening for us, and he and I started comparing flutes. We got on to one of the Native courting flutes which used to be made from human bone and somehow from there he started telling me about a legend they have in the Southwest about this old fat woman who wanders through the mountains and arroyos, collecting bones from the desert that she brings back to her cave."

"What does she collect them for?"

"To preserve the things that are in danger of being lost to the world," Cerin said.

"I don't get it."

"I'm not sure of the exact details," Cerin went on, "but it had something to do with the spirits of endangered species."

"Giving them a new life," Meran said.

"Or a second chance."

"But there's no desert around here," I said. "What would this Bone Woman be doing up here?"

Meran smiled. "I remember John saying that she's as often been seen riding shotgun in an eighteen-wheeler as walking down a dry wash."

"And besides," Cerin added, "any place is a desert when there's more going on underground than on the surface."

That described Newford perfectly. And who lived a more hidden life than the street people? They were right in front of us every day, but most people didn't even see them anymore. And who was more deserving of a second chance than someone like Ellie, who'd never even gotten a fair first chance?

"Too many of us live desert lives," Cerin said, and I knew just what he meant.

⟶

The gig went well. I was a little bemused, but I didn't make any major mistakes. Amy complained that her regulators had sounded too buzzy in the monitors, but that was just Amy. They'd sounded great to me, their counterpointing chords giving the tunes a real punch whenever they came in.

The Kelledys' set was pure magic. Amy and I watched them from the stage wings and felt higher as they took their final bow than we had when the applause had been directed at us.

I begged off getting together with them after the show, re-gretfully pleading tiredness. I *was* tired, but leaving the thea-ter, I headed for an abandoned factory in the Tombs instead of home. When I got up on the roof of the building, the moon was full. It looked like a saucer of buttery gold, bath-ing everything in a warm yellow light. I heard a soft voice on the far side of the roof near the Bone Woman's squat. It wasn't exactly singing, but not chanting either. A murmur-ing, sliding sound that raised the hairs at the nape of my neck.

I walked a little nearer, staying in the shadows of the cor-nices, until I could see the Bone Woman. I paused then, lay-ing my fiddlecase quietly on the roof and sliding down so that I was sitting with my back against the cornice.

The Bone Woman had one of her skeleton sculptures set out in front of her and she was singing over it. The dog shape was complete now, all the bones wired in place and gleaming in the moonlight. I couldn't make out the words of her song. Either there were none, or she was using a lan-guage I'd never heard before. As I watched, she stood, rais-ing her arms up above the wired skeleton, and her voice grew louder.

The scene was peaceful—soothing, in the same way that the Kelledys' company could be—but eerie as well. The Bone Woman's voice had the cadence of one of the medicine chants I'd heard at a powwow up on the Kickaha Reservation—the same nasal tones and ringing quality. But that powwow hadn't prepared me for what came next.

At first I wasn't sure that I was really seeing it. The empty spaces between the skeleton's bones seemed to gather volume and fill out, as though flesh were forming on the bones. Then there was fur, highlighted by the moonlight, and I couldn't deny it any more. I saw a bewhiskered muzzle lift skyward, ears twitch, a tail curl up, thick-haired and strong. The powerful chest began to move rhythmically, at first in time to the Bone Woman's song, then breathing of its own accord.

The Bone Woman hadn't been making dogs in her squat, I realized as I watched the miraculous change occur. She'd been making wolves.

The newly animated creature's eyes snapped open and it leapt up, running to the edge of the roof. There it stood with its forelegs on the cornice. Arching its neck, the wolf pointed its nose at the moon and howled.

I sat there, already stunned, but the transformation still wasn't complete. As the wolf howled, it began to change again. Fur to human skin. Lupine shape, to that of a young woman. Howl to merry laughter. And as she turned, I recognized her features.

"Ellie," I breathed.

She still had the same horsy features, the same skinny body, all bones and angles, but she was beautiful. She blazed with the fire of a spirit that had never been hurt, never been abused, never been degraded. She gave me a radiant smile and then leapt from the edge of the roof.

I held my breath, but she didn't fall. She walked out across the city's skyline, out across the urban desert of rooftops and chimneys, off and away, running now, laughter trailing behind her until she was swallowed by the horizon.

I stared out at the night sky long after she had disappeared, then slowly stood up and walked across the roof to where the Bone Woman was sitting outside the door of her squat. She tracked my approach, but there was neither welcome nor dismissal in those small dark eyes. It was like the first time I'd come up to her; as far as she was concerned, I wasn't there at all.

"How did you do that?" I asked.

She looked through, past me.

"Can you teach me that song? I want to help, too."

Still no response.

"Why won't you *talk* to me?"

Finally her gaze focused on me.

"You don't have their need," she said.

Her voice was thick with an accent I couldn't place. I waited for her to go on, to explain what she meant, but once again, she ignored me. The pinpoints of black that passed for eyes in that round moon face looked away into a place where I didn't belong.

Finally, I did the only thing left for me to do. I collected my fiddlecase and went on home.

⸺

Some things haven't changed. Ellie's still living on the streets, and I still share my lunch with her when I'm down in her part of town. There's nothing the Bone Woman can do to change what this life has done to the Ellie Spinks of the world.

But what I saw that night gives me hope for the next turn of the wheel. I know now that no matter how downtrodden someone like Ellie might be, at least somewhere a piece of her is running free. Somewhere that wild and innocent part of her spirit is being preserved with those of the wolf and the rattlesnake and all the other creatures whose spirit-bones *La Huesera* collects from the desert—deserts natural and of our own making.

Spirit-bones. Collected and preserved, nurtured in the belly of the Bone Woman's song, until we learn to welcome them upon their terms, rather than our own.

PAL O' MINE

—

1

Gina always believed there was magic in the world. "But it doesn't work the way it does in fairy tales," she told me. "It doesn't save us. We have to save ourselves."

2

One of the things I keep coming back to when I think of Gina is walking down Yoors Street on a cold, snowy Christmas Eve during our last year of high school. We were out Christmas shopping. I'd been finished and had my presents all wrapped during the first week of December, but Gina had waited for the last minute, as usual, which was why we were out braving the storm that afternoon.

I was wrapped in as many layers of clothing as I could fit under my overcoat and looked about twice my size, but Gina was just scuffling along beside me in her usual cowboy boots and jeans, a floppy felt hat pressing down her dark curls and her hands thrust deep into the pockets of her pea jacket. She simply didn't pay any attention to the cold. Gina was good at that: ignoring inconveniences, or things she wasn't particularly interested in dealing with, much the way—I was eventually forced to admit—that I'd taught myself to ignore the dark current that was always present, running just under the surface of her exuberantly good moods.

"You know what I like best about the city?" she asked as we waited for the light to change where Yoors crosses Bunnett.

I shook my head.

"Looking up. There's a whole other world living up there."

I followed her gaze and at first I didn't know what she was on about. I looked through breaks in the gusts of snow that billowed around us, but couldn't detect anything out of the ordinary. I saw only rooftops and chimneys, multicolored Christmas decorations and the black strands of cable that ran in sagging geometric lines from the power poles to the buildings.

"What're you talking about?" I asked.

"The 'goyles," Gina said.

I gave her a blank look, no closer to understanding what she was talking about than I'd been before.

"The gargoyles, Sue," she repeated patiently. "Almost every building in this part of the city has got them, perched up there by the rooflines, looking down on us."

Once she'd pointed them out to me, I found it hard to believe that I'd never noticed them before. On that corner alone there were at least a half-dozen grotesque examples. I saw one in the archway keystone of the Annaheim Building directly across the street—a leering monstrous face, part lion, part bat, part man. Higher up, and all around, other nightmare faces peered down at us, from the corners of buildings, hidden in the frieze and cornice designs, cunningly nestled in corner brackets and the stone roof cresting. Every building had them. *Every* building.

Their presence shocked me. It's not that I was unaware of their existence—after all, I was planning on architecture as a major in college; it's just that if someone had mentioned gargoyles to me before that day, I would have automatically thought of the cathedrals and castles of Europe—not ordinary office buildings in Newford.

"I can't believe I never noticed them before," I told her.

"There are people who live their whole lives here and never see them," Gina said.

"How's that possible?"

Gina smiled. "It's because of where they are—looking down at us from just above our normal sightline. People in the city hardly ever look up."

"But still . . ."

"I know. It's something, isn't it? It really is a whole different world. Imagine being able to live your entire life in the middle of the city and never be noticed by anybody."

"Like a baglady," I said.

Gina nodded. "Sort of. Except people wouldn't ignore you because you're some pathetic street person that they want to avoid. They'd ignore you because they simply couldn't *see* you."

That thought gave me a creepy feeling, and I couldn't suppress a shiver, but I could tell that Gina was intrigued with the idea. She was staring at that one gargoyle, above the entrance to the Annaheim Building.

"You really like those things, don't you?" I said.

Gina turned to look at me, an expression I couldn't read sitting at the back of her eyes.

"I wish I lived in their world," she told me.

She held my gaze with that strange look in her eyes for a long heartbeat. Then the light changed and she laughed, breaking the mood. Slipping her arm in mine, she started us off across the street to finish her Christmas shopping.

When we stood on the pavement in front of the Annaheim Building, she stopped and looked up at the gargoyle. I craned my neck and tried to give it a good look myself, but it was hard to see because of all the blowing snow.

Gina laughed suddenly. "It knows we were talking about it."

"What do you mean?"

"It just winked at us."

I hadn't seen anything, but then I always seemed to be looking exactly the wrong way, or perhaps *in* the wrong way, whenever Gina tried to point out some magical thing to me. She was so serious about it.

"Did you see?" Gina asked.

"I'm not sure," I told her. "I think I saw something. . . ."

Falling snow. The side of a building. And stone statuary that was pretty amazing in and of itself without the need to be animated as well. I looked up at the gargoyle again, trying to see what Gina had seen.

I wish I lived in their world.

It wasn't until years later that I finally understood what she'd meant by that.

3

Christmas wasn't the same for me as for most people—not even when I was a kid: My dad was born on Christmas day; Granny Ashworth, his mother, died on Christmas day when I was nine; and my own birthday was December 27. It made for a strange brew come the holiday season, part celebration, part mourning, liberally mixed with all the paraphernalia that means Christmas: eggnog and glittering lights, caroling, ornaments and, of course, presents.

Christmas wasn't centered around presents for me. Easy to say, I suppose, seeing how I grew up in the Beaches, wanting for nothing, but it's true. What enamored me the most about the season, once I got beyond the confusion of birthdays and mourning, was the idea of what it was supposed to be: peace and goodwill to all. The traditions. The idea of the miracle birth the way it was told in the Bible and more secular legends like the one telling how, for one hour after midnight on Christmas Eve, animals were given human voices so that they could praise the baby Jesus.

I remember staying up late the year I turned eleven, sitting in bed with my cat on my lap and watching the clock, determined to hear Chelsea speak, except I fell asleep sometime after eleven and never did find out if she could or not.

By the time Christmas came around the next year I was too old to believe in that sort of thing anymore.

Gina never got too old. I remember years later when she got her dog Fritzie, she told me, "You know what I like the best about him? The stories he tells me."

"Your dog tells you stories," I said slowly.

"Everything's got a voice," Gina told me. "You just have to learn how to hear it."

4

The best present I ever got was the Christmas that Gina decided to be my friend. I'd been going to a private school and hated it. Everything about it was so stiff and proper. Even though we were only children, it was still all about money and social standing and it drove me mad. I'd see the public school kids, and they seemed so free compared to all the boundaries I perceived to be compartmentalizing my own life.

I pestered my mother for the entire summer I was nine until she finally relented and let me take the public transport into Ferryside where I attended Cairnmount Public School. By noon of my first day, I realized that I hated public school even more.

There's nothing worse than being the new kid—especially when you were busing in from the Beaches. Nobody wanted anything to do with the slumming rich kid and her airs. I didn't have airs; I was just too scared. But first impressions are everything, and I ended up feeling more left out and alone than I'd ever been at my old school. I couldn't even talk about it at home—my pride wouldn't let me. After the way I'd carried on about it all summer, I couldn't find the courage to admit that I'd been wrong.

So I did the best I could. At recess, I'd stand miserably on the sidelines, trying to look as though I was a part of the linked fence, or whatever I was standing beside at the time, because I soon learned it was better to be ignored than to be noticed and ridiculed. I stuck it out until just before Christmas break. I don't know if I would have been able to force myself to return after the holidays, but that day a bunch of boys were teasing me and my eyes were already welling with tears when Gina walked up out of nowhere and chased them off.

"Why don't you ever play with anybody?" she asked me.

"Nobody wants me to play with them," I said.

"Well, I do," she said and then she smiled at me, a smile so bright that it dried up all my tears.

After that, we were best friends forever.

5

Gina was the most outrageous, talented, wonderful person I had ever met. I was the sort of child who usually reacted to stimuli; Gina created them. She made up games, she made up stories, she made up songs. It was impossible to be bored in her company, and we became inseparable, in school and out.

I don't think a day went by that we didn't spend some part of it together. We had sleepovers. We took art and music and dance classes together, and if she won the prizes, I didn't mind, because she was my friend and I could only be proud of her. There was no limit to her imagination, but that was fine by me, too. I was happy to have been welcomed into her world, and I was more than willing to take up whatever enterprise she might propose.

I remember one afternoon we sat up in her room and made little people out of found objects: acorn heads, seed eyes, twig bodies. We made clothes for them and furniture and concocted long, extravagant family histories so that we ended up knowing more about them than we did our classmates.

"They're real now," I remember her telling me. "We've given them lives, so they'll always be real."

"What kind of real?" I asked, feeling a little confused because I was at that age when I was starting to understand the difference between what was make-believe and what was actual.

"There's only one kind of real," Gina told me. "The trouble is, not everybody can see it and they make fun of those who can."

Though I couldn't know the world through the same perspective as Gina had, there was one thing I did know. "I would never make fun of you," I said.

"I know, Sue. That's why we're friends."

I still have the little twig people I made, wrapped up in tissue and stored away in a box of childhood treasures; I don't know what ever happened to Gina's.

We had five years together, but then her parents moved out of town—not impossibly far, but far enough to make our getting together a major effort, and we rarely saw each other more than a few times a year after that. It was mainly Gina's doing that we didn't entirely lose touch with each other. She wrote me two or three times a week, long chatty letters about what she'd been reading, films she'd seen, people she'd met, her hopes of becoming a professional musician after she finished high school. The letters were decorated with fanciful illustrations of their contents and sometimes included miniature envelopes in which I would find letters from her twig people to mine.

Although I tried to keep up my side, I wasn't much of a correspondent. Usually I'd phone her, but my calls grew further and further apart as the months went by. I never stopped considering her as a friend—the occasions when we did get together were among my best memories of being a teenager—but my own life had changed, and I didn't have as much time for her anymore. It was hard to maintain a long-distance relationship when there was so much going on around me at home. I was no longer the new kid at school, and I'd made other friends. I worked on the school paper, and then I got a boyfriend.

Gina never wanted to talk about him. I suppose she thought of it as a kind of betrayal; she never again had a friend that she was as close to as she'd been with me.

I remember her mother calling me once, worried because Gina seemed to be sinking into a reclusive depression. I did my best to be there for her. I called her almost every night for a month, and went out to visit her on the weekends, but somehow I just couldn't relate to her pain. Gina had always seemed so self-contained, so perfect, that it was hard to imagine her being as withdrawn and unhappy as her mother seemed to think she was. She put on such a good face to me that eventually the worries I'd had faded and the demands of my own life pulled me away again.

6

Gina never liked Christmas.

The year she introduced me to Newford's gargoyles we saw each other twice over the holidays: once so that she could do her Christmas shopping, and then again between Christmas and New Year's when I came over to her place and stayed the night. She introduced me to her dog—Fritzie, a gangly, wirehaired, long-legged mutt that she'd found abandoned on one of the country roads near her parents' place—and played some of her new songs for me, accompanying herself on guitar.

The music had a dronal quality that seemed at odds with her clear high voice and the strange Middle Eastern decorations she used. The lyrics were strange and dark, leaving me with a sensation that was not so much unpleasant as uncomfortable, and I could understand why she'd been having so much trouble getting gigs. It wasn't just that she was so young and since most clubs served alcohol, their owners couldn't hire an underage performer; Gina's music simply wasn't what most people would think of as entertainment. Her songs went beyond introspection. They took the listener to that dark place that sits inside each and every one of us, that place we don't want to visit, that we don't even want to admit is there.

But the songs aside, there didn't seem to be any trace of the depression that had worried her mother so much the previous autumn. She appeared to be her old self, the Gina I remembered: opinionated and witty, full of life and laughter even while explaining to me what bothered her so much about the holiday season.

"I love the *idea* of Christmas," she said. "It's the hypocrisy of the season that I dislike. One time out of the year, people do what they can for the homeless, help stock the food banks, contribute to snowsuit funds and give toys to poor children. But where are they the rest of the year when their help is just as necessary? It makes me a little sick to think of all the money that gets spent on Christmas lights and parties and presents that people don't even really want in the first place. If we took all that money and gave it to the people who need it simply to survive, instead of throwing it away on ourselves, we could probably solve most of the problems of poverty and homelessness over one Christmas season."

"I suppose," I said. "But at least Christmas brings people closer together. I guess what we have to do is build on that."

Gina gave me a sad smile. "Who does it bring closer together?"

"Well . . . families, friends . . ."

"But what about those who don't have either? They look at all this closeness you're talking about, and it just makes their own situation seem all the more desperate. It's hardly surprising that the holiday season has the highest suicide rate of any time of the year."

"But what can we do?" I said. "We can't just turn our backs and pretend there's no such thing as Christmas."

Gina shrugged, then gave me a sudden grin. "We could become Christmas commandos. You know," she added at my blank look. "We'd strike from within. First we'd convince our own families to give it up and then . . ."

With that she launched into a plan of action that would be as improbable in its execution as it was entertaining in its explanation. She never did get her family to give up Christmas, and I have to admit I didn't try very hard with mine, but the next year I did go visit the residents of places like St.

Vincent's Home for the Aged, and I worked in the Grasso Street soup kitchen with Gina on Christmas day. I came away with a better experience of what Christmas was all about than I'd ever had at home.

But I just couldn't maintain that commitment all year round. I kept going to St. Vincent's when I could, but the sheer despair of the soup kitchens and food banks was more than I could bear.

7

Gina dropped out of college during her second year to concentrate on her music. She sent me a copy of the demo tape she was shopping around to the record companies in hopes of getting a contract. I didn't like it at first. Neither her guitar-playing nor her vocal style had changed much, and the inner landscape the songs revealed was too bleak, the shadows it painted upon the listener seemed too unrelentingly dark, but out of loyalty I played it a few times more and subsequent listenings changed that first impression.

Her songs were still bleak, but I realized that they helped create a healing process in the listener. If I let them take me into the heart of their darkness, they took me out again as well. It was the kind of music that while it appeared to wallow in despair, in actuality it left its audience stronger, more able to face the pain and heartache that awaited them beyond the music.

She was playing at a club near the campus one weekend, and I went to see her. Sitting in front were a handful of hard-core fans, all pale-faced and dressed in black, but most of the audience didn't understand what she was offering them any more than I had the first time I sat through the demo tape. Obviously her music was an acquired taste— which didn't bode well for her career in a world where, more and more, most information was conveyed in thirty-second sound bites and audiences in the entertainment industry demanded instant gratification, rather than taking the time to explore the deeper resonances of a work.

She had Fritzie waiting for her in the claustrophobic dressing room behind the stage, so the three of us went walking in between her sets. That was the night she first told me about her bouts with depression.

"I don't know what it is that brings them on," she said. "I know I find it frustrating that I keep running into a wall with my music, but I also know that's not the cause of them either. As long as I can remember I've carried this feeling of alienation around with me; I wake up in the morning, in the middle of the night, and I'm paralyzed with all this emotional pain. The only people that have ever really helped to keep it at bay were first you, and now Fritzie."

It was such a shock to hear that her only lifelines were a friend who was hardly ever there for her and a dog. The guilt that lodged inside me then has never really gone away. I wanted to ask what had happened to that brashly confident girl who had turned my whole life around as much by the example of her own strength and resourcefulness as by her friendship, but then I realized that the answer lay in her music, in her songs that spoke of masks and what lay behind them, of puddles on muddy roads that sometimes hid deep, bottomless wells.

"I feel so . . . so stupid," she said.

This time I was the one who took charge. I steered her toward the closest bus stop and we sat down on its bench. I put my arm around her shoulders and Fritzie laid his mournful head upon her knee and looked up into her face.

"Don't feel stupid," I said. "You can't help the bad feelings."

"But why do I have to have them? Nobody else does."

"Everybody has them."

She toyed with the wiry fur between Fritzie's ears and leaned against me.

"Not like mine," she said.

"No," I agreed. "Everybody's got their own."

That got me a small smile. We sat there for a while, watching the traffic go past until it was time for her last set of the night.

"What do you think of the show?" she asked as we returned to the club.

"I like it," I told her, "but I think it's the kind of music that people have to take their time to appreciate."

Gina nodded glumly. "And who's got the time?"

"I do."

"Well, I wish you ran one of the record companies," she said. "I get the same answer from all of them. They like my voice, they like my playing, but they want me to sexy up my image and write songs that are more upbeat."

She paused. We'd reached the back door of the club by then. She put her back against the brick wall of the alley and looked up. Fritzie was pressed up against the side of her leg as though he was glued there.

"I tried, you know," Gina said. "I really tried to give them what they wanted, but it just wasn't there. I just don't have that kind of song inside me."

She disappeared inside then to retune her guitar before she went back on stage. I stayed for a moment longer, my gaze drawn up as hers had been while she'd been talking to me. There was a gargoyle there, spout-mouth open wide, a rather benevolent look about its grotesque features. I looked at it for a long time, wondering for a moment if I would see it blink or move the way Gina probably had, but it was just a stone sculpture, set high up in the wall. Finally I went back inside and found my seat.

8

I was in the middle of studying for exams the following week, but I made a point of it to call Gina at least once a day. I tried getting her to let me take her out for dinner on the weekend, but she and Fritzie were pretty much inseparable and she didn't want to leave him tied up outside the restaurant while we sat inside to eat. So I ended up having them over to the little apartment I was renting in Crowsea instead. She told me that night that she was going out west to try to shop her tape around to the big companies in L.A., and I didn't see her again for three months.

I'd been worried about her going off on her own, feeling as she was. I even offered to go with her, if she'd just wait until the semester was finished, but she assured me she'd be fine, and a series of cheerful cards and short letters—signed by either her or just a big paw print—arrived in my letterbox to prove the point. When she finally did get back, she called me up and we got together for a picnic lunch in Fitzhenry Park.

Going out to the West Coast seemed to have done her good. She came back looking radiant and tanned, full of amusing stories concerning the ups and downs of her and Fritzie's adventures out there. She'd even got some fairly serious interest from an independent record label, but they were still making up their minds when her money ran out. Instead of trying to make do in a place where she felt even more like a stranger than she did in Newford, she decided to come home to wait for their response, driving back across the country in her old station wagon, Fritzie sitting up on the passenger seat beside her, her guitar in its battered case lying across the back seat.

"By the time we rolled into Newford," she said, "the car was just running on fumes. But we made it."

"If you need some money, or a place to stay . . ." I offered.

"I can just see the three of us squeezed into that tiny place of yours."

"We'd make do."

Gina smiled. "It's okay. My dad fronted me some money until the advance from the record company comes through. But thanks all the same. Fritzie and I appreciate the offer."

I was really happy for her. Her spirits were so high now that things had finally turned around, and she could see that she was going somewhere with her music. She knew there was a lot of hard work still to come, but it was the sort of work she thrived on.

"I feel like I've lived my whole life on the edge of an abyss," she told me, "just waiting for the moment when it'd finally drag me down for good, but now everything's changed. It's like I finally figured out a way to live some place else—away from the edge. *Far* away."

I was going on to my third year at Butler U. in the fall, but we made plans to drive back to L.A. together in July, once she got the okay from the record company. We'd spend the summer together in La La Land, taking in the sights while Gina worked on her album. It's something I knew we were both looking forward to.

9

Gina was looking after the cottage of a friend of her parents' when she fell back into the abyss. She never told me how she was feeling, probably because she knew I'd have gone to any length to stop her from hurting herself. All she'd told me before she went was that she needed the solitude to work on some new songs and I'd believed her. I had no reason to worry about her. During the two weeks she was living out there I must have gotten a half-dozen cheerful cards, telling me what to add to my packing list for our trip out west and what to leave off.

Her mother told me that she'd gotten a letter from the record company, turning down her demo. She said Gina had seemed to take the rejection well when she called to give her daughter the bad news. They'd ended their conversation with Gina already making plans to start the rounds of the records companies again with the new material she'd been working on. Then she'd burned her guitar and all of her music and poetry in a firepit down by the shore, and simply walked out into the lake. Her body was found after a neighbor was drawn to the lot by Fritzie's howling. The poor dog was shivering and wet, matted with mud from having tried to rescue her. They know it wasn't an accident, because of the note she left behind in the cottage.

I never read the note. I couldn't.

I miss her terribly, but most of all, I'm angry. Not at Gina, but at this society of ours that tries to make everybody fit into the same mold. Gina was unique, but she didn't want to be. All she wanted to do was fit in, but her spirit and her muse wouldn't let her. That dichotomy between who she was and who she thought she should be was what really killed her.

All that survives of her music is that demo tape. When I listen to it, I can't understand how she could create a healing process for others through that dark music, but she couldn't use it to heal herself.

10

Tomorrow is Christmas day and I'm going down to the soup kitchen to help serve the Christmas dinners. It'll be my first Christmas without Gina. My parents wanted me to come home, but I put them off until tomorrow night. I just want to sit here tonight with Fritzie and remember. He lives with me because Gina asked me to take care of him, but he's not the same dog he was when Gina was alive. He misses her too much.

I'm sitting by the window, watching the snow fall. On the table in front of me I've spread out the contents of a box of memories: the casing for Gina's demo tape. My twig people and the other things we made. All those letters and cards that Gina sent me over the years. I haven't been able to re-read them yet, but I've looked at the drawings and I've held them in my hands, turning them over and over, one by one. The demo tape is playing softly on my stereo. It's the first time I've been able to listen to it since Gina died.

Through the snow I can see the gargoyle on the building across the street. I know now what Gina meant about wanting to live in their world and be invisible. When you're invisible, no one can see that you're different.

Thinking about Gina hurts so much, but there's good things to remember, too. I don't know what would have become of me if she hadn't rescued me in that playground all those years ago and welcomed me into her life. It's so sad that the uniqueness about her that made me love her so much was what caused her so much pain.

The bells of St. Paul's Cathedral strike midnight. They remind me of the child I was, trying to stay up late enough to hear my cat talk. I guess that's what Gina meant to me. While everybody else grew up, Gina retained all the best things about childhood: goodness and innocence and an endless wonder. But she carried the downside of being a child inside her as well. She always lived in the present moment, the way we do when we're young, and that must be why her despair was so overwhelming for her.

"I tried to save her," a voice says in the room behind me as the last echo of St. Paul's bells fades away. "But she wouldn't let me. She was too strong for me."

I don't move. I don't dare move at all. On the demo tape, Gina's guitar starts to strum the intro to another song. Against the drone of the guitar's strings, the voice goes on.

"I know she'll always live on so long as we keep her memory alive," it says, "but sometimes that's just not enough. Sometimes I miss her so much I don't think *I* can go on."

I turn slowly then, but there's only me in the room. Me and Fritzie, and one small Christmas miracle to remind me that everything magic didn't die when Gina walked into the lake.

"Me, too," I tell Fritzie.

I get up from my chair and cross the room to where he's sitting up, looking at me with those sad eyes of his. I put my arms around his neck. I bury my face in his rough fur, and we stay there like that for a long time, listening to Gina sing.

WHERE DESERT SPIRITS CROWD THE NIGHT

—

*If your mind is attuned to beauty,
you find beauty in everything.*
                        —Jean Cooke,
            in an interview in *The Artist's
                and Illustrator's Magazine,*
                            April 1993

*All I ask of you
Is that you remember me
As loving you*
                        —traditional Sufi song

Each of us owes God a death.
—attributed to Humphrey Osmond

1

Sophie didn't attend the funeral. She hadn't met Max yet, couldn't have known that his lover had died. On the afternoon that Max stood at Peter's gravesite under a far too cheerful sky, she was in her studio in Old Market, preparing for a new show. It wasn't until the opening, two months later, that they met.

But even then, Coyote was watching.

2

There is a door in my dreams that opens into a desert. . . .
    where the light is like a wash of whiskey over my vision;
    where the color of the earth ranges through a spectrum of

dusty browns cut with pale ochre tones and siennas;

where distant peaks jut blue-grey from the tide of hills washing up against the ragged line the mountains make at the horizon, peaks that are shadowed now as the sun sets in a geranium and violet glory behind me;

where the tall saguaro rise like sleepy green giants from the desert floor, waving lazy arms to no one in particular, with barrel cacti crouching in their shadows like smaller, shorter cousins;

where clusters of prickly pear and cholla offer a thorny embrace, and the landscape is clouded with mesquite and palo verde and smoke trees, their leaves so tiny they don't seem as much to grow from the gnarly branches as to have been dusted upon them;

where a hawk hangs in the sky high above me, a dark silhouette against the ever deepening blue, gliding effortlessly on outspread wings;

where a lizard darts into a tight crevice, its movement so quick, it only registers in the corner of my eye;

where an owl the size of my palm peers at me from the safety of its hole in a towering saguaro;

where a rattlesnake gives me one warning rattle, then fixes me with its hypnotic stare, poised to strike long after I have backed away;

where the sound of a medicine flute, breathy and soft as a secret, rises up from an arroyo, and for one moment I see the shadow of a hunchbacked man and his instrument cast upon the far wall of the gully, before the night takes the sight away, if not the sound;

where the sky, even at night, overwhelms me with its immensity;

where the stillness seems complete . . .

except for the resonance of my heartbeat that twins the distant-drum of a stag's hooves upon the dry, hard ground;

except for the incessant soughing cries of the ground-doves that feed in the brushy vegetation all around me;

except for the low sound of the flute which first brought me here.

The sweet scent of a mesquite fire in the middle of a dry wash draws me down from the higher ridges. The grounddoves break like quail with a rushing thrum of their wings as I make my way near. A figure is there by the fire, sitting motionless, head bent in shadow. I stand just beyond the circle of light, uncertain, uneasy. But finally I step forward. I sit across the fire from the figure. In the distance, I can still hear the sound of the flute. My silent companion gives neither it nor my presence any acknowledgment, but I can be patient, too.

And anyway, I've nowhere else to go.

3

Given her way in the matter, Sophie would never attend one of her own openings. She was so organized and tidy that she never really thought that she looked like the typical image of what an artist should be, and she always felt awkward trying to make nice with the gallery's clients. It wasn't that she didn't like people, or even that she wasn't prone to involved conversations. She simply felt uncomfortable around strangers, especially when she was supposed to be promoting herself and her work. But she tried.

So this evening as The Green Man Gallery filled with the guests that Albina had invited to the opening, Sophie concentrated on fulfilling what she saw as her responsibility in making the evening a success. Instead of clustering in a corner with her scruffy friends, who were doing their best not to be too rowdy and only just succeeding, she made an effort to mingle, to be sociable, the approachable artist. Whenever she felt herself gravitating to where Jilly and Wendy and the others were standing, she'd focus on someone she didn't know, walk over and strike up a conversation.

An hour or so into the opening, she picked a man in his late twenties who had just stopped in front of *Hearts Like Fire, Burning*—a small oil painting of two golden figures holding hands in a blaze of color that she'd meant to represent the fire of their consummated love.

He was tall and slender, a pale, dark-haired Pre-Raphaelite presence dressed in somber clothes: black jeans, black T-shirt, black sportsjacket, even black Nike sneakers. What attracted her to him was how he moved like a shadow through the gallery crowd and seemed completely at odds with both them and the bright, sensual colors of the paintings that made up the show. And yet he seemed more in tune with the paintings than anyone else—perhaps, she thought wryly as she noticed the intensity of his interest in the work, herself included.

Hearts Like Fire, Burning, in particular, appeared to mesmerize him. He stood longest in front of it, transfixed, his features a curious mixture of deep sadness and joy. When she approached him, he looked slowly away from the painting and smiled at her. The expression turned bittersweet by the time it reached his eyes.

"So what do you think of this piece?" he asked.

Sophie blinked in surprise. "I should probably be asking you that question."

"How so?"

"I'm the artist."

He inclined his head slightly in greeting and put out his hand. "Max Hannon," he said, introducing himself.

"I'm Sophie Etoile," she said as she took his hand. Then she laughed. "I guess that was obvious."

He laughed with her, but his laugh, like his smile, held a deep sadness by the time it reached his eyes.

"I find it very peaceful," he said, turning back to the painting.

"Now that's a description I've never heard of my work."

"Oh?" He regarded her once more. "How's it usually described?"

"Those that like it call it lively, colorful, vibrant. Those that don't call it garish, overblown. . . ." Sophie shrugged and let the words trail off.

"And how would you describe it?"

"With this piece, I agree with you. For all its flood of bright color, I find it very peaceful."

"It reminds me of my lover, Peter," Max said. "We were in Arizona a few months ago, staying with friends who have a place in the desert. We'd sit and hold hands at this table they had set up behind their house and simply let the light and the sky fill us. It felt just like this painting—full of gold and flames and the fire in our hearts, all mixed up together. When I look at this, it brings it all back."

"That's very sweet."

Max turned back to the painting. "He died a week or so after we got back."

"I'm so sorry," Sophie said, laying a hand on his arm.

Max sighed. "It doesn't hurt to talk about him, but God do I miss him."

You can say it doesn't hurt, Sophie thought, but she could see how bright his eyes had become, only just holding back a film of tears. The openness with which he'd shared his feelings with her made her want to do something special in return.

"I want you to have this painting," she said. "You can come pick it up when the show's over."

Max shook his head. "I'd love to buy it," he said, "but I don't have that kind of money."

"Who said anything about you having to pay for it?"

"I couldn't even think of . . ." he began.

But Sophie refused to listen. "Look," she said. "What would be the point of being an artist if you only did it for the money? I always feel weird about selling my work anyway. It's as though I'm selling off my children. I don't even know what kind of a home they're going to—there's no evaluation process beforehand. Someone could buy this painting just for the investment and for all I know it'll end up stuck in a closet somewhere and never be seen again. I can't tell you how good it would make me feel knowing that it was hanging in your home instead, where it would mean so much to you."

"No, I just couldn't accept it," Max told her.

"Then let me give it to Peter," Sophie said, "and you can keep it for him."

Max shook his head. "This is so strange. Things like this don't happen in the real world."

"Well, pick a world where it could happen," Sophie said, "and we'll pretend that we're there."

Max gave her a curious look. "Do you do this a lot?"

"What? Give away paintings?"

"No, pick another world to be in when you don't happen to like the way things are going in this one."

Now it was Sophie's turn to be intrigued. "Why, do you?"

"No. It's just . . . ever since you came over and started talking to me, I've felt as though we've met before. But not here. Not in this world. It's more like we met in a dream. . . ."

This was too strange, Sophie thought. For a moment the gallery and crowd about them seemed to flicker, to grow hazy and two-dimensional, as though only she and Max were real.

Like we met in a dream . . .

Slowly she shook her head. "Don't get me started on dreams," she said.

4

"There are sleeping dreams and waking dreams," Christina Rossetti says in her poem "A Ballad of Boding," as though the difference between them is absolute. My dreams aren't so clearly divided, not from one another, and not from when I'm actually awake either. My sleeping dreams bleed into the real world; actually, the place where they take place seems like a real world, too—it's just not one that's as easily accessed by most people.

The experiences I have there aren't real, of course, or at least not real in the way people normally use the word. What happens when I fall asleep and step into my dreams can't be measured or weighed—it can only be known—but that doesn't stop these experiences from influencing my life and leaving me in a state of mild confusion so much of the time.

The confusion stems from the fact that every time I turn around, the rules seem to change. Or maybe it's that every time I think I have a better understanding of what the night side of my life means, the dreams open up like a Chinese puzzle box, and I find yet another riddle lying inside the one I've just figured out. The borders blur, retreating before me, deeper and deeper into the dreamscape, walls becoming doors, and doors opening out into mysteries that often obscure the original question. I don't even know the original question anymore. I can't even remember if there ever was one.

I do remember that I went looking for my mother once. I went to a place, marshy and bogled like an old English storybook fen, where I found that she might be a drowned moon, pinned underwater by quicks and other dark creatures until I freed her from her watery tomb. But I came back from that dreamscape without a clear answer as to who she was, or what exactly it was that I had done. What I do know is that I came back with a friend: Jeck Crow, a handsome devil of a man who, I seem to remember, once bore the physical appearance of the black-winged bird that's his namesake. Is it a true memory? I don't know, he won't say, and our relationship has progressed to the point where it doesn't really matter anymore.

I only see him when I sleep. I close my eyes and step from this world to Mabon, the city that radiates from Mr. Truepenny's, the bookstore/art gallery I made up when I was a kid. Or at least I thought I'd made it up. It was the place I went when I was waiting for my dad to come home from work, a haven from my loneliness because I didn't make friends easily in those days. Not having anyone with whom I could share the fruits of my imagination, I put all that energy into making up a place where I was special, or at least had access to special things.

Faerie blood—courtesy of a mother who, Jilly is convinced, was a dream in this world, a moon in her own—is what makes it all real.

5

"Who was that guy you spent half the night talking to?" Jilly wanted to know as she and Sophie were walking home from the restaurant where they'd all gone to celebrate after the opening. Sophie had asked Max to come along, but he'd declined.

"Just this guy."

Jilly laughed. " 'Just this guy.' Oh, please. He was the best-looking man in the place and he seemed quite smitten with you."

Sophie had to smile. Only Jilly would use a word like smitten.

"His name's Max Hannon," she told Jilly, "and he's gay."

"So? This means you can't be friends?"

"Of course not. I was just pointing out that he's not potential boyfriend material."

"It's possible to be enamored with someone on an intellectual or spiritual level, you know."

"I know."

"And besides, you already have a boyfriend."

Sophie sighed. "Right. In my dreams. That doesn't exactly do much for me in the real world."

"But your dreams are like a real world for you."

"I think I need something a little more . . . substantial in my life. My biological clock is ticking away."

"But Jeck—"

"Isn't real," Sophie said. "No matter how much I pretend he is. And Mabon isn't a real city, no matter how much I want it to be, and even if it seems like other people can visit it. You can talk all you want about consensual reality, Jilly, but that doesn't change the fact that some things are real and some things aren't. There's a line drawn between the two that separates reality from fantasy."

"Yeah, but it's an imaginary line," Jilly said. "Who really decides where it gets drawn?"

They'd been through variations on this conversation many times before. Anyone who spent any amount time with Jilly did. Her open-mindedness was either endearing or frustrating, depending on where you stood on whatever particular subject happened to be under discussion.

"Well, I'll tell you," Jilly went on when Sophie didn't respond. "A long time ago a bunch of people reached a general consensus as to what's real and what's not and most of us have been going along with it ever since."

"All of which has nothing to do with Max," Sophie said in an attempt to return to the original topic of their conversation.

"I know," Jilly said. "So are you going to see him again?"

"I hope so. There's something very intriguing about him."

"Which has nothing to do with the way he looks."

"I told you," Sophie said. "He's gay."

"Like Sue always says, the best ones are either married or gay, more's the pity."

Sophie smiled. "Only for us."

"This is true."

6

The desert dream starts in the alley behind Mr. Truepenny's shop—or at least where the alley's supposed to be. I'm in the back of the store with Jeck, poking around through the shelves of books, when I hear the sound of this flute. It goes on for a while, sort of lingering there in the back of my mind, until finally I get curious. I leave Jeck digging for treasure in a cardboard box of new arrivals and step past the door that leads into the store's small art gallery. The music is sort of atonal, and the instrument appears to have a limited range of notes, but there's something appealing about it all the same. I walk down a long narrow corridor, the walls encrusted with old portraits of thin, bearded men and women in dresses that appear far too stiff and ornately embroidered to be comfortable. The soles of my shoes squeak on the wooden floor in a rhythmic counterpoint to the music I'm following. I stop at the door at the far end of the hall. The music seems to be coming from the other side of it, so I open the door and step out, expecting to find myself in a familiar alleyway, but the alley's gone.

Instead, I'm standing in a desert. I turn around to see that the door through which I came has disappeared. All that I can see on every side of me is an endless panorama of desert, each compass point bordered by mountains. I seem to be as far from Mabon as that city is from the place where my body sleeps.

"What is this place?" I say.

My voice startles me, because I didn't realize I was speaking aloud. What startles me more is that my rhetorical question gets answered. I turn to see the oddest sight: There's a rattlesnake coiled up under a palo verde tree. The pale color of the tree's branches and twigs awakes an echoing green on the snake's scales which range through a gorgeous palette of golds and deep rusty reds. That's normal enough. What's so disconcerting is that the snake has the face of a Botticelli madonna—serene smile, rounded features enclosed by a cloud of dark ringlets. *The Virgin and Child With Singing Angels* comes immediately to mind. And she's got wings—creamy yellow wings that thrust out from the snake's body a few inches below the face. All that's lacking is a nimbus of gold light.

"A dreaming place," is what the snake has just said to me.

For all her serenity, she has an unblinking gaze which I doubt any of Botticelli's models had.

"But Mabon's already a dreaming place," I find myself replying, as though I always have conversations with snakes that have wings and human faces.

"Mabon is your dreaming place," she says. "Today you have strayed into someone else's."

"Whose?"

The snake doesn't reply.

"How do I get back to Mabon?"

Still no reply—at least not from her. Another voice answers me. This time it's that of a small owl, her feathers the color of a dead saguaro rib, streaks of silver-grey and black. She's perched on the arm of one of those tall cacti, looking down at me with another human face nestled there where an owl's beak and round eyes should be, calm madonna features surrounded by feathers. At least wings look normal on her.

"You can't return," she tells me. "You have to go on."

I hate the way that conversation can get snarled up in a dream like this: Every word an omen, every sentence a riddle.

"Go on to where?"

The owl turns her head sharply away then turns back and suddenly takes off from her perch. I catch a glimpse of a human torso in her chest feathers—breasts and a rounded belly—and then she's airborne, wings beating until she catches an updraft, and glides away. A stand of mesquite swallows her from my sight and she's gone. I turn back to the rattlesnake, but she's gone as well. The owl's advice rings in my mind.

You have to go on.

I look around me, mountains in every direction. I know distance can be deceiving in the open desert like this, in this kind of light, with that immense sprawl of sky above me. I feel as though I could just reach any one of those ranges in a half-hour walk, but I know it would really be days.

I find my sense of direction has gone askew. Normally, I relate to a body of water. In Newford, everything's north of the lake. In Mabon, everything's south. Here, I feel displaced. There's no water—or at least none of which I'm aware. I can see the sun is setting toward the west, but it doesn't feel right. My inner compass says it's setting in the north.

I turn slowly in place, regarding the distant mountain ranges that surround me. None of them draws me more than the other, and I don't know which way to go until I remember the sound of the flute that brought me here in the first place. It's still playing, a sweet low music on the edge of my hearing that calms the panic that was beginning to lodge in my chest.

So I follow it again, hiking through what's left of the afternoon until I don't feel I can go any further. The mountains in front of me don't seem any closer, the ones behind aren't any further away. I'm thirsty and tired. Every piece of vegetation has a cutting edge or a thorn. My calves ache, my back aches, my throat holds as much moisture as the dusty ground underfoot. I don't want to be here, but I can't seem to wake up.

It's the music, I realize. The music is keeping me here.

I've figured out what kind of flute is being played now: one of those medicine flutes indigenous to the Southwest. I remember Geordie had one a couple of years ago. It was almost the size of his Irish flute, with the same six holes on top, but it had an extra thumb hole around back and it didn't have nearly the same range of notes. It also had an odd addition: up by the air hole, tied to the body of the flute with leather thongs, was a saddle holding a reed. The saddle directed the air jet up or down against the lower reed, and it was adjustable. The sound was very pretty, but the instrument had next to no volume. Geordie eventually traded it in for some whistle or other, but I picked up a tape of its music to play when I'm working—medicine flute, rattles, rainstick and synthesizers. I can't remember the last time I listened to it.

After carefully checking the area around me for snakes or scorpions or God-knows-what else might be lurking about, I sit down on some rocks and try to think things through. I'd like to believe there's a reason for my being here, but I know the dreamlands don't usually work that way. They have their own internal logic; it's only our presence in them that's arbitrary. We move through them with the same randomness as the weather in our world: basically unpredictable, for all that we'd like to think otherwise.

No, I'm here as the result of my own interference. I followed the sound of the flute out the door into the desert of my own accord. I've no one to blame but myself. There'll be no escape except for that which I can make for myself.

I'm not alone here, though. I keep sensing presences just beyond my sight, spirits hovering in the corners of my eyes. They're like the snake and the owl I saw earlier, but much more shy. I catch the hint of a face in one of the cacti, here one moment, gone the next; a ghostly shape in the bristly branches of a smoke tree; a scurry of movement and a fleeting glimpse of something with half-human skin, half-fur or -scale, darting into a burrow: little madonna faces, winged rodents and lizards, birds with human eyes and noses.

I don't know why they're so scared of me. Maybe they're naturally cautious. Maybe there's something out here in the desert that they've got good reason to hide from.

This thought doesn't lend me any comfort at all. If there's something they're scared of, I don't doubt that I should be scared of it, too. And I would be, except I'm just too exhausted to care at the moment.

I rest my arms on my knees, my head on my arms. I feel a little giddy from the sun and definitely dehydrated. I came to the desert wearing only sneakers, a pair of jeans and a white blouse. The blouse is on my head and shoulders now, to keep off the sun, but it's left my arms, my lower back and my stomach exposed. They haven't so much browned as turned the pink that's going to be a burn in another couple of hours.

Something moves in the corner of my eye and I turn my head, but not quickly enough. It was something small, a flash of pale skin and light brown fur. Winged.

"Don't be scared!" I call after it. "I won't hurt you."

But the desert lies silent around me, except for the sound of the flute. I thought I caught a glimpse of the player an hour or so ago. I was cresting a hill and saw far ahead of me a small hunched shape disappear down into the arroyo. It looked like one of those pictographs you sometimes see in Hopi or Navajo art—a little hunchbacked man with hair like dreadlocks, playing a flute. I called after him at the time, but he never reappeared.

I hate this feeling of helplessness I have at the moment, of having to react rather than do, of having to wait for answers to come to me rather than seek them out on my own. I've walked for hours, but I can't help thinking how, realistically, all that effort was only killing time. I haven't gotten anywhere, I haven't learned anything new. I'm no further ahead than I was when I first stepped through that door and found myself here. I'm thirstier, I've got the beginning of a sunburn, and that about sums it up.

The air starts to cool as the sun goes down. I take my blouse off my head and put it back on, but it doesn't help much against the growing chill. I hear something rustle in the brush on the other side of the rocks where I'm sitting, and I almost can't be bothered turning my head to see what made the noise. But I look around all the same, and then I sit very still, hoping that the Indian woman I find regarding me won't be startled off like every other creature I've met since the owl gave me her cryptic advice.

The woman is taller than I am, but that's not saying much; at just over five feet tall, I'm smaller than almost everyone I meet. Her features have a pinched, almost foxlike cast about them, and she wears her hair in two long braids into which have been woven feathers and beads and cowrie shells. She's barefoot, which strikes me as odd, since this isn't exactly the most friendly terrain I've ever had to traverse. Her buckskin dress is almost a creamy white, decorated with intricate beadwork and stitching, and she's wearing a blanket over her shoulders like a shawl, the colors of which reflect the surrounding landscape—the browns and the tans, deep shadows and burnt siennas—only they're much more vibrant.

"Don't run off on me," I say, pitching my voice low and trying to seem as unthreatening as possible.

The woman smiles. She has a smile that transforms her face; it starts on her lips and in her dark eyes, but then the whole of her solemn copper-colored features fall easily into well-worn creases of good humor. I realize that hers is the first face I've seen in this place that didn't look as though it had been rendered by a Florentine painter at the height of the Italian Renaissance. She seems indisputably of this place, as though she was birthed from the cacti and the dry hills.

"Why do you think I would do that?" she asks. Her voice is melodious and sweet.

"So far, everybody else has."

"Perhaps you confuse them."

I have to laugh. "*I* confuse *them?* Oh please."

The woman shrugs. "This is a place of spirits, a land where totem may be found, spirits consulted, lessons learned, futures explored. Those who walk its hills for these reasons have had no easy task in coming here."

"I could show them this door I found," I start to joke, but I let my voice trail off. The crease lines of her humor are still there on her face, but they're in repose. She looks too serious for jokes right now.

"You have come looking for nothing," she goes on, "so your presence is a source of agitation."

"It's not something I planned," I assure her. "If you'll show me the way out, I'll be more than happy to go. Really."

The woman shook her head. "There is no way out— except by acquiring that which you came seeking."

"But I didn't come looking for anything."

"That presents a problem."

I don't like the way this conversation is going.

"For the only way you can leave in such a case," the woman goes on, "is if you accompany another seeker when their own journeying is done."

"That . . . that doesn't seem fair."

The woman nods. "There is much unfairness—even in the spirit realms. But obstacles are set before us in order that they may be overcome." She gives me a considering look. "Perhaps you are simply unaware of what you came seeking?"

She makes a question of it.

"I heard this flute," I say. "That's what I followed to get here."

"Ah."

I wait, but she doesn't expand beyond that one enigmatic utterance.

"Could you maybe give me a little more to go on than that?" I ask.

"You are an artist?" she asks.

The question surprises me, but I nod.

"Kokopelli," she says, "the flute-player you heard. He is known for his—" she hesitates for a moment. "—inspirational qualities."

"I'm not looking for ideas," I tell her. "I have more ideas than I know what to do with. The only thing I'm ever looking for is the time to put them into practice."

"Kokopelli or Coyote," she says. "One of them is responsible for your being here."

"Can they help me get back?"

"Where either of them is concerned, anything is possible."

There's something about the way she tells me this that seems to add an unspoken "when hell freezes over," and that makes me feel even more uneasy.

"Can you tell me where I might find them?"

The woman shrugs. "Kokopelli is only found when he wishes to be, but Coyote—Coyote is always near. Look for him to be cadging a cigarette, or warming his toes by a fire."

She starts to turn away, but pauses when I call after her.

"Wait!" I say. "You can't just leave me here."

"I'm sorry," she tells me, and she really does seem sorry. "But I have duties that require my attention. I came upon you only by chance and already I have stayed too long."

"Can't I just come along with you?"

"I'm afraid that would be impossible."

There's nothing mean about the way she says it, but I can tell right away that the question is definitely not open to further discussion.

"Will you come back when you're done?" I ask.

I'm desperate. I don't want to be here on my own anymore, especially not with night falling.

"I can't make you a promise of that," she says, "but I will try. In the meantime, you would do better to look within yourself, to see if hidden somewhere within you is some secret need that might have brought you to this place."

As she starts to turn away again, I think to ask her what her name is.

"Since I am Grandmother to so many here," she says, "that would be as good a name as any. You may call me Grandmother Toad."

"My name's Sophie."

"I know, little sister."

She's walking away as she speaks. I jump to my feet and follow after her, into the dusk that's settling in between the cacti and mesquite trees, but like everyone else I've met here, she's got the trick of disappering down pat. She steps into a shadow and she's gone.

A vast emptiness settles inside me after she's left me. The night is full of strange sounds, snuffling and rustles and weird cries in the distance that appear to be coming closer.

"Grandmother," I call softly.

I wonder, how did she know my name?

"Grandmother?"

There's no reply.

"Grandmother!"

I run to the top of another ridge, one from which I can see the last flood of light spraying up from the sunset. There's no sign, no trace at all of the Indian woman, but as I turn away, I see the flickering light of a campfire, burning there, below me in a dry wash. A figure sits in front of it. The sound of the flute is still distant, so I make the educated guess that it isn't Kokopelli hanging out down there. Grandmother's words return to my mind:

Look for him to be cadging a cigarette, or warming his toes by a fire.

I take one last look around me, then start down the hill toward Coyote's fire.

7

Sophie awoke in a tangle of sheets. She stared up at a familiar ceiling, then slowly turned her head to look at her bedside clock. The hour hand was creeping up on four. Relief flooded her.

I'm back, she thought.

She wasn't sure how it had happened, but somewhere in between leaving Grandmother Toad and starting down towards Coyote's fire, she'd managed to escape the desert dream. She lay there listening to the siren that had woken her, heard it pass her block and continue on. Sitting up, she fluffed her pillow, then lay down once more.

No more following the sound of a flute, she told herself, no matter how intriguing it might be.

Her eyelids grew heavy. Closing her eyes, she let herself drift off. Wait until she told Jeck, she thought. The desert she'd found herself in had been even stranger than the fens where she and Jeck had first met—if such a thing was possible. But when she fell asleep she bypassed Mr. Truepenny's shop and found herself scrambling down a desert incline to where a mesquite fire sent its flickering shadows along a dry wash.

8

"Little cousin," Coyote says after we've been sitting together in silence for some time. "What are you doing here?"

I can't believe I'm back here again. I would never have let myself go back to sleep if I'd thought this would happen. Still, I can't stay awake forever. That being the case, if every time I dream I'm going to find myself back here instead of in Mabon, I might as well deal with it now. But I'm not happy about it.

"I don't know," I tell him.

Coyote nods his head. He sits on his haunches, on the far side of the campfire. The pale light from the coals makes his eyes glitter and seem to be of two different colors: one brown, one blue. Except for his ears, his silhouette against the deep starry backdrop behind him belongs to a young man, long black hair braided and falling down either side of his head, body wrapped in a blanket. But the ears are those of the desert wolf whose name he bears: tall and pointed, lips quivering as they sort through the sounds drifting in from the night around them.

Wind in the mesquite. Tiny scurrying paws on the sand of the dry wash. Owl wings beating like a quickened breath. A sudden squeal. Silence. The sound of wings again, rising now. From further away, the soft grunting of javalinas feeding on prickly pear cacti.

When Coyote turns his head, a muzzle is added to his silhouette and there can be no pretending that he is other than what he is: a piece of myth set loose from old stories and come to add to the puzzle of my being here.

"So tell me," he says, a touch of amusement in his voice. "With your wise eyes so dark with secrets and insights lying thick about you like a cloak . . . what *do* you know?"

I can't tell if he's making fun of me or not.

"My name's Sophie," I tell him. "That's supposed to mean wisdom, but I don't feel very wise at the moment."

"Only fools think they're wise; the rest of us just muddle through as we can."

"I'm barely managing that."

"And yet you're here. You're alive. You breathe. You speak. Presumably, you think. You feel. The dead would give a great deal to be allowed so much."

"Look," I say. "All I know is that I stepped through a door in another dream and ended up here. I followed this Kokopelli's flute-playing and Grandmother Toad told me I have to stay here unless I either discover some secret need inside me that can be answered by the desert, or one of you help me find my way back."

"Kokopelli," Coyote says. "And Grandmother Toad. Such notable company to find oneself in."

Now I know he's mocking me, but I don't think it's meant

to be malicious. It's just his way. Besides, I find that I don't really care.

"Can you help me?" I ask.

"Can I help? I'm not sure. Will I help? I'll do my best. Never let it be said that I turned my back on a friend of both the flute-player and Nokomis."

"Who?"

"The Grandmother has many names—as does anyone who lives long enough. They catch on our clothes and get all snarled up in a tangle until sometimes even we can't remember who we are anymore."

"You're confusing me."

"But not deliberately so," Coyote says. "Let it go on record that any confusion arose simply because we lacked certain commonalities of reference."

I give him a blank look.

"Besides," he adds, "it was a joke. We always know who we are; what we sometimes forget are the appellations by which we come to be known. There are, you see, so many of them."

"I just want to get out of this place."

Coyote nods. "I must say, I have to admire anyone with such a strong sense of purpose. No messing about, straight to the point. It's refreshing, really. You wouldn't have a cigarette, would you?"

"Sorry, I don't smoke."

It's hard to believe that this is the same person who sat in silence across the fire from me for the better part of an hour before he even said hello. I wonder if archetypal spirits can be schizophrenic. Then I think, just being an archetype must make you schizophrenic. Imagine if your whole existence depended on how people remember you.

"I gave it up myself," Coyote says. Then he proceeds to open up a rolling paper, sprinkle tobacco onto it and roll himself a cigarette. He lights it with a twig from the fire, then blows a contented wreath of smoke up into the air where it twists and spins before it joins the rising column of smoke from the burning mesquite.

I'm beginning to realize that my companion's not exactly the most truthful person I'm going to meet in my life. I just hope he's more reliable when it comes to getting a job done or I'm going to be stuck in this desert for a very long time.

"So where do we start?" I ask.

"With metaphor?"

"What?"

"The use of one thing to explain another," Coyote says patiently.

"I know what it means. I just don't get your point."

"I thought we were trying to find your secret need."

I shake my head. "I don't *have* any secret needs."

"Are you sure?"

"I . . ."

"Are you sexually repressed?"

I can't believe I'm having this conversation.

"What's that got to do with *anything?*"

Coyote flicks the ash from the end of his cigarette. "It's this whole flute-player business," he says. "It's riddled with sexual innuendo, don't you see? He's a fertility symbol, now, very mythopoetic and all, but it wasn't always that way. Used to be a trader, a travelling merchant, hup-two-three. That hunched back was actually his pack of trading goods, the flute his way of approaching a settlement, *tootle-toot-toot,* it's only me, no danger, except if you were some nubile young thing. Had a woman in every town, you know—they didn't call him Koke the Poke for nothing. The years go by and suddenly our randy little friend finds himself elevated to minor deity status, gets all serious, kachina material, don't you know? Becomes a kind of erotic muse, if you will."

"But—"

"Ah, yes," Coyote says. "The metaphorical bit." He grinds his cigarette out and tosses the butt into the fire. "Your following the sound of his flute—*his* particular flute, if you get my meaning—and well, I won't say he's irresistible, but if one were to be suffering for a certain particular *need,* it might be quite difficult *not* to be drawn, willy-nilly, after him."

"What are you saying? That all I have to do is have sex here, and I get to leave?"

"No, no, no, no. Nothing so crass. Nothing so obvious. At this point it's all conjecture. We're simply exploring possibilities, some more delightful than others." He pauses and gives me a considering look. "You're not a nun, are you? You haven't taken one of those absurd vows that cut you off from what might otherwise be a full and healthy human existence?"

"I don't know about nuns," I tell him, "but I'm outta here."

I stand up, expecting him to make some sort of protest, but he just looks at me, curiously, and starts to roll another cigarette. I don't really want to go out into the desert night on my own, but I don't want to sit here and listen to his lunacy either.

"I thought you were going to help me," I say finally.

"I am, little cousin. I will."

He lights his cigarette and then pointedly waits for me to sit down again.

"Well, you haven't been much help so far," I say.

"Oh, right," he says, laying a hand theatrically across his brow. "Kill the messenger, why don't you."

I lean closer to the fire and take a good long look at him. "Is there *any* relevance to anything you have to say?" I ask.

"You brought up Kokopelli. You're the one who followed the music of his randy little flute. You can't blame me for any of that. If you've got a better idea, I'm all ears."

He cups his hands around those big coyote ears of his and leans forward as well. I try to keep a straight face, but all I can do is fall back on the ground and laugh.

"I was beginning to think you didn't have any sort of a sense of humor at all," he says when I finally catch my breath.

"It's not that. I just want to get away from here. When I dream, I want to go to Mabon—to where *I* want to go."

"Mabon?" Coyote says. "Mabon's yours? Oh, I love Mabon. The first time I ever heard the Sex Pistols was in Mabon. That was years ago now, but I couldn't believe how great they were."

Whereupon he launches into a version of "My Way" that's so off-key and out of time that it makes the version Sid Vicious did sound closer to Ol' Blue Eyes than I might ever have thought possible. From the hills around us, four-legged coyote voices take up the song, and soon the night is filled with this horrible caterwauling that's so loud it's making my teeth ache. All I want to do is bury my head or scream.

"Great place, Mabon," he says when he finally breaks off and the noise from his accompanists fades away.

Wonderful, I think. Not only am I stuck with him here, but now I find out that if I ever do get out of this desert, I could run into him again in my own dreaming place.

9

"I've got to figure out a way to sleep without dreaming," Sophie told Jilly.

They were taking a break from helping out at a bazaar for St. Vincent's Home for the Aged, drinking tea and sharing a bag of potato chips on the back steps of the old stone building. The sun was shining brightly, and it made Sophie's eyes ache. She hadn't slept at all last night in protest of how she felt Coyote was wasting her time.

"Still visiting the desert every night?" Jilly asked around a mouthful of chips.

Sophie gave her a mournful nod. "Pretty much. Unless I don't go to sleep."

"But I thought you liked the desert," Jilly said. "You came back from that vacation in New Mexico just raving about how great it was, how you were going to move down there, how we were all crazy not to think of doing the same."

"This is different. All I want to do is give it up."

Jilly shook her head. "I'm so envious of the way you get to go places when you dream. I would *never* want to give it up."

"You haven't met Coyote."

"Coyote was your favorite subject when you got back."

Sophie sighed. It was true. She'd become enamored with the Trickster figure on her vacation and had even named her last studio after a painting she'd bought in Santa Fe: Five Coyotes Singing.

"This Coyote's not the same," she said. "He's not all noble and mystical and, oh I don't know, mischievous, I suppose, in a sweet sort of a way. He's more like the souvenirs in the airport gift shop—fun if you're in the right mood, but sort of tacky at the same time. And definitely not very helpful. The only agenda he pursues with any real enthusiasm is trying to convince me to have sex with him."

Jilly raised her eyebrows. "Isn't that getting kind of kinky? I mean, how would you even do it?"

"Oh please. He's not a coyote all of the time. Mostly he's a man." Sophie frowned. "Mind you, even then he'll have the odd bit of coyote about him: ears, mostly. Sometimes a muzzle. Sometimes a tail."

Jilly reached for the chip bag, but it was empty. She shook out the last few crumbs and licked them from her palm, then crumpled the bag and stuck it in the pocket of her jacket.

"What am I going to *do*?" Sophie said.

"Beats me," Jilly said. "We should go back inside. Geordie's going to think we deserted him."

"You're not being any help at all."

"If it were up to me," Jilly said, "I'd join you in a minute. But it isn't. Or at least, we've yet to find a way to make it possible."

"He's going to drive me mad."

"Maybe you should give him a taste of his own medicine," Jilly said. "You know, act just as loony."

Sophie laughed. "Only you would think of that. And only you could pull it off. I wish there *was* some way to bring you over. Then I could just watch the two of you drive each other mad."

"You could always just sleep with him."

"I've been tempted—and not simply because I think it'd drive him away. He's really quite attractive, and he can be very . . . persuasive."

"But," Jilly said.

"But, I feel as though it'd be like eating the fruit in fairyland—if I give in to him, then I'll never be able to get away."

10

So every night when I dream, I come to the desert and Coyote and I go looking for my way out. And every night's a trial. My night-nerves are shot. I'm always on edge because I never know what's going to happen next, what he's going to want to discuss, when or if he's going to put a move on me. We never do find Kokopelli, but that's not the worst of it. The worst thing is that I'm actually getting used to this: to Coyote and his mad carrying-on. Not only used to it, but enjoying it. No matter how much Coyote exasperates me, I can't stay mad at him.

And my desert time's not all bad by any means. When Coyote's being good company, you couldn't ask for a better friend. The desert spirits aren't shy around him, either. The aunts and uncles, which are what he calls the saguaro, tell us stories, or sing songs, or sometimes just gossip. All those strange madonna-faced spirits drop by to visit us, in ones and twos and threes. Women with fox-ears or antlers. Bobcat and coati spirits. Cottontails, jack rabbits and pronghorns. Vultures and grouse and hawks. Snakes and scorpions and lizards. Smoke-tree ghosts and tiny fairy-duster sprites. Twisty cholla spirits, starburst yucca bogles and mesquite dryads draped in cloaks made of a thousand perfectly shaped miniature leaves.

The mind boggles at their variety and number. They come in every shape and size, but they all have that madonna resemblance, even the males. They're all that strange mix of human with beast or plant. And they all have their own stories and songs and dances to share.

So it's not all bad. But Kokopelli's flute-playing is always there, sometimes only audible when I'm very still, a Pied Piper covenant that I don't remember agreeing to, but it keeps me here. And it's that loss of choice that won't let me ever completely relax. The knowledge that I'm here, not because I want to be, but because I have to be.

One night Coyote and I are lying on a hilltop looking up at the stars. The aunts and uncles are murmuring all around us, a kind of wordless chant like a lullaby. A black-crested phainopepla is perched on my knee, strange little Botticelli features studying mine in between groomings. Coyote is smoking a cigarette, but it doesn't smell like tobacco—more like piñon. A dryad was sitting on an outcrop nearby, her skin the gorgeous green of her palo verde tree, but she's drifted away now.

"Grandmother Toad told me that this is a place where people come to find totem," I say after a while. I feel Coyote turn to look at me, but I keep my own gaze on the light show overhead. So many stars, so much sky. "Or they come to consult spirits, to learn from them."

"Nokomis is the wisest of us all. She would know."

"So how come we never see anybody else?"

"I'm nobody?" the little phainopepla warbles from my knee.

"You know what I mean. No people."

"It's a big desert," Coyote says.

"The first spirits I met here told me it was somebody else's dreaming place—the way Mabon is mine. But they wouldn't tell me whose."

"Spirits can be like that," Coyote says.

The phainopepla frowns at the both of us, then flies away.

"Is it your dreaming place?" I ask him.

"If it was my dreaming place," he says, "when I did this—" He reaches a hand over and cups my breast. I sit up and move out of his reach. "—you'd fall into my arms and we'd have glorious sex the whole night long."

"I see," I say dryly.

Coyote sits up and grins. "Well, you asked."

"Not for a demonstration."

"What is that frightens you about having sex with me?"

"It's not a matter of being frightened," I tell him. "It's the consequences that might result from our doing it."

He reaches into his pocket and pulls out a condom. I can't *believe* this guy.

"That's not quite what I had in mind," I say.

"Ah. You're afraid of the psychic ramifications."

"Say what?"

"You're afraid that having sex with me will trap you here forever."

Am I that open a book?

"The thought has crossed my mind," I tell him.

"But maybe it'll free you instead."

I wait, but he doesn't say anything more. "Only you're not telling, right?" I ask.

"Only I don't know," he says. He rolls himself another cigarette and lights up. Blowing out a wreath of smoke, he shoots me a sudden grin. "I don't know, and you don't know, and the way things are going, I guess we never will, hey?"

I can't help but react to that lopsided grin of his. Frustrated as I'm feeling, I still have to laugh. He's got more charm than any one person deserves, and when he turns it on like this, I don't know whether to give him a hug or a bang on the ear.

11

A week after her show closed at The Green Man Gallery, Sophie appeared on Max Hannon's doorstep with *Hearts Like Fire, Burning* under her arm, wrapped in brown paper.

"You didn't pick it up," she said when he answered the bell, "so I thought I'd deliver it."

Max regarded her with surprise. "I really didn't think you were serious."

"But you will take it?" Sophie asked. She handed the package over as though there could be no question to Max's response.

"I'll treasure it forever," he said, smiling. Stepping to one side so that she could go by him, he added, "Would you like to come in?"

It was roomier inside Max's house than it looked to be from the outside. Renovations had obviously been done, since the whole of the downstairs was laid out in an open layout broken only by the necessary support beams. The kitchen was off in one corner, separated from the rest of the room by an island counter. Another corner held a desk and some bookcases. The remainder of the room consisted of a comfortable living space of sprawling sofas and armchairs, low tables, Navajo carpets and display cabinets.

There was art everywhere—on the walls, as might be expected: posters, reproductions and a few originals, but there was even more three-dimensional work. The sculptures made Sophie's heartbeat quicken. Wherever she looked there were representations of the desert spirits she'd come to know so well, those strange creatures with their human features and torsos peeping out from their feathers and fur, or their thorny cacti cloaks. Sophie was utterly entranced by them, by how faithful they were to the spirits from her desert dream.

"It's funny," Max said, laying the painting she'd given him down on a nearby table. The two ocotillo cacti spirit statues that made up the centerpiece seemed to bend their long-branched forms toward the package, as though curious about what it held. "I was thinking about you just the other day."

"You were?"

Max nodded. "I remembered why it was that you looked so familiar to me when we met at your opening."

If her desert dream hadn't started up after that night, Sophie might have expected him to tell her now that he was one of its spirits and it was from seeing her in that otherworldly realm that he knew her. But it couldn't be so. She hadn't followed Kokopelli's flute until after she'd met Max.

"I would have remembered it if we'd ever met," she said.

"I didn't say we'd actually met."

"Now you've got me all curious."

"Maybe we should leave it a mystery."

"Don't you dare," Sophie said. "You have to tell me now."

"I'd rather show you than tell you," Max said. "Just give me a moment."

He went up a set of stairs over by the kitchen area that Sophie hadn't noticed earlier. Once he was gone, she wandered about the large downstairs room to give the statues a closer look. The resemblances were uncanny. It wasn't so much that he'd captured the exact details of her dream's desert fauna as that his sculptures contained an overall sense of the same spirit; they captured the elemental, inherent truth rather than recognizable renderings. She was crouched beside a table, peering at a statue of a desert woodrat with human hands, when Max returned with a small painting in hand.

"This is where I first saw you," he said.

Sophie had to smile. She remembered the painting. Jilly had done it years ago: a portrait of Wendy, LaDonna and her, sitting on the back steps of a Yoors Street music club, Wendy and LaDonna scruffy as always, bookending Sophie in a pleated skirt and silk blouse, the three of them caught in the circle of light cast by a nearby streetlight. Jilly had called it *The Three Muses Pause to Reconsider Their Night*.

"This was Peter's," Max said. "He loved this painting and kept it hanging in his office by his desk. The idea of the Muses having a girl's night out on the town appealed to the whimsical side of his nature. I'd forgotten all about it until I was up there the other day looking for some papers."

"I haven't thought of that painting in years," Sophie told him. "You know Jilly actually made us sit for it at night on those very steps—at least for her initial sketches, which were far more detailed than they had any need to be. I think she did them that way just to see how long we'd actually put up with sitting there."

"And how long did you sit?"

"I don't know. A few hours, I suppose. But it *seemed* like weeks. Is this your work?" she added, pointing to the statues.

Max nodded.

"I just love them," she said. "You don't show in Newford, do you? I mean, I would have remembered these if I'd seen them before."

"I used to ship all my work back to the galleries in Arizona where I first started to sell. But I haven't done any sculpting for a few years now."

"Why not? They're so good."

Max shrugged. "Different priorities. It's funny how it works, how we define ourselves. I used to think of myself as a sculptor first—everything else came second. Then when the eighties arrived, I came out and thought of myself as gay first, and only then as a sculptor. Now I define myself as an AIDS activist before anything else. Most of my time these days is taken up in editing a newsletter that deals with alternative therapies for those with HIV."

Sophie thought of the book she'd seen lying on one of the tables when she was looking at the sculptures. *Staying Healthy With HIV* by David Baker and Richard Copeland.

"Your friend Peter," she said. "Did he die of AIDS?"

"Actually, you don't die of AIDS," Max said. "AIDS destroys your immune system and it's some other illness that kills you—something your body would have been able to deal with otherwise." He gave her a sad smile. "But no. Ironically, I was the one who tested positive for HIV. Peter had leukemia. It had been in remission for a couple of years, but just before we went to the desert it came back and we had to go through it all again: the chemo treatments and the sleepless nights, the stomach cramps and awful rashes. I was sure that he'd pulled through once more, but then he died a week after we returned."

Max ran his finger along the sloped back of a statue of a

horned owl whose human features seemed to echo Max's own. "I think Peter had a premonition that he was going to die, and that was why he was so insistent we visit the desert one more time. He had a spiritual awakening there after one of his bouts with the disease and afterwards, he always considered the desert as the homeground for everything he held most dear." Max smiled, remembering. "We met because of these statues. He would have moved there, except for his job. Instead, I moved here."

Sophie got a strange feeling as Max spoke of Peter's love for the desert.

"Remember we talked about dreams at the opening?" she said.

Max nodded. "Serial dreams—what a lovely conceit."

"What I was telling you wasn't something I made up. And ever since that night I've been dreaming of a desert—a desert filled up with these." Sophie included all of the statuary with a vague wave of her hand. "Except in my desert they aren't statues; they're real."

"Real."

"I know it sounds completely bizarre, but it's true. My dreams are true. I mean, they're not so much dreams as me visiting some other place."

Max gave her an odd look. "Whenever someone talked about what an imagination I must have to do such work, Peter would always insist that it was all based on reality—it was just a reality that most people couldn't see into."

"And are they?"

"I . . ." Max looked away from her to the statues. He lay his hand on the back of the owl-man again, fingers rediscovering the contours they had pulled from the clay. "I should show you Peter's office," he said when he finally looked up.

He led her up to the second floor which was laid out in a more traditional style, a hallway with doors leading off from it, two on one side, three on the other. Max opened the door at the head of the stairs and ushered her in ahead of him.

"I haven't been able to deal with any of this yet," he said. "What to keep . . . what not . . ."

A large desk stood by the window, covered with books, papers and a small computer, but Sophie didn't notice any of that at first. Her attention was caught and trapped by the rooms' other furnishings: the framed photographs of the desert and leather-skinned drums that hung on the walls; a cabinet holding kachina figures, a medicine flute, rattles, fetishes and other artifacts; the array of Max's sculptures that peered at her from every corner of the room. She turned slowly on the spot, taking it all in, until her gaze settled on the familiar face of one of the sculptures.

"Coyote," she said softly.

Max spoke up from the doorway. "Careful. You know what they say about him."

Sophie shook her head.

"Don't attract his attention."

"Why?" Sophie asked, turning to look at Max. "Is he malevolent? Or dangerous?"

"By all accounts, no. He just doesn't think things through before he takes action. But while he usually emerges intact from his misadventures, his companions aren't always quite so lucky. Spending time with Coyote is like opening your life to disorder."

Sophie smiled. "That sounds like Coyote, all right."

Her gaze went back to the cabinet and the medicine flute that lay on its second shelf between two kachinas. One was the Storyteller, her comical features the color of red clay; the other was Kokopelli. The medicine flute itself was similar to the one that Geordie had traded away, only much more beautifully crafted. But then everything in this room had a resonance of communion with more than the naked eye could see—a sense of the sacred.

"Did Peter play the flute?" she asked.

"The one in the cabinet?"

"Mmm."

"Only in the desert. It has next to no volume, but a haunting tone."

Sophie nodded. "I know."

"He'd play that flute and his drums and rattles. He'd go

to sweats and drumming nights when we were down there. I used to tease him about trying to be an Indian, but he said that the Red Road was open to anyone who walked it with respect."

"The Red Road?"

"Native spiritual beliefs. I went with him sometimes, but I never really felt comfortable." He touched the nearest statue, an intricate depiction of a prickly pear spirit. "I love the desert, too, but I've never been much of a joiner."

"Did that disappoint Peter?"

Max shook his head. "Peter was one of the most open-minded, easygoing individuals you could ever have met. He always accepted people for what they were."

"Sounds like Jilly. No wonder they got along."

"You mean because of the painting?"

Sophie nodded.

"Peter never met her. I bought it for him at one of her shows. He fell in love with it on the spot—much as I did with the painting you gave me today." An awkward smile touched his lips. "I had more money in those days."

"Please don't feel guilty about it," Sophie told him, "or you'll spoil the pleasure of my giving it to you."

"I'll try."

"So did Peter have desert dreams?" Sophie asked. "Like mine?"

"He never told me that he had serial dreams, but he did dream of the desert. What are yours like?"

"This could take a while."

"I've got the time."

So while Max sat in the chair at Peter's desk, Sophie walked about the room and told him, not only about the desert dream and Coyote, but about Mabon and Jeck and the whole strange life she had when she stepped into her dreams.

"There's something odd about Coyote referring to Noko-mis," Max said when she was done.

"Why's that?"

"Well, everything else in your desert relates to the Southwest except for her. Nokomis and Grandmother Toad—those are terms that relate to our part of the world. They come from the lexicon of our own local tribes like the Kickaha."

"So what are you saying?"

Max shrugged. "Maybe Coyote was the woman who sent you looking for him in the first place."

"But why would he do that?"

"Who knows why Coyote does anything? Maybe he just took a liking to you and decided to meet you in a roundabout way."

"So was he Kokopelli as well?" Sophie asked. "Because it's the flute-playing that got me there in the first place."

"I don't know."

But Sophie thought perhaps she did. She stood before the cabinet that held Peter's medicine flute. It was too much of a coincidence—Max's sculptures, Peter's interest in the desert. The feeling came to her that somehow she'd gotten caught up in unfinished business between the two, neither quite willing to let the other go, so they were haunting each other.

She turned to look at Max, but decided she needed one more night in her desert dream before she was ready to bring up that particular theory with him.

"It feels good being able to talk about this with someone," she said instead. "The only other person I've ever told it to is Jilly and frankly, she and Coyote are almost cut from the same cloth. The only difference is that Jilly's not quite as outrageous as he is, and she's not always talking about sex. Everything Coyote wants to talk about eventually relates to sex."

"And *have* you slept with him?"

Sophie smiled. "I guess there's a bit of Coyote in you, too."

"I think there's a bit of him in every one of us."

"Probably. But to answer your question: No, I haven't. I'll admit I've come close—he can be awfully persuasive—but I have the feeling that if I slept with him, I'd be in more trouble than I already am. I'd be trapped in those dreams forever and I can't see that being worth one night's pleasure."

Max shook his head. "I hate it when people try to divorce sex from the other aspects of their life. It's too entwined with everything we are for us to be able to do that. It's like when some people find out that I have HIV. They expect me to disavow sex. They tell me that promiscuity got me into this position in the first place, so I should just stop thinking about it, writing about it, doing it. But if I did that, then I'd be giving up. My sexuality is too much a part of who I am, as a person and as an artist, for me not to acknowledge its importance in my life. I may not be looking for a partner right now. I may not live to be forty. But I'll be damned if I'll live like a eunuch just because of the shitty hand I got dealt with this disease."

"So you think I should sleep with him."

"I'm not saying that at all," Max replied. "I'm saying that sex is the life energy, and our sexuality is how we connect to it. Whether or not you sleep with Coyote or anyone else isn't going to trap you in this faerie otherworld, or even get you infected with some disease. It's *why* you have sex with whoever you've chosen as your partner. The desire has to include some spiritual connection. You have to care enough about the other person—and that naturally includes taking all the necessary precautions.

"How often or with how many people you have sex isn't the issue at all. It's not about monogamy versus promiscuity; it's about how much love enters the equation. If there's a positive energy between you and Coyote, if you really care about him and he cares for you, then the experience can only be positive—even if you never see each other again. If that energy and caring isn't there, then you shouldn't even be thinking about having sex with him in the first place."

12

So now I'm feeling cocky. I think I've got the whole thing figured out. Those first spirits told me the truth: This isn't my dreaming place. It's either Peter's or Max's, I don't know which yet. One of them hasn't let go of the other, and whichever one of the two it is, he's trying to hang on to the other one. Maybe the desert belongs to Max and he doesn't know it. Maybe it's his way of keeping Peter alive, and I just tumbled into the place through having met him that night at my opening. Or maybe it belongs to Peter; Peter wearing Kokopelli's guise in this desert, calling me up by mistake instead of Max. He probably got me because I'm such a strong dreamer, and when he saw his mistake, he just took off, leaving me to fend for myself. Or maybe he doesn't even know I'm here. But it's got to be one or the other, and talking to Kokopelli is going to tell me which.

"No more fooling around," I tell Coyote. "I want to find Kokopelli."

"I'm doing my best," he says. "But that flute-player—he's not an easy fellow to track down."

We're sitting by another mesquite fire in another dry wash—or maybe it's the same one where we first met. Every place starts to look the same around here after a while. It's a little past noon, the sun's high. Ground-doves fill the air with their mournful *coo-ooh, coo-ooh* sound, and a hawk hangs high above the saguaro—a smudge of shadow against the blue. Coyote has coffee brewing on the fire and a cigarette dangling from the corner of his mouth. He looks almost human today, except for the coyote ears and the long stiff whiskers standing out from around his mouth. I keep expecting one of them to catch fire, but they never do.

"I'm serious, Coyote."

"There's people put chicory in with their coffee, but it just doesn't taste the same to me," he says. "I'm not looking for a smooth taste when I make coffee. I want my spoon to stand up in the cup."

He looks at me with those mismatched eyes of his, pretending he's as guileless as a newborn babe, but while my father might have made some mistakes in his life, raising me to be stupid wasn't one of them.

"If you'd wanted to," I say, "we could have found Kokopelli weeks ago."

The medicine flute is still playing, soft as a distant breeze. It's always playing when I'm here—never close by, but never so far away that I can't hear it anymore.

"You could take me to him right now . . . if you wanted to."

"The thing is," Coyote says, "nothing's as easy as we'd like it to be."

"Don't I know it," I mutter, but he's not even listening to me.

"And the real trouble comes from not knowing what we really want in the first place."

"I know what I want—to find Kokopelli, or whoever it is playing that flute."

"Did I ever tell you," Coyote says, "about the time Barking Dog was lying under a mesquite tree, just after a thunderstorm?"

"I don't want to hear another one of your stories."

13

But Coyote says:

Barking Dog looks up and the whole sky is filled with a rainbow. Now how can I get up there? he thinks. Those colors are just the paints I need for my arrows.

Then he sees Buzzard, and he cries: "Hey, Uncle! Can you take me up there so that I can get some arrow paint?"

"Sure, nephew. Climb up on my back."

Barking Dog does and Buzzard flies up and up until they reach the very edge of the sky.

"You wait here," Buzzard says, "while I get those paints for you."

So Barking Dog hangs there from the edge of the sky, and

he's hanging there, but Buzzard doesn't come back. Barking Dog yells and he's making an awful racket, but he doesn't see anyone and finally he can't hang on any more and down he falls. It took Buzzard no time at all to get to the edge of the sky, but it takes Barking Dog two weeks to fall all the way back down—bang! Right into an old hollow tree and he lands so hard, he gets stuck and he can't get out.

A young woman's walking by right about then, looking for honey. She spies a hole in that old hollow tree and what does she see but Barking Dog's pubic hairs, sticking out of the hole. Oh my, she's thinking. There's a bear stuck in this tree. So she pulls out one of those hairs and goes running home to her husband with it.

"Oh, this comes from a bear, don't doubt it" her husband says.

He gets his bow and arrows and the two of them go back to the tree. The young woman, she's got an axe and she starts to chop at that tree. Her husband, he's standing by, ready to shoot that bear when the hole's big enough, but then they hear a voice come out of the tree:

"Cousin, make that hole bigger."

The young woman has to laugh. "That's no bear," she tells her husband. "That's Barking Dog, got himself stuck in a tree."

So she chops some more and soon Barking Dog crawls out of that tree and he shakes the dust and the dirt from himself.

"We thought you were a bear," the young woman says.

Her husband nods. "We could've used that meat."

Barking Dog turns back to the tree and gives it a kick. "Get out of there, you old lazy bear," he cries and when a bear comes out, he kills it and gives the meat to the young woman and her husband. Then he goes off, and you know what he's thinking? He's thinking, I wonder what ever happened to Buzzard.

14

"Was I supposed to get something out of that story," I ask "or were you just letting out some hot air?"

"Coffee's ready," he says. "You want some?"

He offers me a blue enameled mug filled with a thick, dark brown liquid. The only resemblance it bears to the coffee I'd make for myself is that it has the same smell. I take the mug from him. Gingerly, I lift it up to my lips and give it a sniff. The steam rising from it makes my eyes water.

"You didn't answer me," I say as I set the mug in the dirt down by my knee, its contents untouched.

Coyote takes a long swallow, then shrugs. "I don't know the answer to everything," he says.

"But you told me you could find him for me."

"I told you I would try."

"This is trying?" I ask. "Sitting around a campfire, drinking coffee and smoking cigarettes and telling stories that don't make any sense?"

He gives me a hurt look. "I thought you liked my company."

"I do. It's just—"

"I thought we were friends. What were you planning to do? Dump me as soon as we found the flute player?"

"No. Of course not. It's just that I want . . . I need to have some control over my dreams."

"But you do have control over your dreams."

"Then what am I doing here? How come every time I fall asleep, I end up *here*?"

"When you figure that out," Coyote says, "everything else will fall into place."

"What do you think I've been trying to do all this time?"

Coyote takes another long swallow from his mug. "The people of your world," he says, "you live two lives—an outer life that everyone can see, and another secret life inside your head. In one of those lives you can start out on a journey and reach your destination, but when you take a trip in the other, there's no end."

"What do you mean there's no end?"

Coyote shrugs. "It's the way you think. One thing leads to another and before you know it you're a thousand miles from where you thought you'd be, and you can't even remember where it was you thought you were going in the first place."

"Not everybody dreams the way I do," I tell him.

"No. But everybody's got a secret life inside their head. The difference is, you've got a stage to act yours out on."

"So none of this is real."

"I didn't say that."

"So what are you saying?"

Coyote lights another cigarette, then finishes his coffee. "Good coffee, this," he tells me.

15

"And these stories of his," Sophie said. "They just drive me crazy."

Jilly looked up from her canvas to where Sophie was slouching in the window seat of her studio. "I kind of like them. They're so zen."

"Oh please. You can keep zen. I just want something to make sense."

"Okay," Jilly said. She set her brush aside and joined Sophie in the window seat. "To start with, Barking Dog is just another one of Coyote's names."

"Really?"

Jilly nodded. "It's a literal translation of *Canis latrans,* which is Coyote's scientific name. That last story was his way of telling you that the two of you are much the same."

"I said sense," Sophie said. "You know, the way the rest of the world defines the term?"

"But it does make sense. In the story, Coyote's looking for arrow paints, but after he gets sidetracked, all he can do is wonder what happened to Buzzard."

"And?"

"You were following this flute music, but all you can think of now is finding Kokopelli."

"But *he's* the one playing the flute."

"You don't know that."

"Nokomis told me it was either Coyote or Kokopelli who tricked me into this desert dream. And she told me that it was Kokopelli's flute that I heard."

Jilly nodded. "But then think of what Max told you about how out of context she is. You've got a dream filled with desert imagery, so what's a moon deity from the eastern woodlands doing there?"

"Maybe she just got sidetracked."

"And maybe she really was Coyote in another guise. And if that's true, can you trust anything she told you?"

Sophie banged the back of her head against the window frame and let out a long sigh. "Great," she said. "That's just what I needed—to be even more confused about all of this than I already am."

"If you ask me," Jilly said, "I think it's time you left Coyote behind and struck out on your own to find your own answers."

"You don't know how good he is at sulking."

Jilly laughed. "So let him tag along. Just take the lead for a change."

So that night Sophie put on the tape she'd bought around the time Geordie was messing around with his medicine flute. *Coyote Love Medicine* by Jessita Reyes. She lay down on her bed and concentrated on the sound of Reyes's flute, letting its breathy sound fill her until its music and the music that drew her into the desert dream became one.

16

Coyote's stretched out on a rock, the brim of his hat pulled down low to shade his eyes. Today he's got human ears, a human face. He's also got a bushy tail of which he seems inordinately proud. He keeps grooming it with his long brown fingers, combing out knots that aren't there, fluffing out parts that just won't fluff out any further. He lifts the brim of his hat with a finger when he sees me start off.

"Where are you going?" he asks.

"I've got an appointment."

From lying there all languid in the sun, with only enough energy to roll himself a cigarette and groom that fine tail of his, suddenly he bounds to his feet and falls into step beside me.

"Who're you going to see?" he wants to know.

"Kokopelli."

"You know where he is?"

I shake my head. "I thought I'd let him find me."

I hold the music of the medicine flute in my mind and let it draw me through the cacti and scrub. We top one hill, scramble down the dusty slope of an arroyo, make our way up the next steep incline. We finally pull ourselves up to the top of a butte, and there he is, sitting crosslegged on the red stone, a slim, handsome man, dark hair cut in a shaggy pageboy, wearing white trousers and a white tunic, a plain wooden medicine flute lying across his knees. A worn cloth backpack lies on the stone beside him.

For the first time since I stepped into this desert dream all those weeks ago, I don't hear the flute anymore. There's just the memory of it lying there in my mind—fueled by the cassette that's playing back in that world where another part of me is sleeping.

Kokopelli looks from Coyote to me.

"Hey, Ihu," he says. "Hey, Sophie."

I shoot Coyote a dirty look, but he doesn't even have the decency to look embarrassed at how easy it was for me to track Kokopelli down.

"How do you know my name?" I ask the flute-player.

He gives me a little shrug. "The whole desert's been talking about you, walking here, walking there, looking everywhere for what's sitting right there inside you all the time."

I'm really tired of opaque conversations, and I tell him as much.

"Your problem," he says, "is that you can't seem to take

anything at face value. Everything you're told doesn't necessarily have to have a hidden meaning."

"Okay," I say. "If everything's going to be so straightforward now, tell me: Which one are you? Peter or Max?"

Kokopelli smiles. "That would make everything so easy, wouldn't it?"

"What do you mean?"

"For me to be one or the other."

"You said this was going to be a straightforward conversation," I say.

I turn to Coyote, though why I expect him to back me up on this, I've no idea. Doesn't matter anyway. Coyote's not there anymore. It's just me and the flute-player, sitting up on the red stone of this butte.

"I didn't say it would be straightforward," Kokopelli tells me. "I said that sometimes you should try to take what you're told at face value."

I sigh and look away. It's some view we have. From this height, the whole desert is lain out before us.

"This isn't about Peter or Max, is it?" I say.

Kokopelli shakes his head. "It's about you. It's about what you want out of your life."

"So Coyote was telling me the truth all along."

"Ihu was telling you a piece of the truth."

"But I followed your flute to get here."

Kokopelli shakes his head again. "You were following a need that you dressed up as my music."

"So all of this—" I wave my hand to encompass everything, the butte, the desert, Kokopelli, my being here. "—Where does it fit in?"

"It's different for everyone who comes. When you travel in a dream, you can bring nothing across with you; you can bring nothing back. Only what is in your head."

And that's my real problem. I know my dream worlds are real, but it's a different kind of real from what I can find in the waking world. I work out all of my problems in my dreams—from my mother abandoning me to my never seeming to be able to maintain a good relationship. But the solutions don't have any real holding power. They don't ever seem to resonate with the same truth in the waking world as they do in my dreams. And that's because I can't bring anything tangible back with me. I have to take it all on faith and for some things, faith isn't enough.

"Perhaps you expect too much," Kokopelli says when I try to explain this to him. "We are shaped by our experiences, and no matter where those experiences occur, they are still valid. The things you have seen and done don't lose their resonance because you can only hold them in your memory. In that sense there is little difference between what you experience when you are awake or when you dream. Keepsakes, mementos, tokens . . . their real potency lies in the memories they call up, rather than what they are in and of themselves."

"But I don't always understand the things I experience."

Kokopelli smiles. "Without mysteries, life would be very dull indeed. What would be left to strive for if everything were known?"

He picks up his flute and begins to play. His music carries us through the afternoon until the shadows deepen and twilight mutes the details of the desert around us. Although I don't hear a pause in the music, at some point he's put on his pack and I look up to see him silhouetted against the sunset. For a moment I don't see a man, but a hunchbacked flute-playing kachina.

"Tell Max," he says, "to remember me as loving him."

And then he steps away, into the night, into the desert, into the sky—I don't know where. I just know he's gone, the sound of his flute is a dying echo, and I'm left with another mystery that has no answer:

If he was Peter, how did he know so much about me?

And if he wasn't, then who was he?

17

"I've been thinking a lot about the desert lately," Max said.

He and Sophie were having a late dinner in The Rusty

Lion after taking in a show. They had a table by the window and could watch the bustling crowds go by on Lee Street from where they sat.

"Are you thinking of moving back to Arizona?" Sophie asked.

Max shook his head. "I probably will one day, but not yet. No, I was thinking more of the desert as a metaphor for how my life has turned out."

Sophie had often tried to imagine what it would be like to live with a terminal disease, and she thought Max was probably right. It would be very much like the desert: the barrenness, the vast empty reaches. Everything honed to its purest essence, just struggling to survive. There wouldn't be time for anything more. She wondered if she'd resent the rich forests of other people's lives, if she knew her own future could be cut short at any time.

"I think I know what you mean," she said.

Max laughed. "I can tell by the way you look that you've completely misunderstood me. You're thinking of the desert as a hopeless place, right?"

"Well, not exactly hopeless, but . . ."

"It's just the opposite," Max said. "The desert brings home how precious life is and how much we should appreciate it while we have it. That life can still flourish under such severe conditions is a miracle. It's an inspiration to me."

"You're amazing, you know that?"

"Not really. We all know we're going to die someday, but we like to pretend we won't. Given the hand I've been dealt, I don't have the luxury of that pretense. I have to live with the reality of my mortality every day of my life. Now I could just give up—and I won't pretend to you that I don't have my bad days. But when I tested positive, I made myself a promise that I was going to dedicate whatever time I have left to two things: to fight the stigmas attached to this disease, and to squeeze everything I can out of life."

The waitress came by with their orders then and for a while they were kept busy with their meals.

"You look a little gloomy," Max said later, when they

were waiting for their coffees. "I hope I didn't bring **you** down."

"No, it's not that."

"So tell Uncle Max what's bothering you."

"My problems seem so petty compared to what you have to put up with."

"Doesn't make them any less real for you, though. So 'fess up. Are you having man trouble again? We can be such bitches, can't we?"

"I suppose," Sophie said with a smile, then her features grew serious. "I just get tired of arguing. Everything starts out fine, but it always ends up with me having to adjust my life to theirs and I'm just not ready to do that anymore. I mean, I know there's going to be compromise in a relationship, but why does it always have to be on my side?"

"Compromise is necessary," Max agreed, "so long as you never give up who you are. That isn't compromise; that's spiritual death. You have to remain true to yourself."

"That's what I keep telling myself, but it doesn't make it any easier."

"Somewhere there is someone who'll love you for who are, not what they think you should be."

"And if there isn't?" Sophie said. "If I never connect with that person?"

"Then you'll be alone."

"Alone."

Sophie sighed. She was too familiar with what it meant to be alone.

"It's hard to be alone, isn't it?" Max said.

Sophie nodded.

"But better to be alone than to settle for less than what you need . . . less than what you deserve."

"I suppose."

"Here," Max said. He reached down under his chair for the package he'd carried into the restaurant when he'd arrived. "Maybe this'll cheer you up."

He put the package on the table between them. Sophie looked at him.

"What is it?" she asked.

"Open it up and find out."

Inside was one of Max's sculptures—a new one. Sophie recognized herself in one small figurine that made up the tableau, only she was decked out in a leather cap from which sprang a deer's antlers giving her a very mythic air. She stood in front of a saguaro on which was perched a tiny owl with a woman's face. Lounging on a rock beside her was a familiar figure in jeans, shirt and vest, coyote features under the cowboy hat. On the ground between them lay a medicine flute.

"It's beautiful," she said, looking up at Max.

"It's for you."

"I just—"

"Don't you even dare say you can't accept it."

"I just love it," Sophie said.

"Like I said," Max told her. "I've been thinking a lot about the desert lately."

"Me, too."

18

Sometimes when I'm in Mabon, walking its streets while my body's sleeping a world away, I'll get a whiff of smoke that smells like piñon and then somewhere in the crowd I'll spot a lean man who I swear has coyote ears poking up out of his hair, but he's always gone before I can get close enough to be sure.

Coyote was right about one thing: The journeys we take inside our heads never end.

I never thought I'd say this, but I miss him.

DREAM HARDER,
DREAM TRUE

—◆—

*Man is a genius when he dreams. Dream
what you're capable of. The harder you
dream it, the sooner it will come true.*
          —attributed to Akira Kurosawa

1

The best artists know what to leave out. They know how
much of the support should show through as the pigment is
applied, what details aren't necessary. They suggest, and let
the viewer fill in whatever else is needed to make the communication complete. They aren't afraid to work with a
smaller palette, to delete excess verbiage or place rests on
the musical staff, for they know that almost every creative
endeavor can be improved with a certain measure of under-
statement. For isn't it the silence between the notes that
often gives music its resonance? What lies between the lines
of the poem or story, the dialogue the actor doesn't speak,
the pauses between the dancer's steps? The spaces can be
just as important as what's distinctly portrayed.

So it's not important where the angel came from, or how
she broke her wing. Only that she was there for Jean to find.

2

I'm not saying the city was perfect back then, but it was
safer. There were still jobs to be had, and every neighbor-

hood had its own sense of community. The streets and alley-ways were swept clean on a regular basis, and it actually made a difference. There was crime, but its reporting was met with shock rather than a shrug. The state sanatoriums had yet to release the majority of their inmates and put them out onto the street—a seeding of homelessness that spread in the streets the way weeds will in an untended garden. Some might say it was a different world entirely through which Jean Etoile made his way home that autumn day.

Jean was a nondescript individual, neither short nor tall, neither ugly nor handsome; the sort of man you might pass on the street even now and never give a second glance: plain grey suit, white shirt and dark tie, briefcase in hand. Brown hair and eyes, with a pleasant smile, though he showed it rarely. When he passed the time of day with his neighbors, he spoke of the weather, of baseball scores and, yes, wasn't it a pity about old Mrs. Rather down the street, may she rest in peace. Not at all the sort of person one would imagine might bring home a prostitute to live with him in his apartment.

To be fair, Jean didn't know for certain that Candida was a prostitute. It was merely the assumption he'd made when he went to put out his garbage the night before and found her hiding by the back steps of his apartment building in Lower Foxville.

Jean had a secret addiction to mystery and pulp novels—stories by Mickey Spillane, Richard S. Prather, Lionel White and the like; stories about tough criminals and tougher cops, hard-boiled PIs and big-hearted hookers—so he felt he knew more than most about the dark side of the city, the side ruled by the night, with its wet streets and neon lights, deals going down in alleyways and pimps running their women, broad-shouldered men with guns under their sportsjackets. And in their hearts, the need to see justice served. When he saw such a beautiful woman in her tight, short dress and stiletto heels, eyelids dark with shadow, rouged cheeks and cherry-red lips, hiding there by his back steps, of all places, he knew she was on the run. Knew she needed help. And while he had neither broad shoulders nor a gun, he did carry in his heart a need to see justice done. It was why the books appealed to him in the first place.

"Don't be frightened," he said when she realized he had seen her. "I won't hurt you."

"I'm not frightened."

Jean was too much the gentleman to point out that her hands were trembling so much that she had to make an effort to hold them still on her lap. Instead he asked, "What's your name?"

"Candida."

Jean nodded. Of course. An exotic given name—if it even was her own—and no surname. This was how the stories always started.

"Do you need some help?" he asked.

"I need a place to stay."

Jean nodded again. He put his paper bag full of garbage into the bin beside the steps, then turned back to her. She was sitting on the steps now, back straight, hands still clasped together on her lap.

"I've got an extra bed," he said. "You can use it for as long as you need."

"Really? You don't know anything about me."

"I know you need help. Isn't that enough?"

Candida gave him a long considering look, then smiled and followed him up the steps to his apartment.

3

Needless to say, Jean had a good heart. If Candida hadn't been beautiful, or even a woman, he would still have offered his help. And it was, as I said, a more innocent time. But his mystery novels about the seamier side of life were no more real than the protagonists after which he was now modeling his actions. Private detectives were rarely larger than life, and even more rarely solved murder investigations that had left the police baffled—it was as true then as it is now. Nor were real prostitutes the unblemished beauties that could be found on the covers of those same pulp novels. Walking the streets leaves scars, as many visible as hidden.

Jean's secret passion was misled, as romantic as a fairy tale. By such token, Candida might well have been something more exotic still: A faerie, perhaps, strayed from some enchanted forest glen. Or a wounded angel, fallen from heaven. For she had wings. Hidden from ordinary sight, it's true, but she did have them. When she rose to follow him up the apartment steps, they could be seen lifting from her shoulderblades, one a majestic sweep of feathers as imagined by da Vinci, or Manet; the other broken, hanging limp.

They could be seen, if you had more than ordinary sight. Or you might see only what you expected to see, what you wished to see. Jean saw a prostitute on the run, in trouble with the law, or with her pimp; perhaps both. Standing at her kitchen window, Hannah Silverstein looked up from her sinkful of dishes to see her neighbor befriend a pretty girl in a pink sweater and a modest skirt that hung just below her knees. The stranger had thick chestnut hair falling free to her shoulders, eyes that seemed as luminous as moonlight, and Hannah was happy for Jean because she had always thought of him as such a nice, pleasant man, but too old at twenty-seven to be living on his own. Too lonely. It was time he met himself a nice girl like this and settled down.

That was what Hannah saw, but then Hannah had her own preconceptions concerning what she expected to see in the world. She once met the great god Pan at the reception following Janet Carney's wedding and thought him a quaint little man who had imbibed perhaps too much wedding cheer.

"Pan is dead," he told her, lifting his glass to clink its rim against hers. "Long live Pan."

But she thought he'd said, "What a spread—long live Jan."

Perhaps it was his accent. Or perhaps, as many of us will, she used a similar filter to listen to him as the one through which she viewed the world.

4

Jean's own perception of his houseguest changed as he came to know Candida. That first autumn day when he returned home from work, not even expecting her to be in his apartment anymore, she had already undergone a slight alteration from the woman he remembered meeting the previous night. She was still sexy, he could still picture her gracing the cover of an issue of *Spicy Detective Stories,* but she no longer seemed cheap, her sexiness was no longer so blatant. She must have gone out while he was at work, he thought, for while she hadn't even been carrying a purse last night, today the tight dress and heels were gone, the makeup far more subdued. She wore, instead, a loose cotton dress with a flower print more suitable to summer than the fall.

"You look different," he said.

"So do you."

It was true. Last night he'd been wearing casual slacks and a short-sleeved polo shirt. But the difference seemed to run deeper in her—beyond a mere change in clothing.

"That's not what I meant," he began.

He was going to go on to tell her that he was dressed for work now, while last night he hadn't been, that he had a chest of drawers and closet full of different clothes into which he could change, while she'd come into his apartment with only what she was wearing, nothing more. But then he smelled the air.

"You made dinner," he said, unable to hide his delight. The last time he'd come home to dinner was when he was still living with his parents, years ago. He looked in the oven, his smile broadening. "Shepherd's pie. It's my favorite."

"I know."

And Jean forgot the anomaly of her wardrobe, never thought to ask how she might know his favorite dinner. It was as though someone had found the room in his mind that housed his curiosity and simply turned off the light and closed the door quietly behind them as they left. The riddles remained, but his questions were gone, just like that.

5

In older, more superstitious days, it might have been said that Candida had bewitched him, for theirs was a whirlwind romance—especially at that time, in that community. They met in September, but the odd circumstances of that meeting had been forgotten. They were married in January, a quiet civil ceremony, because neither had any other family. They had their first and only child late the next September and named her Sophie.

Jean didn't read his detective novels and magazines anymore—he didn't need other stories. At night when they lay in bed, Candida would tell him hers. She had an impossible storehouse of tales tucked away behind her eyes; like Scheherazade, she had so many, she never had to repeat one. In response, Jean felt an unfamiliar stirring in his own mind, a need to communicate his love for his wife and their child, a desire to share with them dreams that were his own, instead of the fantasies he had borrowed from his books and magazines.

Once he had carried a secret life inside him, an ongoing adventure in which he was the tall man in the trenchcoat with the brim of his hat pulled down low over his eyes, who acted when others stood by helpless, to whom the hurt and lost were drawn that he might find them justice, to whom men looked with respect and women with desire. Now the hat and trenchcoat were put aside. Now he had a child who had offered him her unconditional love from the moment he first saw her in the hospital. Now he had a wife who was not only his partner and his lover, but also his best friend. His life was so complete that he had no need for that old secret life.

6

But there was still something unusual about Candida, even if Jean could no longer see it. Though he wasn't alone in that particular blindness, for no one did—not in their circle of friends, not in the neighborhood, though no one ever did remember her quite the same. To some she was tall, to others she was of medium height. To some she had a classical beauty, others thought her a little plain. Some, when they looked at her, marveled at how she retained an unaffected girlishness, belying her motherhood and maturity; others were reminded of their mothers, or their grandmothers.

She was a charming conversationalist, and an even better listener, but it was only to Jean that she told her stories; stories, and cryptic remarks to which Jean never gave much thought until much later.

Because he'd been bewitched, some would say.

7

"Where does she go when she sleeps?" Candida murmured one evening, leaning on the windowsill in their bedroom, looking out at the moon where it hung above the brownstones of Upper Foxville. "Does she go into another world? Or does she only dream?"

She often watched the moon, noting its phases, her eyes not so much reflecting the light as absorbing it. But that night Jean wasn't looking at her. He sat on the bed, giving Sophie her bottle, and thought Candida spoke of the baby.

"If she's dreaming," he said, "I hope they're sweet dreams."

"Oh yes," Candida said, still looking at the moon. "We can only hope they're so sweet as mine."

8

Another time she told him, "If I should ever go, it won't be for lack of loving you—not you, not Sophie. It will be because I am called away. It will be because I will have no choice."

Jean thought she spoke of her death. He didn't like to consider death, little say speak of it. He held her closer to him.

"Don't even think about it," he told her.

He felt her sigh.

"Sometimes I can think of nothing else."

9

One time Jean asked her how she knew so many stories, and she replied that they came from her dreams.

"We have to believe in our dreams," she said, "because without them we are nothing. Dreams are how we make sense of the world, but they're also how we remember it. When your dreams are real—if only to you—when you believe in them and make them a part of the story that is your life, then anything is possible. You can go anywhere, be anyone, mend any hurt—even a broken wing."

"A broken wing?" Jean replied, puzzled.

"We fly in our dreams. But if we break a wing, we have to work that much harder to keep them real, or they fade away." She gave him a sad smile. "But the trouble is, sometimes we heal ourselves so well that we go away all the same."

Jean shook his head. "You're not making sense tonight."

"Just promise me you'll believe in your dreams. That you'll teach Sophie to believe in hers."

"But—"

"Promise me."

For a moment Jean felt as though he didn't know the woman lying in bed beside him. A sliver of moonlight came in through the window, casting strange shadows across Candida's face, reshaping the familiar planes and contours into those of a stranger.

"It's important, Jean. I need to be able to remember this."

"I . . . promise," he said slowly.

She moved out of the moonlight and the familiar features all fell back into place. The smile that touched her lips was warm and loving.

"When we look back on these days," she said, "we'll remember them as mythic times."

"What do you mean?"

"It's as though we stand in the dark of the moon and anything is possible. We're hidden from the sun's light, from anything that might try to remind us that we only borrow these lives we live, we don't own them."

"If we don't own our lives," Jean asked, "then who does?"

"The people we might become if we stop believing in our dreams."

10

Years later, Jean had trouble remembering all the stories Candida had told him. When he tried to tell them to Sophie, he got them mixed up, transposing this beginning to that ending, the characters of this story into that one, until finally he gave up and read her stories out of books the way other parents did. But he never forgot to remind her to believe in her dreams.

11

Candida went to the store to get some milk one evening, almost three years to the day that they had first met on the back steps of the brownstone, and she never came back, leaving Jean's life as mysteriously as she'd first come into it. He remembered looking at her as she turned back from the

doorway to ask if there was anything else she should pick
up, and being astounded at the vision he beheld. For one
long glorious moment he imagined he saw her bathed in a
nimbus of radiant light that shone from her every pore, gold
as honey, bright as flames. Wings rose up behind her, huge
magnificent feathered wings, each with a span twice her
height.

The vision held, one moment, another, and then it was
gone, and it was Candida standing there in the doorway, the
Candida he'd married and who was the mother of their
child. But it was that vision of her that he remembered—as
an angel, a faerie, a shaft of moonlight, a gift of wonder that
had strayed into his world from some nevernever, drawn by
his need, or perhaps her own, to weave the strands of her
dreams with his, his with hers. Their time together was too
short, far too short, but at least they had had that time together. That was what he reminded himself whenever despair threatened to overwhelm him. The memories . . . and
Sophie . . . were all that enabled him to carry on.

He remembered Candida as others remember the myths
of their ancestors, and he taught their daughter to believe in
her dreams. Because in time he came to understand what
Candida had meant when she told him that stories begin in
dreams and without the stories that we dream, we live someone else's life rather than our own. It wasn't something he
realized all at once; instead, he happened upon the fragments of the puzzle, one piece at a time, finding them in the
spaces that lay between his memories and his dreams, until
one day, when he was sitting alone on the back steps of his
apartment building after having put Sophie to bed, the puzzle pieces all came together and he understood.

He smiled then, one of his rare smiles, as sad as it was
sweet, but no one was there to see. There were only the stories, the tangled skein of the city's stories, waiting to be
shaped by our dreams.

THE POCHADE BOX

——

*The essential thing in art
cannot be explained.*
—Pierre-Auguste Renoir

1

—What's it like when you're dead?
—You still dream.

2

One grey September day, Jilly Coppercorn decided to try to
break herself of a bad habit she'd managed to acquire over
the years. She'd been working on increasingly larger canvases, which was fine, she had no problem with that, but in
the process she'd let herself get so finicky that the clarity of
her work was getting bogged down with unnecessary detail.
She stood back to look at the bewildering complexity of her
latest work-in-progress and realized that, despite the near-
perfect rendering of the individual sections, the painting as a
whole made no sense whatsoever.

What was the point in developing an ideal composition,
she thought, when the detailing eventually came to overwhelm the main point of interest to such an extent that it
was subservient to all the fussy specifics around it? The
viewer's eye, it was plain, could only become confused as it

traveled about the canvas trying to find a point of reference amidst the barrage of detail. All she was going to succeed in doing with work such as this was make the viewer look away and walk over to the next piece hanging on the gallery wall, for relief.

So that day she stopped working in the studio, where the temptation to use big canvases would remain a constant niggle in the back of her head. Instead she took to painting on the street, using her pochade box as a studio. It held everything she needed: six tubes of paint for her limited palette, rag, tissues, a turp can, and a couple of brushes with the handles cut down so that they'd fit into the box. Out on the street, she could hold the box with one hand as though it were a palette, the thumb of her left hand poking up through a small hole in the bottom of the box. When the box was open, the lid formed an easel for the small six-by-eight-inch panels she painted. She used the box's tray for her palette, and, to make sure she didn't get too precious, the smallest brush she took with her was a number 8 oxhair filbert. Her only other equipment was a small drying box to carry her panels and a camp stool that folded flat and could be hung on her shoulder by its strap.

She gave herself thirty minutes per painting, working wet-in-wet, on-site, minimal sketching, minimal detail, looking for the heart of each composition, suggesting detail, not rendering it, concentrating on values and shapes. Most of her time was spent studying her subjects, really thinking through what was important and what wasn't, before she'd squeeze the first dollop of pigment onto her palette. She averaged three to four paintings a day, but quantity didn't interest her. All she was really trying to do at this point was get back to the place she'd been with her art before her preoccupation with detail had taken over.

The habits she'd fallen into were hard to break, but as September drifted into a chilly October and she was well into her second week out on the streets, she was finally making some progress. Rough though the finished pieces were, she was happy with the results she was beginning to get. The small six-by-eight panels forced her to ignore inconsequential details and concentrate instead on essentials: the larger shapes of light and dark, the broader color relationships and the overall composition. She was relearning the ability to portray a scene as a whole, rather than rendering its details piecemeal.

The afternoon she met Tommy Flood, she was sitting on her stool, trying to ignore the brisk nip in the wind as she painted the sweeping lines of St. Paul's Cathedral. She'd lucked into a cloudless day and this late in the afternoon, the light was wonderful. Bundled up against the chill, hands warming in fingerless wool gloves, she was so intent on the play of shadow and light on the cathedral's steps that she didn't realize she had company until Tommy spoke.

"Pretty," he said.

Jilly looked up and smiled at the large man who loomed above her. It was hard to place his age, but she thought he might be in his early thirties. He had the slack features of the simpleminded and returned her smile with one of his own, utterly charming and as innocent as a child's. Around his legs pressed an entourage of scruffy, but amazingly well-behaved dogs: an old black lab, one that looked like a cross between a dachshund and a collie, a couple that had a fair amount of German Shepherd in their mix and one that was mostly poodle.

"Thank you," Jilly told him. "It's not done yet."

"My name's Tommy," he said, thrusting out his hand.

He slurred his words a little when he spoke, but not enough so that Jilly had trouble following him. She laid her brush down on top of her palette. Gravely, she shook hands with him and introduced herself.

"Does it have a story?" Tommy asked as Jilly picked up her brush once more.

"What? This painting?"

"No. The box."

Jilly gave him an odd look. "Now how would you know that?" she asked.

"Everything has a story."

3

—So what do the dead dream about?

—I can't speak for others, only myself. Since my death, I've found myself existing in an odd state of mind, one that seems to lie somewhere between sleep and waking. In this place even my dreams don't seem to play fair with my sense of equilibrium. Often I feel that what I dream is real, while a moment such as this—conversing with you—is the dream.

—I think I know exactly what you mean.

—Do you now?

—I have a friend whose dreams are real—they're just real somewhere else.

—I see.

—But you haven't told me yet what it is that you dream about.

—*Heaven.*

—You mean like angels and the pearly gates and all?

—Hardly. *Heaven* was the name of the first painting I ever did which seemed to make the leap from mind to canvas without losing anything in the translation.

—So you're an artist.

—I *was* an artist. That was how I categorized myself, and it was through the terms of my art that I lived my life. In my present existence there appear to be only two classifications of being: the living and the dead. When you must count yourself among the latter, you soon realize that your career options are severely limited. Nonexistent, you might say.

—It sounds horrible.

—You get used to it.

—I'm an artist.

—Are you now? Well, I hope you don't let art consume your life the way I did.

—What do you mean?

—I was so single-minded in my work that the details of my life became a meaningless blur—a *sfumato* backdrop upon which I painted, but no longer experienced. In the end, when even my art was taken away from me, I had nothing left. I understood all too well how Monet, grieving at the death bed of his beloved wife Camille, could still find himself automatically studying the arrangement of colored gradations that death was imposing upon her lifeless features. Before he ever had the idea of recording the moment in a painting, his reflexes had involved him in memorizing the tonal succession. Blue, yellow, grey.

—*Camille on Her Death Bed.*

—Exactly. But while Monet went on to redeem himself in Giverny, striking a balance between the demands of his artistic genius and actually experiencing life, I painted myself into oblivion.

4

"Tommy!"

They all looked up at the figure running down the pavement toward them—Jilly, Tommy and five sleepy dogs who were suddenly almost comically alert. The approaching young woman was in her late teens or early twenties, a slim figure not much taller than Jilly with light brown hair flowing out from under an old black fedora. She wore jeans and sneakers and a short quilted jacket with white shirttails dangling below its hem. Running along beside her was a funny-looking little wirehaired dog.

It wasn't until she got closer that Jilly could see the weariness in her features, the dark circles under her eyes. The woman didn't appear so much exhausted as stretched too tightly, the way Jilly knew she looked the week before she had a show to hang and she was working day and night trying to get the last few pieces done.

"Oh-oh," Tommy said.

"Do you know her?"

Tommy nodded. "She's my sister, Maisie."

There wasn't much family resemblance between them, Jilly thought, but then whoever said everybody in a family had to look the same?

"Where have you *been*?" Maisie cried as she reached them. "I was so worried."

"Just walking, Maisie. I was just walking."

Maisie sighed. Jilly got the idea that she did that a lot when it came to Tommy.

"He wasn't bothering you, was he?" she asked, turning to Jilly.

"Not at all. He's been very sweet."

"He scares people sometimes—because he's so big and they don't understand that he's not crazy, he's just simple."

"And happy," Tommy put in.

Maisie laughed and gave him a quick hug. "And happy," she agreed.

"Jilly's going to tell me a story," Tommy informed her.

Maisie looked at Jilly, eyebrows lifting.

"It's okay," Jilly said.

Neither Maisie nor Tommy were dressed well—too busy worrying about when they were going to eat and keeping a roof over their heads to worry about buying new clothes as well, she decided. It must be especially tough making do when you had a big brother like that with special needs. The least Jilly thought she could do was entertain Tommy with a story.

"Tommy wanted to know about my pochade box," she said. "I can sit with him over on the steps there if you've got some stuff you want to do."

But Maisie's gaze had gone to the box. "Pochade," she said. "That's French for 'rapid sketch,' isn't it?"

Jilly nodded, trying to hide her surprise. Not many of her artist friends had known that—she'd had to provide the definition.

"I read a lot," Maisie explained.

Something clicked in Jilly's mind then, and she realized that she'd heard about Maisie Flood and her extended family of foundlings before.

"You know Angel, don't you?" she asked.

Maisie nodded. "Yeah, she's got me back into school and stuff."

"Welcome to the club," Jilly said. "I'm another one of her successes."

"Really?"

"Though I guess my time goes back further than yours."

"What about the story?" Tommy asked.

"There's two things Tommy loves," Maisie told Jilly. "Pictures and stories. If you can tell a story as well as you paint, you'll have a friend for life."

"Well, I'd probably argue about the criteria involved," Jilly said, "but I love making new friends."

She led the way over to the cathedral's steps, carrying the pochade box as Tommy brought along her stool and the drying box, which held the two paintings she'd done this morning along with a number of unused gessoed panels she'd prepared for other paintings. The dogs followed in what seemed like an undulating wave of fur, settling themselves around and upon Tommy, Maisie and the steps as though they were big, floppy beanbag toys instead of real dogs.

"I really don't mind looking after Tommy if you've got some things to do," Jilly said.

Maisie shook her head. "Are you kidding? Where do you think he got his love for stories from?"

"It's not that great a story—doesn't really have much of a beginning or an end. It's just sort of weird."

"You're stalling."

Jilly laughed. "Only partly. Mostly what I'm doing is offering up the apologia beforehand so that you don't ask for your money back when I'm done."

"We don't have any money to give you," Tommy said, looking disappointed, as though he thought that now they weren't going to get the story.

"It's just an expression," Maisie assured him. "Like letting the cat out of the bag—remember?" She turned to Jilly. "Tommy tends to take things pretty literally."

"I'll keep that in mind," Jilly said.

5

—What do you mean by oblivion?

—You have to be remembered. People have to think about you. If they don't, you just disappear. That's what happens to all those people who vanish mysteriously. Not enough people were thinking about them and eventually they faded away. They were simply forgotten, remembered only when they disappeared—BECAUSE they disappeared— and then it was too late, of course. You can't bring back what doesn't exist anymore.

—Too late for those of us left behind, maybe, but you still exist somewhere, or I wouldn't be talking to you, would I?

—Sometimes I can't decide if I am actually dead—or alive, but somehow become invisible. Unheard, unseen, unable to taste or feel . . .

—I can't see you, but I can hear you.

—Perhaps you are imagining my voice. Perhaps you are dreaming.

—I think I'd know if I was asleep or not. Besides, I never have dreams this interesting.

—I'm happy to realize I can still be amusing.

—I'm sorry. I don't mean to trivialize your situation. Is there anything I can do to help you?

—You could riddle me this: Is it still existence, when one resides in limbo?

6

"Okay," Jilly said. "I guess it started when Geordie got back from his last trip to England. I wasn't expecting him back for another—"

"Who's Geordie?" Tommy wanted to know.

Maisie sighed. "Tommy tends to interrupt," she apologized. "He doesn't mean to be rude."

"That's all right. It's ruder to just expect everybody to know who you're talking about, without stopping to explain. Geordie's a friend of mine," she added, turning to Tommy. "He plays the fiddle and that summer—I guess it was in the mid-seventies—he went on a busking vacation of the British Isles."

"What's—"

"Busking is when you play music on the street and hope people will give you money because they like what they're hearing."

"We've seen people doing that, haven't we, Maisie?"

"We sure have."

"Is Geordie good?" Tommy wanted to know.

"Very good," Jilly assured him. "The next time he's playing somewhere, I'll take you to see him." She caught Maisie shaking her head, and realized why. "It's okay," she said. "I wouldn't make the promise unless I was going to keep it."

"It's just that people mean well . . ."

"You'll have to trust me on this," Jilly said. Maisie shrugged noncommittally, which was about as much as you could expect, Jilly thought, given how they'd only just met. "Anyway," she went on, "I'm working in my studio one morning and right out of nowhere, Geordie shows up, weeks before I thought I'd be seeing him. Seems he got caught gigging with an Irish band in a London club, except he didn't have a work permit, so he got the boot."

"They made him come back home," Maisie explained to Tommy before he could ask.

"I never got the boot until Maisie found me," Tommy said. "Before that I never had a home."

"I know what you mean," Jilly said. "It's not fun, is it?" Tommy shook his head. "But we have fun now."

"So did Geordie bring you the box back from England?" Maisie asked.

Jilly nodded. "He got it at something called a car boot sale—it's like a flea market, except it's out in a field somewhere and everybody just sells stuff out of the trunks of their cars."

"Why do they call car trunks 'boots'?" Maisie wondered.

"I don't know. Why do we call chips French fries and

crisps 'chips'? Anyway, I thought it was very sweet of him to get it for me. It was pretty grungy, with oil paint caked all over the insides and the tray you use for a palette was broken in two, but I'd never seen anything like it before. If I closed my eyes I could almost picture the turn-of-the-century artist who'd owned it, out somewhere in the English countryside painting *en plein*—outside, on location as opposed to in the studio. The pochade box is like a little studio, really, only in miniature."

She opened the box as she spoke and showed Tommy how it worked and how everything could be stowed away in it once you were done painting.

"After Geordie left that night, I cleaned it up. Scraped away all the dried paint, glued the palette tray back together again and sanded it down so I could start off fresh with my own palette. It took me most of the day before I had it all fixed up—not quite new, but certainly serviceable. I loaded it up with some tubes of paint, rags and a few old brushes cut down to fit inside, and I was ready to head out myself, just the way I imagined its original owner had. But somehow I never did. I set it up on a windowsill, and except for taking it out into the country a few times, it's been sitting there collecting dust for years. Until I started using it again a couple of weeks ago."

Tommy looked at her expectantly when she fell silent. After a few moments, he couldn't hold it in anymore.

"Is that it? Is that the whole story?"

"Well, no," Jilly said, and then she hesitated again. "It gets a little weird after that."

"We can take weird," Maisie assured her.

The wirehaired terrier sprawled out on her lap looked up at Jilly and yipped as though in agreement. Jilly laughed and roughed the stiff fur on the top of its head.

"After I was done fixing the box up," she said, "I sat with it on my lap in the window seat of my studio. I wasn't thinking of anything, just holding the box and staring out the window, watching the light change in the alley below. I can't see the sunset from there, but that alleyway seems to hold the light long after the sun's actually set. I never get tired of watching it."

"I know places like that," Maisie said. "Doesn't matter if they're in the middle of nowhere and there's trash everywhere, they just seem magical."

Jilly nodded. "I'm fascinated by what can't be explained—or at least what can't be explained through the facts most of us have decided are true. So when I had this . . . visitation, I wasn't scared or anything. Just curious."

"What kind of visitation?"

"I can't really explain it. I was alone, sitting there with the box on my lap, and then there was this ghostly presence in the studio with me, and I ended up having a long conversation with it. I can still remember most of what we talked about, word for word."

7

—I don't know about limbo, but I had a friend once—a dancer. She used to tell her boyfriends that every second step she danced, she danced for them.

—But that would only be half the dance.

—I know. She said you have to keep something for yourself. You can't give everything away.

—I'm not sure I understand how this relates to me.

—You put everything into your paintings. You didn't keep anything for yourself.

—I still don't see the relevance.

—I think you're still doing it, and that's why you're in limbo. You're not painting anymore, but even as a ghost, you're not hanging onto anything for yourself. Maybe if you did, you'd be able to let go and move on.

—I'm not sure I have the courage to move on.

—Unfortunately, I can't help you there.

8

"What happened then?" Maisie asked.

Jilly shrugged. "Nothing, really. We talked a little more and then he was just gone. He never came back—at least not so as I ever noticed. I don't know if he went on, or if he's still stuck in limbo and I just can't hear him anymore."

"Sad," Tommy said.

He looked so glum that Jilly began to regret having said anything about the pochade box having a story. But before she could think of something more cheerful to talk about, Tommy sat up straighter on the steps and suddenly brightened up on his own. He pointed down the pavement to where a vendor had set up a cart selling hot pretzels.

"Oh, look!" he cried.

He gave Maisie a long hopeful look until finally she relented. She carefully counted out the change he'd need, then stowed the remainder back in the pocket of her jacket. Jilly had been about to offer to treat them all, but reconsidered when she realized that it might be taken wrong. Maisie struck her as prideful enough to mistake generosity for charity, and Jilly didn't want to chance losing their new friendship over something like that. She was enjoying their company and wanted to get to know them better. So she sat back and let it play out, waiting there on the steps with Maisie and watching Tommy run eagerly to the pretzel cart, the dogs scrambling about at his heels.

"Do you think Tommy would like it if I gave him this painting when it's done?" she said.

Maisie shrugged. "It's hard to say. When I said he likes pictures, it's mostly stuff from magazines. He has me cut out the people in the pictures and then he uses them as dolls to make up little stories. He's never had a painting before, so I don't know what he'd do with it."

Jilly decided that she would give Tommy a painting, except it would be one of him and his sister and their dogs. She had a good enough memory that she knew she'd be able to do it back in her studio without their needing to sit for it.

"That was an odd story," Maisie said.

"What there was of it," Jilly said.

Her companion gave her a considering look. "If I didn't know better," she said, "I'd think that Angel had set this up—sort of a morality play, you know?"

Jilly shook her head.

"Well, she's always telling me I've got to get a life for myself—meet people, maybe get a boyfriend, that kind of thing. I can't seem to get her to understand that being with Tommy and the dogs is what I *want* to do."

"But she's got a point."

"And that is?"

"If you lose sight of yourself, then what've you got to offer Tommy and the dogs? You'll be as bad as my ghost, giving of yourself until there's nothing left to give and you simply fade away. You'll end up stuck in the same limbo."

"You don't get it either. I *want* to be with them."

Jilly sighed. "I do get it. But maybe it'd be good for them to have some other input as well. I'm not saying Tommy can be self-sufficient—I don't know him well enough, what his limitations might be. But if you're always there doing things for him, how's he supposed to learn to do anything for himself?"

"But that's how I found him. He was like that. He's not my brother, I just kind of adopted him. He got dumped on the streets because nobody else wanted him and let me tell you, without me, he wouldn't have survived."

"I believe you. But maybe whoever he was with before wasn't giving him any slack either." Jilly held up her hand to forestall Maisie's protest. "Look, I'm not saying you're right or wrong, just that you might want to think about it—for Tommy, if not for yourself. Maybe you need Tommy as much as he needs you. I don't know. It's not for me to say, is it?"

"That's right. It's not for you to say."

Jilly sighed. "Now you think I'm trying to tell you how to take care of Tommy."

"Aren't you? You're beginning to sound the same as everyone else I meet—you all know better."

"No, I don't," Jilly said. "The only thing I know about Tommy is that I intend to treat him like anybody else I know. I don't have some hidden agenda; I was talking about you. Maybe you know how to take care of Tommy and the dogs, but do you know how to take care of yourself? I'm not talking about making a living or going back to school, or any of that. I'm talking about what goes on in here—" she touched a hand between her breasts "—in your heart."

"What's that supposed to mean?"

"It's like my painting," Jilly said. "I'm out here on the streets with this pochade box because I was overloading my work with detail—so much so that while all the various parts of a painting would be good, the excessive details made the final painting way too busy. I was losing sight of what I was trying to say with each painting in the first place."

"So?"

"I've done the same thing with my life. Concentrated so much on the details, that I would lose sight of the overall direction of where I was going—of the fact that I even wanted to go somewhere in the first place. I've got friends who work with people with special needs. I've even done some volunteer work myself. The thing is, it's so easy to wrap your whole life around the details of theirs, that you become invisible in the process. People like Tommy can't help needing so much from us. But we've got to have something to give them, and if we spend all our time wrapped up in what we see as our responsibility, our relationships with them end up becoming burdens instead of gifts."

At first Maisie looked angry, and Jilly thought she'd gone too far. She didn't know anything about either Maisie or Tommy beyond what she'd picked up in the past hour, so who was she to be blithely handing our advice the way she was? But then Maisie's features softened and she gave another one of her sighs.

"Am I that transparent?" Maisie asked.

Jilly shook her head. "Only if you know what to look for.

You seem really tired, almost worn out."

"I am. But what I said was true. I don't resent the time I spend with Tommy. I like being with him, but sometimes it gets to be too much, trying to juggle school and work and time with him. . . ." Her gaze met Jilly's. "But I can't not do it. And I don't want to just foist Tommy off somewhere so that I can have some time to myself."

"Because you think Tommy would feel hurt?"

"Partly. But I also get scared that if it looks like I can't take care of him properly, somebody'll try to take him away from me."

Jilly nodded understandingly. "Maybe you're looking at this from the wrong angle, losing the overall picture for the details. Instead of thinking of it as foisting Tommy off on other people, you should think of it as allowing Tommy to enrich their lives and for Tommy to get some different takes on the world than the way he sees it when he's only with you."

Maisie looked down the pavement to where Tommy was talking excitedly with the vendor as he waited for his pretzel.

"People don't think of time with Tommy as being enriching," she said. "I mean, even my landlady—she looks after him when I'm working or at school, and she's crazy about him—even she doesn't give me the impression that she gets anything out of the relationship."

"Have you ever asked her?"

Maisie shook her head.

"I'd like to see Tommy again," Jilly said. "I think I could learn a lot from him. And I'm sure if you talked to Angel she could help you work things out so that there'd be other people to lend you a hand without anyone thinking that you're not fit to be taking care of Tommy anymore."

"It's hard," Maisie said. "Always asking, always standing there with your hand out."

Jilly nodded. "That's one way of looking at it. But you know, the best thing I ever learned from Angel is that there's nothing wrong with asking for help. If we're not here to look out for each other, then what are we doing here?"

"Living in limbo," Maisie said.

"Exactly. Just like my ghost."

"So what do you think I should do?"

"Well, for a start, what's Tommy doing tomorrow?"

Maisie's brow furrowed. "Let's see. I've got to work until two, but after that I think—"

"Not you," Jilly told her. "Just Tommy. Do you think he'd like to come with me and see Geordie while he's busking?"

Maisie hesitated for a long moment. She looked back at the pretzel vendor to see that Tommy was on his way back, pretzel in hand, dogs running around him, hoping he'd drop a piece of it.

"I don't know," she said. "Why don't we ask him?"

9

—Since you brought up Monet earlier, maybe you should remember what he's supposed to have told Georges Clemenceau when Clemenceau was visiting him at Giverny.

—Refresh my memory.

—'Your mistake is to want to reduce the world to your measure, whereas by enlarging your knowledge of things, you will find your knowledge of self is enlarged.'

—I see. And where did a woman as young as yourself gain such wisdom?

—From making mistakes. I make a lot of them. The trick is not making excuses for them, or trying to pretend they never happened, but learning from them.

—You see the world without shades of grey.

—Hardly.

—Then how can you make it sound so effortless?

—Are you kidding? Life's like art. You have to work hard to keep it simple and still have meaning. It's so much easier just to deal with everything in how it relates to yourself. You have to really concentrate to keep an open mind, to pay attention to the broader view, to stay aware of what's going on outside your own skin.

—And if you don't?

—Think of all you've got to lose.

COYOTE STORIES

—

Four directions blow the sacred winds
We are standing at the center
Every morning wakes another chance
To make our lives a little better
—Kiya Heartwood, from "Wishing Well"

This day Coyote is feeling pretty thirsty, so he goes into Joey's Bar, you know, on the corner of Palm and Grasso, across from the Men's Mission, and he lays a nugget of gold down on the counter, but Joey he won't serve him.

"So you don't serve skins no more?" Coyote he asks him.

"Last time you gave me gold, it turned to shit on me," is what Joey says. He points to the Rolex on Coyote's wrist. "But I'll take that. Give you change and everything."

Coyote scratches his muzzle and pretends he has to think about it. "Cost me twenty-five dollars," he says. "It looks better than the real thing."

"I'll give you fifteen, cash, and a beer."

"How about a bottle of whiskey?"

So Coyote comes out of Joey's Bar and he's missing his Rolex now, but he's got a bottle of Jack in his hand and that's when he sees Albert, just around the corner, sitting on the ground with his back against the brick wall and his legs stuck out across the sidewalk so you have to step over them, you want to get by.

"Hey, Albert," Coyote says. "What's your problem?"

"Joey won't serve me no more."

"That because you're indigenous?"

"Naw. I got no money."

So Coyote offers him some of his whiskey. "Have yourself a swallow," he says, feeling generous, because he only paid two dollars for the Rolex and it never worked anyway.

"Thanks, but I don't think so," is what Albert tells him. "Seems to me I've been given a sign. Got no money means I should stop drinking."

Coyote shakes his head and takes a sip of his Jack. "You are one crazy skin," he says.

That Coyote he likes his whiskey. It goes down smooth and puts a gleam in his eye. Maybe, he drinks enough, he'll remember some good time and smile, maybe he'll get mean and pick himself a fight with a lamppost like he's done before. But one thing he knows, whether he's got money or not's got nothing to do with omens. Not for him, anyway.

⟶

But a lack of money isn't really an omen for Albert either; it's a way of life. Albert, he's like the rest of us skins. Left the reserve, and we don't know why. Come to the city, and we don't know why. Still alive, and we don't know why. But Albert, he remembers it being different. He used to listen to his grandmother's stories, soaked them up like the dirt will rain, thirsty after a long drought. And he tells stories himself, too, or pieces of stories, talk to you all night long if you want to listen to him.

It's always Coyote in Albert's stories, doesn't matter if he's making them up or just passing along gossip. Sometimes Coyote's himself, sometimes he's Albert, sometimes he's somebody else. Like it wasn't Coyote sold his Rolex and ran into him outside Joey's Bar that day, it was Billy Yazhie. Maybe ten years ago now, Billy he's standing under a turquoise sky beside Spider Rock one day, looking up, looking up for a long time, before he turns away and walks to the nearest highway, sticks out his thumb and he doesn't look back till it's too late. Wakes up one morning and everything he knew is gone and he can't find his way back.

Oh that Billy he's a dark skin, he's like leather. You shake his hand and it's like you took hold of a cowboy boot. He knows some of the old songs and he's got himself a good voice, strong, ask anyone. He used to drum for the dancers back home, but his hands shake too much now, he says. He doesn't sing much anymore, either. He's got to be like the rest of us, hanging out in Fitzhenry Park, walking the streets, sleeping in an alleyway because the Men's Mission it's out of beds. We've got the stoic faces down real good, but you look in our eyes, maybe catch us off guard, you'll see we don't forget anything. It's just most times we don't want to remember.

———

This Coyote he's not too smart sometimes. One day he gets into a fight with a biker, says he going to count coup like his plains brothers, knock that biker all over the street, only the biker's got himself a big hickory-handled hunting knife and he cuts Coyote's head right off. Puts a quick end to that fight, I'll tell you. Coyote he spends the rest of the afternoon running around, trying to find somebody to sew his head back on again.

"That Coyote," Jimmy Coldwater says, "he's always losing his head over one thing or another."

I tell you we laughed.

———

But Albert he takes that omen seriously. You see him drinking still, but he's drinking coffee now, black as a raven's wing, or some kind of tea he brews for himself in a tin can, makes it from weeds he picks in the empty lots and dries in the sun. He's living in an abandoned factory these days, and he's got this one wall, he's gluing feathers and bones to it, nothing fancy, no eagle's wings, no bear's jaw, wolf skull, just what he can find lying around, pigeon feathers and crow's, rat bones, bird bones, a necklace of mouse skulls strung on a wire. Twigs and bundles of weeds, rattles he makes from tin cans and bottles and jars. He paints figures on the wall, in between all the junk. Thunderbird. Bear. Turtle. Raven.

Everybody's starting to agree, that Albert he's one crazy skin.

Now when he's got money, he buys food with it and shares it out. Sometimes he walks over to Palm Street where the skin girls are working the trade and he gives them money, asks them to take a night off. Sometimes they take the money and just laugh, getting into the next car that pulls up. But sometimes they take the money and they sit in a coffee shop, sit there by the window, drinking their coffee and look out at where they don't have to be for one night.

And he never stops telling stories.

"That's what we are," he tells me one time. Albert he's smiling, his lips are smiling, his eyes are smiling, but I know he's not joking when he tells me that. "Just stories. You and me, everybody, we're a set of stories, and what those stories are is what makes us what we are. Same thing for whites as skins. Same thing for a tribe and a city and a nation and the world. It's all these stories and how they braid together that tells us who and what and where we are.

"We got to stop forgetting and get back to remembering. We got to stop asking for things, stop waiting for people to give us the things we think we need. All we really need is the stories. We have the stories and they'll give us the one thing nobody else can, the thing we can only take for ourselves, because there's nobody can give you back your pride. You've got to take it back yourself.

"You lose your pride and you lose everything. We don't want to know the stories, because we don't want to remember. But we've got to take the good with the bad and make ourselves whole again, be proud again. A proud people can never be defeated. They lose battles, but they'll never lose the war, because for them to lose the war you've got to go out and kill each and every one of them, everybody with even a drop of the blood. And even then, the stories will go on. There just won't be any skins left to hear them."

This Coyote he's always getting in trouble. One day he's sitting at a park bench, reading a newspaper, and this cop starts to talk big to one of the skin girls, starts talking mean, starts pushing her around. Coyote's feeling chivalrous that day, like he's in a white man's movie, and he gets into a fight with the cop. He gets beat up bad and then more cops come and they take him away, put him in jail.

The judge he turns Coyote into a mouse for a year so that there's Coyote, got that same lopsided grin, got that sharp muzzle and those long ears and the big bushy tail, but he's so small now you can hold him in the palm of your hand.

"Doesn't matter how small you make me," Coyote he says to the judge. "I'm still Coyote."

Albert he's so serious now. He gets out of jail and he goes back to living in the factory. Kids've torn down that wall of his, so he gets back to fixing it right, gets back to sharing food and brewing tea and helping the skin girls out when he can, gets back to telling stories. Some people they start thinking of him as a shaman and call him by an old Kickaha name.

Dan Whiteduck he translates the name for Billy Yazhie, but Billy he's not quite sure what he's heard. Know-more-truth, or No-more-truth?

"You spell that with a 'K' or what?" Billy he asks Albert.

"You take your pick how you want to spell it," Albert he says.

Billy he learns how to pronounce that old name and that's what he uses when he's talking about Albert. Lots of people do. But most of us we just keep on calling him Albert.

One day this Coyote decides he wants to have a powwow, so he clears the trash from this empty lot, makes the circle, makes the fire. The people come but no one knows the songs anymore, no one knows the drumming that the dancers need, no one knows the steps. Everybody they're just standing around, looking at each other, feeling sort of stupid, until Coyote he starts singing, *Ya-ha-hey, ya-ha-hey,* and he's stomping around the circle, kicking up dirt and dust.

People they start to laugh, then, seeing Coyote playing the fool.

"You are one crazy skin!" Angie Crow calls to him and people laugh some more, nodding in agreement, pointing at Coyote as he dances round and round the circle.

But Jimmy Coldwater he picks up a stick and he walks over to the drum Coyote made. It's this big metal tub, salvaged from a junkyard, that Coyote's covered with a skin and who knows where he got that skin, nobody's asking. Jimmy he hits the skin of the drum and everybody they stop laughing and look at him, so Jimmy he hits the skin again. Pretty soon he's got the rhythm to Coyote's dance and then Dan Whiteduck he picks up a stick, too, and joins Jimmy at the drum.

Billy Yazhie he starts up to singing then, takes Coyote's song and turns it around so that he's singing about Spider Rock and turquoise skies, except everybody hears it their own way, hears the stories they want to hear in it. There's more people drumming and there's people dancing and before anyone knows it, the night's over and there's the dawn poking over the roof of an abandoned factory, thinking, these are some crazy skins. People they're lying around and sitting around, eating the flatbread and drinking the tea that Coyote provided, and they're all tired, but there's something in their hearts that feels very full.

"This was one fine powwow," Coyote he says.

Angie she nods her head. She's sitting beside Coyote all sweaty and hot and she'd never looked quite so good before.

"Yeah," she says. "We got to do it again."

～

We start having regular powwows after that night, once, sometimes twice a month. Some of the skins they start to making dancing outfits, going back up to the reserve for visits and asking about steps and songs from the old folks. Gets to be we feel like a community, a small skin nation living here in exile with the ruins of broken-down tenements and abandoned buildings all around us. Gets to be we start remembering some of our stories and sharing them with each other instead of sharing bottles. Gets to be we have something to feel proud about.

Some of us we find jobs. Some of us we try to climb up the side of the wagon but we keep falling off. Some of us we go back to homes we can hardly remember. Some of us we come from homes where we can't live, can't even breathe, and drift here and there until we join this tribe that Albert he helped us find.

And even if Albert he's not here anymore, the stories go on. They have to go on, I know that much. I tell them every chance I get.

See, this Coyote he got in trouble again, this Coyote he's always getting in trouble, you know that by now, same as me. And when he's in jail this time he sees that it's all tribes inside, the same as it is outside. White tribes, black tribes, yellow tribes, skin tribes. He finally understands, finally realizes that maybe there can't ever be just one tribe, but that doesn't mean we should stop trying.

But even in jail this Coyote he can't stay out of trouble and one day he gets into another fight and he gets cut again, but this time he thinks maybe he's going to die.

"Albert," Coyote he says, "I am one crazy skin. I am never going to learn, am I?"

"Maybe not this time," Albert says, and he's holding Coyote's head and he's wiping the dribble of blood that comes out of the side of Coyote's mouth and is trickling down his chin. "But that's why you're Coyote. The wheel goes round and you'll get another chance."

Coyote he's trying to be brave, but he's feeling weaker and it hurts, it hurts, this wound in his chest that cuts to the bone, that cuts the thread that binds him to this story.

"There's a thing I have to remember," Coyote he says, "but I can't find it. I can't find its story. . . ."

"Doesn't matter how small they try to make you," Albert he reminds Coyote. "You're still Coyote."

"*Ya-ha-hey,*" Coyote he says. "Now I remember."

Then Coyote he grins and he lets the pain take him away into another story.

THE FOREVER TREES

If you understand, things are just as
they are. If you do not understand,
things are just as they are.
—Zen saying

1

In the end, what she remembers isn't her name, not at first, who she was or even how and where she lived her life. What she remembers is this:

When I was a child I had this ability to simply go somewhere. It wasn't a good place or a bad place—just *another* place. I wouldn't hide there, but when I was there, I couldn't be found. I didn't have to walk there, I'd just be there, in that ghost place.

Sometimes now I think it was a part of me, a piece of my mind where I'd go when things were bad. But then I remember: I went there when things were good, too.

2

Tasha never stops thinking, thinking. She's a visual artist but her mind's always full of words, scuttling around inside her head like mice in an old house when the sun goes down, the eyelids are drawn, the shutters fastened, the body still sleeping, but that secret part of her where the spirit candle burns the brightest is busy-busy, talking to itself, remembering, dreaming. She paints because of those words.

It's like this: She sees colors for words, like a light mottled grey touched with soft green and purple for *whisper*. *Free* is a Prussian blue that goes on forever, acquiring a hint of violet just before it vanishes from sight. *Cacti* is a deep fuchsia, but *cactus* is a warm buttery yellow with streaks of olive green and greenish browns. *New* is the electric color of a kingfisher's wing and *ford* is the coppery red of an old pen nib, but *Newford* is a grey with highlights of henna and purple.

Joe doesn't pretend to understand. He looks at her art. He knows that her paintings are fragments of stories, conversations, essays, all chasing down those mice in her head, trying to put them into some semblance of order, but he doesn't get the translation. All he sees is color on the canvas, random patterns that make no sense even after Tasha reads them to him.

But it doesn't stop them from being friends.

They're just friends. Good friends.

"I don't want to exchange bodily fluids with you," she tells him once. "It always spoils things."

He wonders at the time if that's how she really meant to put it, or if she just liked the way the words looked as she said them, but he understands what she means. Sex is good. Sex is fun. There's no better place to be, he thinks, than in the middle of a relationship when most of the awkwardness is gone and you're still crazy about each other. But one person always loves the other more, and the imbalance undermines the best of intentions and eventually it all falls apart. He's seen it happen. He's had it happen. Lovers have come and gone in his life, but Tasha's constant. She's not one of the guys, not even close. She brings out the best in him, the way a friend should, but too often doesn't. Asks hard questions, but doesn't answer them for him. Lets him work them out for himself. The way he does for her.

"Men always want to fix everything," she tells him another time, "and I can't figure out why. I'd settle for simply understanding things."

Gets to where he knows exactly what she means. She talks about men, he talks about women, they're generalizing, like you do, but they're not talking about each other. It's not that they're sexless. The gender thing is there, it's part of what endears them to each other, the insights they get into what each is not, but the attraction's strictly platonic. Which makes it all the more confusing when Joe finds himself thinking not about her, Tasha, his friend, but about the curve of her neck and the way her hennaed hair lies so soft against it, how she fills her sweater and jeans with perfect contours that he wants to explore, palm to skin; soft, she'd be so soft, so smooth, like silk; touching her would be like touching silk, but warm.

He'd give anything to taste her lips, and all of a sudden everything's way too complicated and he wants to fix what's going on instead of understanding it.

3

To get to that ghost place, first I'd have to find the meadow. Summer growth slaps my knees as I follow the long slope up from the bottom of the hill where the hedge is an unruly thicket tangled up in heaps of gathered fieldstone. It's been years since the slope was ploughed, but not so long that the forest has resettled the open ground. The weeds are never too tall, and there are always wildflowers in bloom, great stuttering sweeps of color that twist and wind in spiraling paths up and down the slope of the hill. Sometimes there's a hawk, high up, floating in the sky, but I don't see it right away, rarely look for the grey-brown cut of its wings against the blue. As I make my way up the slope, my gaze is always on the forest.

It's a crown of trees on the crest of the hill, trunks and fallen snags slow-dancing around the granite outcrops, a hundred-acre wood, but Pooh doesn't live there and I'm not Christopher Robin. I wouldn't even want to be. I liked being a girl and I like being a woman.

Under the trees, the air is cool and dark and rich with the

wet smell of old damp wood, of ferns and mushrooms and
the moss that cushions my footfalls. Not far from where the
edge of the meadow and the forest blurs, a natural spring
bubbles up from a leak in the granite and trickles pell-mell
through the leaf mold and around the stones. The water
hurries with a jigging and reeling rush that's long since cut a
narrow cleft through the dark red earth as it ribbons its way
down the slope. All the trees seem to lean down to listen to it
as it goes by.

What kind of trees? I don't know. I never had a name for
them. They're big, some of them. Bigger than redwoods.
But gnarled like old oaks or elms. And kind. I can't really
explain. There's a kindness about them. They always welcome me. I know they're older than the stars, thick with
mystery and wind-music rustlings and shadow. Written on
their bark are the histories of ancient times, long lost, and a
thousand forgotten stories that they must remember, but
they always have time for me. Child, girl, woman. I only
ever felt kindness in that hundred-acre wood.

Nim called them the forever trees.

4

So Joe's redefined their relationship, but Tasha doesn't
know. She comes over that evening to watch a video with
him and feels something different in the air. Innocent in a
white T-shirt and snug jeans that make her seem anything
but, she looks around his apartment to see what's changed.
The bookcase still stands on one wall, its shelves stuffed
with paperbacks, magazines and found objects like a tattered slipper or a chipped coffee mug that have been there so
long they've acquired squatters' rights and would look out
of place anywhere else. The sofa still faces the old cedar
chest that holds Joe's TV set and stereo. The same posters
are on the wall, along with the small reproduction of a
Hockney print in its narrow metal frame. The same worn
Oriental carpet underfoot. The two beers Joe brings from
the kitchen are given temporary refuge on the same apple

crate that usually serves as his coffee table.

Nothing's different, but everything has changed. Joe seems—not edgy, but he can't stop moving. His usual stillness has dissolved, leaving behind the bare bones of nervous energy that makes his fingers twitch, his toes tap. Tasha tucks a loose lock of red hair back behind her ears and sits down on the sofa. She leans back, draws her knees up to her chin, smiles over them at Joe, who's hovering about in the middle of the carpet until finally he sits down as well.

The video he's picked is *Enchanted April.* They've seen it before, but tonight the holidaying women don't absorb him. He's constantly stealing glances at her until Tasha begins to wonder if she's got a bit of her dinner stuck to her chin or lodged in between her teeth. A scrap of egg noodle. An errant morsel of snow pea. She explores the spaces between her teeth with her tongue, surreptitiously gives her chin a wipe with the back of her hand.

When she puts her feet down for a moment to reach for her beer, Joe is suddenly right beside her. She turns to look at him, confused, their faces only inches apart. He leans closer. As their lips touch, all the clues Tasha hadn't realized were clues go tumbling through her mind, rearranged in their proper order, the mystery solved, the confusion now embracing what had brought this change to their relationship—and how could she have missed it? But then she lets the confusion go away and enjoys the moment, because Joe's a better kisser than she had ever imagined, and she finds she likes the feel of his back and shoulders as she returns his embrace, likes the press of his chest against her, especially likes the touch of his lips and the tingling that wakes in her belly as the tips of their tongues explore each other.

"This is nice," she murmurs when they finally come up for air.

Nice hangs behind her eyes, all chicory blue, like when the sun first pulls the petals awake, and speckled like a trout. The movie plays on, forgotten except for the flickering glow it throws upon their faces.

"It's weird," Joe tells her. "I just haven't been able to stop thinking about you." The parade of his words kaleidoscopes through her. "It's like we've been friends for what—eight, nine years?—and all of a sudden I'm seeing you for the first time, and I can't believe that I've ever been the least bit interested in another woman."

It takes Tasha a moment to separate the meaning of what he's saying from the colors.

"Are you saying you love me?" she asks, not sure how she wants him to answer, for all that she's been thoroughly enjoying the intimacy of the past ten minutes.

Joe gives her an odd look, as though he hadn't thought things through quite that far. But then he smiles.

"I guess I am," he says.

The words wake a warm flood of color in Tasha's mind, a mingling of rose and pale violet like a coneflower's bloom in the twilight.

"How do you feel?" he asks.

"I'm not sure," she says softly. "It's all so sudden. It's . . ." She can't find the color to tell him what she feels because she's not sure herself; she puts a hand behind his head and draws his lips back toward hers. "Kiss me again," she murmurs just before their lips meet.

The words float in their colors through her mind but Joe doesn't need the invitation.

5

I guess I have to explain everything, don't I? Nim lives in the hundred-acre wood. At least I think she does, because that's the only place I've ever seen her. Actually, I'm not even sure she's a she. I just always think of her as female, but as I try to describe her I realize she's asexual, androgynous. No breasts, but no body hair or Adam's apple either. Her long curly hair is always filled with seeds and twigs and burrs, but it's still soft as duck down. Skinny, she's so skinny you'd think she was made of sticks, but her limbs are pliant. She's the first person I've ever met who's as double-jointed as me.

Maybe more. And she hears colors, too.

"But not sounds," she said when we're talking about it one time. "Just words."

Like me.

6

Joe knows he's screwed up big time. Tasha stays the night and they sleep together. They don't make out, they just sleep together, but somehow that makes everything seem more intimate instead of less. He wakes up to find her lying there beside him, still asleep. He traces the contour of her cheek with his gaze, and he sees a friend, not a lover; all the little fireworks have packed up and gone. He still thinks she's beautiful, ethereal and earthy, all mixed up in one red-topped bundle, but desire has fled. Making love to her would be like making love to a relative.

She opens her eyes and smiles at him, her warmth washing over him in a gentle pulsing tide until the guilt he's feeling registers, the smile droops, worry flits across her eyes.

"What's wrong?" she asks.

"This is a mistake," he tells her. "This is a serious mistake."

"But you said—"

"I know. I . . ."

He can't face her. He's feeling bad enough as it is. The hurt that's growing in her eyes is going to devastate him. He gets out of bed and starts dressing, fast, doesn't even look to see what he's putting on.

"I've got to get to work," he says, for all that it's a Saturday morning. He combs his hair with his hands, give her an apologetic look. "We'll talk about it," he adds, knowing how lame it sounds, but he can't seem to do any better. "Later."

And then he's gone. Tasha stares at the door of the bedroom through which he's fled. She's sitting up in the bed, has the bedclothes pulled up to her chin, but they don't do anything for the shivering chill he's left behind, the blank spot that seems to have lodged in the middle of her chest. It's hard to breathe, hard to think straight. Harder still when she starts to cry and she can't stop, she just can't stop.

7

The thing is, I don't ever have to come back if I don't want to. I could stay forever the way Nim does and never grow any older. What brings me back? It used to be my puppy—Topy. I'd come back for Topy, but then one day I let her stay and she's lived in the hundred-acre wood with Nim ever since. Nobody could understand why I wasn't sad that she'd run away, but they didn't understand that she hadn't run away from me. I could see her any time I wanted to. I still can.

What brought me back after that? I don't know. Different things. I like this world, but sometimes everything gets to be too much for me in it. Like it's hard just having simple conversations when you have to be constantly separating the meanings of what's being said from its colors. I can't argue with people. By the time I've worked out what we're fighting about, everything's usually gotten way more complicated, gotten so tangled up and knotted that it'll never make sense again. At least not for me. The hundred-acre wood gives me a break from that. Gives me a chance to catch my breath so that when I come back to this world I fit in a little easier.

Nim knows what I mean. She's never going back, she says. She wants to become a forever tree herself and sometimes, when I look at her, all twig-thin with that wild bird's-nest of hair on top, I think she's halfway there.

8

Tasha makes her way home, crawls into her own bed, pulls the covers over her head, but can't stop the chill, can't stop the tears. It hurts too much—not because Joe redefined the relationship and then, after she tentatively embraced its new parameters, he went and backed off. She enjoyed necking with him last night, but she wasn't exactly making a lifetime commitment herself. No, it's that he didn't stay to talk. To explain. She hasn't been betrayed by a lover she's just met; she's been betrayed by one of her oldest friends.

She waits for him to call, but the phone stays silent by her bed. Saturday night. All day Sunday. Maybe it's better that way. She's never been good on the phone. Without a face to concentrate on, without being able to watch the lips move, or absorb the subtext that resonates in eyes and facial tics and twitches, conversation too often turns into nothing more than a confusing porridge of color.

So Sunday evening she gets out of bed, dresses, tries to fix her face so that it doesn't look as though she's been crying for most of the weekend, sets off for Joe's apartment. Dreading it. Already knowing it'll be a disaster when she attempts to filter word-sense from the color flood of what they'll say to each other. But they've been friends too long for her not to try.

Friends, she thinks. Friends don't treat each other this way. Her ability to trust is undergoing a test of faith. Once the masks drop, anything could be waiting there. That's something she's always known. The shock is finding a mask where she didn't expect one to be. She'd never realized that Joe could have been wearing a mask all this time.

But friends make mistakes, she told herself, and she clung to those words, spoke them aloud. Saw yellow ochre veined with madder and blues. The grey underbelly of a summer cloud, winging across it, a flock of magenta and yellow-gold flowers.

But the colors couldn't disguise the fear that no matter what happened tonight, she was never going to be sure if Joe was wearing a mask or not. There was just no way to *know*.

9

I guess the hardest thing to explain is how the hundred-acre wood is a real place, that I really go there, that when I'm walking under the forever trees, I'm not here anymore. It's not like I've shut my eyes and gone to some place inside my head. That's what I thought it was at first. Well, not at first. When I first went, I was too young even to wonder about that kind of thing.

My parents knew there was something wrong with me, but no one could figure out what it was. It wasn't until years later that anyone even came up with a name for my condition: synaesthesia. Everyone just thought I was a slow learner, that the connections in my head weren't all wired the right way, which is true I guess, or I'd be like everybody else, right?

I didn't talk until I was five because it took me that long to realize that it was words people used to communicate with each other—not colors. Because I *was* communicating, you see. Right from the first. But it was with crayons and watercolor paints, and nobody could understand what I was saying. When I finally started to use words it was like having to translate everything from a foreign language.

That's what so seductive about the hundred-acre wood. When I talk with Nim, I'm communicating directly with her. I don't feel like I'm muddling around with translations. I never get the feeling that she's impatient with the long pauses in our conversations, because she hears and sees everything the same as me. When I show her one of my paintings she knows exactly what I'm saying with it—the same way that somebody else can read a page from a book.

I guess one day I'll go and I won't come back. I'll become a raggedy wild girl like Nim with twigs and burrs in my hair. Maybe we'll both end up as forever trees. Maybe that's where they came from. Maybe we're both dryads and we just haven't matured from tree spirits into proper trees yet.

The idea of it makes me smile. If we were forever trees, we'd have *really* slow conversations, wouldn't we?

10

Joe is not a bad guy. Like Tasha said, even friends make mistakes. He never wore a mask around her, and that was part of the problem that night when he told her he thought they should be lovers *and* friends. Maybe he should have waited, kept it to himself a little longer until he'd really worked it out in his own head, dealt with it in a way that wouldn't have hurt Tasha before sharing his feelings with her. But maybe it took his sharing those feelings for him to work it out.

He knew it hadn't been fair to her, but he hadn't meant to hurt her. Not that night. Not when he fled the next morning. He'd just gotten confused, couldn't think straight, but he meant to make it right. He meant to call her and apologize for screwing up the way he had, screwing up big time, and he hoped she'd forgive him because maybe they weren't supposed to be lovers, but nothing in his life meant more to him than Tasha's friendship.

So he phones her, Sunday night, lets the phone ring and ring, but there's no answer. He keeps trying up until midnight, then he finally goes over to her apartment, lets himself in with the key she gave him so long ago, but she really isn't there, she wasn't just ignoring the phone, she really isn't home. But she isn't anywhere else either.

Days go by and she's never home, never at her studio, nobody has seen her, nobody ever sees her again.

Joe's sitting in his apartment, cradling one of Tasha's paintings on his lap, and he's remembering holding her one night when she's having a stress attack, when all the words turned into too many colors and everything inside her just shut down for a while so that she didn't even know who or where she was; he's remembering what she told him that night, about a ghost place she can visit, a hundred-acre wood of forever trees. He believed she could go there, didn't ask for proof. That's what friends do—they accept each other's secrets and marvels and hold them in trust.

So Joe knows where Tasha has gone, running up a long meadowed slope with a wild girl and a puppy, vanishing into the embrace of a forest of forever trees, and he misses her, more than anything, he misses her, and what he regrets, what he regrets the most, is that he never asked her how to get there himself, so that he could see her again.